your
worst
nightmare

your worst nightmare

FROM THE TRILOGY
"Through It All"

JK

K. J. Tyrrell

Cover design by Jeffrey Stasko
Front Cover Photo by Polly Tyrrell
Author's Photo by Hannah Balta
Book design by The Troy Book Makers

Printed in the United States of America

The Troy Book Makers • Troy, New York • thetroybookmakers.com

To order additional copies of this title,
contact your favorite local bookstore
or visit www.tbmbooks.com

ISBN: 978-1-61468-295-0

Acknowledgements

Writing this novel has been an amazing experience for me! The inspiration for much of the story comes from my life as a person with cerebral palsy. Charlie's character goes through many things that I have experienced in daily life. Other characters are based on my amazing siblings and many of my good friends.

Two people that have helped me greatly with this project are my personal assistants, April and Amy! They have spent many hours typing, taking dictation, and editing. I am very thankful for the support and encouragement that I have received from family and friends as I have worked on this.

KJT

ONE

"RUSS, STOP THE CAR, STOP, please!" Lucas begged the burly man to pull over, but instead he took another swig from the brown-bagged bottle he clutched tightly as he drove.

Lucas' mom in the passenger seat slurred her speech drunkenly, "Russ, maybe you should slow down."

"Shut up and let me drive!" Russ growled, swinging a thick arm toward the woman's head.

"Mom!" Lucas cried, jumping forward from the back to block the blow.

Suddenly, the car was careening out of control. A loud crash pierced the night, and Lucas was airborne. Thrown from the vehicle, he landed harshly on the pavement a few feet away.

"Russ!" Lucas could hear his mom screaming for her boyfriend.

Lucas opened his eyes as heat began to roll over him. Flames erupted from the car Russ had crashed into. Though Lucas felt dizzy and light headed, he could still see the form of a car seat about to be engulfed by flames.

Sirens screamed as police arrived on the scene, but Lucas had no time to waste. Forcing himself to his feet, he stumbled to the car. Miraculously, the doors were unlocked. Ignoring the burning metal, he tore open the car door and tugged on the baby's car seat. The little child screamed and coughed as smoke filled his face. Lucas couldn't yank the car seat free. He had no choice but to reach over into the burning car and unbuckle it. Lucas covered his mouth and nose with his shirt and lurched over the seat. The smoke blinded him and stung his eyes. Tears clouded his eyes as he felt around for the seat belt buckle. His burning fingers finally found the hot metal buckle, and he pushed. The car seat came free, and Lucas tumbled to the ground with it.

"Good job, kid," someone was encouraging as he grasped under his arms and pulled him away from the scene.

Lucas handed the car seat up to the emergency personnel standing over him. He knew Russ was nearby, reeking of alcohol. Russ grabbed this moment to try to escape with a nearby vehicle, while the emergency personnel were distracted.

"Come on, kid," Russ grabbed him by the collar of his burned shirt and hauled him to his feet.

Still choking from the smoke, Lucas had no strength left to resist.

"Hey, stop!" a police officer called out as Russ made a break towards the car.

Lucas dragged his feet, trying to stall Russ.

"You stupid kid! Get in the car!" Russ cussed out Lucas, pulling him along. They had made it to the car door. Lucas refused to get in. Police were close on their heels.

"I said get in!" Russ lost his patience and drew back his fist. Lucas felt his head snap back, and his world went black just long enough for Russ to shove him in and slam the door. Lucas heard the ignition clicking as Russ tried desperately to drive away. Lucas blacked out again, and when he awoke, he was lying on a stretcher. The police were escorting Russ away from the vehicle.

"He doesn't need to be seen, I'll take care of him," Lucas heard his mom insist.

"Ma'am, he needs medical treatment immediately. I do not recommend that you attempt to treat him on your own." Lucas heard the paramedic's tone change as he realized Lucas' mom had no intention of treating her son.

"No, he's my son. I'll take care of him," his mom insisted again, trying to speak clearly.

Lucas closed his eyes again, wishing the paramedics would just take him away. A few moments later, someone helped him up and into a vehicle.

"Sorry, kid, we did everything we could. You were really brave out there," one of the paramedics apologized as he helped lay Lucas on the backseat of a taxi.

Lucas curled up into a ball and tried to shut out the world. His drunken mom slid in beside him, making no effort to soothe him. Lucas wished he were somewhere far away from this horrible place, but it would be another awful four years before anything would change for him.

TWO

TEARS STREAMED DOWN HIS FACE as blood trickled from his nose. He lay shaking underneath the blankets on his bed. Angry words flew back and forth between his mom and her boyfriend. The man had already punched him once, and he was terrified of getting hurt again. He heard his name being called, but he burrowed further under the blankets. Footsteps thundered down the hall and the doorknob turned. He thought his heart would stop in his chest. He hoped it would, but in his heart he knew nothing could stop what was coming. The door opened, and he heard the man storm in. He was drunk. Lucas could tell by the way he slammed into everything calling his name. Lucas huddled in a ball as the covers were ripped off. The man clutched a knife in one hand. In the other, he gripped a belt. With anger in his eyes, he reached for Lucas who scrambled desperately to get away. "Please... don't!" Lucas cried covering his eyes.

Lucas woke screaming. After a moment, he realized it was just a dream as the faces and voices faded from his mind. His eyes adjusted to the darkness and he remembered where he was. The park was empty at this time of night. The city was fast asleep. All he could hear was the crickets chirping in the few small bushes scattered through the park. Struggling to get comfortable on the frigid bench, he rolled over onto his back and stared at the stars trying to go back to sleep.

The next morning, he awoke at six o' clock, before most of the city was awake. He yawned and picked up his backpack. Another long night had passed, and it was time for work again. The sun was just rising as he jogged to the community college. Their showers opened for the athletes at five a.m. He walked into the bathrooms and used the open showers while the runners were out.

Even though he was only seventeen, his dark clothes and couple day's worth of stubble made him look old enough to be one of the college students. He showered quickly and shaved. He checked his watch and quickly dashed for the door. He had to make it by seven today!

Two weeks had gone by with him being late every day. The boss said it couldn't happen again or he would be fired, and he couldn't afford that. He ran to the bus stop and caught the bus just before it left.

Today was his ten-hour day at Happy Hearts Nursing Home. Nothing about it was very happy, but it was a job, and the utility bill wasn't going to pay itself. He wondered about his mom as the bus made its way through town. He hoped she would get rid of her newest boyfriend before he returned home. This new boyfriend was a heavier drinker than the last one and rougher, too. Lucas' eye still hurt from the fight they had gotten into last week.

The bus arrived right at six forty-five, and Lucas had just enough time to run into the huge nursing home facility and make it to the check-in just before seven.

"Early today," remarked the security guard, leaning back in his chair. The rickety chair creaked as it held all his weight.

Lucas ignored him and pushed through the doors to the elevator. He took it to the third floor where he had spent most of his high school life. The doors opened, and he almost tripped over Mrs. Wygoni, a seventy-year-old woman from Japan who had arrived in America just last year.

"Hello, Mrs. Wygoni. How are you today?" Lucas yelled as he stepped off the elevator.

She was mostly deaf in both ears and constantly forgot she had to wear her hearing aids. The night nurse never failed to forget to put them in.

She reached up, took his face in her hands, and kissed his cheeks on both sides, uttering something in Japanese. Lucas smiled and nodded as if he understood.

"Yep, let's go get your hearing aids, Mrs. Wygoni," he said, taking her arm in his.

For each step he took, she had to take three little steps. He was patient, talking kindly as they slowly made their way down the hallway. Mr. Quackinbush shuffled towards them, pushing his walker out too far.

"Oh, Mr. Quackinbush, you have to keep up with the walker! You're always letting it run away," Lucas reminded him, hurrying to his side before he fell. The elderly man's brown sweater hung loosely from his shoulders, and his missing teeth made him almost look like he was quacking when he talked.

"Have you heard about the ship? It was a great big one! It sunk, by golly." Mr. Quackinbush began the same story he told every morning. All Lucas did was smile and nod and say, "Yep, that's correct. It was on the news this morning."

"Where can I find a copy of the newspaper? I want to see it on the front page," Mr. Quackinbush said, looking through the papers in the nurses' station.

"What should I do... or say?" Lucas asked himself, never sure whether to play along or tell him the truth. "Oh, look at that, it's right there on the front page!" Lucas decided to play along, grabbing the newspaper.

He helped Mr. Quackinbush sit in a nearby chair. Lucas knew he had forgotten how to read, so only pictures mattered. As luck would have it, a boat had sunk on the lake near them that day. The town the nursing home was in was pretty small, so if a car ran over a cat, it would probably be in the news.

Lucas thought to himself, "I will never live in a small town."

He didn't like anyone knowing his business, and in small towns, all that seemed to entertain people was talking about other people's business. The day seemed to drag on. Patients asked him endless questions. He fed them breakfast, lunch, and dinner before his shift was finally over.

He took the bus back to his house, forty-five minutes downtown. When he got to his street, Lucas was filled with dread. He hated his house. There was almost always some sort of fight going on. A beat-up pickup sat in the driveway, and empty beer cans littered the broken cement sidewalk outside their apartment. Little kids dodged in and out of the alleyways between the houses.

He stepped over two girls playing on the ground and walked up the steps to the apartment. Pushing open the door, he immediately wished he were somewhere else. His mom was already drunk, her words slurring as she pointed a finger in her boyfriend's face.

"I saw you with someone else!" she cried and yelled at the same time.

The boyfriend's face hardened, and he grabbed her by the arm.

"Hey!" Lucas interrupted as he strode over to them. He broke the man's grip on his mom's arm. "What do you want, Kyle?" he demanded, stepping in front of his mom who sank to the couch, sniffling.

"She's accusing me of cheating, and you best stay out of it boy or I'll make sure you have matching eyes this time."

Lucas felt his pulse hammer as Kyle towered over him.

"Leave her alone," Lucas said firmly, tensing his fists.

"Don't fight, please," his mom begged, her voice thick. "Kyle didn't mean it. Don't hit him again, Luke," she begged.

"Mom, he hurt you! He's going to hurt you again, just like last time!"

"Just leave!" his mom cried, trying to point to the door.

"Fine, but just remember who takes care of you, mom. I'll be back because I have to pay the utility bill tomorrow! Don't bother to miss me," he seethed.

"Don't touch her," he warned Kyle.

Kyle stumbled backwards as Lucas shoved him before turning and walking out the door. He let the screen door slam behind him. Lucas ran down the steps and saw Scott walking out of his house. Scott had been his best friend since tenth grade. Scott got a little drunk once in awhile – well, mostly every day—he was usually able to hide it except from people who knew him well.

"Hey, are we partying tonight?" Scott called out, holding up a six-pack.

"Yeah buddy!" Lucas cheered, pretending to be excited.

"You missed the last couple," Scott accused, playfully slapping him on the back.

"I got to work, dude," Lucas responded.

"But you're free tonight," Scott said, fist bumping him.

"Yay," Lucas replied sarcastically.

"Come on, let's go!" Scott announced, putting an arm around him. His heart heavy, Lucas followed along.

They took the bus over to Lamont's house. It was just getting dark as they arrived. Lucas followed them down the shadowed alleyway to the apartment Lamont shared with his girlfriend. Trash was scattered around the few grassy patches that grew in the broken pavement. Three more people Lucas didn't know met them at the door.

"Hey guys!" One of them greeted Scott, holding up a six-pack of beer.

Scott grinned and threw a fist in the air. "Yeah boy, we gonna party tonight," he whooped and threw an arm around Lucas and towed him inside.

"I can't drink too much tonight, man, I got to work tomorrow," Lucas told Scott as he handed him a beer.

"Work, smirk, it's a Friday night! Relax a little!" he demanded, shaking Lucas' shoulders. "You're always so tense. It's like you carry the world around or something."

Lucas pushed him away. "Get off me, and go easy on the beer. I'm not carrying you home again tonight," Lucas warned, smiling at the memory of his friend's last drunken adventure.

"I know you Lucas. You always got everyone's back except your own. Carry me piggyback this time! The over-the-shoulder carry is a little uncomfortable," Scott laughed, punching him playfully before walking off.

Lucas sighed and looked around at all the people who were crowding into the small apartment. More arrived every couple of minutes. Maybe Scott was right. Maybe he was a little too tense. He thought of his mom and everything that he knew was going to happen tonight. She would get trashed, provoke her boyfriend into an argument, get beat up, and Lucas would be there to pick up the pieces before he went to work. Tonight, though, was still tonight. He wouldn't worry about it until tomorrow.

"Lucas, come join the party. Why are you just standing there? Come on! It's Friday!" one of his old high school buddies called from the other room.

"To Friday!" Lucas cheered holding up his beer. Inside his heart he locked the pain away and joined his friends.

"Hey, Lamont," Lucas greeted his old friend.

"Where ya been?" Lamont exclaimed handing Lucas another beer as Lucas finished off the first.

"Working, man," Lucas responded snapping the top off the bottle. Beer dripped down his hand as he took a swig from the top.

"Working? Pfff, who needs to work? You're supposed to be in school having fun with us. Ponytail Abbey has been asking about you," Lamont laughed, opening his third beer.

Lucas grinned, "Oh yeah? I must have lost her number somewhere."

Lamont threw his head back laughing, "She probably searched all over town for you."

"I bet she did," Lucas responded, taking another swig of beer.

"Come on, seriously, man, where ya been?" Lamont patted him on the back, spilling some of his beer on the floor.

"Hey watch it, that's good beer you're wasting," Lucas chided.

"Come on, I want to know. Why don't you come back with us?" Lamont insisted, plopping himself onto one of the living room couches. Lucas sat carefully trying not to spill the beer. "I dropped out, dude. We need the money," Lucas confided.

"Money? For that crazy drunk mother of yours? Come on, man, she's been dragging you along since we were in kindergarten. Just get rid of her, you can come live with me."

Lucas chuckled. "Oh sure, we can both sleep in a box on the street after your parents kick you out for having all these parties!"

Lamont punched his arm, "Hey what they don't know won't hurt 'em. Cheers to the high school dropout," Lamont held his beer up, and they toasted. Tipping their heads back, they emptied their bottles. They sat in silence for a long moment.

"Beer pong?" Lamont suggested.

"Don't mind if I do." Lucas stood and followed Lamont downstairs to the basement. They joined Scott and teamed up. Lucas, Lamont, and Scott won the first round.

"One more!" Scott cheered, stumbling to pick up all the cups.

"No, no, no, we gotta get goin," Lucas declined.

Lamont groaned, "Come on, man, work can wait."

Lucas shook his head, "Maybe another night. I got to go."

Lamont nodded, "You're a good kid, Lucas. Hey! We're thinking of getting together down by the beach on Monday. You down?"

"I'll let you know," Lucas responded, looking around for Scott. He spotted him over by the stereo tripping over the cords as he tried to change the song.

"Come on, man, we gotta go. I have to work tomorrow, remember?" Lucas yelled over the music to Scott. Scott yelled back something Lucas couldn't understand. Lucas pushed his way through the crowd of people and grabbed Scott by his shirt.

"Come on, we're leaving," Lucas said firmly. Scott stumbled along, cheering. Lucas got to the door and released his friend. "If you don't come out right now, I'm leaving you here," Lucas warned, taking out his pack of cigarettes.

"All right, all right! I need my shoes," Scott's words slurred together as he leaned on the wall for support.

"Your shoes are on your feet! Now come on," Lucas said, dragging Scott along.

"Wait up, Scott, we'll come with you. This party's getting old," one of their friends staggered over.

"Party at my house!" Scott announced, his words running together. A couple of people cheered.

Lucas sighed. "I'm going out to smoke a cigarette. Hurry up!"

Outside, the night air was warm and humid. He crossed the street and waited for Scott and his buddies. Lucas leaned down to light his cigarette.

"Excuse me," a polite, quiet voice interrupted him. He looked up and met a pair of wide brown eyes. He raised his eyebrows, signaling for her to ask her question as he took a drag on his cigarette.

"Where is the bus stop for Western Town?" she asked, looking disgustedly at his cigarette.

He blew the smoke to the side, away from her. As he straightened, he looked her over. She didn't look like she belonged downtown. Her simple jeans and t-shirt told him she wasn't looking for another party.

She watched him, waiting for an answer as she nervously played with her long black ponytail.

"Down there, on the corner," he answered finally. She appeared confused so he pointed past Lamont's house to the corner where the sign for the bus stop stood under a flickering street lamp.

"Oh, thanks," she said, hurrying towards it.

He watched her leave, taking another drag on his smoke. He hoped she wouldn't run into trouble. She seemed like a nice girl.

He waited five more minutes and looked at his watch. If he didn't leave soon, he would be too exhausted for work tomorrow. Ten more minutes passed, and Scott didn't show. Lucas decided it was time for Scott to worry about himself. He had to get home. He tossed the cigarette and shoved his hands deep into his pockets.

Halfway down the street, he heard the same soft voice cry out. He couldn't make out the words, but she sounded distressed. Lucas kept walking, but heard the same voice again, louder, and more upset. He looked to his left and saw two guys standing too close to the girl. The girl appeared to be about sixteen. She had a black curly ponytail, with tan skin. It definitely was the same girl, he thought. Lucas saw Scott saunter over. He was completely drunk, and bent on getting her attention. She clearly didn't want to give it. This seemed to anger Scott. Scott shoved her, and the other two closed in. Lucas wasn't sure why he was suddenly afraid for the girl, but his heart pounded in his chest. He ran over and pushed his way to the middle, just as Scott roughly grabbed her arm.

"Hey, lay off. She's just trying to get home," Lucas commanded, breaking Scott's grip on her arm.

Scott let go, and the girl rubbed her red wrist. "Come on, Lucas. We were just having fun with her," Scott laughed.

"You have had enough fun for tonight! Get out of here!" Lucas demanded, glaring at Scott.

"Fine man, we'll go, just chill out! We were headed back to party anyway. I just came out to tell you I'm not coming with you," Scott defended, wobbling back towards the apartment.

Lucas kept his fists tense until the other two followed Scott. He waited until they got out of earshot before he turned to the girl.

Her hands shook, though she tried to hide it by clutching her purse with both hands. "Thanks," she said, trying to keep her voice steady.

Lucas stood there, watching her silently.

"Thank you for saving me," she repeated, waiting for his response.

Lucas nodded.

"That's it? No 'you're welcome'?" she questioned, unsure of the boy's intent. She stared up at him as he watched her. "Hello, anyone in there?" she asked, waving her hand in front of his face.

Lucas reached for his cigarettes without speaking.

She sighed, "Well anyway, thanks for saving me. I guess this is good-bye," she said, sticking her hand out for him to shake.

He let her hand stay there as he lit a cigarette.

She crossed her arms, annoyed. "Okay Superman, at least tell me your name," she demanded.

He lit his cigarette as she glared angrily. She huffed as he took a drag from the cigarette and blew the smoke out behind him.

"Excuse me, it's polite to answer a lady when she's talking to you," the girl lectured.

Lucas finally laughed, "Okay, okay, fine. It's Lucas. You?"

"Kayla. Why didn't you answer me?" she demanded angrily.

"Didn't know such a pretty girl could be so pushy. Most people give up after the first five minutes," he smiled as her mouth opened in shock.

"Well, if I am so pushy then you can just go. I'll be fine," she turned her back to him, as the bus pulled up.

"Nope, you won't, you'll die probably," Lucas retorted stepping forward.

She looked offended and opened her mouth to say what she thought just as the bus doors opened.

Lucas took her hand, "Two for uptown please," he told the bus driver politely. The bus driver rolled his eyes. Kayla tried to interrupt him, but he ignored her and pulled out his wallet to pay.

"But I want to…" she started, but he pulled her onto the bus.

"Quiet, honey, you'll wake the drunks," he chided, walking by various people passed out in their seats.

She ripped her hand away as they sat. "Excuse me," she glared at him.

He just smiled, putting out his cigarette. "Why are you even down here, anyway?" he asked as the bus started.

"If you must know, I got a little lost," she huffed.

"Well that was clear! I meant why you were even in the area?" he grinned as her face turned three different shades of angry.

"I know my way around downtown. What do you think, I'm some snobby country girl?"

"Maybe not country," Lucas agreed.

She glared at him until he smiled. When he smiled, Kayla thought it was the most adorable smile she had ever seen. She broke into a laugh despite herself.

"I was down visiting a good friend, and I got lost trying to find the right bus stop," she explained. "What about you?"

He laughed. "I basically live here. My mom and her boyfriend are…" he paused, searching for the right word. "Annoying," he said finally. He decided she didn't need to know the personal details of his nightmare.

"So because your parents are annoying, you wander the streets until three in the morning?" she asked, her eyebrows raised. She knew there was something he wasn't telling her.

"Pretty much," he answered, shrugging. She wanted to ask him more, but the bus was turning onto her street.

"This is my stop," she explained, standing. He walked her to the door of the bus. "Thanks again," she said, turning to leave.

The bus stopped and Lucas found himself wishing she didn't have to go. He looked out the door at her house. It was a two story white house with a small building adjacent to it. The neighbors were few and far between. The woods stretched out for miles behind her house. He knew they had nothing in common. She deserved better. He nodded as she walked out the door.

"Goodbye Lucas," she waved.

The bus driver shut the doors.

"Wait until she gets in, please," Lucas asked the bus driver. The bus driver waited, the engine idling. Lucas waited until the lights turned on and her father came out waving his arms angrily.

"You can go," Lucas said ducking back into the seat. The last thing he needed tonight was an angry, rich parent after him.

The bus turned and headed back for Lucas' town. Lucas tried not to sleep during the twenty-minute drive, but his eyelids were heavy. He had no idea how he was going to get up in three hours and get to work.

The bus driver pulled up to his street and let him off. Lucas ambled home, thinking about the girl. He couldn't get those big brown eyes out of his mind. But as he walked closer to his house, fear filled his mind and consumed his thoughts. He crept up the stairs and cautiously pushed open the door. His mom lay passed out on the couch. Kyle was slumped on the couch snoring loudly. Lucas breathed a sigh of relief. He snuck by them to his room and curled up under the covers. The last face he saw was Kayla's as his eyes closed. He drifted off to sleep.

THREE

LUCAS WOKE TO HIS VIBRATING phone alarm—set to wake him but not the angry drunks in the house. He groaned as he rolled over and tried to find his phone buried in the covers. At once, he realized it was far too light outside. Lucas dragged himself out of bed, brushed his hair, and raced out the door without bothering to change his clothes. The bus was just pulling away as Lucas rounded the corner to the bus stop.

"Hey!" he screamed, waving his arms. The bus creaked to a stop, and the doors opened. Lucas boarded the bus, breathing heavily from the run.

"You again?" the bus driver questioned tiredly. Lucas nodded stumbling to his seat. "Well, we're in the same boat kid. I haven't gotten off this bus since I picked up you and girlie last night," the bus driver sighed.

Lucas counted the minutes until they reached the nursing home. He jumped up as soon as the bus stopped.

"Good luck, kid, see ya later," the bus driver yelled after him as Lucas ran toward the nursing home.

"You're late again!" the boss snarled as Lucas rushed into the office.

"I'm sorry, I…" Lucas started to explain.

"No more buts, kid, after this shift you're done. The whole floor is late because you weren't here to wake everyone up. Get to work," the boss turned on his heel and stalked out.

Lucas stood there stunned.

"Hey, Lucas, you better get to work," Lily, one of his co-workers, told him with a hand on his shoulder.

"Oh, right," Lucas responded dully. He trudged towards Mr. Quackinbush's room.

"Hey, Lucas, I have a present for you," the old man laughed.

Lucas sighed and snapped on a pair of gloves, "Let's get you cleaned up," he responded.

"Hey, did you hear about the Titanic?" Mr. Quackinbush began again.

Lucas worked for ten hours straight. He didn't dare take his break and face his boss again. At five o'clock, his shift finally ended. Lucas could hardly walk. He was so exhausted.

"You'll receive your last paycheck next week!" the boss yelled after him as Lucas walked out.

He let the door slam behind him. He took the bus home and barely made it to his front steps before he felt dizzy. He heard the fighting before he even got in the door. Preparing himself, he tensed his fists and walked in. Kyle stood in the kitchen breathing heavily. The apartment reeked of alcohol. Lucas looked around. Empty bottles lay scattered everywhere. He walked in and saw his mom lying on the floor crying.

"Lucas, help me!" she cried, holding a hand to her black eye. Anger surged through Lucas. The stress of all that had gone on clouded his mind and, without thinking, he let the rage explode.

"I told you not to touch her!" Lucas screamed and charged him.

He turned, and Lucas punched him in the jaw. Kyle stumbled drunkenly, and Lucas pushed him down. They wrestled on the floor. Even drunk, Kyle was strong and twice the weight of Lucas. Lucas got a few good shots in, but began to lose strength when Kyle continually punched him in the face. Lucas faded in and out of consciousness as Kyle kicked and pummeled him. He felt all the breath going out of his lungs. Blood trickled from every place on his body.

His mom pulled on Kyle's arm until he stopped. "Lucas, go! Leave, please!" she begged.

Kyle finally paused, his fist upraised.

When Lucas didn't move, his mom tried again. "He will kill you!" she drunkenly lunged for Kyle, desperate to thwart his next punch.

Kyle himself seemed to be out of strength.

Without waiting for another warning, Lucas struggled to his feet and stumbled out the door. His body ached and pain overwhelmed him.

Scott was waiting outside for him. "Lucas I…" he stopped mid sentence, his mouth opening in horror. "What just happened in there?"

Lucas shook his head, hanging on the railing for support.

"Come on, man, a few good drinks will take care of your pain," Scott encouraged, helping Lucas down.

He put Lucas' arm around his shoulder and helped him to the bus stop. Scott sat him down on the bench and held him up. Lucas' head ached, but the spinning abated.

When the bus pulled up, Scott reached out a hand to help him up. Lucas pushed it away and stood.

"That's my boy, come on. You don't have to work tomorrow. Just forget about them. Lamont's having a party down by the beach," Scott coaxed, hoping Lucas wouldn't ruin his plans for the night.

Lucas just led the way onto the bus in response.

"Yes!" Scott cheered.

They rode down to the beach. Lucas' mind slowly came back into focus, and he could think clearly. He realized the passengers next to him were staring at the blood. He pulled his sweatshirt hood over his head and slumped down in the seat. Once they arrived, he stumbled off the bus.

"Hey!" Lamont met them as they exited the bus. "What happened to you?" Lamont demanded anxiously. Blood was dripping from Lucas' nose and lip.

"Nothing, he just needs a few good drinks, that's all," Scott replied quickly slinging an arm around Lucas.

Scott didn't want to have to sit in the ER all night instead of partying.

Lucas didn't care anymore. He needed to forget. He needed to forget everything.

A swarm of partiers descended on them carrying a cooler full of beer.

Scott handed Lucas a beer can. "I bet you can't drink this in one swig," Scott dared Lucas as Lucas opened the top.

Scott hoped Lucas would take the bait and just enjoy himself. He was so tense all the time; it was obnoxious.

Lucas didn't want to remember what happened to him that day, so he decided to have a little fun and drink. He chugged the can in ten seconds.

"Oh yeah, the Lucas party is on!" Scott cheered, encouraging Lucas to do it again.

They decided to have some fun and make a contest out of it. Scott's friends got out two six packs. One was for Scott and one was for Lucas. Scott opened up the boxes. Lucas was already opening a bottle.

"Ready. Set. Go!" Lamont yelled, and they began drinking.

"Chug, chug, chug," the crowd chanted.

They watched amazed as Lucas finished two bottles ahead of Scott.

"Who's next?" Lucas slurred, tripping over his own feet.

Another person raised his hand, and Scott stumbled off, throwing up. Lucas didn't remember when he blacked out. He only remembered finding a tree, throwing up, and then lying down—replaying the horrible memories of his life.

FOUR

KAYLA COULDN'T STOP THINKING ABOUT Lucas. She replayed their encounter over and over in her mind during school, on the bus ride home, and as she got her little brother Charlie ready to go to the park.

"Dad, do you really have to go to another meeting today?" she sighed.

"Yes, it's very important, Honey. I'm sorry, I know you had plans to go to the mall, but I have to have someone to watch Charlie," responded Mr. Maxwell.

"Where's his assistant? Can't she do it?" Kayla begged as she put on Charlie's shoes.

"She called in…again…" her father sighed.

It was the third time that week that he had had to ask his daughter to stay home and watch Charlie. But he had to go. Things were getting dangerous, and they needed an extra person for downtown patrol.

"Look, Sweetie," he said, kneeling next to her as she laced Charlie's shoes. "I love you very much. I couldn't ask for a better daughter than you. Your mother would be proud of you," he said teary-eyed.

Kayla hugged her father tightly.

"I love you, Dad. Don't be too late tonight! Don't worry about us - I have something fun for us to do." They smiled at each other.

"Bye, Kiddo. I love you, too," he said to Charlie, ruffling his hair.

"Bye, Dad. I'll just have fun torturing Kayla," he giggled as Kayla pretended to attack him. Their father laughed and pulled Charlie into his arms.

"Now you leave your sister alone," he said, putting him into his wheelchair.

"Never!" Charlie exclaimed, giggling.

Kayla rolled her eyes and buckled him into the wheelchair. She hooked her purse and his backpack on the back of the wheelchair.

"Off we go," Mr. Maxwell said, opening the front door for them.

They watched as their dad got into the car and waved as he drove away. Kayla pushed the wheelchair to the bus stop and waited. She wasn't really sure if her father would approve of her plan for the day, but she had to do it. She wanted to see Lucas again. There was a park she knew of close to where she and Lucas had met. He said he lived around that spot. The park had some swings specially made for kids with disabilities as well as a small place to play in the water. It had waterspouts and other equipment for the kids to cool off in. She knew Charlie would love it, but she secretly hoped Lucas would be there. She realized he probably wouldn't be, but she had to try.

The bus pulled up and she helped the driver load Charlie in. She recognized him from the night before.

"Where to, Miss?" he asked settling Charlie in.

"Downtown park, please," she responded.

"Haven't you gotten yourself into enough trouble down there?" he asked, raising an eyebrow.

"I can handle myself," she said firmly.

"Of course—as you wish," he replied, shaking his head.

He climbed back into the driver's seat and drove toward the city. As the bus reached the park, she searched for Lucas' face through the window. It was a hot day. People were everywhere trying to cool off and hang out in the shade. Her heart sank. Of course! Why would he be here? He was probably hanging out in a gang somewhere and smoking his cigarettes. Maybe he was dangerous. Maybe he never even wanted to see her again….

"What am I even doing here?" she thought to herself as she pushed Charlie onto the sidewalk. She tried not to let her disappointment show. She wanted Charlie to have a good time.

"Well, here we are," she announced.

Charlie looked up at her. "Here?" he questioned.

"Yeah, there's a water park or something—somewhere."

Charlie rolled his eyes. "For someone who is so much older, she isn't a whole lot smarter," he thought to himself.

She walked along the outside of the park, trying to find where the water equipment was. When she finally spotted it, she tried to make her way over. The crowd was really thick and people didn't seem to understand that they needed to move in order for her to be able to push the wheelchair through. Halfway there, she gave up in frustration.

"Let's eat lunch on the grass first. Maybe some people will clear out by then," she decided and pushed Charlie over toward the only open picnic table.

As she sat, she noticed a man curled up underneath one of the trees. He wore a tattered shirt and filthy jeans. She looked closer and saw that his clothes were stained with blood. He had several cuts and bruises on his face. She worried that he was hurt, but she was too afraid to see if he needed help. She remembered how afraid she'd felt when the other three boys had almost attacked her. The boy with the deep blue eyes who had rushed to save her flooded her memory. Wait! There was a reason that shirt looked familiar! She saw the pack of cigarettes and lighter in the back pocket of his jeans and everything clicked.

"Stay here Charlie," she commanded, locking his chair. She ran over to the boy and knelt beside him. "Lucas," she whispered horrified. She gently put her hand on his cheek as tears filled her eyes.

Lucas awoke to a familiar pair of wide brown eyes staring into his.

"What happened to you?" she whispered, touching one of the cuts on his swollen cheek.

Kayla? When had she gotten here? How long had he been asleep? He couldn't remember what happened. Then he felt the pain in his body. He remembered the fight with Kyle, then drinking with his friends and lying down in the park, but not Kayla being there. He could feel the dried blood on his face and was ashamed.

"You shouldn't be here," he whispered, his voice hoarse.

"Neither should you. What happened?" she pressed.

"Just go home, Kayla." He tried to sound convincing as his strength faded. He was losing consciousness again.

"Nope, you'll probably die if I do," she repeated his phrase from the other night. He rolled over to ignore her. "Oh no, you don't! Come on!" she hauled him to his feet.

He staggered as she half-supported, half-dragged him back to where Charlie was. Lucas saw the little boy through swollen eyes.

In his wheelchair, the little boy gazed at him nervously.

"Don't worry, kid, I'm not going to hurt you," Lucas teased between painful breaths. "Does your sister always pick up homeless teenagers?"

Charlie laughed. "Sometimes. Daddy says she attracts trouble,"

"Clearly," Lucas answered.

"Hey, I am the one saving your life, you know," she retorted, attempting to hold him on his feet in his weakened condition.

"I can handle myself," he imitated her high-pitched voice as his knees started to buckle.

"Stay with me," she insisted, grabbing him around the waist just before they both collapsed.

"I'm trying," he said weakly.

"Okay, we have to at least get to the bus stop."

He nodded, and they made a slow procession over to the sidewalk where the bus had dropped her off earlier. The crowd parted for them once they saw Lucas' face. Kayla struggled to push Charlie and hold up Lucas with the other arm as he staggered along, but somehow they made it. Lucas tried to stay upright, but the world kept spinning.

"Lucas," Kayla started, but Lucas had already passed out cold, the weight of his unconscious body pulling her down.

"Is he dead? Kiss him! Maybe he will wake up like in Snow White!" Charlie cried as Kayla knelt beside him.

She leaned in to try and shake him back into consciousness.

"I was just kidding!" Charlie said nervously. "A kiss won't do anything when you're dead!"

As Charlie started to get upset, Lucas opened his eyes. Kayla begged to call an ambulance, but Lucas refused, knowing there was no way to pay for emergency services. With Kayla's help, he carefully stood up, steadying himself with the back of the wheelchair.

Thankfully, the bus pulled up. The doors opened and Kayla looked up at the bus driver. His arms were already crossed.

The bus driver shook his head. "I see you found trouble."

"Can you help me get him on?" Kayla fretted.

The bus driver sighed and got out of his chair. "I don't get paid enough for this job," he told her as he descended to the sidewalk. He hefted Lucas into his arms and carried him onto the bus.

Kayla followed him and helped him lay Lucas on the seat in the back.

"I'll get the kid," the bus driver said.

Kayla nodded, putting her arm around Lucas to keep him from falling off the seat.

"Dad's going to kill you, you know that, right?" Charlie asked forebodingly as the bus driver loaded him in.

"Yeah, I know. Maybe I'll tell him we were playing the Good Samaritan."

"I don't think he will buy that. In church, we just use puppets," Charlie informed her.

The bus driver drove them back home and half-carried Lucas inside the house.

"You can just put him on the couch," Kayla pointed towards the living room.

Charlie sighed, "Great, we find a bloody man and help him, and now we're letting him move in with us, all in one hour. Perfect. Dad's gonna love you, Kayla."

"Yeah, yeah," she said, pushing his wheelchair into the living room.

She put him on the floor to crawl around in front of Sesame Street and thanked the bus driver.

"No problem, you were my last passengers anyway. See you around," the bus driver tipped his hat and let himself out.

Kayla filled a bowl of warm water in the kitchen and got some washcloths from the bathroom. She walked back to where Lucas still lay unmoving on the couch. She pulled up a chair next to him. She dipped the washcloth in the water and gently wiped the cheek that wasn't as swollen. Lucas felt her touch but wasn't fully awake yet. The warm water seemed to relieve some of the soreness, and he was grateful for that. She cleaned up most of the dried blood and started to work on the cuts. Pain finally awakened him and he winced.

"You're awake," she smiled.

"Unfortunately," he replied.

"Hold still, we are almost done," she instructed.

He opened his eyes. Her forehead creased in concentration as she examined the cut on his cheek.

"How did you get this?" she demanded.

"Where are we?" Lucas ignored her question as he curiously looked around.

"We're at my house," Kayla responded, wiping some more blood off his cheek.

"How did you get me here?"

"Eh, it wasn't hard. I only had to ask the bus driver to help me carry you while pushing my brother up a hill. But don't worry about it, just a simple thank you will be good, I think," Kayla laughed, dabbing more warm water onto his face.

"Thank you," he said sincerely as he looked into her eyes.

She blushed and he smiled. She pushed the washcloth more firmly on the cut to stop the bleeding. He sucked in his breath.

She smiled. "Not one for pain, are you?"

He laughed a harsh, short laugh. "You have no idea."

"Hi kids, I'm home!" Mr. Maxwell swung the door open and stepped into the foyer.

Kayla ran to the door and tried to stall him from walking into the room where Lucas was.

"So, Dad how was your day?"

"Okay, I guess."

"I need to show you something in the kitchen." She led him to the kitchen, looking intensely at Charlie.

She whispered, "Take care of him, I'll be back."

Charlie nodded in agreement.

"So...uh...Dad?" Kayla tried stalling him from going into the living room.

"Yes?" he asked slowly, turning around so he was eye-to-eye with her.

"Hi, Daddy." Kayla smiled her sweetest smile. Her dad raised an eyebrow at her.

"What do you want, dearest darling whom I know is trying to get something out of me?"

"Remember that boy I told you about who rescued me?"

Her father walked past her into the kitchen. He took off his holster and put it on the table. Lucas' eyes widened as he watched nervously.

"M-hmm," her father nodded, unbuttoning the top button of his collared shirt.

Kayla wasn't sure how to begin. "Well...he's on our couch in the living room," Kayla said quickly, smiling.

Her father's back went rigid. "What did you say?"

"Um...well," Kayla stuttered, backing away from his angry glare. Lucas was terrified. He rolled off the couch and stood ready to run.

"Wait, don't go," Kayla calmed him. "Dad won't hurt you. He just seems scary."

Lucas' heart was pounding in his chest. Mr. Maxwell turned and met Lucas' terrified eyes. He examined Lucas' appearance. The boy looked like he hadn't eaten in days. His clothes were ripped and dirty, he needed a shave, and he reeked of alcohol.

"Are you drunk?" he demanded of Lucas.

"No, no, sir," Lucas stammered.

Mr. Maxwell moved closer to look over his injuries. "Sit down, boy. Let Kayla clean those wounds, and we will talk over dinner."

Lucas felt frozen. Kayla put a light hand on his shoulder and gently pushed him down.

"Thank you, Dad. I'll make dinner right after I finish cleaning him up," Kayla promised.

Mr. Maxwell was already walking away. "All right – good" he called over his shoulder. He whistled his way upstairs, and they heard a door shut and the shower turn on.

"You didn't tell me your Dad was a cop!" Lucas whispered tensely.

"Lie back," Kayla instructed. Lucas reluctantly obeyed. "Well, I didn't want to scare you."

"Too late for that," Lucas sighed. "When he took the gun off I thought I was going to have a heart attack."

Kayla guided Lucas to the kitchen. She dampened a towel and sat down next to Lucas at the table.

"Close your eyes," she instructed. Tenderly she dabbed the cut above his eye with the warm cloth. He winced.

"Sorry," she apologized.

"It's okay," he replied, trying not to pull away from her as she pulled open the wound.

"It doesn't look too deep to me," she announced, applying gauze to stop the bleeding.

"That's good," Lucas sighed.

"Can I be with you guys?" Charlie called from the other room.

"Sure, bud, hang on one minute!" Kayla called back.

"I'll get him," Lucas stood.

"Are you sure?" Kayla replied. Lucas nodded and went in to get Charlie.

"You're not Kayla," Charlie observed.

"True, I'm not," Lucas responded. He winced in pain as he knelt down to Charlie's eye level.

"You wanted to come hang out with us?" Lucas questioned.

"No, I'm hungry," Charlie answered honestly.

Lucas laughed.

"Want a ride? I'll carry you out."

Charlie looked at him skeptically, "You're not going to murder me, are you?"

Lucas became very solemn.

"Only if you're not going to be my friend," Lucas responded. Charlie's eyes widened. "I'm just kidding, bud! Come on, we will go get some food."

He held his arms out to Charlie who was still wary of him. "Ready? Here comes the rocket ship!"

He winced in pain as he picked up Charlie. His bones and muscles ached all over, but he was anxious to show Kayla he was okay. He zoomed Charlie into the kitchen.

"Where does astronaut Charlie sit?" Lucas asked in an army voice.

Kayla laughed, "In his wheelchair at the table."

"Astronaut Charlie would like something to eat," Charlie announced.

"Oh, what a shock! We *only* fed you an hour ago!" Kayla teased, tickling him.

"Astronauts work hard and they eat a lot," Charlie explained.

"Well, let me get Lucas some ice for his eye, and I'll get you young men some food," Kayla replied patiently.

Out of the freezer she took some ice and wrapped it in a clean washcloth. Lucas reached out to take it from her, and she pressed it into his hands.

"Leave it on. It will help with the swelling," she instructed firmly as she held his blue eyes with hers.

He stared back at her for a moment, watching the way the light in the kitchen played with the light in her eyes.

"Look, Charlie, I'm a pirate." Lucas made a hook with his finger and squinted with his good eye.

Charlie sighed, "You can't be a pirate. You don't have a parrot."

Kayla laughed, "Lucas' parrot is in the living room. You two can play after dinner."

"What's for dinner?" Charlie asked.

"Astronaut food," Kayla replied.

Lucas held back a smile. "Astronauts can only eat Jell-O," Lucas reminded him. Charlie's eyes widened.

"I can only eat Jell-O?"

Kayla hit Lucas lightly on the shoulder.

"He's just kidding! We are having hot dogs and mac and cheese tonight, and I made a pie for dessert," Kayla told him excitedly.

"Yay!" Charlie exclaimed.

"I hope we aren't having spinach again…" Mr. Maxwell called to Kayla as he came downstairs.

Lucas froze. The smile faded from his face and his body became rigid as he waited.

Mr. Maxwell stopped in the kitchen doorway rubbing his eyes. "Work has been so long lately. There are just not enough people to shoot in this town." He sighed for effect, watching Lucas for his reaction.

"Daddy!" Kayla hissed angrily motioning with her eyes towards Lucas.

"He really did shoot someone," Charlie added.

Lucas wished he could shrink into the floor and disappear as Mr. Maxwell gazed steadily at him.

"Daddy, stop teasing. You know that man was threatening to hurt a young girl and her child with a gun. You never would have shot him if you didn't absolutely have to," Kayla reminded, trying to reassure Lucas.

"Yes, I do have a particular anger toward men out to hurt women," Mr. Maxwell responded, still staring at Lucas.

Lucas swallowed uncomfortably.

"So…tell me about yourself, Lucas. What brings you to our house this lovely evening?" Mr. Maxwell finally broke his gaze and picked up the hot dog Kayla placed in front of him.

Lucas swallowed nervously again.

Mr. Maxwell leaned back leisurely in his chair and chewed, patiently waiting for Lucas' response.

"I....um....," Lucas started. His stomach turned as he spoke. He forced his voice to remain steady. "I had a little trouble at home. Your daughter.... well...she..." Lucas struggled with how to tell him the state she found him in.

"And I invited him home with me..." Kayla jumped to his rescue, and Lucas nodded in agreement.

"Oh, did she? Kayla, are you in the habit of bringing strange young men home when I am away at work?" Mr. Maxwell questioned with his brow raised.

"No, he rescued me. He wasn't a stranger. I knew who he was when I saw him," Kayla insisted. Lucas stared down at the table.

"Did you save my daughter?" Mr. Maxwell finished his hot dog and reached to pour himself a drink of water.

Lucas cleared his throat, "I didn't save her really. She seemed perfectly capable of handling herself... I just told the other guys to back off," Lucas stammered.

"Oh, I was under the impression that you also paid for her bus fare and brought her safely home to me?" Mr. Maxwell stated it as a question. Lucas didn't answer.

"Is that true?" Mr. Maxwell pressed.

Lucas wrung his hands in his lap, "Yes...yes, that is true."

"Well then," Mr. Maxwell paused to drink his water. "You are very welcome in my home. Do you need a place to stay?"

Lucas' terrified mind was reeling in all different directions. Should he accept the offer? What did the father really want? He wouldn't really just offer him a place to stay...would he? Lucas' heart raced as quickly as his thoughts.

Mr. Maxwell smiled, "What's wrong, son? I'm a cop. I know what could have happened to my daughter that night if you hadn't stepped in. That kind of heroism and chivalry do not go unrewarded in this house. You're welcome here anytime you want."

Lucas glanced nervously at Kayla. She nodded and smiled in encouragement. Lucas cleared his throat and turned to face Mr. Maxwell.

"I do need a place to stay, but I wouldn't ask you to take me in without giving you something in return," Lucas answered his question steadily.

Mr. Maxwell took another hot dog roll from the table and turned it over thoughtfully in his hands.

"Well, I could use someone to help supervise Charlie for a few hours while I work and Kayla is at school. You could do that for a couple of weeks while you look for another job," Mr. Maxwell offered.

Lucas took a deep breath. What did he have to lose anyway? He was out of a job and he didn't want to stay at home. If he felt uncomfortable he could always leave, right?

"What do you say, Lucas?" Mr. Maxwell extended his hand across the table.

Lucas reached out and shook it.

"Thank you, Mr. Maxwell. You won't be disappointed," Lucas promised.

"I sure hope not, Lucas. You seem like a good kid to me. Now, let's finish dinner and I'll take you to get your things."

"I don't need to get my things," Lucas replied immediately as fear filled him.

"Nonsense, we have to get your clothes, son. What are you going to wear? Kayla's clothes are too small for you," he laughed as Kayla chucked a paper plate at him.

"Does he really have to go back there?" Kayla questioned softly to avoid Charlie hearing. "What if they hurt him again?"

"Oh, no worries, darling. My buddy and I have to do a patrol over in that part of town anyway. We'll see to it nothing happens," Mr. Maxwell reassured her and stood.

"I'm going back upstairs to change. Be ready in a few minutes, Lucas. I want to get over there before dark," Mr. Maxwell instructed.

"Yes, officer," Lucas replied, standing to help Kayla clear the table.

"It's Mr. Maxwell to you, Lucas. You're a guest, not a criminal, here," Mr. Maxwell reminded him and jogged up the stairs.

Lucas' shoulders slumped, and Kayla hugged him.

"It will be okay; Dad won't let anyone hurt you. He always keeps his promises," Kayla tried to reassure him, but Lucas had retreated to a deep place inside his heart. He helped her clean up in silence.

"Ready to go?" Mr. Maxwell stuck his head into the kitchen to ask.

Lucas jumped and sent soapsuds and drops of water everywhere. Kayla shielded herself from a good drenching.

"Sorry! I'm really sorry!" Lucas apologized profusely, trying to wipe up the water. Kayla laid her hand on his back as he stooped over to wipe up the floor.

"It's okay, Lucas. You go. I'll clean up," Kayla encouraged.

Lucas nodded and tried to stand. They left the house in silence. Lucas tried to keep his hands from shaking as anxiety coursed through him. He could barely open the door of the police car. Mr. Maxwell slid into the front seat and started the car.

"You seem nervous," Mr. Maxwell remarked as they pulled out of the driveway and started down the street. Lucas swallowed hard.

"Yes, sir," he responded, locking his hands together in his lap.

"You don't need to be. You're Lucas McMullan right? From Helf's Park High School?" Lucas nodded numbly. "You saved my son from that car fire three and a half years ago. I knew when I saw you that I had seen you before. It took me a while to remember because I never got a chance to meet you," Mr. Maxwell explained.

Lucas stared at Mr. Maxwell in amazement. He remembered that day clearly. The sound of the cars crashing still rang in his ears.

"Th...that was your son?" Lucas stammered as the memories flashed in his mind.

"Yes. Charlie." Mr. Maxwell added solemnly.

Lucas remembered screaming for his mom's boyfriend to pull the car over, but he was too drunk to care. The bright red stoplight still pierced Lucas' eyes as he remembered flying through the intersection. The crushing impact of the two cars colliding rolled through his mind. He couldn't remember much after that.

"I know you did, son. I saw everything. You were thrown from the car and as soon as you got up, you ran toward the fire to save my son."

"I'm sorry, sir, I don't remember much about it. I remember the little boy in my arms and then handing him to someone."

"You don't remember the man driving the car trying to haul you away? He punched you in the face and told you to get in the car. You were badly injured, but they wouldn't let the paramedics treat you. The man who was driving was arrested, but your mom took you home. I learned everything I could about you. Social services was called, but I never knew what happened to you."

Lucas was silent. They were getting closer and closer to his part of town.

"I know those bruises didn't come from a fight with another kid, Lucas. You are welcome at my house as long as you need to stay," Mr. Maxwell assured him.

"What if they're home?" Lucas questioned his voice close to a whisper.

"I'll come in with you. No one will hurt you while I'm with you," he replied as he drove onto Lucas' street. "Which house?"

"That one," Lucas pointed out, trying not to shake.

"Now, you go in and get your things and I'll be right behind you," Mr. Maxwell instructed as he parked in front of the house.

Lucas didn't reply. He forced himself to get out of the car and walk towards the front door. He pushed open the front door and reluctantly stepped inside.

Kyle turned as the door opened. "What are you doing here? I thought I kicked you out last night? You back again?" He walked threateningly towards Lucas.

Mr. Maxwell stepped in behind him and glared at the man.

"You brought the cops?" Kyle seethed.

"Go ahead, Lucas," Mr. Maxwell encouraged. "Get your things."

Lucas hurried to his room and quickly packed. He could hear Kyle's voice escalating. He grabbed the few clothes he owned and stuffed them into his pillowcase. When he came back out, he froze. Mr. Maxwell stood face to face with the drunken man.

"What did you say to me?" Kyle demanded, anger flashing in his eyes.

"I said, if you ever touch that boy again I will press criminal charges," Mr. Maxwell replied steadily.

Lucas turned from the scene to gaze at his mom. She lay passed out on the couch. Lucas walked over slowly.

"Mom?" he called out quietly. She didn't stir. "I'm leaving, Mom. I love you," he whispered. Tears threatened to spill over onto his cheeks. Still there was no reply.

"If you're going to leave, you better go," Kyle warned.

"Bye, Mom," Lucas whispered, touching her cheek.

Lucas stalked over to where Kyle was facing Mr. Maxwell.

"You better take care of her," Lucas firmly reminded.

"Let's go, Lucas," Mr. Maxwell tugged on Lucas' arm.

Kyle smiled widely, "Of course. I always take care of that piece of trash."

Lucas threw down his clothes and attacked the abusive alcoholic.

"Lucas, it's not worth it!" Mr. Maxwell screamed over Lucas' cries of rage.

He wrapped his arms around Lucas' waist and hauled him off. The drunken man scrambled to his feet and Mr. Maxwell shoved Lucas outside.

Lucas collapsed against the side railing. He heard a gun click and Mr. Maxwell's low and steady command.

"Step back, sir, or I will be forced to shoot."

Kyle swore profusely, but Mr. Maxwell backed out of the house safely. He pulled Lucas to his feet and they hurried towards the car. Lucas jumped into the front seat and Mr. Maxwell peeled out of the alleyway, his tires screeching.

"I'm sorry! I'm sorry!" Lucas cried, covering his face as he sobbed.

"You have nothing to be sorry about, kid," Mr. Maxwell replied quietly.

He drove home and helped Lucas inside. Everyone was already asleep.

"You can sleep on the couch tonight. We have a small apartment on the property where my mother used to live when she was alive. Tomorrow, I'll help you move in, free of charge, of course, as long as you're looking after Charlie," Mr. Maxwell told him gently as he helped Lucas onto the couch.

Shuddering with sobs, Lucas lay there without reply. Mr. Maxwell took off Lucas' shoes and covered him with a blanket. Lucas slowly quieted.

"Is it okay if I pray with you, Lucas?" Mr. Maxwell requested as he knelt beside him.

Lucas nodded.

"Dear, God, I pray for Lucas tonight. His heart has been through a lot. I pray that You will show him Your love and care tonight. Amen."

Mr. Maxwell felt Lucas' breathing even out, and he opened his eyes to find Lucas already asleep.

"Poor kid," he shook his head and went upstairs, trying to shake the last couple of horrible hours from his mind.

FIVE

LUCAS OPENED HIS SORE EYES. His whole body felt like somebody had hit him with a ton of bricks.

"Hello," Charlie stuck his head up from where he was kneeling on the floor near the couch.

Lucas jumped at the sudden sound.

"Oh, Charlie, right? That's your name?" Lucas asked kindly, trying to slow his heartbeat.

"Yes, I'm five," Charlie answered with his slurred speech.

Lucas squinted as if it would help him understand the boy better.

"Um, what?" Lucas questioned, smiling.

"I'm *FIVE,*" Charlie tried to annunciate the word.

Lucas smiled and nodded like he understood. "Oh, really?" Lucas replied.

"*F-I-V-E,*" Charlie tried hard to say each letter clearly.

"Uh huh," Lucas smiled again.

Charlie attempted to hold up five fingers for Lucas to see and accidentally smacked him in the face.

Lucas jumped back. "Okay, okay, you don't have to hit me!" Lucas held his arm up over his face.

Charlie yelled something he couldn't understand, and Kayla popped her head around the corner.

"What's wrong, Charlie?" Kayla leaned on the doorframe, wiping flour-covered hands on her apron.

"Tell him I'm five, please," Charlie requested, letting his arm fall to his side.

Kayla laughed at the panicked look on Lucas' face. "He was telling you he is five. It's okay if you need to ask him to repeat," Kayla assured Lucas.

"Ohhhhh," Lucas nodded in understanding. "Got it! You're Charlie and you're five years old," Lucas smiled at Charlie.

"Yes, wanna play blocks?" Charlie replied.

Lucas smiled and nodded, but looked to Kayla for clarification when Charlie wasn't looking.

"Blocks," Kayla whispered, smiling.

Lucas nodded in understanding and knelt down next to Charlie. Kayla observed them for a few minutes and then returned to the kitchen. Lucas moved cautiously around her little brother as if he wasn't sure what to do. Charlie helped Lucas build the blocks, and Lucas laughed when Charlie knocked them all down.

The oven timer went off. Charlie yelled and fell backwards. Lucas sat there shocked. Kayla rushed in and lifted Charlie up.

"Are you okay?" she questioned Charlie as she hugged him.

"I'm fine, Mother," Charlie rolled his eyes.

Kayla turned to Lucas whose eyes were wide.

"I didn't do it. We were just sitting here and he flew backwards," Lucas quickly explained.

"He gets startled by sudden noises. It wasn't your fault," Kayla laughed patting Lucas on the back as she stood.

"What's for breakfast, sis?" Charlie yawned.

"Nothing if you keep scaring Lucas like that," Kayla teased walking back into the kitchen.

"It's not my fault he doesn't know anything about CP!" Charlie yelled.

Lucas couldn't understand what Charlie said, so he just sat nodding. Charlie sighed. It would be a very long Saturday, Charlie determined.

"I'm going in the kitchen to help your sister," Lucas told Charlie as he stood to his feet.

"Okay," Charlie responded. "Tell her to put chocolate chips in whatever she's making," Charlie requested.

"You can't have chocolate chips in eggs!" Kayla yelled from the kitchen.

"Yes, I can. It's a Saturday, come on!"

"No!"

Lucas paused, unsure of what Charlie was saying.

"I'll get Lucas to do it for me," Charlie yelled knowing Lucas couldn't understand him.

Kayla popped her head in the door and grabbed Lucas by the collar of his shirt, dragging him into the kitchen.

"No, Charlie. Final answer."

"Fine," Charlie sighed.

"Don't mind Charlie, he can be pushy," Kayla told Lucas.

Lucas rubbed his neck.

"He must take after his sister," he mumbled just loud enough for her to hear.

"I heard that," she answered as she sauntered back over to the counter.

Lucas grinned.

Silence fell between them for a moment as she beat the eggs. Lucas glanced around the kitchen in awe. The sunlight streaming in through the open window reflected off the black marble countertop and danced on the white tiles. Outside, the Florida sun was just peeking through the newly budded trees. The smell of freshly mown grass floated in on the breeze as the birds sang their morning song. Lucas drank in the peacefulness of the house.

"You want eggs?" Kayla asked from across the room.

Lucas didn't respond for a moment. Kayla glanced over at him as she poured the eggs into the pan. He was staring out the window with a blank expression. The bruises on his face seemed worse in the sunlight, and the cuts stood red against his lightly tanned skin. Tears welled up in her eyes as sadness filled her heart for him. She took the eggs off the burner and crossed the kitchen to where he was sitting.

"Lucas?" she said quietly and softly placed her hand on his back.

Startled, Lucas drew back quickly from her touch. His fear-filled eyes met hers, and she rubbed his back.

"It's okay, I was just seeing if you wanted eggs," Kayla reassured.

Lucas' eyes held hers for a moment before he looked away. "I'm sorry, I was just –" Lucas started to say.

"Don't worry about it," Kayla smiled at him.

He let out a breath he didn't know he was holding in.

"So eggs, or no eggs?" she asked again as she paced back over to the stove.

"Eggs, please," Lucas responded politely.

"With chocolate chips," a little voice whispered from the floor.

"Charlie?" Lucas whispered back as the little boy crawled around the corner.

"Shhhhh," Charlie raised up his arm and pointed to his lips.

Lucas nodded and winked, having understood him for the first time.

"Can I have chocolate chips in mine?" Lucas requested.

Kayla spun around with the spatula in her hand and spotted Charlie on the floor. Charlie screeched as Kayla pretended to chase him around the kitchen. Charlie scooted across the floor, using his knees since his legs were too weak to walk on. Finally, he fell over in a fit of giggling. Kayla scooped him up in her arms and tickled him.

"Stop, stop!" Charlie begged breathlessly.

"Only if you stop trying to get Lucas to ask for chocolate in his eggs!" Kayla demanded playfully.

"Okay, okay," Charlie agreed, trying to catch his breath from laughing so hard.

Kayla turned her head, and Charlie shook his head at Lucas. Lucas laughed, understanding what Charlie meant. Both of them went silent as Kayla turned around. Kayla hung Charlie upside down by his ankles and held him there.

"Lucas, say 'no chocolate' or Charlie dies by tickling," Kayla threatened as she winked at Lucas.

Lucas glanced from Kayla's eyes to Charlie who was shaking his head and mouthing something he couldn't understand.

"What?" Lucas mouthed back.

Charlie's sandy brown hair grazed the floor as he shook his head and mouthed the same word again. Lucas left his chair and knelt beside Charlie to hear him.

"I said, 'attack', and hurry before I die from all this blood in my head!"

Lucas glanced up at Kayla who winked again.

"You're not going to attack me, are you?" she asked, pretending to sound furious.

Lucas grinned and lunged towards her. He wrapped his arms around her shoulders. She gripped Charlie's legs tighter.

"Let him go!" Lucas commanded valiantly.

"No, I don't want chocolate in the eggs!" Kayla shouted, giggling as Lucas pried Charlie from her grip.

She let go, and Lucas acted as if she had shoved him backwards. He staggered around the kitchen with Charlie still upside down in his arms.

"I gotcha, buddy! We're gonna make it!" Lucas stumbled into the living room and collapsed onto the couch gasping for air. He held onto Charlie who lay sideways on his lap.

"Did we do it? Did she agree to put the chocolate in our eggs?" Charlie asked Lucas as Lucas helped him sit up.

"Already did," Kayla came out from the kitchen with a plate.

"Ew, chocolate in eggs? What a freak," Lucas said to Charlie jerking his thumb in Kayla's direction. He grinned and ducked as she smacked him over the head.

"Come on you two, let's eat before it gets cold," Kayla rolled her eyes.

Lucas carried Charlie into the kitchen and sat him in his wheel-chair. Lucas started to stand up.

"I'm not buckled," Charlie reminded him.

"Oh, right," Lucas mumbled picking up the two straps. His eyebrows scrunched together in concentration as he tried to clip them the wrong way three times.

Kayla amusingly observed him before she finally stepped in. "Here, I'll help you," she put a hand on his back. A warm, happy feeling spread through Lucas at her gentle touch.

"Thank you, I thought I would never get food," Charlie sighed.

"He'll get it eventually. We have awhile to teach him," Kayla smiled as she buckled Charlie and put his little feet in the footplates. The thought that he would be around to know more about Charlie and to be with her warmed Lucas even more. He offered a hand to help her up. She took it, and he helped her to her feet. She blushed as he smiled at her. He held her gaze for a moment.

"Well...let's get breakfast on then, shall we?" she cleared her throat as embarrassment washed through her. His smile melted her heart and she could feel the melting in her cheeks as they turned bright red.

"I hope you made regular eggs too. Chocolate in eggs sounds gross," Lucas wrinkled his nose as Kayla laughed and passed him the bowl of regular eggs.

They ate breakfast and Kayla demonstrated how to feed Charlie.

"See, you have to feed him in small bites. Because of his CP, he has difficulty swallowing and can choke," Kayla explained, placing a spoonful of the chocolate eggs in Charlie's mouth.

She showed Lucas how to give Charlie a drink.

"You always have to use a straw that bends to give him a drink. It's the best way for him to be able to drink it. If you try to get him to sip from a cup it will end up all over both of you," she warned.

"Do you always have to feed him?" Lucas inquired, wondering if maybe there were foods Charlie could pick up on his own.

"Sometimes we put food on a plate and he drops his face into it, but it tends to get messy. He can't use his hands much or his legs either. That is part of the CP," Kayla described.

Lucas nodded, feeling slightly overwhelmed. He had a lot of questions for her like why couldn't Charlie walk? Or why was his speech so hard to understand? What could he do by himself? But Lucas decided to wait until they were alone to ask. He didn't want to embarrass or upset Charlie.

After breakfast Lucas helped Kayla clear the table.

"You go watch a couple shows with Charlie. I'll clean up." Kayla shooed him out of the kitchen.

"Are you sure?" Lucas questioned.

Kayla opened her mouth to tell him he didn't need to do everything for her when she was interrupted.

"I pooped!" Charlie yelled from his wheelchair at the table.

"Charlie! That's rude!" Kayla reproached.

"What did he say?" Lucas asked, taking the plate from Kayla and beginning to wash it.

"He said, it's time for Lucas to learn the best part of this job," Kayla sighed. "Come on."

Lucas followed her as she lifted Charlie from his wheelchair and brought him to the living room. She handed Charlie to Lucas and spread a changing pad on the floor.

"Lay him down on his back and I'll get the changing stuff," Kayla instructed.

Lucas grimaced as the perfume of Charlie's overly full pull-up wafted around him.

"What's wrong?" Charlie smiled.

Lucas carefully laid Charlie on the floor without answering him. He didn't want to be rude to Charlie, but he couldn't help covering his nose.

Kayla came back with an arm full of supplies. Lucas took a step back.

"Oh no, Lucas! You are jumping right in today because I have school on Monday, and I'm not coming home just because you can't change a messy diaper!"

Kayla grasped his arm and tugged him back over.

"Okay, sit down here with me. I'll help you through it the first time," Kayla patted his back in reassurance.

She taught him how to change the pull-up and how to put a new one on.

"Here, you get the honor of throwing it in the garbage outside," Kayla said enthusiastically as she handed him the plastic bag in which she had put the dirty diaper.

"Thanks," Lucas replied sarcastically.

He carried the diaper outside and threw it in the garbage bin near the garage. A light breeze picked up and whispered through the leaves of the trees. He stood for a moment, breathing in the fresh air. Sunlight filtered through the woods that surrounded the house.

It was the first time he had seen the house in the light. The black shutters stood out from the white siding that lined the house. In the small front yard there stood a large oak tree whose branches spread out and hung over the house.

Lucas ambled along the stone steps that led to the house. He glanced over at the small apartment adjoining the property, curious about his new place. Lucas thought back over the events of the past twenty-four hours and felt relieved. It was as if a huge weight had lifted off of his chest. In one day, he had a new family, a job, and a place to stay. Though he felt overwhelmed at the thought of taking care of his dream girl and her little handicapped brother, he was exceedingly full of joy.

He crossed the porch and stepped back into the house. Kayla was spinning in circles spraying the whole house with air freshener. Lucas had a feeling she was doing it to entertain Charlie.

"It's not working, I can still smell it!" she cried as she turned a circle a little too fast and tripped into Lucas.

Without thinking, he put out his arms to catch her and held her tight as she started to fall.

"Lucas and Kayla sitting in a tree, K-I-S-," Charlie continued with the song as Kayla gazed up at Lucas.

"Thanks," she breathed softly.

"You're welcome," he replied, a smile slowly spreading across his face as her cheeks flushed red again.

He stood her up and steadied her on her feet.

"I think you used enough spray," he coughed as he inhaled the strong scent of lemon.

"Sorry, I hate it when the whole house smells," she apologized, tossing the can on the couch.

Charlie started to sing the kissing song again.

"You can feel free to stop, anytime," Kayla spoke quietly through clenched teeth.

Charlie stopped and grinned widely.

"Who, me?" he asked innocently.

"Yes, you. Now what do you want to do today?" Kayla asked as a distraction. She picked him up and sat him on her lap on the couch.

"The mall?"

"I don't know if Lucas is feeling up to the mall, Charlie. He might be tired," Kayla reminded Charlie.

"Pleeease," Charlie begged, tugging on Lucas' shirt.

"Charlie, that's rude," Kayla scolded.

"No, no, it's okay. I don't mind. I'm not that tired," Lucas smiled at Charlie who cheered.

Kayla sighed, "Okay, the mall it is I guess. Build-A-Bear again?"

"Yes, we have to make a bear to remember Lucas' first day here," Charlie replied as if Kayla was missing the obvious.

"Oh, okay," Kayla sighed again, glancing over Charlie's head to wink at Lucas.

"But this time Lucas is doing the dance."

"Yea!" Charlie cheered.

Lucas shrugged, wincing as the muscles in his shoulder pulled painfully against the bone. Kayla noticed and sympathetically placed a hand on his back.

"Thanks," she mouthed to him.

He smiled widely at the thought that she was happy with him.

"Alright, let's get going. I'll show you how to put Charlie's chair in the van," Kayla swung Charlie up into her arms and grabbed his diaper bag from the closet.

Lucas pushed the chair slowly behind Kayla as he followed her out to the van. Kayla stood shocked as Lucas picked up the chair without waiting for the lift and strapped the buckles on all four sides of the wheelchair. He struggled for a minute with the buckles that held the chair in place, but quickly figured it out.

"Wow, you're good," Kayla remarked.

Lucas stepped back so she could put Charlie in his chair.

"He's okay," Charlie replied sarcastically. Lucas ruffled his hair from behind.

"Why don't you drive? We will test your skills," Kayla smiled.

"Are you doubting my skills?" Lucas asked incredulously.

"Yes, that's why it's called a test."

"Oh, well then, I hope you have your stickers ready because I deserve an A," Lucas grinned.

"M-hmm, here's the first test. What comes next when you're driving a lady anywhere?"

"Hmmmm," Lucas leaned on the open passenger door with a hand on his chin.

She crossed her arms.

"Oh well, guess I'll think of it on the way," Lucas announced decidedly and shoved the passenger door to close it. He ran around to his side and hopped in, smiling as he heard her disgruntled remarks from outside the car.

"What took you so long?" he pretended to yawn as she climbed in.

"You failed test number one."

"Oh no," Lucas groaned dramatically.

"Just drive! I've already started test number two," she tapped a pen on the dashboard.

"Yes, sir," Lucas replied wincing as she smacked his shoulder.

"Sorry!" Kayla apologized quickly as she remembered how badly he had been hurt the day before.

"Ahhh! I think you broke my shoulder," Lucas moaned, slowly moving his shoulder blade back and forth as he drove.

"I'm sorry, I didn't remember!" she cried distraught.

"Oh, how will I ever recover? It's so painful!" Lucas cried dramatically.

Kayla opened her mouth to apologize again when she noticed the slight smile on his face.

"I hate you!" she replied as he began to laugh. She lifted her arm to hit him again.

"Okay, okay, I'm sorry! I was kidding," he reached over and touched her shoulder apologetically.

Though it only lasted a second, his touch sent butterflies flitting through her heart. She was sure he could hear her heartbeat, but if he did, he didn't show it.

He held the steering wheel with one hand and let the other rest in his lap as he easily navigated the traffic. Lucas seemed content to drive in silence. He stopped at a stoplight. They slowly turned to glance at each other. Kayla was admiring Lucas' lightly tanned skin that brought out the brilliant blue hue of his eyes. She quickly looked away and switched on the radio.

Lucas grinned. He had caught her staring at him, and he could tell she was embarrassed by the way her cheeks were flushing slightly pink. Her slender fingers nervously fiddled with the knobs.

"Need help there?" he teased as he tried to focus on driving.

The slow twang of a country lullaby filled the car as she sat back in her seat. He listened to the melody for a moment and snuck a glance at her. She had a hand out the window, playing with the wind as she softly sang along. He wanted to turn the music down so he could hear her sing, but he didn't want to ruin the moment for her. The song was clearly one she enjoyed, and one he vaguely knew from a different time in his life – a happier one.

"My mom used to sing me to sleep with that song when I was a baby," Lucas told her when the song ended.

"It was my favorite song as a child," Kayla replied distantly as if still in a memory Lucas couldn't see.

The silence hung for a moment, both of them lost in time.

"Are we almost there? I really want to build a bear and get a corn dog!" Charlie interrupted excitedly.

"Corn dogs? You can't get corn dogs in the mall," Lucas laughed.

"But I'm starved!" Charlie exclaimed.

"Well, we'll see what the Rainforest Café has," Kayla told him.

Lucas pulled into the parking lot of the mall and searched the rows of cars.

"Wow, busy place," he remarked as he maneuvered around people and cars.

"What are you doing?" Kayla questioned as Lucas drove by the open handicapped space for the third time.

"Trying to find a parking spot."

"There's three right there." Kayla pointed out the windshield at the three open handicapped spots.

"But that's…"

"Handicapped?" she interrupted him with a brow raised.

"Oh, right," Lucas said after a minute.

Kayla shook her head and took out the handicapped tag from the dashboard compartment.

"You have to park in one with the extra room for loading," Kayla instructed as Lucas drove to the spots.

"Which one is that?"

"The one with the blue lines next to the parking spot. It's so we can use the ramp," Kayla explained.

"Oh, well that's handy," Lucas agreed.

"Handy - capped," Charlie added laughing.

Kayla showed Lucas how to unsnap the buckles and maneuver the wheelchair backwards down the ramp. She let Lucas take over pushing Charlie after they were out of the van.

"Last one to Build-A-Bear has to dance for the Build-A-Bear workers!" Charlie shouted once they had crossed the parking lot.

"You're on!" Kayla shouted and took off.

"What did you say?" Lucas asked Charlie. Lucas leaned down to hear him better.

"Run!" Charlie shouted in his ear. Lucas looked up at Kayla who was motioning for him to come.

"Hang on Charlie," Lucas warned and shoved the wheelchair forward.

Charlie squealed as Lucas set off jogging. People stared as they flew past – Charlie screaming in excitement, and Lucas huffing as he carefully steered the wheelchair around throngs of people. When they reached the store, they found Kayla perched on a bench outside waiting.

"What took you so long?" she teased as Lucas gasped for air.

" Oh, just trying to push a wheelchair with a million people in the way!" Lucas retorted when he could breathe.

Charlie was grinning from ear to ear.

"We get to dance, Lucas!" he cheered. Kayla put an arm around Lucas as he followed them into the store.

It wasn't very crowded, but all the attendants flocked to Charlie. A worker came, bent down to Charlie, and looked at him eye to eye.

"WOULD YOU LIKE TO BUILD A BEAR?" The worker spoke slowly and loudly as if Charlie were deaf and couldn't understand him.

Charlie nodded and moaned really loudly while Kayla and Lucas tried not to burst out laughing. The worker smiled a wide-toothed grin and patted Charlie's shoulder.

"LET'S MAKE A BEAR," the young man suggested.

Charlie looked up at Kayla and yelled, "Mommy! Can we build a bear?"

Lucas burst out laughing at her irritated expression.

"What's so funny, Daddy?" Charlie yelled.

All of the three were trying not to burst out laughing as they finally sat down and started stuffing a soft brown teddy bear.

"Aw, look at its nose, it looks like a heart," Kayla cooed holding up the bear up for Charlie to see.

"How do you stuff this thing?" Lucas questioned skeptically as he stared at the deflated furry body of the bear Kayla was tenderly holding.

"Oh, I'll show you," the attendant offered.

Lucas still wasn't sure how the little piece of fur would become a bear, but he loved watching Charlie grin, so he went along.

They picked out a heart for it and the attendant held it out to Charlie.

"*OKAY, READY TO SING THE SONG?*" he yelled, leaning in close to Charlie.

"YES!" Charlie screamed back.

The attendant winced as Charlie's high-pitched yell pierced his ears. Lucas was becoming annoyed with how the worker was treating Charlie.

"Okay then," the worker replied rubbing his head.

Lucas held back a laugh. Kayla unbuckled Charlie from his wheelchair and held him out to Lucas.

"Time to dance," she smiled.

Lucas' quizzical expression made her giggle.

"Okay – hands in the air, spin around!" the worker instructed. Lucas stood there skeptically.

The worker twirled his pointer finger slowly, "SPIN," he annunciated to Lucas as if Lucas couldn't understand. Lucas stepped forward into the bright florescent lights. The worker stepped back as he clearly saw Lucas' cut face and black eye.

"What would you like us to do?" Lucas requested, his tone firm.

"Well….ummm….when you spin, it gives the hearts love and kindness," the man stuttered.

"Come on, Lucas, spin! We have to give the teddy love and kind thingies," Charlie insisted clapping his hands.

"You want to spin, then we'll spin," Lucas replied happily, twirling Charlie in slow circles.

"Now, jump up and down ten times," the worker instructed quietly.

Lucas jumped with Charlie. Kayla laughed as Charlie screamed in delight.

"Now, I'll stuff the bear with his new heart full of kindness and…" Lucas narrowed his eyes at the man.

"And joy," the man squeaked as Lucas sat down next to him.

Kayla couldn't help feeling safer with Lucas. The attendant was wary of Lucas, who seemed to not notice, and kept his distance. After the bear was stuffed and sewn together, Lucas pushed Charlie out of the store while Kayla paid.

"Wasn't that fun?" Charlie squealed.

"It was a lot of fun wasn't it?" Lucas smiled as Charlie grinned widely.

"You know, you didn't have to terrify the Build-A-Bear worker," Kayla chuckled as she came out of the store with the completed bear and its cardboard box house.

"Yes, I did. They shouldn't treat Charlie like he's deaf or can't understand them if they don't know what his disability is," Lucas responded angrily.

"It happens a lot...he's used to it," Kayla shrugged.

"Well, he shouldn't have to be," Lucas replied, glaring at the worker in the store who was still staring at them.

Kayla turned around just in time to see the worker duck his head.

Kayla took Lucas' arm and tugged him along, "Come on, before you give him a heart attack."

Lucas took over pushing the wheelchair for Kayla.

"I'm hungry," Charlie whined as they walked toward the car.

"We just had breakfast!" Kayla exclaimed.

"That was four hours ago," Charlie moaned.

"No, it was only an hour and a half."

"Lucas, please?" Charlie begged, looking up at him from the wheelchair.

"I already rescued you once this morning! I'm not crossing your sister again," Lucas threw up his hands in surrender as Kayla glowered at him.

"Where would you like to go, Prince Charlie?" Kayla teased, rolling her eyes. She could never say no to Charlie, even though she didn't have a whole lot of money to be eating out for the third time that week.

"McDonalds!"

"McDonalds!" Kayla echoed Charlie as she jokingly slapped her forehead in disbelief.

"You want to go there again? That's the second time this week!"

"But I'm loving it," Charlie pouted, trying not to laugh at his own joke about the mega-chain slogan.

Lucas laughed as Kayla rolled her eyes at her witty little brother's persistence.

"Okay, we can show Lucas your favorite McDonalds – you know, the one with the big playroom."

They drove to McDonalds and Lucas fed Charlie for the first time by himself. Kayla showed him how to cut everything into little pieces because of Charlie's swallowing difficulties.

"Okay, go," she encouraged as Lucas held a small piece of chicken between his fingers. He attempted to put the chicken in Charlie's mouth but didn't pull back quick enough.

"Ow!" he yelled as Charlie's teeth found his finger. "You bit me!" he accused, rubbing his finger.

"Sorry," Charlie shrugged, munching on the chicken.

"That happens sometimes, you'll get the hang of it," Kayla laughed.

Once they had finished lunch there, Lucas drove them home.

They unloaded Charlie from the van and brought him inside.

"You're a natural P.A. – a personal assistant," Kayla commented as she watched Lucas unbuckle Charlie from his wheelchair and set him on his knees on the floor.

Kayla sat down next to Charlie on the floor.

"What exactly does a PA do?" Lucas asked sitting down next to both of them.

Kayla rolled her eyes. "Pretty much everything – laundry, feeding, dressing. Night times are easy. He just has seizures once in awhile, but no worries," Kayla laughed.

"Oh, thank you for telling me that after I took the position," Lucas laughed rolling his eyes.

"Don't worry, Dad sleeps with him at night," she said, patting his shoulder.

"Good luck."

"What does that mean?" Lucas asked a little nervously.

"Oh, let's just say Charlie looks sweet and wonderful, the first time you meet him. Just give him a week or two, and you'll know what I'm talking about," Kayla laughed. He looked at Charlie and he grinned widely.

"Uh huh," Lucas answered.

SIX

KAYLA SPENT MOST OF THE rest of the day teaching Lucas how to change, feed, and help Charlie. It was dinnertime, and the second time that Lucas was supposed to feed Charlie without Kayla's help. The dinner was soup. Kayla rolled her eyes.

"This is the worst meal to start off on, but okay. Good luck," she smiled.

"What's wrong with soup?" he asked, giving Charlie a scoop of it in his bowl. Charlie whacked the spoon out of his hand and the spoon went flying.

Kayla looked at Lucas, "Told ya."

"Thanks," he responded sarcastically. Lucas got most of the soup on Charlie's clothes. When they finished eating, Kayla grinned "Well at least you can practice dressing him,".

They brought Charlie into the living room and Kayla laid him on the floor.

"Okay, getting his clothes off is tricky at first, but you can do it," she encouraged. She showed Lucas how to pull the sleeves over Charlie's rigid arm.

"Okay, you do the other side," she nodded her head at Lucas. Reluctantly, Lucas grasped the sleeve of Charlie's shirt and pulled.

"Ow, you're killing me!" Charlie whined loudly, pretending to be in pain.

"Charlie," Kayla warned.

"What? I'm just kidding," Charlie grinned as Lucas finally pulled his arm free of the sleeve.

"Okay, now have Charlie roll over so you can pull the shirt off of his shoulders and over his head. Charlie will whine about rolling over, but don't listen to him," she informed Lucas.

"I would *never* do that," Charlie responded, acting insulted.

"Just roll over," Kayla sighed, rolling her eyes.

"Ah! It's so painful!" Charlie screeched as he rolled to the side.

"Oh, please," Kayla huffed sarcastically as Lucas pulled the shirt over Charlie's head.

"You're so mean," Charlie pouted, rolling so his back was flat on the floor again.

"Yeah, yeah. Now, we have to put the shirt on," Kayla smiled as Lucas gave her an exasperated look. "This part isn't as hard, just put one of his hands in the first sleeve and pull it on, then put it over his head, then do the other arm," she tried to demonstrate, but the shirt got stuck on Charlie's left arm.

"It's really easy," she grunted with effort, trying to wrestle Charlie's arm away from his body.

Charlie's tense muscles coiled and held fast. Finally, she managed to pull his arm down just far enough to get the sleeve across his elbow. She finished putting his shirt on and sat back panting.

"Now for the pants," she sighed, after a few moments.

Lucas hung his head pretending to be exhausted already.

"Come on, then we can watch a show," she encouraged.

She showed him how to thread Charlie's kicking legs through the pant legs and had him lift up as she drew the pants up to his waist. Lucas watched her, unsure if he would ever understand how to do it.

Finally, Charlie was changed and Kayla sat him in front of Sesame Street.

"When he sits, you have to put him on his knees so he can balance himself. He can't sit or lay on his stomach like other kids. Sometimes when he is on his knees, he tips over, like he did earlier, but you don't have to freak out. He is usually okay. Just pick him up as soon as you can," Kayla explained, sitting next to Lucas on the floor.

"What is CP?" Lucas asked when Charlie was distracted watching Sesame Street.

"It means Cerebral Palsy. Mom had a complicated pregnancy. She died while giving birth. At some point when the doctors were trying to get him out, Charlie lost oxygen to his brain and it affected the part of the brain that controls his arm and leg muscles. He also had brain damage to the area that controls his speech. Poor Charlie spent the first 10 days of his life in the intensive care unit at the hospital because he was having seizures almost constantly. He gets startled easily and loses control of his muscles, which is why he will probably whack you ten times a day, but he doesn't mean it. Just learn to dodge quickly," she laughed.

"Your mom died while giving birth?" he asked.

She nodded.

"I'm sorry," Lucas said.

"It's okay, it was a long time ago. Do you miss your parents?" she questioned. He turned his head away and shrugged. She knew he didn't want to talk about it.

"Do you have any other questions?" she asked, trying to make up for the silence.

Lucas paused. He wasn't sure how to ask.

"It's okay. It's natural for people to have questions about things they don't understand," Kayla offered, waiting for Lucas to respond.

"I don't want this to sound mean and I don't want you to get the wrong idea. I just don't want to treat Charlie like he doesn't understand me, if he does, you know what I mean?" Lucas squirmed trying to find a way to ask.

"Oh, you want to know if Charlie is 'all there'? If all the cookies are in the box? If the elevator goes to the top?" Kayla joked. Lucas smiled in relief.

"I asked because I don't want to play baby games with him if he can do a puzzle or play pretend, you know?" Lucas explained.

"Actually that's really thoughtful of you. Most people who don't know him assume the CP affected his intelligence as well. He's very smart and knows exactly what everyone is saying – probably more than the average five-year-old. The CP only affects his muscles and speech. That's why he can't walk or move around, besides scooting. It really frustrates him when people pretend to understand him and don't ask him to clarify himself. He wants to have conversation and talk to people. A lot of people assume he can't hear well. That's why that guy in the shop spoke like that to him. Charlie's used to it – it happens all the time."

"I don't like that. It isn't fair for people to assume like that."

"Well, having a handicapped family member is like speaking a different language. People who love you and know you can speak it, but other people can't," Kayla shrugged.

"Still, people shouldn't try to speak it without at least trying to understand about it first," Lucas huffed.

"True! Well, I have to do homework for school on Monday. You should spend some time with Charlie. You two can get to know each other better. You can learn to speak his language," Kayla grinned.

Lucas smiled in return, and she went into her bedroom. Lucas walked into the living room and sat down next to Charlie.

"Want to play a game?" Lucas asked Charlie.

When Kayla came out for a break two hours later, she saw Lucas laughing and playing Candy Land with Charlie. It was the first time in a long time that she had seen Charlie so happy. Kayla watched Lucas do everything for Charlie. When he needed a drink, Lucas would get it right away – though he still struggled trying to get the straw in his mouth and keep it there when Charlie's head moved around. If he looked bored, Lucas would invent another fun way to play the game. Kayla blushed when he turned and caught her staring.

"Want to play? You can be the pink one," he picked up the piece and slowly put it in her hand. When he put it in her hand, he froze. The skin on her hand was soft and warm.

She blushed as he smiled into her eyes and let go.

"Your move, Princess," he smiled.

Charlie cheered, and they played three rounds. Lucas watched her care for her brother. Her long, black, curly hair fell over her shoulders as she took it out of her usual ponytail. Once again, Lucas let out a breath he didn't realize he was holding in. He had never seen her with her hair down before. It framed her face in pretty waves as she held Charlie's hand and helped him move his piece around the board.

He watched her laugh as Charlie knocked her piece over and she tickled him. He remembered her gentle touch as she cleaned the cuts on his face, her terrified face when he saved her from Scott, and her insistence on independence, even when he knew she was scared. As she looked up and met his eyes, he realized he liked her... a lot. It was a feeling he hadn't ever felt for anyone before. They both shyly looked down again.

They played until Charlie's bedtime, and Kayla showed him how to get Charlie ready for bed.

"See, you brush his teeth with a regular toothbrush, but his mouth is kind of a moving target. Just don't get bitten. Circle around his teeth like this," she showed Lucas how to move the toothbrush in circles on Charlie's teeth.

"He will spit when he's done, and he likes a drink after," she explained.

"Does he sleep with pajamas on?" Lucas wondered as they moved Charlie from the bathroom to his bedroom upstairs.

"Only a shirt and a diaper," she replied, as they tucked Charlie in. Once Charlie was safely asleep, they tiptoed back downstairs to pick up the living room. Lucas picked up the board game while Kayla straightened the blankets and pillows. He stood and accidentally bumped into Kayla. He caught her before she fell.

"You should probably watch where you're walking," he suggested, laughing. Her heart beat faster at his touch.

"I'll try," she smiled.

He didn't let her go.

"Thanks for taking care of me and letting me stay," he said looking into her eyes.

"Thank you for rescuing me," she replied, smiling and moving closer.

"You could have saved yourself," he teased.

"I'm sure, but I'm glad you did," she whispered, looking up at him.

Lucas' heart felt as if it was beating out of his chest.

"Well, I should go. Your Dad said the keys to the apartment are over the doorway. I should go move my things in."

"Okay, see you tomorrow," Kayla smiled.

Kayla let him out and watched him walk to his apartment across the yard.

He lugged his few personal belongings up the stairs to one of the empty rooms. Exhaustion overcame him as he set everything down. He hadn't realized how tired he was until now. The bed that stood already made for him was too much of a temptation. He decided to leave all the unpacking and arranging for tomorrow.

Climbing into the big fluffy bed, he was amazed. A bed so soft had never been his alone before. It was amazing. He could hardly believe it was real.

Lucas lay awake, staring at the ceiling. He wondered where his mom was, what she was doing, and if she was okay. His shoulders and stomach still hurt from the beating, but his heart hurt the worst. He knew he couldn't go back. This was the last time she would put him through this for a long time, he determined. She had to learn how to handle herself sometime. Kayla and Charlie were all that mattered to him now. They needed him, and he never let down the people who needed him most. His mom didn't need him anymore. She had made her own choice and now she would have to live with it. He would miss Scott, but not the partying. He hated all the people, all the trouble it caused, and all the people he had to pretend to be friends with. He thought about Mr. Quackinbush and the other residents of the nursing home. They probably wouldn't even remember his name by next week. For the first time, he was doing what he wanted to. The girl he was falling in love with was the one he wanted to be with, and he would stay as long as she needed him, he decided.

SEVEN

OVER THE NEXT WEEK, CHARLIE and Lucas became inseparable. Lucas quickly learned how to take care of him while Kayla and Mr. Maxwell were away.

The house settled into a quiet routine. Lucas helped Charlie get up and ready for the day at seven while Mr. Maxwell got ready for work, and while Kayla dressed for school. They all ate breakfast together and prayed. Lucas had never heard of God the way they talked about Him before, but he liked the genuine feel of their prayers. They prayed as if God was actually listening rather than the stuffy prayers Lucas had heard others pray before. Kayla arrived home around three and did her homework until Mr. Maxwell arrived home from work. They ate dinner around seven, and enjoyed time as a family until it was time for bed.

Lucas loved the routine and settled into it right away. Lucas also loved playing with Charlie, although he learned right away that five-year-olds always win – or maybe it was just Charlie, he wasn't sure.

"You can't take all the poker chips! You have to use only your pile," Lucas tried explaining to Charlie.

"These are mine." Charlie pointed to the poker chips scattered on the table.

Lucas sighed.

"I win!" Charlie announced, reaching a small arm out and pulling all the chips in the middle towards himself.

"You win again? How?"

"Because, I win," Charlie smiled, piling the chips in his lap.

"Let's play Candy Land – you can't cheat at that game," Lucas suggested, beginning to pick up the piles of cards.

The doorbell rang loudly, interrupting their quarrel and sending a startled Charlie jumping a mile high.

"I'll get it!" Kayla yelled from the living room where she was folding clothes.

She had just arrived home from school and was doing chores before her homework.

"May I help you?" she asked in a polite tone, stepping on to the front porch.

A few minutes later, the boys heard the front door shut with a bang. Lucas stopped shuffling cards and turned to listen. He could hear Kayla trying to catch her breath as she slowly tried to make her way to the kitchen. Finally appearing at the kitchen door, she leaned heavily on the doorframe, a tear trickling down her cheek. Even though Lucas didn't know this girl very well, he knew she needed comfort. He stood to his feet, waiting for the news.

"What's wrong, Kay?" Charlie anxiously asked.

Kayla quietly walked to Charlie and held his hand, trying not to burst into tears.

"Charlie...buddy...." Kayla started.

Charlie grew anxious as he waited for her words. He had never seen his sister this upset.

"What's wrong?" Lucas asked carefully. Kayla broke down, unable to speak.

"Daddy won't be coming home..." She forced the words out through her sobs.

Charlie's five-year-old mind was confused. "Huh?" Charlie looked up at Lucas for clarification.

Kayla wondered how to explain what the officers had told her. How do you tell a child his dad got shot? Charlie didn't even know that most kids his age have a father *AND* a mother.

She tried to be brave for Charlie, but couldn't. Lucas caught her as she collapsed, devastated, onto the cold tiled floor.

"I'm so sorry," Lucas whispered, pulling her close to his chest.

"I'll be okay, just in shock," she lied to him as she looked away.

"You don't have to pretend. It's okay," Lucas reassured.

"I don't think I can go to school and take care of Charlie. What am I going to do?" she sobbed.

Lucas wasn't sure what to say. How could her Dad be dead? They had just talked to him on the phone hours before. It didn't seem real, but he knew one thing. He had to take care of them as long as they needed him. He hated seeing her cry.

"I'll do whatever I can to help," Lucas promised, but Kayla didn't seem to hear.

Lucas sat down on the floor and held her close. He had no words for her pain. Kayla felt depression drowning her body. Her sobs filled the house. Charlie sat still in his chair. Lucas wasn't sure if he understood Kayla or not, but he wasn't going to repeat it. Her cries broke his heart. Lucas almost didn't hear the phone ringing.

"I'll answer it, Kay," he whispered, rubbing her shoulders. He left her on the floor and quickly crossed the hall to the kitchen. He fought to steady his voice as he answered the phone.

"Hello?" he answered.

"Who is this?" a male voice demanded.

"Lucas, the new PA for Charlie," Lucas stammered.

"Is Kayla there?" the strict voice continued.

"Yes, she's here with me and Charlie," Lucas forced himself to reply.

"Tell her Uncle Bobby is on his way over. I'll be there in ten minutes."

The phone went dead. He carefully hung it up and walked back over to Kayla.

"Your uncle will be here in ten minutes," Lucas announced nervously.

Kayla continued to sob on the floor. Lucas felt helpless. He didn't know what to do for her, for them. The minutes passed. Suddenly, the front door flew open. Uncle Bobby had arrived.

"Who are you?" he glared at Lucas who slowly backed up.

"M-my name is Lucas," he stuttered as the man advanced closer.

"What are you doing in this house?"

Lucas' heart started to race. "Mr. Maxwell hired me." Lucas struggled to hold his voice steady as the man got closer.

The Uncle shook his head furiously. "That's my brother, hiring some kid off the street to take care of his kids," he said, with some emotion in his voice.

Kayla sniffed and stood to her feet, stepping in front of Lucas.

"He's the one who rescued me, Uncle. Please talk to Charlie! I can't tell him about Dad! I can't!" she cried.

The Uncle turned and went to Charlie who looked terrified. Kayla buried her face in Lucas' shoulder. He rubbed her back comfortingly. Lucas felt as if he were a character in a movie he didn't belong in. This girl needed someone who knew how to comfort. He didn't have any words for her pain.

"Kayla, I can go, if you want family to stay instead," Lucas whispered. She shook her head against his chest.

"I don't want you to go. None of my relatives know how to take care of Charlie, and none of them liked my father very much. My father only had one brother who stayed around – Uncle Bobby. My mom's family said Dad was crazy for working so much overtime and leaving us alone. They haven't spoken to us in years," Kayla wept. "I can't live with them. I want to be here in Dad's house, with Charlie."

Lucas nodded. Uncle Bobby was watching them warily. Lucas stepped away from Kayla as he came back over to them.

"I told him. How about you comfort him now, Kayla? I'm going to talk to your... boyfriend? Is that what he is?"

"No, he's the new PA for Charlie. I don't want him to leave. I can't take care of Charlie on my own."

"Don't be ridiculous, you will come live with me," Uncle Bobby said firmly.

Kayla burst into tears again. "I don't want to leave Daddy's house. Please, Uncle Bobby. Let me stay. Lucas will take good care of us, and I'll take good care of Charlie. I don't want to leave."

Uncle Bobby nodded and clamped a hand on Lucas' shoulder. "I'll talk to Lucas about it. You go comfort Charlie, he's pretty upset." Kayla went to Charlie's side. Lucas' heart felt like it was going to beat out of his chest. He was sure this was when he was to be banished forever or beat up. They walked out the front door and onto the porch where they could talk privately. Uncle Bobby let go of Lucas and sighed heavily as his shoulders slumped.

"I can't make her leave. I know my fool-headed brother would let her stay. Maybe it's best for them. I know they need each other, but they can't stay here alone. I could move in," the Uncle offered.

"It's fine. I got it covered," Lucas said, feeling overwhelmed. Lucas didn't want anyone around who could hurt him again.

"Are you sure? They are going to need a lot of comfort and looking after."

Lucas tried to sound confident. "I've looked after my family my whole life, sir. I can do it."

The Uncle was already nodding. "Consider yourself hired for the next year, and anything you need will be paid for. Thank you for rescuing my niece that night. She told me how you took care of her. Now that we've talked, you seem like a fine young man to me. Don't prove me wrong," he warned sternly, holding Lucas' gaze.

Lucas nodded quickly and looked down. "Yes, sir, I will take care of them and see to it that they're safe."

"Of course you will," Uncle Bobby said, clapping him on the shoulder. "I've got to go make the funeral arrangements. I'll call you guys shortly."

Lucas nodded and watched him leave. Whatever his life was before, he knew it was changed for good now. He just hoped he could live up to his promise. He walked into the living room where Charlie and Kayla were.

"Do we…have to move out?" Kayla gulped, her voice miserable.

"We're staying here… together," Lucas' serious look faded into a smile.

"Really?" Kayla yelled, jumping up and running towards Lucas.

"Well, unless you want me to call him back and tell him to take you," Lucas smiled slightly, trying to lighten the mood.

"Nope, that's okay. I'm good here. It will be hard without Dad," she looked down, tears threatening to spill over again.

Lucas felt like he needed to be the man of the house now. He had no idea what to do, but he thought Kayla and Charlie would help him to learn.

Charlie looked up at Kayla and Lucas red-eyed. "Kayla?"

"Yes?" Kayla answered, kneeling by his side to comfort him.

"What was Mom like?" Charlie asked crawling into her lap.

She combed his short, smooth hair with her fingers. "Mom, actually, was a worship leader."

"Is that why you don't go to church anymore?" Charlie asked, his five-year-old mind trying to figure everything out.

"How did he know that?" Kayla thought to herself. "Of course not," she said, lying to him. She hated lying to him, but it was the best thing to do at that moment.

Lucas joined them on the floor. Kayla immediately burst into tears again. "I can't do this by myself."

Lucas laid his hand on her back. "I'm here," he whispered. "I'm going to try to take care of you and Charlie. Your uncle left me in charge," Lucas told her.

"Okay," she agreed.

"Do you want some time alone?" Lucas asked her after a few moments of silence had passed.

"Yes, that would be helpful, thanks," she whispered.

"Would you take Charlie to your apartment for a little while?" she asked as Lucas started to leave.

"Of course, anything you need," Lucas comforted. "Come on, Charlie, you're coming to hang out with me for a little while."

Lucas picked Charlie up. Charlie laid his head on Lucas' shoulder and Lucas carried him to his apartment. "I'm sorry, I don't have any toys here," he apologized.

Charlie didn't respond, he only clutched Lucas shoulder with little fists.

"You want to watch a movie?" Lucas asked. He could feel Charlie nod.

Lucas turned on the TV and found a PBS Kids' movie playing. Carefully, he sat down and pulled Charlie from his shoulder to his lap. Charlie curled up against his chest.

Charlie knew something terrible had happened, but he couldn't understand what it was. Dad would be home soon, he knew, and Dad would explain everything.

Lucas rubbed Charlie's back and held him for a long time. Night fell quickly, and Lucas worried about Kayla alone in the house. Charlie was fast asleep in his arms. Lucas wasn't sure where to put him so he placed him in his own bed and covered him up. Lucas dialed Kayla's home phone.

"Hello?" she sniffed as she answered the phone.

"Hi, it's Lucas. How are you holding up?"

"I'm okay. How's Charlie?"

"He's asleep in my bed. Did you want him home with you?"

"No, if he is already asleep, don't wake him. Do you mind staying with him tonight?"

"No, of course not. Is there anything else I can do for you?" Lucas asked, wishing he could help Kayla more.

"No, not tonight. Uncle Bobby called and said the wake and funeral will likely both be tomorrow. You might watch Charlie so he doesn't have to go."

"Okay, that will be fine. Get some sleep, Kay," Lucas offered her the only advice he could give.

"Thanks," she whispered hoarsely and hung up the phone.

Lucas opened the small window in the apartment and took out a cigarette. He needed time to think - to process - all that had happened in the last week. He had left everything he knew behind to become a PA, and instead he became a family caretaker overnight. What did he know about families? He knew an awful lot about taking care of his mom, but not a special needs child. Kayla would need time to grieve, but for how long? What could he say to comfort her? All he knew was that there were no answers to his questions. He had lost one of the only people who had ever cared about him. Their father had taken him under his wing and now he was dead. Lucas hadn't known him long, but the ache was still real. He didn't know what to do.

Suddenly, a cry pierced the quiet night. Lucas quickly put out the cigarette and ran into his room where Charlie lay screaming on the bed.

"Hey, buddy, it's okay," Lucas soothed.

"Where's Daddy? Daddy always sleeps with me," Charlie cried.

"Oh, buddy, Daddy isn't..." Lucas swallowed hard, "coming home. He went to heaven today."

"Will you stay with me until Daddy gets back from heaven?" Charlie sobbed.

"Of course," Lucas agreed sliding into bed beside him. He let Charlie curl up next to him and held him until he fell asleep. Lucas lay awake for a while contemplating how he was going to take care of this precious little boy.

EIGHT

Hundreds of pieces of glass *shattered everywhere as the man threw another* *beer bottle at his head. Covered in glass and blood, Lucas tried hard not to* *scream. Making any noise at all would anger him further. Lucas curled into a* *ball as the sound of heavy footsteps on the creaky apartment floor came closer.*

Lucas sat straight up in bed, breathing heavily. For a moment, he didn't realize where he was. As his eyes adjusted to the darkness, his breathing slowly calmed. He remembered. He was at his new apartment. Lucas looked down to find Charlie scooting lower into the sheets.

"I'm sorry, I was just hungry," said Charlie.

"Oh Charlie, I'm sorry. I get nightmares at night. It wasn't you." Lucas said softly, feeling horrible.

"Okay. Can I have Oreos and Peanut butter?"

Lucas nodded. "Of course," he mumbled, ripping off the sheets.

He went into the kitchen and grabbed the peanut butter and Oreos. Helping Charlie sit up, he fed him and gave him a drink of water.

"Thanks," Charlie whispered before drifting back off to sleep.

Lucas put the food on the bedside table. He lay down next to Charlie and hoped the nightmares would go away.

A few short hours later, Lucas was roused from his sleep by a loud ringing. He rolled over and picked up the phone.

"Hello?" he answered sleepily.

"Lucas? It's Kayla. The wake and funeral are both today. Uncle says we will be over in about an hour so he can tell Charlie. Could you have him ready?" Lucas nodded before realizing she couldn't see him.

"Yes, yes, that would be fine," Lucas answered, unsure of what to do.

The phone clicked and he laid there with it in his hand for a moment. Slowly, he hung up the phone and rolled out of bed. The clock read seven a.m. Lucas decided to let Charlie sleep while he got dressed.

He took a shower and tried to find some decent clothes to wear. After several minutes, he chose the only pair of clean jeans he owned and a collared shirt. He wished that he could look nicer for Kayla, but it was all he had. He buttoned the top two buttons and leaned over to shake Charlie awake.

"Hey, kiddo, come on wake up. We have to talk to your uncle," Lucas spoke softly as Charlie's eyes fluttered open.

"Hey, there's my man. Come on, let's go," Lucas pulled the covers back as Charlie stretched.

Lucas managed to find a pair of sweat pants and t-shirt for him in his supply backpack.

"How do these go on?" he wondered out loud as he tried to put Charlie's leg through the armhole.

"Ow! That's a shirt, not pants," Charlie moaned as Lucas stopped trying to wrestle with his leg.

"Oh, right," he said. He finally got the shirt on, but realized it was backwards.

"This is awkward," Charlie said as Lucas clumsily tried to put his pants on.

"Sorry," Lucas apologized, finally sliding the pants on. Lucas went to fix the shirt and Charlie shook his head.

"Don't worry about it."

Lucas nodded and carried him to the kitchen to put him in his chair. They ate breakfast in silence. Lucas didn't know what to say and Charlie still wasn't sure what was going on.

"When is my sister getting here?" he asked for the third time as Lucas was clearing the dishes.

"Soon," Lucas answered, also for the third time.

Charlie wished Kayla would hurry up. After what seemed like hours, the door opened and Kayla ran to Charlie. She threw her arms around his neck and hugged him tightly. Uncle Bobby followed closely behind. He stopped in the doorway of the living room and motioned to Lucas. Lucas hesitantly came forward. He still wasn't sure where he stood with Uncle Bobby.

"What do you think we should do about Charlie?" Uncle Bobby whispered to Lucas.

Lucas looked confused.

"I mean for the funeral today. Do you think he should be there?"

Lucas wasn't sure how to answer. He had no idea how little kids thought or felt about death. He thought Uncle Bobby should know better than he would, but Uncle Bobby just shrugged along with Lucas.

They stood in silence for a few moments watching Kayla hold Charlie as she cried.

Charlie's face was blank. He didn't seem to understand. Lucas was worried about Charlie. Would he be able to handle seeing all the policemen and people crowding to say goodbye to his father? Lucas didn't want Charlie to be more upset than he was.

"What if I just kept Charlie with me today?" Lucas offered.

"Would you mind? I really think it would be too much on the boy," Uncle Bobby sighed in relief as Lucas nodded in agreement.

Lucas was glad he wouldn't have to try to find something to wear. He wished he could be there for Kayla, but she would have her family there. She probably didn't need him to be there.

Uncle Bobby pulled Kayla aside and explained the plan.

"Thank you, Lucas." She hugged him tightly. Her tears wet his neck as he held her close.

"No problem, Kayla. He will be okay," Lucas reassured her.

Uncle Bobby told Charlie he would be with Lucas for the day. Charlie nodded and Uncle Bobby left with Kayla to get ready.

"What do you want to do today, Charlie?" Lucas asked after the door had shut.

"I want to remember Daddy," Charlie whispered as he laid his head on the table.

Lucas knelt down in front of him.

"We will always remember your daddy. You never have to forget him."

"What if I do?" Tears welled up in Charlie's eyes.

Lucas picked him up and held him. He wasn't sure what to say to him. Nothing would make it better, but he wanted to try and help him.

"We could talk about your daddy a lot so you never forget," Lucas suggested.

"Okay. Want to see our project?"

"You had a project?"

"Yeah, it's in the back of the house."

"Okay, let's go." Lucas put him on his shoulders and carried him out of the apartment and downstairs.

Charlie showed Lucas the little path through the woods in the back of the house. After a few minutes, they came to a clearing where a small workshop had been set up. Lucas could hear water running nearby.

"See, there it is!" Charlie pointed to a giant tree.

Lucas could see the beginning of a platform between two thick branches.

"That's the wheelchair ramp," Charlie explained. He pointed to a set of boards nailed in a row on the ground.

"That looks like it was a lot of fun to help your dad build," Lucas remarked.

Charlie nodded.

"I wish we had gotten to finish it," he sighed.

Lucas looked around at the stack of boards and nails. He had never built anything in his life, but how hard could it be?

"We could finish it in honor of your dad?" Lucas suggested.

"Okay!" Charlie brightened for the first time that day. "Can we start right now?" he begged.

"Sure," Lucas agreed.

He would do anything to make Charlie feel better and to keep his own mind occupied. Lucas thought Mr. Maxwell's death wouldn't upset him so much because he hadn't known Mr. Maxwell that long. But the more he thought about it, the worse he felt. He was glad to have a distraction.

They worked for a couple hours on drawing a design. Lucas tried his hand at hammering, but only ended up with a sore thumb. He fed Charlie lunch, and they played games until dinner. Kayla stumbled through the door as Lucas was putting on a movie for Charlie.

"Whoa, careful there," Lucas warned as he caught Kayla. She held several large trays of food in her hands.

"Here, I got it," Lucas assured as he put his hand on her back.

"Thanks," she sighed.

He could tell she had been crying. Her eyes were bloodshot, and her face reddened. He wished he could do more for her than just carry the eight additional tins of food that Uncle Bobby lugged in.

She went straight to her room and shut the door.

"How did it go?" Lucas questioned Uncle Bobby while Charlie was watching TV.

"All the guys from the police force were there. It was a pretty big ceremony. Poor Kayla held it together until the end. She had just had it. Everyone and his brother wanted to talk to her and give their condolences. I felt terrible that she had to do it alone."

Lucas felt a pang of guilt. He felt like he should have been there for her.

As if reading his mind, Uncle Bobby laid a hand on his shoulder.

"There was nothing you could have done. She had to do it. She will be okay. You did the hardest part and that was staying with Charlie. I know he must have asked some hard questions."

"He did, but we worked it out."

"Good. How are you doing with all this?" Uncle Bobby looked seriously into Lucas' eyes as he waited for a response.

Lucas looked down. "It's harder than I thought it would be. I didn't know him very long, but he was the nicest anyone has ever been to me in a long time," Lucas admitted. He took a deep breath to keep the tears from falling as sadness welled in his chest.

"I know. If you need anything, just call. I'm here for you, okay? Keep an eye on Kayla. She will try to pretend she's okay, but I know this is really hard on her."

Lucas nodded and Uncle Bobby took out his wallet.

"This is for anything you need this week. I'll send more each week. Anything and everything you need will be covered," Uncle Bobby promised. He pressed the money into Lucas' hand.

Lucas knew it was his time to take charge of this little family now. Closing his fist around the money, he thanked Uncle Bobby and walked him to the door. As he heard him drive away, he wondered what lay ahead.

NINE

"Lucas!" His mother screamed, her voice sounding desperate. "Help!"

He slowly opened the front door dropping his schoolbag on the ground. He could see his mom lying on the floor in a pool of blood. "Lucas!" she screamed again. His legs felt stuck to the floor as he tried to run closer. The man standing over her pointed the gun toward her. Lucas wasn't fast enough.

Panting, Lucas woke in a cold sweat.

"Is that how you're going to wake up every morning?" Charlie wondered, looking up at him.

Blinking, Lucas wiped the sweat from his forehead and tried to calm his breathing.

"You'd think I would get used to waking up to you," he joked lightly, ruffling Charlie's hair.

Charlie smiled, "Breakfast?"

Lucas nodded, his heart still racing. He stood cautiously. Putting Charlie's clothes on, he wheeled him from the apartment to Kayla's house. They charged into the front door and raced into the kitchen, stopping short, as an oversized man and woman stared at him from the kitchen.

"And this is…Lucas," Kayla turned and pointed at Lucas. "He's the new PA for Charlie. He comes in the mornings."

Lucas opened his mouth, and Kayla glared and drew her finger across her neck.

"Lucas was just leaving," Kayla smiled her fake smile and motioned towards the doorway with her eyes.

"Well son, don't just stand there. Come introduce yourself like a real man," the man's command echoed through the house.

Lucas froze, looking to Kayla for help. Her eyes widened, and she motioned for him to move forward.

"Lucas, this is Uncle Carl and Aunt Karen."

Lucas slowly came around the wheelchair, nodding. Kayla pointed to her head and twirled her finger.

"These must be the crazy relatives she was talking about," Lucas thought to himself as Kayla made several more silly faces.

The man wore tattered overalls with a filthy white beater underneath. What was left of his hair stuck out in five different directions. Aunt Karen's hair was red and wild underneath her straw hat. Uncle Carl turned to Kayla and she replaced the silly faces with a smile.

"Nice to meet you," Lucas said nervously, extending his hand.

"What you afraid of boy? Ain't no one here gonna hurt ya, unless of course you be up to no good," the Uncle tightened his grip and stared at Lucas.

Lucas shook his head quickly. "No, I'm all good...up to good, I mean....I'm..." he stuttered.

"He's not only a PA, Uncle, he's..." Charlie started, but Lucas interrupted.

"I'm also a..." Lucas paused.

"Plumber," Kayla added quickly.

"Ah, yes...plumber," Lucas said with a grin.

"Good! Hope you can fix the kitchen sink then! Y'all don't look like no plumber to me. Y'all look like some city slicker."

"He's actually a really good cook, too" Charlie interjected, trying to save Lucas.

Kayla rolled her eyes. If this lie got any bigger their noses would start to grow.

Lucas headed for the door.

"Well, enough chatting! Let's have some breakfast, shall we?" Kayla threw one last look out the door to Lucas who waved.

"Come back soon," she mouthed.

"I won't be far," he mouthed back.

"Give me two hours," she said, joining him for a minute on the front porch.

He nodded.

"I'll miss you," she whispered, looking sad.

"I'll miss you more," he smiled and she grinned.

"Where's that breakfast, Kay?" Uncle Carl yelled from the kitchen table.

She rolled her eyes, and Lucas smiled as he left.

Lucas couldn't take the car - that would look suspicious. Thankfully, he had his bus pass in his back pocket. He couldn't run errands; he didn't grab his wallet from his room. He walked down to the bus stop, planning to go to the city park.

The bus pulled up and squealed to a stop. The doors opened and the same bus driver he had met when he rescued Kayla greeted Lucas.

The driver rolled his eyes when Lucas got on. "No funny business this time."

"No promises," Lucas joked, walking to the back.

He sat down and looked out the window. He found himself thinking about his nightmare. The more he thought about it, the more he worried. With Kayla and Charlie safe, he decided he could at least check on his mom. He still loved her; even after all she had put him through. Family is family. Lucas never abandoned family. Besides, the utility bills had stopped coming. He decided he should at least see why.

He got off at the park, waving to the bus driver who just shook his head.

Lucas walked down the familiar streets to what used to be his apartment. He stepped over all the usual trash, but felt strange. Something was different. It was silent. There was no fighting or yelling or crashing coming from the house.

He crept quietly up the steps and pushed open the door. What he saw next scared him more than he had ever had been scared, even growing up.

The apartment was sparkling clean. It was empty of all the tattered furniture and beer stains on the walls. There was no sign of a struggle or fight.

He slipped in quietly, constantly looking over his shoulder. There was no creaking to let him know someone was there, there were no cries for help, and there was no blood. Silence filled the house. It was deafeningly loud to him. He checked each room. Each was cleaned out, straightened up, and swept clean. Even the few things he had kept in his room were gone. She didn't even leave a note.

Lucas' chest felt tight. Tears were forming in his eyes. She left him. It couldn't be! She loved him enough to at least tell him, didn't she?

Suddenly he found himself panicking. He ran out of the house and onto the street, looking around wildly. He spotted Scott walking along the street.

"Scott!" he called, running up to him.

Scott turned around, and Lucas stopped dead. His friend's face was puffy and bruised. There were stitches around his mouth and above his left eye.

"What happened?" Lucas gasped.

Scott glared at him.

"You! You happened to me!" he yelled.

Lucas was shocked as he realized his friend was slurring his words.

"Are you drunk? It's only ten in the morning!" Lucas said, putting a hand on Scott's shoulder.

"Don't touch me," Scott growled, shoving his hand away.

"I'm sorry, I just came to see what happened to my mom. Do you know where she is?" Lucas asked worriedly.

"Of course you came about your loser mother. Her and whatever guy she picked up moved out of here a couple of days ago."

"What? How could she?" Lucas stepped back, stunned.

"I'm happy to see you're so concerned about your own friend," Scott said sarcastically.

"I'm sorry! I'm just..."

"Whatever. You want to know how this happened? On my way home from that party, I was jumped. Three guys jumped me. I went out to look for you because you were pretty messed up after that drinking contest," Scott yelled, getting closer to Lucas.

"Wow, Scott, I'm really sorry," Lucas apologized. "I was hurtin' pretty bad. Kayla found me...you know, that girl you were threatening the other night?"

Scott smiled an eerie smile, "I wasn't gonna hurt her, I was just going to show her whose territory she walked into."

Lucas stepped closer to Scott and glared. "Don't ever speak about her like that again."

"Oh, she your girlfriend now? All of a sudden you leave everyone who has ever helped you? For a girl? An ugly girl at that."

Scott fell to the ground as Lucas landed a punch to his jaw. Scott's eyes hardened with anger.

"You think you can take me?" Scott stood to his feet and towered over him.

"Don't speak about her like that, and I won't have to." Lucas said firmly, tensing his fists.

"What if I said she was a loser - like you, like your mom, like your whole family? I watched out for you, and you just left!" Scott screamed in Lucas' face.

Something in Lucas snapped, and he couldn't contain the words that were raging in his head.

"You never watched out for me! You were always dragging me to parties I never even wanted to go to! Look at you, you're drunk at ten in the morning!" Lucas shouted.

For a second, he saw pain register in Scott's eyes as the words sunk in. Guilt consumed Lucas as soon as the words were out of his mouth. There were times that Scott had been there for him when no one else was.

"You don't have to do this, Scott. You are more than just a drunk," Lucas tried, his tone softening.

Scott had always been someone to take his mind off things, but never had taken care of him. If anything, Lucas had gotten into more trouble with him. Still, he knew Scott was a good person deep inside. He wanted Scott to find something good, just like he had found Kayla.

"There's more to life than parties, Scott. I found a family who loves each other. Kayla loves me for who I am."

"Well, she must like losers then," Scott retorted, getting to his feet.

Lucas was silent, as Scott stood up.

Without warning, Scott punched Lucas full in the face.

Lucas flew backwards and hit the ground hard. As he fell, Scott advanced closer, his eyes full of hate.

Lucas rolled away and got quickly to his feet. Scott attacked him, arms flailing. They both went down, and Lucas shielded his face as Scott tried to punch him again and again. Lucas shoved him off and hit him in the nose. Scott groaned and rolled over, holding his bloody nose in his hands.

Lucas took that opportunity to make an escape.

"I'll come after you, Lucas! You are going to pay for this!" Lucas heard Scott yell as he turned the street corner.

The bus was leaving the curb as Lucas reached it. He ran, waving his arms. It lurched to a stop and the doors opened. The bus driver crossed his arms.

"Not a word," Lucas said, putting a hand to his bloody lip and walking to the back.

Shaking his head, the bus driver closed the doors. As the bus pulled up near his house, Lucas desperately hoped the aunt and uncle had left.

"Are you okay?" the bus driver asked as Lucas stood to get off.

Lucas nodded.

"You deserve better than that, kid. Keep your head up! It gets better."

Lucas nodded, and the bus driver let him off. As he walked back to the house, he realized the driveway was empty of cars besides Kayla's.

He breathed a sigh of relief.

Kayla was outside watering the flowers as he came up.

"Hey," she greeted him with a smile. As she came closer, her smile turned to a frown. "What happened to you?" she pleaded for an answer as he walked past her up the stone walkway.

"It's nothing."

"Yes, it is. Let me see," she insisted following after him. She reached out and grabbed his arm. Her gentle touch stopped him, and he turned to face her.

"Let me see," she requested less forcefully, but still determined.

Lucas took his hand away from his lip.

She dabbed at the blood with her sleeve. "What happened?"

"I went back to see my mom. I know I shouldn't have, but I was worried about her. Scott was there. He was drunk again, and he let me have it. He told me mom left. He was angry because after I left that drinking party, he got jumped when he came to look for me."

"So he beat you up?"

"No, I beat him up," Lucas smiled.

Kayla stepped back and shook her head. "Come on, Superman, I'll get you a cold cloth." She began to pull him by the hand inside the house.

"Hold on, I need a smoke." He pulled back and reached for the cigarettes.

She yanked his arm more forcefully. "No, you're quitting."

"When?" he demanded as he fumbled about, trying to open the box with one hand.

"Now. Let's go." She took the box from his hands and threw it across the yard.

"Hey, you're throwing away my sanity there!"

"Well, you're throwing away mine what with all the fights you keep getting in," she retorted.

He obediently followed her inside and sat at the kitchen table.

"Scott was one of the ones who threatened me, right?" Kayla questioned as she wet yet another cloth for him.

"Yes, he was there. So were Josh and Erik. They were the three that tried to attack you that night," Lucas answered.

"You knew them?"

"Yeah, I did. That's why they backed off. That and they were very drunk. Which reminds me, what were you really doing there at two in the morning, Miss Goody Two-Shoes? I know you weren't leaving a party," he teased, trying to keep her from questioning him further.

She crossed her arms, "Maybe I was."

Lucas laughed. "You looked like you were dressed for Bible class. I knew you weren't from around there the moment I saw you. Come on, what were you really doing there?"

"Oh, Bible class, huh? How do you know I wasn't, you know, what's that word?"

"Trashed, smashed, loaded, under the influence?" Lucas offered with a grin.

"Yeah, that. I was loaded under the influence, you just couldn't tell."

Lucas tried to hold back a laugh.

"Come on, you couldn't have given them a bruise even if you'd wanted to. Please, tell me," Lucas pretended to beg desperately.

Kayla gave in to his persistence. "Okay, okay. I was helping out at the homeless shelter."

"Until two in the morning?" Lucas asked skeptically.

"Well, we work at night handing out food and Bibles to the homeless people around the city."

"They just let you walk home by yourself after that?"

"No, I had caught a ride there with a friend. I was supposed to call my dad, but I knew he had worked overtime the night before, and I didn't want to wake him and Charlie."

"So…you just decided you would try to catch a bus home in the worst part of the city? Alone?" Lucas shook his head.

"Hey, they said it would only be a couple minutes before the bus arrived. I thought I would be fine," she said defensively.

"Well, good thing I was there to protect you." Lucas smiled widely as she hit him with a dishtowel.

"I could have handled myself."

"Well, that purse is a scary weapon. Who knows what's inside there." He jumped out of the chair as she came after him.

They chased each other around the kitchen, until Lucas caught her in his arms. For a moment, he held her there.

"Thank you… for everything," she thanked him sincerely, as he suddenly released her.

"You're welcome," he shrugged.

Kayla liked the way he cared so much about her, and she wondered if he was just a really nice guy, or if…maybe…he was starting to have feelings for her. As he smiled at her, she hoped it was for the latter.

The rest of the day passed quickly, and all too soon, it was time for her to get ready for school the next day. Though she acted fine, Kayla was worried about school. She worried that the three boys who had threatened her might show up at school. Lucas had expressed that he didn't feel comfortable with her going back, but she wanted to try and finish the year. Reluctantly he had agreed. With an anxious heart, she laid out her clothes and packed her school bag, hoping there wouldn't be any more trouble.

The morning came quicker than she expected. Even she found herself wishing she had listened to Lucas.

Lucas and Charlie drove Kayla to school in silence. They pulled up along the curb and he put the car in park.

"Are you sure you're going to be okay?" Lucas worried.

"I'll be fine." Her voice shook, though she tried to steady it.

Lucas noticed. "Call me if you need me. I'll be back to pick you up at three," he assured.

"Thanks." She half-smiled as she shut the car door.

Lucas watched her until she got inside. Suddenly out of the corner of his eye, he caught sight of Scott, Josh, and Erik. Fear flipped his stomach as the three boys caught sight of him as well and glared. Lucas pulled away from the curb uneasily. He hoped she would be okay, but if she wasn't, he was determined that he would fix it. No one was going to push him around anymore - or the people he loved. He knew he was responsible for Charlie and Kayla now and that gave him courage.

"Why are those guys lookin' at us funny?" Charlie questioned from the backseat as they drove away.

"Because they want to pick a fight, Charlie."

"Then fight them. You can do it. You're strong like Daddy was," Charlie encouraged.

Lucas looked in the rearview mirror at Charlie who smiled. Lucas was touched. He felt honored to be counted as brave as Charlie's father was. He had to protect Kayla. It was what their father would have wanted.

"You might be right, Charlie. We'll see. But right now, we are going to have some fun!"

"Yay! I hope there will be ice cream," Charlie sighed in desire.

Lucas chuckled.

"Sometimes you sound like you're thirty," Lucas laughed.

He tried to have fun with Charlie, but Kayla was on his mind all day. After three unanswered text messages, he knew something was wrong. He forced himself to wait until two thirty and quickly got Charlie ready and into the car.

"Let's go pick up Kayla, and then we will get ice cream, okay?" Lucas promised Charlie as he drove to the school.

They arrived a couple minutes early and parked outside the school to wait.

A few minutes after three, his phone rang. Kayla's picture ID popped up on the screen, and he answered on the first ring.

"Lucas!" he heard her cry before the line went dead. Lucas' pulse quickened and his heart pounded.

"Lucas!" He jumped as a small blonde girl banged on the window of the van. He rolled the window down.

"You have to help Kayla," she spoke frantically as her glasses slipped down over her nose.

Lucas was already out of the car. "Where is she?" he demanded, grabbing the small girl's shoulders.

"By the park. Scott's girlfriend and a couple other guys are there. Be careful!" she called after him as he took off running.

"Stay with Charlie!" Lucas yelled back over his shoulder. The small girl peeked into the back where Charlie was sitting in his wheelchair.

"Want to see me eat a booger?" he grinned.

Lucas was nearing the park when he spotted them. Two of the boys from earlier that morning stood by watching the fight. Lucas rammed into them from behind, taking them by surprise.

"Kayla!" he screamed.

Kayla was holding her own against Alexis who was throwing punches crazily.

Josh knocked Lucas to the ground.

"You traitor!" Josh screamed and aimed a kick at Lucas' stomach. Lucas rolled away from it just in time.

"You were our friend, and now we find out you were living with the cop that busted our joint!"

Lucas' was breathing heavily as he rolled to his knees.

"I'm glad that cop got shot. He deserved it. I bet you told him right where we were, too," Josh accused, leaning down to punch him.

Lucas blocked his blow with one arm and stumbled to his feet.

"I didn't tell anyone anything!" Lucas shouted in defense as they closed in.

"Because of you, Lamont is dead," Erik hissed, shoving Lucas backwards.

"Lucas!" Kayla screamed as Alexis bore down on her.

"You made your own choices, Erik. I wanted a better life. The drugs and the drinking aren't all there is to life. I'm sorry about Lamont, but I didn't tell their father anything!"

"We are going to make you pay," Josh seethed.

"Lucas!" Kayla screamed again as she watched them close in. Anger coursed through Lucas' veins. Power rushed through his hands as courage burst from his heart. He was driven by a sole intent – to protect Kayla. Lucas brought his fist back and punched Erik in the face. Erik fell, holding a bloody nose. Josh rushed in, but the two were no match for Lucas' strength. He knocked them to the ground. While they lay catching their breath, Erik started to get up. Lucas drew back his foot and kicked him in the face. The boy fell to the ground, unconscious.

Lucas took his chance and ran to Kayla. Though she had gotten a couple of punches in, it was clear that Alexis had the upper hand. Alexis had a fist full of Kayla's hair in her hand when Lucas grabbed her from behind.

"Let her go," he commanded.

Terrified, she let go and backed away.

"Are you alright?" Lucas knelt next to Kayla whose face was streaked with blood from several vicious scratches.

"I know you were trying to kiss Scott! He told me you attacked him! You will pay, Kayla!" Alexis screamed.

Lucas helped Kayla to her feet and supported her as they ran. They made it to the car, aware that sirens were approaching.

"Get in!" Lucas directed. Kayla stumbled in, and Lucas slammed the door shut.

"Thanks for watching Charlie for us," he said to the frightened girl who seemed frozen in the driver's seat. She scrambled out, and Lucas started the car.

"Bye, Lucy! Hope you have fun at your grandparents' tonight," Charlie called.

They pulled away just as the police arrived with sirens screaming. "Did you get them?" Charlie asked excitedly.

Lucas was still trying to catch his breath.

"Yes, Charlie, we got them," Lucas reassured.

He drove home quickly and carried Charlie in.

"You play with your toys here for a few minutes, okay? I'm going to help your sister in."

Lucas helped Charlie get into a kneeling position on the floor and jogged outside to Kayla.

She sat in the car staring straight ahead.

"Come on, we have to go inside," he encouraged as he took her arm.

She let him help her get out of the car. Lucas kept his arm around her as they walked slowly into the house. He sat her down in the kitchen.

"I'm okay," she insisted, covering her face with her hands.

He gently took her hands in his and pulled them away from her face.

"It's my turn to take care of you. Relax, I have to make sure we don't need to go to the ER," Lucas instructed.

She watched him warily as he looked over her face.

"Do your arms or legs hurt?" he questioned, looking over her scraped hands.

"Yes, but they're just bruised, I think," Kayla rasped. Her voice was raw from screaming. The scratches on her face were still dripping blood and her eye was beginning to blacken.

"Here, hold this cloth to your eye. Sit forward," he instructed.

He could tell by her sniffing that she was starting to cry.

"I'm sorry you got hurt," he whispered as he held her hand.

She laid her head against his chest. He held her close.

"It's okay. They will never hurt you again," Lucas promised.

He felt so guilty that they had attacked her because of him. What kind of a caretaker was he? Guilt consumed him.

"Why don't you go lie down?" he suggested.

She nodded, and he helped her over to the couch. He covered her with a blanket and headed to the kitchen for an ice pack.

She was exhausted. Her whole body felt like it was bruised. As Lucas rummaged around in the kitchen, she thought about how amazing he was. He was sweet and gentle and kind, but also courageous and protective. She heard the freezer door shut with a bang, and she watched as he approached her. The expression on his face was serene. Her heart fluttered in her chest, and her throat felt closed when he spoke.

"Here, close your eyes," he coached quietly. He carefully laid the ice pack over her black eye.

"Leave it on. I'm going to take Charlie back to my apartment and feed him and put him to bed. I'll call and check on you later, okay?"

She looked up at him with her one good eye, and he smiled. She looked so small and frail lying there. He hesitated a moment and gazed into her deep brown eyes. Slowly, he leaned down and brushed her hair out of her face.

"I hope you feel better," he said quietly.

"Thanks," she whispered.

He paused a moment. He wanted to kiss her, but he wasn't sure if he should. Did she feel the same way about him?

"Lucas, I'm hungry," Charlie whined from where he was playing on the floor.

The moment was broken and he thought better of the kiss. "I'm coming, I'm just checking on her your sister," Lucas assured him.

He got the wheelchair ready and picked up Charlie. "Let's go back to my apartment, and we'll watch some Sesame Street," Lucas suggested.

He looked down at Kayla who snuggled further into the blankets. His heart melted as she winced in pain. He wished he could do more for her. But he was just a friend...what could he do? He left the house and walked across the lawn to where she had thrown his box of cigarettes.

"Those are bad for you," Charlie reprimanded as Lucas pocketed them.

"Isn't it past your bedtime?"

"It's only five!"

"Crap," Lucas sighed and tickled him.

He took Charlie back to the apartment and let him watch Sesame Street until eight. He microwaved a couple of hot dogs he had grabbed for Charlie from Kayla's kitchen. After he fed him, he tucked him into bed.

Lucas could hardly wait to call her. He quickly bid Charlie a goodnight and hunted around the apartment for the phone. He couldn't think of what to say. He wished he were there in person so he could comfort her.

Anxiety filled his chest when she didn't answer on the first ring. Lucas paced back and forth debating whether to call her a second time. He reached for his cigarettes with shaking hands. Lucas leaned on the windowsill and dialed her number again. He inhaled the smoke as she answered.

"Hi."

"Hey, how are you?" Lucas blew the smoke to the side as he spoke.

"I'm okay," she replied groggily.

"I'm sorry if I woke you," he apologized. His breathing calmed once he realized she was all right.

"It's okay. Thanks for checking on me." She smiled even though she knew he couldn't see her.

Silence followed for a few moments. He wasn't sure what to say. She could hear his raspy breathing and the slow inhale of his breath.

"Are you smoking? I thought I threw those across the lawn?" she accused angrily.

"I don't smoke," Lucas teased, blowing the smoke out the open window into the cold night air.

"Lucas, put that cigarette down right now," her hoarse voice commanded.

He loved how ferocious she tried to sound.

"I'm serious," she added after he paused.

"Only if you promise to hang up and get some rest. No homework, no dishes, nothing. I want you to sleep. You had a long day." Lucas grinned. He could almost see her indignant face.

"I'm fine," she retorted.

Lucas inhaled loudly and blew the smoke in the earpiece of the phone.

"I'm getting lung cancer over here," he teased.

"That's not funny!" Kayla couldn't help but laugh. In her mind, she could see the adorable smile spreading across his face.

"Promise?" he waited a moment before he heard her sigh.

"Promise," she agreed, rolling her eyes.

"Good," he answered, taking one last drag on the cigarette.

"Put it out!"

"Okay, okay, deal." He snuffed it out on the windowsill and tossed it out the window.

"Okay," she agreed, her eyes beginning to close. Exhaustion was pulling her mind towards sleep.

"Are you sure you'll be okay?" Lucas asked seriously.

"M-hmm," she mumbled as her body slowly succumbed.

"Okay. Goodnight, Kayla."

His voice sounded so smooth and sincere. Kayla loved the sound of it. The pain seemed bearable knowing she would see his face the next morning. She wanted to say goodnight back, but her body had already given in.

All Lucas heard was the sound of her deep, even breathing. The thought of seeing her when she awoke made him smile. Maybe it was a good thing Charlie was up so early. He clicked the phone off, shut the window, and went to bed dreaming of the girl he was falling in love with.

TEN

"Lucas," Charlie whispered as he peered over at Lucas. Lucas slowly opened his eyes.

"What time is it?" he asked groggily.

"Breakfast for Charlie time," Charlie smiled at Lucas.

"Aren't little kids supposed to need a lot of sleep?"

"Not this one. Come on, I'm hungry. Can you do the air plane ride into the kitchen?"

Charlie rolled over and got to his knees in the bed. Lucas covered his head with a pillow.

"Get up, get up, get up," Charlie chanted in a singsong voice as he jumped on Lucas. Charlie paused when he realized Lucas wasn't moving.

"Lucas?" Charlie called hesitantly.

"*ROAR!*" Lucas playfully attacked Charlie, forming his hands like claws. Lucas flipped him onto his back pretending to tackle him.

"Stop, stop!" Charlie cried between fits of giggles.

"No! You have woken the beast!" Lucas growled as he tickled Charlie with his fake claws.

"I leaked!" Charlie gasped as Lucas tickled him.

"You what?" Lucas responded sitting back on his heels.

"I leaked."

"You leaked? In the bed?"

"Yep, it's still warm." Charlie grinned as Lucas jumped out of the bed.

He looked down at the soaking wet sheets. "Wow, that's a lot of pee," Lucas remarked, removing the sopped covers. He grimaced as the smell began to waft around the room.

"Where does Kayla put the wet bedspreads?" Lucas asked as he gingerly peeled off the sheets with two fingers.

"I don't know, Dad always used to do it."

"Where did Dad put them?"

"Outside, I think," Charlie scrunched up his forehead in thought.

"Works for me," Lucas shrugged and placed all the bedspreads in a basket.

"What are we doing today?" Charlie questioned as Lucas picked out a new outfit for him from the pile of clothes on the dresser.

"Ummm," Lucas answered as he held up a shirt and sweatpants.

"Those match too much," Charlie commented as Lucas brought them over with a new diaper.

"They match too much?" Lucas questioned Charlie skeptically.

"Yes, I like to be unmatching."

"Well, I will make sure to unmatch your clothes next time, Sir Charlie," Lucas responded in a fake English accent and bowed.

"Thank you, sir." Charlie pretended to knight Lucas with his teddy bear.

Lucas changed Charlie and dressed him. He let Charlie watch Sesame Street while he got ready for the day. Lucas took a shower and dressed quickly. He turned off the TV and shut off the lights.

"Ready? Let's go!" Lucas carried Charlie under one arm and held the basket of laundry in the other. He'd come back for the wheelchair if Charlie needed it later.

"I'm flying!" Charlie exclaimed.

He spread his arms out as Lucas ran across the lawn.

"Faster!" Charlie encouraged as Lucas picked up speed.

They charged up the stone walkway, ran up the ramp, and barged into the house.

"Lucas 147 has landed safely!" Charlie pretended to radio in.

Lucas swung him up into his arms and carried him into the living room. Just as they entered the kitchen, he noticed Kayla sitting at the table. Tears ran freely down her cheeks. She covered her face with her hands as Lucas approached.

"Hey, Charlie, why don't we turn on Sesame Street instead and I'll make pancakes. Okay?"

Lucas headed back for the living room and placed Charlie on the floor, turning on the wide flat screen. The channel was already set from the day before. Lucas waited until Charlie wasn't watching and slipped into the kitchen.

Lucas' heart broke as he heard her quiet sobs. She looked up at him from where she was sitting. He opened his arms and she stood as he embraced her.

"Shhh," he quieted as he pulled her head to his chest. She clutched his shirt in her fists as she sobbed. He wrapped his arms around her and held her tightly.

"I miss Dad," she sobbed.

"I know," he whispered as he rocked her.

"I sat by his graveside all night last night. I want him back so badly, it hurts." She heaved deep sobs as Lucas helped her sit back down.

"Hey, you told me you would sleep. And you shouldn't go out alone. I would have gone with you." Lucas brushed her hair out of her eyes.

"I told him. I told him not to work so much overtime in that part of the city. It's dangerous. Why didn't he just listen?" Kayla covered her face with her hands and rested her head on her knees.

"Cause he was trying to protect people. He died saving lives, Kayla," Lucas whispered.

"I know." She took a deep breath trying to calm herself. Lucas went to the sink and filled a glass of water for her.

"Thanks," she sniffed as he handed it to her.

"I'm going to make breakfast, okay? Are pancakes alright?" Lucas asked as he took out a frying pan from the cabinet.

She nodded, still unable to speak for fear of the tears returning. She sat quietly and listened to the soothing sounds of everyday normal life. Her heart ached with pain, but she knew she had to let go of her old life. Dad was gone and she couldn't change that. Tears fell again as she thought of him. How would she continue? She turned her head as Lucas accidentally dropped a pan.

"Ah!" she heard Charlie scream from the other room.

"They're shooting at us, Captain, what do we do?" Lucas yelled to Charlie as he stirred the batter for the pancakes.

"Hit the deck!" Charlie called back.

Lucas spooned the pancakes onto the frying pan and left them to brown while he dropped to the floor and army-crawled to the living room.

"Captain, no enemy fire has been reported. Only friendly fire," Lucas saluted as he crawled in.

"You mean our own people are shooting us?" Lucas gasped.

"No, it was just practice," Charlie explained patiently.

"You mean you made me crawl all the way in here for practice?"

"A Captain must always prepare his men. Oh and…Sergeant…?" Charlie raised an eye brow.

"Yes, Sir?"

"Your pancakes are burning."

Lucas quickly stood to his feet and ran back to the stove where the pancakes were rapidly bubbling. He flipped them over before smoke started to fill the kitchen. Kayla couldn't help but smile as Lucas opened the windows.

"Fire in the hole!" Charlie called.

Lucas laughed as he tossed the pancakes into the garbage.

"Round two," Lucas announced as he poured another batch on.

"Make it quick! This soldier is hungry!" Charlie called.

Kayla rubbed her reddened eyes and tried again to take some deep breaths. After a couple minutes, Lucas came over with a stack of pancakes.

"Want the first one? I made it specially unburnt, just for you," he smiled.

She looked up again into his eyes. He knew she didn't care about the pancakes.

"I'm so sorry about your father, and the fight, and everything that's happened," Lucas spoke sincerely.

"It's okay, I need to get used to him not being around, and you were amazing yesterday. Thanks for helping me," she said, looking into his kind, blue eyes.

Without thinking, he leaned in to kiss her.

Kayla couldn't believe that he was kissing her! She had never been kissed before.

Lucas cupped her cheeks as a tear trickled down. Kayla leaned her face into his palms as he wiped away with his thumb the tear running down her chin.

"I think I love you," Lucas whispered softly, before his head could hold him back from what his heart desired.

Warmth spread through her body at his words. She felt so safe and happy with him. In that moment, she knew she wanted to be with him forever.

"I...I...think I love you too." Fresh tears overflowed her eyes.

"Then why are you crying?" Lucas laughed softly as her tears soaked his hands. She looked so distraught.

"I just wish Dad could have been here to see us be together. He really liked you. He didn't approve of any of the boys I've liked until you."

"Oh, you just like me now?" Lucas teased as she rested her head against his chest.

"Just a little," she admitted.

He laughed that quiet laugh she loved. She listened to the sound of it in his chest. The tears subsided after a few moments and she stepped away to grab a tissue. He waited patiently while she dried her eyes.

"I'm sorry," she apologized.

He looked so cute standing there. It hit her that he was hers. He wanted her. The impulse to run to him was natural and it felt just as natural to Lucas as he caught her in his arms and lifted her off her feet.

"I love you, Kayla," he whispered again.

She laid her head on his shoulder as he spun her around slowly.

"And I always will," he added, pulling her closer.

The next weeks passed rapidly for Lucas, but Kayla was still adjusting to the realization of her father's death. Ever since she decided not to return to school, she felt lost. The weeks seemed to drag by.

She used her time to get to know Lucas better. She really thought this was the right guy for her. He also seemed perfect for Charlie.

She tried hard to be okay because she didn't want to be a burden to Lucas, so she acted happy every time he walked into the room. She didn't feel comfortable crying all the time in front of him. Lucas was sweet about it, but she was sure all the crying would become tiresome. Why would he like someone who is depressed all the time? She reasoned.

Lucas knew she was sad, but she wouldn't open up. He wasn't sure what to do. He decided to talk to her about her life and parents. Maybe then she would open up. He waited until a night where Charlie was asleep on the couch.

Kayla was putting away dishes in the kitchen. Lucas covered Charlie with a blanket and joined her.

"Hey Kay, can I talk to you for a minute before I take Charlie back to the apartment with me?"

Kayla's heart dropped to her stomach. This was where he was going to break up with her. She knew it. Tears welled up in her eyes and she covered her face.

He put his arms around her. She broke down.

"Babe, what's wrong?" Lucas rubbed her back soothingly.

"You're breaking up with me, aren't you?" she sobbed. Lucas drew back and gripped her shoulders.

"Why would you think that?" He demanded quietly as he pulled her closer to him.

"I know I'm no fun to be around. I try to be fun and I just can't. I can't! I miss Dad," she lamented.

"Kay, I don't expect you to just move on with your life. A lot has happened to you over the last couple of months. I would understand if you lie on the couch for the next four months! Of course that doesn't mean that I wouldn't try to bribe you with ice cream just to get you up."

Lucas gently caressed her cheek and was rewarded with a small smile.

"Really? You don't hate that you left your whole life just to live with a depressed, lonely, high school dropout?" She buried her face in his chest as he laughed.

"Oh yes, I wish I lived back with my amazing parents and lived off their million dollars. I just left out of pity for you. It's not like I had no-where to go or anything," he chuckled and she laughed.

"Well, we'll see what adventures we can have," Lucas smiled.

Two months later:

The summer air was hot on her skin. In her hand, Kayla carried a cold cup of iced tea with a slice of lemon floating on the top.

Lucas walked close to her side, carrying Charlie on his shoulders. They crossed a bridge over a small stream. The water was so clear you could see the little pebbles on the bottom and little fish swimming around in the shallow ends. The sun was just beginning to set and the crickets were starting their song.

"I don't see any sticks that would be good enough for the marsh-mallows," Lucas said, looking around at all the tree branches.

"You have too much city blood in you," Kayla teased putting down her tea.

"What are you doing?" he asked as she looked up at the sky.

"I'm getting the sticks," she explained, grabbing a low lying branch.

"How?" Lucas asked nervously, seeing the height of the tree.

"Like this." She smiled as she pulled herself up into the branches.

"Hey! No fair! I want to go up!" Charlie exclaimed excitedly.

"Come on Lucas, climb up."

"Um, I don't know," he started to say but Charlie was excitedly pulling his hair.

Lucas walked to the tree trunk and Kayla reached her arms out.

"Be careful," Lucas warned, supporting most of Charlie's weight as Kayla pulled him into the tree.

"Wow, you're so tall!" Lucas smiled at Charlie and Charlie grinned.

"I am taller than you!"

"No you're not!" Lucas exclaimed, pretending to be upset.

"Yes I am!"

"I'm going to come up there and show you how tall I am," Lucas joked, trying to pull himself into the tree. "You make this look so easy Kay," he laughed as his hands slipped.

"Come on! It's easy!" Charlie yelled.

"Oh, easy for you to say, Mister," Lucas teased.

Lucas finally pulled himself almost all the way up. He went to put his foot in the crotch of the trunk and got it stuck. Charlie almost fell out of Kayla's arms he was laughing so hard.

"Come on city boy, you can do it," Kayla encouraged, watching him struggle to get his foot out of the tight squeeze.

"Hey stop laughing, it's not funny!" He pointed his finger at Charlie and pretended to be serious.

Charlie laughed harder.

Lucas leaned down and freed his foot from the stuck shoe. He scrambled toward Charlie.

"I'm going kill you, Charlie," he laughed, trying to balance on the branch.

Kayla reached out her arm to steady him as he came closer. He thankfully grabbed hold and sat next to Charlie. Kayla then helped him pull Charlie into his lap.

"This is for laughing!" He pretended to be angry as he tickled Charlie who was squirming and giggling.

Smiling, Kayla watched Lucas and her brother. She had never seen Charlie so happy before. Lucas looked up and flashed a smile and Kayla couldn't help but smile back. His kindness made him cuter. His blue eyes sparkled in the fading sunlight, and she found herself staring longingly.

Out of breath, Charlie finally pushed Lucas away and nearly fell over. Lucas balanced him upright and caught Kayla staring.

"I think your sister has become a zombie," he whispered as Kayla jumped.

"No, she gets that way when she really likes a boy," Charlie said, smiling.

"Lucas and Kayla sittin' in a... Hey! We are in a tree! Lucas and Kayla sittin' in a tree K – I...."

"That's enough Charlie," Kayla interrupted, smacking the back of his head gently as she blushed.

Lucas grinned. "Come on, it's getting dark. Let's go back to the campfire."

Lucas handed Charlie to Kayla as he jumped down. He turned so Kayla could put Charlie on his shoulders. She lowered him down then turned to jump. Lucas held onto Charlie with one hand and held out the other for Kayla. Blushing again, she took his hand, and he steadied her as she jumped.

They walked back slowly.

"I wasn't staring," she defended herself suddenly, taking his hand.

"Oh you were definitely staring." Charlie imitated her by tilting his head and opening his eyes wide.

"You were all googley-eyed," Lucas laughed, squeezing her hand.

"Maybe she was just squinting to find a stick," Charlie defended.

"We do have to get a stick," she reminded Lucas.

He looked up and pulled a small branch from a tree. "This good?"

"You know, for a city boy, that was pretty impressive."

"Thanks, I'll make sure to brag about pulling twigs off trees more often."
She just smiled.

Lucas slipped his phone out of his pocket to check the time.

"Wow, I didn't realize it had gotten so late, it's almost your bedtime,
Charlie," Lucas reminded.

"Can I stay up with you?" Charlie begged.

Lucas turned to Kayla who crossed her arms in silent answer. Lucas
stuck out his lower lip and begged her with pleading eyes.

Charlie laughed as Kayla sighed and rolled her eyes. "That look
always gets me!"

"I know," Lucas remarked smugly.

"Can we go to the lake? I want to see how it looks at night!" Charlie
begged.

Lucas kept forgetting there was a lake on the property. They had
only visited it twice. Lucas still had to get over the idea of having a huge
body of water right in their backyard. Other people lived on the far side
of the lake, but most of it belonged to Kayla's family.

"That's a great idea, Charlie. Let's get the rowboat!" Kayla swung
him around excitedly.

"Can I row?" Charlie squealed.

Before Lucas had a chance to answer, Kayla immediately chimed in
and yelled out, "No, you'll run us into a pine tree!"

"Do pine trees grow in the pond?" Lucas asked with his eyebrow raised.

"Shhhh, I just need an excuse not to let him," Kayla whispered,
pretending Charlie couldn't hear.

"Oh," Lucas murmured thoughtfully.

Kayla handed Charlie off to Lucas and disappeared into the night.
She came back dragging a small rowboat. As they were getting into the
boat, Lucas went in first to help Kayla lift Charlie in. Unfortunately, he
never had been in a boat before, so when he stepped in, he lost his balance and it flipped upside down, tossing him into the cold water.

Kayla was holding Charlie in her arms and couldn't help Lucas as
he flailed around in the shallow water.

"Umm…I forgot to tell you something…I don't know how to row a
boat!" Lucas just looked at her, water dripping into his eyes, and burst
out laughing as he waded out of the water.

"Come on, City Boy, we are waiting," Kayla teased as he tried to hoist himself onto the slippery dock.

"Yeah, come on!" Charlie shouted.

Lucas paused, pretending to catch his breath so Kayla would come over and try to help. As planned, Kayla put Charlie down and came over to see if he was okay. He reached out his arms as if to ask her to help him up and as soon as she got there he pulled her into the water with him.

"Not so funny now is it?" he teased, rubbing water off her face as she glared angrily.

They finally got into the boat with Charlie and rowed to the other side of the lake. Fireflies darted over the water. Frogs created a night-time melody.

As they drew closer to the shore, they saw a bobcat staring at them from the edge of the woods. Lucas screamed like a girl, holding Charlie closer.

Charlie screamed right along with Lucas.

"You two are such babies," Kayla laughed as the bobcat disappeared into the darkness.

"I think it's time to go home." Lucas swallowed hard, his heart still pounding in his chest.

"Bobcats don't like the water – we were fine!" Kayla laughed, but allowed Lucas to take the oars.

"Can we do this again?" Charlie asked as they were rowing home.

"Sure, but maybe in the daylight next time," Lucas replied nervously.

His clothes were still soaking wet by the time they reached the shore. Lucas let Kayla carry Charlie back to the house while he dragged the boat up onto land. He met them at the apartment door.

"Goodnight," Lucas murmured, reaching for Charlie.

"Night, Lucas," she whispered, kissing him once quickly before Charlie could protest. She turned and skipped back to the house. Lucas smiled as he watched her leave. He wished the night wasn't so long and that morning would come quickly so he could see her again.

The next day was a cleaning day for Kayla. Lucas and Charlie played games on the floor while she dusted, swept, and generally cleaned the house.

"Lucas, it's been your turn for five minutes," Charlie chided.

Startled, Lucas jumped.

"What?"

"Stop staring at my sister! I want to finish the game! It's your turn!" Charlie sighed, exasperated.

"Sorry," Lucas grinned.

He loved watching her dance around the house in cleaning mode. The sad memories seem to have faded away, and each day had brought new adventures. He loved feeling alive for the first time in his life. Even playing games with Charlie felt to him like the world was a bright and beautiful place.

"Can we do s'mores tonight, outside?" Charlie broke Lucas' train of thought.

"It's a little cold to go into the woods tonight, Charlie. But maybe we could do it on the patio if we could get your sister to stop cleaning for five minutes," Lucas said loudly so Kayla, who was waltzing by, could hear him.

"What was that, Lucas?" she playfully accused with her hands on her hips and a feather duster hanging precariously from her apron.

He looked up at her from his place on the floor.

"I said, you should take a break, and we should have a fire in the pit on the patio. Charlie wants s'mores."

"Oh, you're blaming it on the innocent CP kid? Real mature," she teased, wrapping her arms around his neck and hugging him.

Lucas smiled at Charlie who rolled his eyes.

"Just because you want s'mores, Lucas, doesn't mean you have to pretend it was my idea," Charlie sarcastically chided.

Lucas stood up and snatched him up into his arms.

"Oh yeah?" he growled and swung him around.

"Alright, I could use a break. I'll get the crackers and chocolate, you two go set up the chairs," Kayla directed, shaking her head as she walked away.

Lucas held Charlie in airplane formation and flew him out onto the patio. He set up the chairs while Charlie watched. Kayla came out a few moments later with Charlie's wheelchair. Lucas buckled Charlie safely into his chair and went to work on starting the fire.

The fire crackled and popped. Lucas turned to open the package of marshmallows. Charlie was leaning over to look at the fire closely when suddenly the chair began to tip!

Kayla jumped up, dangerously close to the open flames, just in time to stop the wheelchair from tipping over. Lucas watched the whole scene in slow motion, but couldn't stop it. A flame caught her sleeve, but she had to make sure that Charlie was safe.

Lucas ran over to help Kayla who was flailing around, desperately trying to put out the fire. He ripped off his shirt and smothered her burning arm with it. The flame died down, but not before his shirt caught on fire. The palms of his hands were singed in the process. The burns blistered, but he didn't seem to notice.

"Are you okay, Kayla?" he asked, trying not to panic.

"Yes, I'm alright. My arm is only a little painful. What about you?"

He looked down at his hands to examine the wounds, and she shrieked.

"Lucas, your hands are burned!"

"Oh, look at that," he mused.

"Ew!" Charlie squealed.

Kayla ran inside to get the First aid kit. She ran back out and knelt down beside Lucas.

"Let me see." She gingerly touched the wounds, wincing as she felt her dinner coming up.

"That bad, huh?"

"No," she lied as she dabbed at the blisters with a cloth.

"Ow!" He flinched, drawing away from her touch.

"Stay still! I have to clean it."

"It's fine. I'll be okay."

"Let me take care of it." She emphasized each word as she looked into his eyes.

"Okay," he relented.

He loved the determined look in her eyes as she demanded to take care of him. It wasn't something he couldn't do himself, but he liked her gentle touch and her concern.

She expertly applied burn cream to his palms and covered them with a light bandage.

"Okay, Nurse Kayla." Lucas rolled his eyes as she fiddled with the dressing.

"Your turn." He carefully helped her stand and drew her close to him.

"It's just a little burn," she explained.

He gingerly pulled back her sleeve and examined the reddened blistered area.

"Hmm…," he pretended to think deeply. "I think I have the perfect treatment."

"The cream is right," she started to say.

He leaned down and lightly blew a kiss toward the wound.

Kayla's heart stopped as he looked up at her with serene blue eyes.

"Better?" his perfect smooth voice intoned.

She could only nod.

He grinned at her speechlessness.

"Come on you two love birds, I want a marshmallow," Charlie rolled his eyes.

The rest of the evening passed without excitement – to Lucas' relief.

Kayla changed his bandages once more before the night was over.

"Are you sure you're going to be okay?" she fretted as Lucas hoisted a sleeping Charlie into his arms.

"I'll be fine. I'll just be careful," he assured her.

"Thanks for putting out the fire. I'm sorry. I just panicked! I should have done the drop-roll thingy, and you wouldn't have gotten hurt." She looked down, upset.

Lucas laughed. "I can take care of myself, Kayla. Besides, I couldn't stand and watch you burn. I had to do something to save the princess," he teased, ruffling her hair.

"Go home, Superman, get some rest. I'll see you tomorrow." She ducked out from under his touch.

"Okay. Night," he kissed her and left.

She stood on the doorstep, watching him leave with Charlie draped over his shoulder. Her heart fluttered as she thought of seeing him again. She had always thought love like this was a fairytale, but Lucas was so real. She loved him, and she never wanted it to end.

ELEVEN

SWEAT DRIPPED OFF LUCAS' FOREHEAD. He pounded another nail into the row of two-by-fours lined up underneath him. His t-shirt was soaked through, but he didn't want to stop. He was so close to finishing the last part of the platform that he didn't want to be interrupted by anything.

"Hey there," her beautiful voice rang out over the clanging of his hammer.

"Not now, Babe, the ark is almost built," Lucas yelled over his shoulder.

"Very funny, Noah, come on, take a break. You've been at it all day," she encouraged.

He rose and turned to face her.

She was dressed in a white rose- colored summer dress. Her hair flowed on the slight summer breeze.

Lucas couldn't resist her offer.

"You can still show Charlie the ramp is done. Just take a break for tonight," she insisted.

He hopped down and took her hand.

"Okay, let's go get him. I want to show him and then eat some dinner. Then maybe me and you can spend some time together," he smiled and took her hand as they walked back towards the house.

She moved in closer and he wrapped an arm around her.

''Where's Charlie?" Lucas inquired.

"Finishing his nap in my bed," Kayla replied, sliding open the door to the kitchen.

She began to make dinner as Lucas went off to wake Charlie.

Lucas went into Kayla's room and gently touched Charlie, trying not to scare him as he woke him up. Startled from sleep, Charlie spasmed ten feet off the bed and screamed. They both burst out laughing. Once they caught their breath, Lucas scooped Charlie up out of bed and swung him onto his back.

"Come on, I want to show you something," Lucas whispered.

"Come on, Kayla!" Lucas called as he ran through the kitchen, out the sliding door, and jumped down from the patio, heading toward the woods. He carried Charlie to the tree house.

Charlie gasped as the tree house came into view.

"You did it!" he exclaimed.

"The platform's not quite finished, but you can go up if you want," Lucas offered.

Charlie screamed in excitement.

Lucas carried Charlie piggyback up the ramp. Charlie was almost choking Lucas, he was holding on so tight. Reaching the platform, Lucas put Charlie down.

"Wow, it's so big," Charlie said in awe, looking around.

"Yes, it is," Kayla said quietly.

"How long did it take you to build this?" Charlie asked.

"Ever since you showed me it that one day. You were so sad the last couple months, I wanted to do something for you to remember your dad by," Lucas whispered softly.

He caught Kayla's teary eyes, and he took her hand.

As they stood staring into each other's eyes, Charlie pretended to throw up.

"Ew, keep your romance to yourself! You're ruining the moment!" Charlie teased.

"I forgot something," Lucas said, running out of the tree house and into the house. He came right back with a candle, marshmallows, graham crackers, and chocolate.

As they began roasting s'mores, Kayla started freaking out.

"Don't burn the house down," she warned, both serious and kidding.

Getting burnt by the fire had spooked her. Her mind replayed the memory as they roasted marshmallows.

"You are such a girl," Lucas laughed, wrapping an arm around her.

"Kayla?" Charlie asked after a few moments of silence.

"Yes?"

"When I die, can you wear bright colors to the funeral?"

"What? I thought we were talking about tree houses?" Kayla laughed.

"Yes, we are. I just was thinking about Dad. You wore all those sad colors."

"Ummmm, I guess so. I hope you're not planning to go anywhere… are you?"

"No, I'm just thinking in case I die," Charlie shrugged his shoulders and leaned down to eat a marshmallow.

"Charlie, don't do that," Kayla interrupted while he was swallowing it whole.

Charlie grinned, marshmallow squeezing from his stuffed cheeks.

Lucas laughed.

"Ew, Charlie," Kayla exclaimed dryly.

"What can we wear to my funeral?" Charlie asked again after swallowing.

Kayla looked at Lucas.

"Maybe we should switch topics. Let's talk about it later, okay?" he said, squeezing Kayla's hand for comfort.

She nodded.

"Hey, you're supposed to eat the marshmallow, not play with it," Lucas said, pulling Charlie away from the bag.

"Can I go back to bed? I'm tired," Charlie yawned, rubbing marshmallow into his eyes.

"Okay let's go," Kayla agreed and scooped him up.

After she put him in his bed, she set up the baby monitor and then went back outside where Lucas was sitting on the edge of the tree house.

"You look beautiful," he said, smiling, taking in her natural beauty as she slowly walked up the newly built ramp.

"You're funny," Kayla chuckled, kneeling on the freshly cut wood of the platform.

"No, I'm being honest." Lucas whispered, leaning in closer. "I love you," he said as he leaned back from the kiss.

"I know," she agreed, curling up next to him. "Why do you think Charlie said all that about funerals? I'm worried he thinks too much about Dad dying."

"I think little kids process things differently. He is probably still trying to understand what happened."

"I guess you're right. I don't like him talking about death like that. I can't take one more person dying," Kayla sniffed, wiping tears away as she remembered her parents.

"No one is going to die anytime soon, Kayla. It will be okay," he wrapped his arm around her and pulled her close.

The sound of her quiet crying gave way to steady breathing. Lucas held her as he stared out into the night sky. A couple of minutes went by and she was fast asleep.

Lucas climbed down from the tree house to get her a blanket before the night breeze chilled her. He skimmed though the closet to find the warmest blanket.

"Perfect," he thought to himself, snatching the blanket out of a box.

Feeling peaceful, he walked back up the ramp. Kayla had awakened and was now shivering as she gazed up into the night sky.

"Hey," Lucas whispered draping the blanket over her shoulders.

"I really don't need a blanket." Kayla tried defending herself.

"You're shivering, you need a blanket." Lucas fought back, wrapping the blanket around her.

"Thank you," Kayla finally gave in.

"Do you need anything else?" he asked, tenderly taking her hand.

"Can you just sit with me for a while?"

"Of course." he grinned, pulling her into his chest.

They both gazed up into the night sky and her eyelids began to close again.

"I should check on Charlie and go to bed. You coming in or staying up for a while?" Lucas asked, gently shaking her awake.

"I'll stay up for a while."

"Are you sure?"

"Yes, Lucas, I'm not a baby."

"Yes, but you're my girlfriend, and I love you," Lucas smiled, rubbing her cheek with his thumb.

She shivered as Lucas pulled her in closer for more warmth. She was beginning to believe that she had someone who would love and take care of her.

He pulled her face up towards his and softly kissed her.

"Okay, I'm going in. I'll check on you before I go to sleep," Lucas whispered.

She nodded and watched him walk down the ramp. She needed time to think, to remember. The pain was still fresh in her mind. She missed her father terribly, but she knew God had provided Lucas to take care of her. She prayed and cried out to God as she wished her father were here to see what an amazing man Lucas was.

An hour later, Lucas came back outside to find her sleeping on the tree house floor. He gently woke her.

"Hey, Babe, you got to go inside. You can't stay out here all night," he encouraged as she drowsily stood to her feet.

She leaned heavily on him as he walked her back to the house. He opened the sliding door for her and walked in behind her.

"Go ahead to bed, I'll lock up," he assured her.

She hugged him tightly before stumbling sleepily into her room. He secured the house and gently picked up Charlie, trying not to wake him as he carried him to the apartment. Once inside, he climbed into bed, wishing there was some way he could take away Kayla's pain.

In the middle of the night, Charlie woke up screaming. He was having a string of nightmares lately, but wouldn't tell Lucas what they were about. Lucas held him and tried to get him to talk, but all he wanted to do was go back to sleep. He wondered what the nightmare could be about that it would scare Charlie so badly. But, he thought, kids are kids, and sometimes they are afraid for reasons that can't be understood.

Rolling over, Lucas tried to go back to sleep

TWELVE

THE NEXT MORNING, LUCAS, KAYLA, and Charlie went out to breakfast.

"I heard you had a nightmare last night," Kayla broached cautiously as she put on Charlie's bib.

"I don't want to talk about it," Charlie said firmly, looking away. Kayla met Lucas' eyes in silent communication.

"Look over there," Charlie said, changing the subject. "A flying goat!"

Everyone burst out laughing.

After a few moments of thought, Charlie spoke up again, "I want to meet my daddy."

Lucas and Kayla looked at each other, confused.

"But you already knew Daddy," Kayla explained carefully.

"No, my real daddy is waiting for me at my real home," Charlie insisted.

Kayla looked at Lucas. He took her hand. Neither of them knew what to say. They tried to change subjects, but now it was Charlie who wanted to talk.

The rest of the afternoon was spent trying to keep Charlie off the subject of death. Lucas did everything he could to keep Charlie from talking about it, particularly in front of Kayla. He was never more thankful to put Charlie to bed than he was that night.

Finally, Lucas got ready for bed himself after tucking in Charlie. Pulling the covers back, he rolled in and accidentally rolled on Charlie's head. Thankfully, Charlie stayed asleep. Lucas couldn't stop laughing, but then he got worried. Had he hurt Charlie?

"Charlie, are you okay?"

He tried again.

"Charlie? Charlie?!"

No response.

"Great, I found the girl of my dreams and I killed her brother," he thought, starting to panic.

Lucas stared at Charlie, desperate for a sign that he was okay. At last, Charlie rolled over. Relief washed over Lucas. He vowed to be more careful of him.

As he drifted off to sleep, Lucas wondered why Charlie was talking about death so much. Lucas knew he needed someone to talk to about it. Maybe Charlie was finally realizing that his dad was never coming back. Maybe Charlie was worried Lucas was going to die. Either way, Lucas would make sure to talk about it with him.

The next day, Lucas tried to wake Charlie. After a couple of tries, he knew something was wrong. He dialed Kayla and asked her to come over. By the time she arrived a few moments later, Lucas was frantically pacing back and forth.

"Hey, I tried to wake him up and he's awake but just lying there," Lucas explained anxiously.

Kayla felt Charlie's forehead with the back of her hand.

"Is he going to be okay?" Lucas asked, worried. He was terrified it was his fault for accidentally rolling on him the night before.

"He'll be fine. Sometimes he gets like this. When you or I get a cold, we can deal with it. But with Charlie and his CP, he can't function. When he gets sick, he gets really sick. It does feel like he has a fever. I'll give him some cold medicine, and maybe he'll feel better." Kayla stood up to leave.

"You sure? Maybe I did something. I mean, last night I accidentally rolled on him. I didn't realize how close he was to my side, I just..." Lucas stuttered over his words as he tried to quickly explain to Kayla what had happened.

"No, it wasn't you. He hasn't had a cold in awhile. It happens some-times. Don't worry about it, Lucas," she assured with a hand on his shoulder.

He breathed a sigh of relief. "Okay, I'll go get the cold medicine. You stay with Charlie."

"It's in the medicine cabinet in the bathroom," she yelled after him as he was running out the door.

Kayla took Charlie into her lap and rocked him.

"Hey, Buddy, wake up," she pacified, cradling him.

"I don't feel good," Charlie moaned.

"I know, Honey. Want to go watch cartoons on the couch?"

"Where's Lucas?" Charlie asked without answering her question.

"What? You like Lucas better than your own sister now?" she teased as she carried him out to the living room.

Charlie smiled slightly. Kayla laid him on the couch and wrapped him in a blanket.

"I'm back!" Lucas burst through the door with two boxes of cold medicine.

"Lucas!" Charlie cried out as Lucas came into view.

"Are you okay?" Lucas asked concerned.

"I'm fine," Charlie said with a smile. "I'm just…"

Charlie's voice dropped off as he began to hyperventilate.

"Call 9-1-1!" Kayla yelled.

Lucas whipped out his phone and dialed frantically. The phone seemed to ring forever before someone answered.

"Hello? My girlfriend's brother is having a…" Lucas looked at Kayla quizzically.

"A seizure!" Kayla yelled, beginning to cry.

"He's having a seizure, can you send someone over?" Lucas requested.

The operator asked him a few more questions then hung up.

Lucas ran over to Charlie, put his hand on him and started praying.

''Jesus we need you. Please stop this," Lucas prayed, his voice shaking.

By this time, Charlie had foam coming out of his mouth, and his eyes had rolled back in his head. Lucas stood helpless as Charlie's tiny body began to jerk rhythmically.

"Should I hold him down?" Lucas asked Kayla.

Kayla was desperately trying to keep herself together.

"No, you just have to let him go and try to keep him safe. Hopefully the ambulance will get here soon," she worried as Charlie's body tensed tighter and his legs continued to jerk.

As the ambulance sirens were screaming in the distance, the seizure began to stop. Charlie lay still for a moment before bursting into tears.

"Charlie," Kayla cried, leaning over his body.

Lucas took a deep breath to stop his hands from shaking.

"Come with me, Lucas, don't let them take me by myself!" Charlie whispered as the paramedics knocked and entered the apartment.

"I'm not going anywhere," Lucas whispered softly as the paramedics took over.

Charlie was fighting the oxygen mask strapped on his face and was on the stretcher before Lucas could say another word.

"Kayla, you probably should be the one to ride with Charlie in the ambulance. I'll bring the wheelchair and drive behind you," Lucas directed.

Kayla nodded and followed the paramedics out the door.

After they loaded Charlie in, Lucas helped Kayla board the ambulance as well. The doors shut, and Lucas grabbed the wheelchair and jumped into Kayla's car.

At the hospital, they took Charlie inside, and Lucas and Kayla followed. It was obvious that it had been a rough ride for Charlie. He had always panicked and become extremely agitated by masks of any sort. This time was no exception.

Kayla was sobbing so hard her shoulders shook. Lucas sat next to her and put an arm around her. For two hours, they waited while tests were being done on Charlie. Kayla continued to cry into Lucas' shoulder. His shirt was soaked with her tears by the time a nurse returned to give them an update.

"We did a lot of tests. We are still waiting for the results, but you can see him. The doctor gave him Diastat, so he might be a little groggy."

"What's that?" Kayla asked anxiously as they followed the nurse down the hall.

"It's a muscle relaxant to stop the seizures, but it also makes people really tired. If he goes home today, he might even be groggy tonight. Here he is," the nurse opened a curtain and let them in.

The curtain slipped shut behind them. There was nothing to do but to wait for Charlie to wake up. Lucas wrapped his arm around Kayla. He was terrified. He had never seen Charlie so still.

They cried and prayed for another twenty minutes before Charlie finally opened his eyes.

Charlie opened his eyes slowly. He couldn't figure out where he was. All he saw was Kayla and Lucas and all the bright lights.

"Can I go home now?" Charlie asked groaningly. "Where am I?"

"In the ER. You had a seizure."

"Really?" Charlie asked.

"What did it feel like?" Lucas inquired.

"It felt like I was locked in my own body," Charlie described for him. "It also felt like I was hot and cold on either side. Before the seizure happened, it felt like half of my body was numb."

"Were you scared?" Lucas asked quietly.

"A little," he admitted, looking down.

Kayla rubbed Charlie's back comfortingly.

"It's okay to be scared, Char Char. I was scared, too, and so was Lucas. Right, Lucas?" she asked, elbowing him.

"Oh yeah, I almost fainted," he replied, winking at Charlie and pretending to faint in the chair.

Charlie smiled a little.

"Can we get out of here? I want to go home," Charlie said groggily.

"We have to wait for your nurse to come back and discharge you," Lucas explained, sitting back up in his chair.

"I can go get you something to eat if you want," Kayla offered.

"Or we could get pizza on the way back and eat it in the tree house," Lucas suggested, his blue eyes sparkling.

"We are not bringing him to the tree house after he just had a seizure. We don't want him to have one again and crack his head open falling out," Kayla said, smacking Lucas in the back of the head.

"He'll be fine. If he starts falling, I'll just catch him and break my neck before he does. Easy," Lucas said as Charlie started to laugh.

Kayla's face turned serious.

"No, we are not doing that."

"What was that? You think it's a great idea? Perfect. I'll go get the pizza."

"No, no, that isn't what I said, Lucas," she exclaimed, pulling on his shoulder.

"I think the pizza should have anchovies. That's Kayla's favorite," Lucas said to Charlie as he ducked Kayla's swipe at him.

"And mushrooms," Charlie chimed in.

Kayla saw Charlie's face light up at the thought and gave into Lucas' playful teasing.

"If I have to eat anchovies and mushrooms, you're going to have to clean up after me when I throw up," Kayla said, grinning and running away as Lucas chased her around the hospital room.

"Get her!" Charlie squealed as she ran behind the bed.

"I'm trying!" Lucas exclaimed, dodging Kayla's playful kick.

With a crash, the bedside table knocked over. Lucas leaned over Charlie to pick it up and without warning...*SMACK!* Charlie's fist hit Lucas in the face.

"Oops! CP moment," Charlie laughed as Lucas pretended to have a broken nose.

"Gotcha!" Kayla yelled, grabbing his shoulder.

"Ahem," a deep voice cleared his throat.

Startled, Lucas, Charlie, and Kayla looked up from the bed as apple juice dripped onto the floor. The doctor stood with several nurses observing the chaos.

"And you two are...?" the doctor asked sternly.

"They're Mommy and Daddy," Charlie piped in as Lucas laughed.

Kayla glared. "I am not old enough to be your..." she whispered angrily before the doctor interrupted.

"Mrs. Maxwell, your son is doing well."

Kayla glared again at Charlie before looking at the doctor and smiling.

"Yes, he is. He is a charming, sweet young man."

The doctor paused, "That isn't quite what I meant. I mean he is doing well. He can go home. I am sure he is..." He looked at Charlie who was picking his nose. "Charming."

"Oh yes, he is just wonderful," Kayla said smiling sarcastically.

"Well, Mrs. Maxwell, if he has another seizure, please bring him in for a re-evaluation. I will prescribe Diastat just in case it happens again. The nurse will explain to you how it works. For now, take him home and make sure he gets some rest. But, no food for at least two hours," the doctor instructed.

"Charlie? Rest? Ha! You're funny!" Kayla laughed at the doctor's instructions.

"We're getting pizza and going to the tree house, right?" Charlie questioned.

Lucas shushed him.

"Remember, you're not supposed to eat for another two hours, dear wonderful child," Lucas reminded, trying to keep him quiet.

The doctor shook his head and left the room.

Lucas scooped Charlie up out of the bed and put him in his wheelchair. They pretended to be a rocket as Kayla yelled after them to slow down. Lucas and Kayla loaded Charlie in the car. Charlie licked Kayla's arm as she buckled the seatbelt. She smacked him as she wiped the spit on his shirt.

"You love me," Charlie said grinning.

"It's a good thing I do, or else you would probably be dead," Kayla smiled, ruffling his hair.

Lucas climbed in and took Kayla's hand as they hit the road for home.

They stopped quickly at the pizzeria and grabbed two pizzas. When they arrived home, Lucas got out of the car and wheeled Charlie's wheelchair into the woods.

"Can I hold the pizza on my lap?" Charlie asked.

"Noooo!" Kayla shook her head, holding the box tighter. "I would like to eat it, not wear it."

Charlie laughed, "Well, hurry up! I'm *STARVING*!"

Lucas let go of Kayla's hand to lift Charlie onto his shoulders. He walked up the ramp and brought him inside.

Kayla came up behind them and put the pizza on the table. She found the matches and lit a candle.

"There, a feast by candlelight," she smiled.

"Finally!" Charlie exclaimed.

Lucas cut up the pizza and fed him pieces as they talked and laughed.

After dinner, Charlie wanted to do fireworks. Lucas was shocked.

"Won't your neighbors be upset?"

Kayla smiled and said, "No, we're country, we do this all the time."

She gestured to the large forest and the miles of farms.

"And if we get in trouble, I'll just blame it on you and run away."

"Greaaaaatttttttt. I hope you know how to light fireworks, because if you don't, you're looking at the wrong guy."

"Lucas, I've lived in the country for sixteen years. I'm pretty sure I know how to shoot a firework."

They climbed down from the tree house and went in an open area.

When it was all set up, Charlie asked, "Can I shoot the first firework?"

"Charlie, I've known you all your life, do you really think I would give you a firework with a match?"

"Mmmaaayyybbbeee…probably not. Lucas, can I shoot a firework?"

"I'll make you a deal," said Lucas. "If I run one hundred feet from you right now, you can shoot it."

"Okay."

"Ummm, I was just kidding. I've only known you for about a month or two and I'm pretty sure I figured it out when you punched me in the face today."

"What? That I'm cute and innocent?" Charlie smiled sweetly.

"No, that you're crazy," Lucas teased, tickling him.

"Do the fireworks have ink in them?" Charlie asked.

"You mean, color?" Lucas said laughing. "Yes, they do. I hope they do because otherwise we've been robbed!"

Kayla was really good at lighting the fireworks. Lucas watched her in amazement. A girl, lighting fireworks, in the middle of the woods – he thought that was pretty impressive.

She sat next to him as the last display of colors lit up the summer sky.

Kayla and Lucas smiled at each other. Charlie had fallen asleep on the ground near them.

"So is this another sleep outside night?" Kayla asked.

"I guess so," Lucas answered, taking off his hoodie.

"What are you doing?" Kayla asked, watching him lay it flat on the ground.

"I'm pretending to play picnic," he said sarcastically.

"Really?" she asked, curious.

He shook his head, "No silly, it's for you to sleep on. The ground is wet."

She blushed.

"Oh, t-thanks," she stuttered, lying down. "Where is Charlie going to sleep then?"

"With me," he said, lying down. He reached over and pulled Charlie's small body against his chest.

"If he has another seizure, I want him close so I can make sure he's okay," Lucas explained, wrapping his arm tightly around Charlie.

"Thanks – for everything today." Kayla whispered.

"I didn't do all that much," Lucas said.

"Your shirt still has snot stains," she pointed out, laughing.

He smiled, "Anything for you."

They fell asleep underneath a clear midnight sky.

THIRTEEN

THE NEXT DAY THEY WENT to Farmer Penny's Play Barn.

Lucas looked at Kayla and said, "You realize we're the only teenagers here, right?"

He looked around as adults chased toddlers riding sheep.

Charlie started to rock his body.

"Don't you even think about it," Kayla yelled at Charlie.

"Why not? It's a perfect place to act more handicapped and scare people," Charlie laughed.

"These little kids are the same age as you. Some of them are older even," Kayla explained, moving out of the way as a baby pig ran by.

"Can we at least do something a little mo-o-ore?" Charlie was interrupted by a clown.

He looked up at Kayla and motioned his lips, "Help me."

The clown leaned down and spoke right into Charlie's face, "This is the most *SPECIAL* kid here at Penny's!"

Kayla and Lucas tried not to laugh as the clown was pinching Charlie's cheeks. They knew the clown thought Charlie was mentally handicapped and was trying to make him feel important, so they were polite.

"Yes, he is special," Kayla said with a straight face while Lucas was dying of laughter behind them.

"How – old- are - you?" the clown asked, leaning close to Charlie's face and shouting each word slowly.

"I'm five," Charlie answered.

Lucas and Kayla had all they could do to not burst out laughing.

The clown gave Charlie a balloon and offered a balloon to Kayla and Lucas also.

"Why, thank you so much!" Kayla said grinning.

The clown waddled away and Charlie glared at Lucas and Kayla who were crying from laughing so hard.

"Why didn't you rescue me?" he demanded, trying not to smile.

"How could I deny an innocent clown his wish to help the poor handicapped child? His heart would have been broken," Kayla laughed.

"Come on, let's go find something fun to do before Charlie ends up riding a pig," Lucas suggested, watching a toddler try to climb on the back of a piglet.

"Good idea," Kayla answered. "Let's go."

They quickly dashed off with Charlie so another clown wouldn't stop them!

When they got to the barn they found someone that treated Charlie normally.

"Would you like to ride a horse today?" the ride attendant asked Charlie. "Yes."

"Alrighty! How many people are riding?" the man asked.

Lucas said, "One."

"Two," Kayla interrupted.

The man looked confused.

"How many?"

Lucas said, "Fine…two."

They followed the horse trainer into the stable.

"Pick your horse," the man said.

Kayla saw the white spotted horse first and jumped slightly.

Lucas looked at the horse and thought to himself, "How are we going to put Charlie up there? The horse is five feet tall and he's not even three feet."

"Come on, up you go," the instructor said, lifting Charlie out of his chair and into a special saddle just for kids with special needs.

Lucas was nervous, but the man seemed confident.

"What if the horse spooks and takes off?" Lucas asked, watching Charlie try to stay still in the saddle.

"Oh, Old Brita here? She's almost twenty years old! She doesn't go far, unless she has to. Right old girl?" He asked.

The horse blinked lazily at him as if to say, "Another kid? Really?"

Lucas relaxed a little bit, until he remembered he had to ride, too.

After the horse ride, they went back into the stable to help Charlie dismount. As they were leaving, they saw a clown running toward them.

"Here we go again," Charlie said, rolling his eyes.

Lucas turned the wheelchair, and they ran for the fried dough stand.

"I'm *STARVED*!" Lucas whined.

"Oh yes, because you have been the one doing all the work today," Kayla teased.

"What? I'm a teenage boy, I need food," Lucas defended himself.

"Me too!" Charlie exclaimed.

The fried dough was made just right. The powdered sugar somehow ended up all over Charlie's shirt.

"I knew we forgot something when we left the house," Kayla sighed, trying to get the white powder off of Charlie.

"Next time, we will have a bib for both of you," Kayla laughed, watching Lucas try to get the white powder off of his pants.

They walked around for a bit before settling in to watch a fireworks show.

"I like ours better," she whispered to Lucas.

"Me too," he smiled.

After the fair, they went back to the house.

"You know, we never really made dinner," Lucas suggested.

"You can't be hungry again!" Kayla pretended to be shocked.

"I am! Me! Me! Me!" Charlie yelled.

"Okay, okay. What should we make?"

"Hotdogs!" Charlie exclaimed.

"You can't eat hotdogs at midnight," Kayla said.

"Of course we can. We could make them over a fire," Lucas said excitedly. "I've always wanted to do that."

Kayla shook her head. "Fine, fine, who's going to make the fire?"

"I will," Lucas said, "My friends always used to do bonfires at their parties."

"You can't make fires, city boy," Kayla teased.

"Oh yeah? Watch me! Come on, Charlie, give me a hand," Lucas said, placing him on his shoulders.

"Get the sticks, Kayla! We're making hotdogs!"

He built the fire with twigs and newspaper, but it quickly went out.

"We need some gasoline," he said, looking around.

"That's dangerous!" Kayla exclaimed. "We're country and we don't even do that."

"That's how we do it in the city," he said. "Where is your gas can?"

She went to the shed and came back with a red can. "Please be careful."

"No worries, I'm not going anywhere," he flashed a smile and poured gas over the sticks and logs.

"Now, here's a tip I learned from my grandfather. Most people get hurt because they don't remember gas follows a trail. The way you do it is by lighting a piece of paper and throwing it on top of the wood. That way, there's no trail. Now watch, Charlie! It's like magic!"

He knelt next to Charlie after he threw the paper on.

"It doesn't look like it's doing anything," Charlie complained.

Kayla stood next to Lucas and took his hand.

"Just watch!" He smiled, and the fire caught and lit up high into the sky before burning steadily.

"Whoa, that was so cool!" Charlie said.

"Finally, something that I was right about and you were wrong, Kayla!" Lucas smiled.

"I know I'm amazing," Kayla grinned.

"When can we make hotdogs?" Charlie asked.

"Right now," Lucas replied.

"Can I hold the stick?"

Kayla and Lucas just looked at Charlie.

"What do you think? Would we put a sharp pointy thing in your hand?" Lucas asked.

"Well, maybe if I make you really sleepy, and then ask you, it would work, wouldn't it?" Charlie asked.

"Umm…I don't think a *dead* person would give you a sharp object. Besides, I value my life. *And* if *I* die, you won't have anything to do," Lucas laughed.

After they were done with the hotdogs, they got out fixings for s'mores.

"Can I throw a stick into the fire?" Charlie asked.

"Sure," Lucas said, pushing him closer and giving him a stick.

Charlie leaned forward and threw the stick onto the fire. For a long time, they sat and watched the fire crackle and spark until it was just a pile of smoldering embers.

FOURTEEN

The next day, Charlie woke up and saw Lucas still sleeping.

"Wake up, sleepy head, I'm starving."

Lucas sighed, "Do you ever sleep in?"

"No," Charlie said smiling. "It's boring!"

"If I make cookies, can I go back to sleep?"

"Well, you could, but if you leave me alone, I might trash the house."

"True, I forgot about that. Never mind, I'll stay up," Lucas groaned. He rolled over and pretended to fall back to sleep.

"Noooo," Charlie whined, scooting closer to him. "Get. Up."

Charlie laughed, jumping up and down on Lucas. Lucas waited until Charlie was right on top of him to roll over and grab him.

"Oh, you think it's funny, huh? Getting me up this early?" he playfully tickled Charlie.

"You know, most boys love sleeping, but not you of course! We can't just eat cereal, it has to be pancakes and cookies."

Lucas pretended to be angry and held Charlie high over his head.

"Put me down!" Charlie laughed, out of breath.

"Never!" Lucas retorted. "But…I guess we should get dressed and go see if Kayla wants to join us…"

"Why do we need to get dressed? I already scare everyone with my wheelchair…" Charlie joked. "True, but we don't need to get arrested before breakfast," Lucas reminded. "Good point," said Charlie, allowing Lucas to change and dress him for the day.

"What do you want for breakfast?" Lucas asked as he sleepily unlocked the front door of the main house.

From the quiet, it was obvious that Kayla was still asleep upstairs.

"Candy!"

"Candy?" Lucas echoed, yawning. "You can't have candy for breakfast."

"Yes I can, I can do whatever I want. Remember? You told me I was spoiled. So give me candy!" Charlie grinned mischievously.

"You are so spoiled," Lucas said, rubbing his tired eyes.

"I know, everyone says that to me," Charlie pointed out as Lucas set him on his knees in the kitchen.

"Are you going to give me some candy or not?"

"Fine, once. But if your sister sees me doing this, I'm blaming it all on you."

"What about cookie and candy pancakes?" Charlie asked excitedly.

"Fine, but where do you keep the cookies?"

"Just in the cabinet," responded Charlie.

"Which one?"

"The one that's brown."

"That helps a lot, Charlie," Lucas said sarcastically looking at all the brown cabinets.

"I know," Charlie answered smugly. Lucas tried a couple of different cabinets but couldn't find any cookies.

"Charlie, I don't see any."

Charlie looked at him. "Come on, city boy, you have to bake them yourself."

"What? How?"

"You don't even know how to bake cookies? And you want *me* to tell *you* how to make them? That's scary! I could kill us both. I don't know what even goes *in* cookies…I just eat them. I'm five! Remember?" Charlie said, giggling.

"Well, we could use the internet."

"No, let's make it up!"

"You can't make up a cookie recipe, Charlie."

"Yes you can. We are going to. Right now! Ready? Go!" He grabbed onto Lucas' legs. "Come on, let's go."

"Whoa! Whoa!" Lucas said, trying to catch his balance as Charlie knocked into him.

He reached out to steady himself on the counter and missed. Charlie laughed as he fell.

"That's what you get for not making up a cookie recipe! Come on, a grandma would have been faster than you!" Charlie chided.

"What do cookies need in them?" Lucas asked Charlie.

"Sugar?" Charlie responded, laughing.

"Yes, you called me?" Lucas teased.

He managed to find sugar and flour in one of the cabinets.

"What else goes into cookies?" Charlie asked Lucas.

"Butter? Vanilla?" Lucas responded, trying not to hit his head on the door of the cabinet.

"No! Kit Kats!" Charlie exclaimed pointing to the top of the fridge.

"Fine, you win, but you are so spoiled," Lucas teased.

"How am *I* spoiled?" Charlie smiled.

Lucas rolled his eyes.

"Let me hold them!" Charlie exclaimed, reaching for the Kit Kats.

"Nooooo, you will probably somehow kill me with them," Lucas retorted.

"How?"

"I don't know but everything I give you seems like a weapon."

"Who me?" Charlie asked innocently, pretending to blink cutely.

"The cute look doesn't work for me, just for Kayla," Lucas said, straight faced, trying not to laugh.

"But if I don't have candy I'll...*die*!"

"No, I'm pretty sure you won't, but I'm going to let you have it once."

"Yay!" said Charlie excitedly.

They mixed all the ingredients together with the butter and vanilla and baked them in the oven.

Finally, Kayla woke up and joined them just as Lucas was feeding Charlie the cookie-candy pancake.

"Lucas Josiah, *what* is in that pancake?"

Lucas froze.

Charlie pretended to cry. "He made me eat all this sugar. It's so bad for you. I told him to make me an apple!" He stuck out his lower lip.

"Oh, okay," said Kayla, "You were in this too, then."

"Thank you!" Lucas yelled, hitting Charlie's arm lightly. "Thanks for sticking up for me," Lucas said pretending to be angry.

"Mommy, this horrible candy man is touching me!" Charlie leaned away and reached out for Kayla pretending to cry again.

"Oh, you poor baby! But guess what happens to babies who are covered in candy?" Kayla teased, pushing him away as chocolate dripped from his mouth and onto his cookie-crumb-covered shirt.

"They get more candy?" Charlie asked hopefully.

"Close, but no. It begins with a 'b'."

"Bananas and chocolate?"

"No," Kayla responded.

"Baskets of marshmallows!" Charlie exclaimed, clapping his hands. She put her hands underneath his arms and lifted him off the floor.

"Nope. Try again."

"Baby chocolate bunnies?"

She held him away from her body as sticky candy dripped from his clothes.

"Bob's Diner?"

She turned a corner into the bathroom and set him in the tub. Lucas followed them in, his shoes sticking to candy mess on the floor.

"A bath!" she smiled.

"Noooooo! Help, Lucas!" Charlie squealed, holding his arms out to Lucas.

Lucas looked at him, "Can't help you, Buddy. You *need* a bath!"

"No!" Charlie cried, acting upset.

Kayla cleaned up the kitchen and left Lucas to handle the bath. After all, she reasoned, he was the one to give Charlie cookies and candy.

Lucas felt bad that he made Charlie upset. As Charlie's little lip quivered, he wished he hadn't made the gooey breakfast.

"Don't cry, it's just a bath," he comforted, coming closer and bent down to give him a hug.

Charlie looked at him and smiled. "Wow, you do not know my fake cry compared to my real cry, do you?"

SPLASH! He pulled Lucas into the tub with him. Lucas came thrashing out of the water.

"I'm gonna kill you!" Lucas pretended to be angry and splashed Charlie playfully.

Kayla heard the splash from the kitchen and shook her head. "All this time and he still doesn't know my little brother," she thought to herself, smiling.

An hour later, Lucas came out to the kitchen, soaking wet, with Charlie wrapped in a big towel.

"I think, he wasn't lying about hating the bath," Lucas said.

"Nope, he wasn't," Kayla said.

"Can I go outside without clothes and scare the neighbors?" Charlie begged.

"No. No you can't. You already scare them with clothes *on*. Without clothes on, you're going get *me* in trouble!" Kayla said firmly.

"So? I'll visit you in jail," Charlie smiled.

Lucas covered his mouth with the towel.

"Come on, let Kayla finish cleaning the kitchen. Let's get you dressed," he said, sensing Kayla's annoyance with her brother.

Lucas wrapped Charlie tighter in the towel and opened the front door. Rain poured down from a black sky.

Lucas looked doubtful. "Maybe I should just go and bring your clothes back here?"

"Aw, that's no fun!" Charlie whined.

"Alright, then, you asked for it!" Lucas challenged.

"Ready? Set? Go!" Charlie encouraged as Lucas took off running towards their apartment.

Back at the apartment, Lucas dressed Charlie and changed into a new set of clothes.

"Maybe Kayla will want to race in the rain," Charlie suggested excitedly.

"No way, I just got changed!" Lucas said firmly.

"We take walks in the pouring rain all the time. Don't we Kayla?" Charlie asked his sister as she opened the door to the apartment and stepped inside.

"Yes, we do. And I want to right now. Come on, it will be fun!" Kayla motioned for Lucas and Charlie to go outside with her.

"I just got changed!" Lucas whined, holding out his wet clothes for her to see.

"That's your fault!"

"True, but...fine! Let's go. But if anyone asks why we're out in the middle of a rainstorm, I'm blaming both of you."

"Believe me, Lucas, no one will say that in our town. It's just a little shower," she smiled as he sighed.

Lucas stumbled as he pushed the wheelchair out the door of the apartment. Kayla dashed out into the rain ahead of the boys. Lucas stood under the cover of the roof watching her spin in circles.

"Come on, city boy!" she shouted.

"Come on, Lucas, please?" Charlie begged rocking his torso forward and back as if to encourage Lucas to move.

Lucas took one hesitant step out from under the roof and was drenched in seconds. Kayla's enthusiasm sparked a desire inside of him to enjoy the moment with her.

"Ready, Charlie? Let's go!" Lucas cheered, shoving the wheelchair forward.

They chased after Kayla, heading into the back woods toward the tree house. The water made the path muddy and slippery. Lucas left the wheelchair safely on the back porch and carried Charlie on his shoulders. As they trudged through the mud, Kayla slipped. Lucas held onto Charlie with one hand and reached out with the other just in time to catch her before she fell.

"Thanks," she blushed. "You're always catching me just in time."

"Careful Kayla, Lucas almost dropped me trying to catch you! I just got all clean! I can't take another bath again! I'll die!" Charlie dramatized.

Kayla shook her head. "This is like a giant bath, Charlie," she explained.

"True, but it's a lot warmer with my clothes on," he pointed out.

They raced up the tree house ramp and dried out inside.

Charlie yawned. "I'm tired."

"You can sleep, Little Buddy," Lucas said, laying him on the rug.

"Okay," Charlie agreed, already curling up and falling asleep.

"Guess the bath tired him out," Lucas whispered, laughing quietly.

"Yeah, it must have. He never takes nap."

They sat together and watched the rain make ripples in the pond as Charlie slept for the next hour. She thought about all the reasons she loved Lucas. She remembered how sweet he had been, and how much he cared about Charlie. She loved spending time with him, and he made her smile.

While she was sitting quietly watching the rain, Lucas thought about how much he loved Kayla. She was pretty and had a kind heart. She always put other people before herself, and he loved that about her. They looked into each other's eyes, and he kissed her as the rain was coming down from the sky onto their dangling feet. Lucas held Kayla's hand until he heard Charlie start to stir.

"You awake, Little Buddy?" he called.

"Yeah…I'm hungry," he whined groggily.

"We have to go shopping if you want to eat," Lucas responded.

"I don't want to go anywhere. I want to stay in the tree house," Charlie whined.

"We could order food," Lucas suggested.

Kayla laughed. "You're funny! They don't deliver to tree houses!"

"There's a first time for everything," Lucas said.

"Yay!" Charlie squealed.

Lucas pulled out his cell phone.

"How will they find us?" Kayla worried.

"I'll give them directions."

Lucas ordered a large pizza and salad from Planet of Pizzas and told them how to get to the tree house. They weren't sure at first, but he told them he would tip well and they finally agreed.

The pizza came quickly. Lucas met them at the bottom of the ramp. An annoyed, soaking wet pizza deliveryman waited at the bottom.

"Thanks!" Lucas exclaimed, taking the soggy pizza boxes from the man.

"Sure kid, whatever," he said, trudging back to his car.

Lucas took the food back into the tree house living room. The pizza was a little wet, but it tasted good. As they finished eating, the rain slowed to a drizzle, and finally stopped.

"Look, Lucas!" Kayla exclaimed, glancing up at the sky.

Where the dark rainclouds had gathered earlier, there was a big beautiful rainbow stretching across the clouds. She reached out her hand and he took it in his. For a few long moments, they stared at the colors that shone brightly through the last mist of rain. Kayla squeezed his hand tightly. He turned and smiled that adorable smile that she loved. She turned her face up and he leaned down to kiss her.

"Really?" Charlie sighed as Lucas kissed his sister. "Are you two ever going to not kiss? It's just a rainbow!"

Charlie threw up his hands in exasperation as Lucas ignored him.

"Can we do something fun please?" Charlie asked when the two finally broke apart.

Lucas had an idea. He excused himself and darted inside the house. From Charlie's old room, he grabbed a ball and a bat. When he came outside, Kayla shook her head at him.

"No, you are not giving him a bat."

"Yes! We'll get some distance before he picks it up, and we'll throw the ball from far away."

In spite of Kayla's protests, Lucas carried Charlie out of the tree house and helped him kneel on the wet ground. He set the bat next to Charlie.

"Now, don't pick this bat up until I run away ten feet from you, okay?"

"Okay!" Charlie said, laughing.

Kayla hid behind a tree to protect herself while Lucas prepared to throw the ball.

"Are you ready?" Lucas yelled to Charlie.

"Yep, I'm ready!"

When he threw the ball, it hit Charlie right in the head.

"Ow," Charlie said, laughing as Kayla was running to him to make sure he was okay.

Lucas ran over to him and said, "How about you throw while I hit it?"

"Good idea," Charlie said.

Lucas gave him the ball and ran back with the bat. As Charlie was throwing the ball, he had a CP moment and threw the ball right at Lucas' head.

"Ow! Let's try that again, shall we?" Lucas said, laughing as he rubbed his head. "This time try to aim for the bat."

Charlie threw the ball, and Lucas hit it right at Kayla.

Kayla turned to him and rubbed the spot where Lucas had pegged her with the ball. "That was painful!"

"Are you okay?" Lucas asked, laughing but concerned.

He examined her quickly to be sure he hadn't seriously injured her.

"I'm fine, I just might have a big bruise on my forehead for about a month!" She put her hands on her hips.

"I'm sorry, Babe. You were right, maybe we should do something else," he apologized, kissing her forehead where he had hit it with the ball.

Later that night, hoisted on Lucas' shoulders, Charlie led the brigade to catch fireflies in the woods.

As they walked together, Lucas confessed to them, "I've never even seen a firefly before."

Charlie and Kayla laughed.

"Where did you find this guy?" Charlie wondered aloud.

Lucas wasn't listening to them joke about him, he was too amazed by the fireflies. They walked out to the field where hundreds flew by, lighting up the night.

The crickets were as loud as a symphony.

"Wow," he breathed.

Charlie smiled, "Yay! Bugs!"

Kayla instructed, "They are not bugs! They are flying light bulbs. There's a difference."

"No, there's not," Charlie said.

"Yes, there is."

"I'm right! Look it up on Google! Fireflies are just bugs."

"Bugs or not, they are pretty and fun to catch," Lucas said, putting a few more in the jar Kayla was carrying.

Lucas had cut holes in the lid so that the fireflies had room to breathe and had attached a handle like a lantern. With the firefly lantern lighting the way, they walked down to the beach.

Putting Charlie down on the sand, Lucas looked around and saw a snapping turtle in the water. He didn't know there was a difference between a snapping turtle and a turtle. Lucas went to tap it and pick it up. The snapping turtle popped his head out to bite him. Lucas screamed and jumped back.

"I thought there were no dangerous animals out here!" he exclaimed as the turtle slid back into the water.

"There aren't, if you know which animals are okay to touch. That – that's not okay to touch," Kayla warned.

"Thanks for the warning," he said sarcastically.

"Could it really have bitten me?" he asked, watching the shell glide through the still water.

"Taken your finger clean off," Kayla replied laughing at his expression of horror.

"Come on, maybe fishing will take your mind off it," Kayla said, running back to the house for the fishing equipment.

"Don't be gone too long! Snappy might come back!" he called after her, moving next to Charlie.

"Look! I'm a snapping turtle!" Charlie said, leaning down to pretend to bite Lucas.

"No! Bad turtle! Bad!" Lucas laughed, pulling his arm away from Charlie.

"Help, Kayla! I'm being attacked by wild animals!" Lucas yelled, pretending to run from Charlie.

FIFTEEN

A SHORT WHILE LATER, KAYLA came back with the fishing rods. "Here, I'll show you how it's done."

"Wow, I can't wait to see this!" Lucas said, wincing as she expertly put a worm on the hook.

"Okay, this is how you cast it. Go ahead, pick up a pole and copy me."

"Can I try?" Charlie piped up.

"No, not until we figure out how to keep you from hooking us," she teased.

"Okay, Lucas, pull back," putting her own pole down, she put her hands over his and showed him how far back to go.

"Now release," she commanded, and the line flew out in front of them – far out into the lake.

Picking up her pole, Kayla continued, "Now, very slowly reel it back in. The fish see the worm and latch on thinking it's alive and wiggling."

Lucas watched her reel her line back in, but had no desire to try it himself.

"Come on, you can do it," she encouraged.

"I'll do it!" Charlie insisted, rocking his chair with his excited movement. "Let's go in the boat and try it!"

"Sure, let's do it!" Kayla blurted out, handing her pole to Lucas.

She ran off to get the boat and Lucas stood staring at the pole. All of a sudden the pole jerked out of his hand.

"You got a fish!" Charlie screamed.

Lucas scrambled to grab the rod, which was quickly being pulled towards the water. At the edge of the lake, he managed to grab hold.

"Pull, Lucas!" Charlie encouraged from his chair.

"Easy for you to say!" Lucas yelled back, pulling against the line.

"Use the reel! Come on, it's easy!"

"You try it, then!" Lucas breathed heavily as he tried to pull the line in.

Kayla ran back and took over. She turned the reel and slowly the fish came flopping out of the water. It was a bass and a big one, too.

"No wonder you had a hard time, Lucas, this guy is huge!"

Lucas was feeling a little embarrassed that he had to have Kayla pull the fish in.

"Oh great," he said sarcastically.

"Oh, don't be upset! It was your first fish. You should be proud! I caught a minnow when I first went fishing. Want to hold it?"

The huge, slimy, scaly fish flopped around on the hook. Kayla brought the fish closer to Lucas and he leaned away.

"I'm good! Thanks, though."

"Well, someone is going to have to get him off the hook. I don't know how!"

"You mean we're going fishing, and you don't know how to get the fish off the hook?" Lucas asked.

"Well, Dad always did it for me," she sniffed, letting the pole down a little bit.

"You can't cry now, we have to get the fish back in the lake before it dies!" Charlie yelled.

"I can't," Kayla said, starting to cry.

"Oh, gosh," Lucas said, taking the pole from her.

He didn't want to see her cry, but he didn't want to touch the fish either.

"How do I do this?" he yelled to Charlie.

"You have to hold the fish and pull the hook out!" Charlie yelled. "Hurry, he's not flopping as much now. He's dying!"

Charlie was starting to get upset. Lucas' hands slipped on the fish's slimy body as he tried to hold onto it. The fish dropped to the sand and flopped around.

"You're killing it!" Charlie cried.

"I'm working on it!" Lucas responded, trying not to panic.

He finally pinned the fish down and pulled the hook out.

"Throw it back, quick!" Charlie screamed.

Making a disgusted face, Lucas picked up the huge fish with both hands and stumbled down to the water. He threw it in and watched it swim away.

"Yay!" Charlie cheered.

Kayla was still crying on the sand. Lucas rinsed his hands in the water and wiped them on his pants.

"Come on, a boat ride will cheer you up," he said, putting an arm around her shoulders.

She nodded.

Lucas got the boat ready and loaded Charlie in. Kayla stepped in last and they pushed off. Charlie chattered on about the fish while Lucas comforted Kayla.

"You think Dad is in heaven?" Charlie asked suddenly.

Lucas shrugged.

"Of course he is," Kayla assured Charlie.

"How do you know?" Charlie asked.

Kayla sighed.

"What do you think, Lucas?" Charlie asked innocently.

"I don't know. I don't know that much about God, I'm afraid. Kayla can tell you more."

"I thought you had a Bible?" Kayla asked him.

"I do. It's in my dresser next to all my clothes. The one boyfriend my mom had that I actually liked gave it to me."

"Well, it's not going to do you much good, in with all your clothes," Charlie piped in, making them laugh.

Kayla took out her phone. "Here, I'm going to show you a verse."

She opened her Bible app and flipped through the chapters. She read aloud, "John 3:16: 'For God so loved the world that He gave His one and only Son, that whoever believes in Him shall not perish but have eternal life.'"

She showed it to Lucas.

"Dad used to sing that with me!" Charlie exclaimed, bursting into song.

"John 3:16 for God so loved the world!!!!!" He sang, slightly off-key.

Kayla smiled, "Yes, that one. See? That's how we know Dad's in heaven – because he believed in Jesus."

"Do you believe in Jesus, Lucas?" Charlie stopped singing to ask.

"I don't know," he said honestly.

Kayla wasn't sure what to say, so she started to pray. Even Charlie was silent for a few minutes.

"God has let a lot of bad things happen to me," Lucas said quietly.

"It's hard to believe that there would be a God that allows that."

"What kind of bad things?" Charlie asked before Kayla could quiet him.

"Maybe Lucas doesn't want to talk about it right now," Kayla told Charlie.

"You don't mind telling us, do you Lucas?" Charlie encouraged, patting Lucas' back.

"But you don't have to if you don't want to," Kayla said gently.

Lucas took a deep breath.

"When I was two, my father became a drunk and started abusing me. My mom's boyfriend gave me these scars on my arm when he cut me with a kitchen knife. When I was thirteen, another of her boyfriends made me drink alcohol. I hated it! The whiskey burned my throat. When I choked on it, he just made me drink more. The purple spots are burn scars from cigarettes being put out on my arm. It was all about survival at my old house. I never really told anyone. Scott was a jerk, but he was my first friend."

Kayla was praying as he shared his heart. God put a scripture in her mind for Lucas. She opened the Bible app again and typed in Psalm 34:18.

"When I am going through a hard time, I look to God's word to help me," Kayla said. "The Bible is how God talks to us. This is Psalm 34:18 '*The LORD is close to the brokenhearted and saves those who are crushed in spirit.' This verse means that when you're brokenhearted and you feel like life is falling apart, God is close to you. When my mom died, God showed me this verse so I would know that even though I was sad and upset and hurt, He was there with me. The same is true for you, too. Bad things can't always be explained, but God promises that if you believe in Him, He will be there for you.*"

Lucas nodded, thinking about all the hurt and pain he had been through and about God still being there for him.

"I know it's hard," Kayla comforted. "I didn't understand why God let my mom die and allowed Charlie to be born with a life-altering disability. I was confused at first, because before he was born, I didn't have a clue about what a disability even was. For two years, we weren't sure what was going on with him. When I heard he was never going to walk, I was terrified and depressed. But my mom had always said that God had a plan for everyone, and though she didn't know Charlie would have

CP, I still believed her. God helped us learn how to look after Charlie. He has a purpose and a plan for Charlie's life, too. Even though it seemed sad then, I believe that Charlie will grow up and help other kids who have disabilities."

Kayla hugged her knees to her chest as they talked.

Lucas sat for a moment, thinking about all that she had said. After a long moment of silence, Charlie asked Lucas if he could pray for him.

"Um…sure," Lucas stuttered.

He was slightly uncomfortable with the idea of someone praying for him, but as soon as Charlie began to speak, he relaxed a bit.

"Dear Jesus, I pray that Lucas will know You. Please show him that You are real and that You love him."

Tears ran down Kayla's cheeks as Charlie finished. For the first time, Lucas felt peace.

"Thanks, Charlie. That meant a lot to me." Lucas hugged him tightly.

"You're welcome. Can we go home now? I want cookies and milk before bed time," Charlie requested.

"Of course, Bud, of course." Lucas patted him on the back and steered the boat towards shore.

Back at the house, they fed Charlie and put him into bed. Lucas stood by the bed a long time watching Charlie as he slept.

Suddenly, he dropped to his knees. "What should I do, God? I need You. I've been a sinner my whole life. You can never forgive me," Lucas began to sob.

"*Yes, He can,*" Kayla whispered.

He turned to find her standing quietly behind him.

"Really? How?" Lucas asked, tears still streaming down his face.

"He can forgive you of everything you've done wrong. He died on the cross so that you could go to heaven with Him when you die. See, without believing in God, we would all go to hell. But God sent His son to die so we could go to heaven and be free. With Jesus, we are free to live our lives differently. He wants us to live our lives following Him because He has a plan for all of our lives – no matter how terrible they seem," Kayla explained quietly.

Lucas sat down on the floor. Kayla sat next to him and put her hand on his shoulder.

"Just talk to God the way you do a friend."

Lucas started to pray, "God, I believe in You. I believe that Your Son died for me. I want to know You the way Kayla and Charlie do."

His voice broke as peace washed over him. He felt the sadness inside him lift. He felt new. All the pain he had been carrying for so long seemed to wash away with the words he prayed. Kayla put her arms around him as he sobbed. She prayed for him as he cried.

Lucas felt God come close to him, just like the verse Kayla had read. It was scary, but good. He knew God had seen his pain, and he knew God wanted him to be free – to be a new person. They sat there together for a long time until Lucas could speak.

"Now whose shirt is soaked?" he joked, wiping his eyes.

Kayla laughed and hugged him.

"It's okay, we have our whole lives to get to know God. Right now, let's get some coffee. I'm not tired, and I want to talk."

Lucas smiled and let her pull him to his feet. They talked all night. He told her things he had never told anyone before. For the first time in a long time, he trusted someone. He knew then that she would be the only person he could ever love like this.

"Thank you – for everything," he said to her sincerely, holding her close.

"No, thank *you* for telling *me* your story. You're an amazing person, Lucas."

He kissed her.

"Get some sleep," he whispered as she crossed the floor to the door.

"You too, Lucas," she whispered back with a smile and quietly slipped out.

Lucas climbed into bed with Charlie, thanking God for Kayla and Charlie and for his new faith. For the first time since he could remember, he believed that he could have a good life.

SIXTEEN

"WAKE UP! WAKE UP!" LUCAS awoke to Charlie jumping on him.

"Come on, sleepy head. Kayla made breakfast and we can't eat without you!"

"Charlie, did you wake him?!" Kayla yelled from the kitchen.

"He was already awake when I came in!" Charlie yelled back.

"Come on! Whoa! Why are your eyes all puffy? Did Kayla hit you?" Charlie asked, a little scared.

"No, no, I was just crying a lot," he said, rolling over and hoping to go back to sleep.

"Why were you crying? Crying is for girls," Charlie said, scooting closer. He got ready to jump on Lucas.

"I was crying because I told Jesus I accept Him and I believe Him and I felt Him for the first time," Lucas explained sleepily.

"Really?" Charlie asked and jumped.

He landed on Lucas' stomach. Lucas felt the air leave him as Charlie landed hard. Laughing, Charlie rolled off onto the floor. Lucas remained on the bed gasping for air.

"Kayla, I think I accidentally killed your boyfriend!" he called. He heard the dishes slam and Kayla's feet pounding the floor.

"What did you do?" She demanded and saw Lucas red-faced and gasping.

"Charlie! Did you jump on his stomach?"

"Nope, it was my evil twin," Charlie grinned.

"Lucas, you okay?" Kayla knelt by Lucas and rubbed his stomach.

"I'm okay, just got the wind knocked out of me," Lucas wheezed.

She waited as he caught his breath. As soon as he was feeling better, they got up and ate the breakfast Kayla had made for them.

"Let's take a walk now. It's nice out," Kayla suggested cheerfully as they finished breakfast.

"Lucas, you push Charlie. I'm too lazy to," Kayla whined playfully.

"Okay, but only because I love you," Lucas responded, sighing dramatically.

Charlie grabbed Kayla's hand while Lucas was pushing him out the door.

"Come on! Let's go!"

During their walk, they saw a dead squirrel.

"Let me poke it with a stick," Charlie demanded.

"Noooooo!" Kayla yelled at him.

Charlie looked at Lucas, "Please?" he asked with a pouty face.

"Yes, let's do it!" Lucas yelled.

Kayla rolled her eyes at both of them. "Really?"

"Yeah," Lucas smiled.

Lucas gave Charlie the stick and Charlie poked the squirrel until it opened up and the insides could be seen.

Kayla squealed. "Okay, it's time to go!"

"Fine," Lucas said laughing, pushing away Charlie.

"Do you want to hold the stick?" Charlie asked Kayla.

"No, but thank you for that," she said sarcastically. "I'm not talking to you, Lucas Josiah!"

"That's your middle name?" Charlie asked.

"Yes, Charlie. But Kayla, I think that it's going to be really hard for you not to talk to me. I am your boyfriend now, so…"

Kayla stared. "Fine, you're right… but never do that again or else I'll really dump you."

Lucas rolled his eyes. "I highly doubt that."

Charlie chimed in, "*I'll* still talk to you, Lucas."

"Thank you Charlie. See, Kayla? He agrees with me."

Kayla was silent. They kept walking and she still didn't say anything. Lucas was waiting for her to get over it, but she wouldn't look at him. He stopped pushing Charlie.

"Are you really upset?" he asked.

She kept walking. He ran after her.

"Hey," he said, gently grabbing her arm and pulling her to a stop. "The squirrel was already dead, he didn't feel anything," Lucas tried to reassure her.

"Hey!" Charlie called from a few feet away. "You forgot the CP kid!"

They ignored him for a moment.

"Yeah, but I still didn't want to watch," she said, looking down.

He put his arms around her.

"I'm sorry. I didn't realize it would upset you."

"Hellooooo!" Charlie called as his chair began to roll backward down the small hill.

Kayla and Lucas looked back and, realizing what was happening, ran down the hill toward Charlie.

Suddenly, Lucas tripped and fell.

Kayla kept running.

"Get back here!" Kayla yelled at Charlie, even though she knew he couldn't stop rolling.

"I can't stop!" Charlie yelled back as the chair rolled faster down the hill.

With a final burst of speed, she finally caught up to Charlie and grabbed the edge of his chair just before he toppled over into a ditch.

"Hey! You! Are you going to help me?" Kayla yelled to Lucas.

"I'll be right down!" Lucas yelled, laughing and running down the hill. He helped her push Charlie back up the hill, and they decided to hang out inside the house for the rest of the day. He didn't want to see any more dead squirrels and upset Kayla further. They went home and spent the evening watching a movie.

The end of May passed quickly. Summer was fast approaching. Hopefully the summer would bring some good memories and wash away the bad ones.

SEVENTEEN

KAYLA WOKE UP WITH ONLY one thing on her mind: groceries. The boys had eaten the last of the food the night before. She woke Lucas and Charlie early by banging on the apartment door.

"Come on, let's go!" She yelled, running down the stairs as Lucas opened the door and gave chase.

Lucas put Charlie in the car while Kayla was getting into the driver's seat.

"I'll drive," Lucas offered.

"No way! You're stronger than me, so when Charlie tips over, you can help him up."

"Tips over? Why would he tip over?"

"Well, because Charlie wants to sit in a real seat today, and if you drive, you will tip him over when you go around corners," she smiled, teasing him.

"In my world, we don't allow women to drive," Lucas started to say, but ran when Kayla started to chase him.

Charlie burst out laughing.

"I'm really going to kill you this time," Kayla joked, running after Lucas.

Lucas ran for it around the back of the car. Kayla finally caught up to him, giving him some playful punches.

"Okay, okay, I'm sorry!" he yelled, pretending the punches hurt.

"I'm still over here!" Charlie called, reminding them he was getting bored.

Lucas laughed while Kayla looked at Lucas and said, "Alright now, I'll drive and you sit in the back, but no jokes about women drivers!"

Charlie and Lucas smiled at each other as Lucas helped him in.

"Don't drop him, Lucas," Kayla warned.

"Kayla, I've done this a million times. I know what to do. Go make a sandwich or something."

Kayla looked at him in shock. "What did you say?"

Lucas laughed.

"What's so funny?" Charlie asked.

"It's called a woman joke," Kayla said to him, rolling her eyes.

"Oh, I know one!" Charlie piped in. "What's the difference between a woman driver and a man driver?"

Kayla rolled her eyes.

"We need to work on your woman jokes," Lucas said in the background, laughing.

"What is the difference?" Kayla asked, tapping her foot.

"We arrive at the store alive!" he grinned as Kayla smiled and moved in to tickle Charlie.

"It's a good thing you're cute, or else I would kill you," Kayla teased, shutting the door and getting in the driver's seat.

On the way there, Charlie looked at Lucas who was gazing at Kayla as she drove.

"Are you two making googley eyes again? Because if you are, I would like to get out of the car before I puke."

"Oh yeah?" Kayla teased as she braked for a red light.

Lucas smiled as Kayla leaned back and kissed him.

"EWWWWWWWWWWW!" Charlie squealed, pretending to throw up.

Lucas put an arm around Charlie. "Don't worry, someday you won't find it gross."

When they got to the store, Lucas got the wheelchair out of the back of the van and put Charlie in it. They headed in to the grocery store.

"Can I...." Charlie started to say.

Kayla interrupted, "No. We are not getting candy and sugar cereal," she said.

Lucas interrupted her. "Yes, we are! We're running out! I'll buy some for you, Charlie."

"I hate you," Kayla teased, shaking her head.

Charlie said, "I love you."

Charlie begged for several sugar cereals and picked out three bags of candy before Lucas finally told him enough.

"But we haven't gotten the ingredients for my favorite sandwich yet," Charlie whined.

"What's that?" Lucas asked.

"It's a big piece of Oreo on top and the bottom and in between is candy."

"Don't you just love me, Kayla?" Lucas smiled.

"Not right now, really," Kayla looked at him scowling.

"Well we already have three bags of candy, what else do you need?" Kayla asked Lucas and Charlie.

"No, it needs to be even and we need to have ten packs," Lucas said, smiling.

"I want marshmallows!" Charlie yelled, reaching for the bag in the aisle.

Lucas handed it to him. Kayla followed along behind them as Charlie picked out more candy and sweets.

"Now just the chocolate syrup and we'll be set," Charlie clapped his hands excitedly as he looked at all his treats in the cart.

"Well, we do need some food, so I'm going to get pizza bites, corn dogs, and chicken nuggets," Lucas said.

"That's not food!" Kayla exclaimed, horrified.

"Yes it is. Can you eat it?"

"Yes."

"Can you lick it?"

"Yes."

"Can you smell it?"

"Yes."

"Okay then, it's food," Lucas said.

"All right, smart aleck," Kayla said. "I'm going to get some real food. You boys behave."

Charlie and Lucas shopped for the unhealthiest dinners they could find. They picked up some desserts too. They found some cheap TV dinners on sale and buy-one-get-one-free double stuffed Oreos.

"You know we have to get it, Charlie," Lucas said, grinning.

"Yup, I agree with you, but I'm blaming it all on you," he smiled.

"Fine, I'll let you. Just this once."

They picked up the Oreo packs and walked down the aisle to find Kayla. As they strolled along, they realized they were in the candy aisle again.

Charlie looked around, excited. "Can we get cotton candy?"

"Yes! Definitely, how about chocolate covered raisins?"

"Of course."

"Kit Kat bars?"

"Yes." When they were done raiding the candy aisle for the second time, they looked again for Kayla. Finally, Kayla spotted them and walked over, eyeing the candy and junk food.

"Will you ever grow up, Lucas?" she asked.

"What? It was on sale," Lucas smiled as he defended himself.

"Fine, but when Charlie throws up, it's not my fault – and you're cleaning it up."

"Fine," he said laughing.

They got to the checkout. The bill totaled one hundred and fifty dollars. Lucas and Kayla were shocked, but thankfully Uncle Bobby was sending plenty of money to take care of things.

"First one to the car wins!" she yelled and sprinted for the car with the grocery cart.

"Hurry, Lucas!" Charlie warned as Lucas took off at a run with the wheelchair, watching for traffic.

Kayla made it to the car just before they did.

"Yes!" she exclaimed.

"No fair, I have CP!" Charlie yelled out as Lucas leaned against the car, panting.

"No fair, you were being pushed by the strongest man on earth," Kayla pointed out.

"But I'm cute and wonderful and loving and…"

"Okay, okay, you win," Kayla threw up her hands in defense.

"Boys rule, girls drool," Lucas said, buckling Charlie and hopping in the front seat.

"Will you ever grow up?" Kayla asked both of them as she finished putting the groceries into the trunk.

"No, it's boring," Lucas retorted, smiling as she glared at him from the back.

She shut the trunk and climbed into the front seat.

"Where to?" he asked, putting his sunglasses on as Kayla buckled her seatbelt.

"Beach! Beach! I want a picnic!" Charlie said excitedly.

Lucas looked at Kayla.

"Then, off to the beach we go!" he said in an English accent. "*But first* we bring home the groceries!"

Kayla laughed at his accent and smacked Lucas playfully.

Lucas drove to the beach nearby after making a quick stop at home. He unloaded Charlie while Kayla took out their ingredients for Charlie's crazy sandwich. She put up the umbrella and set out a towel and began to make lunch while Lucas played in the sand with Charlie.

They spent a long time at the beach relaxing and eventually watching the sunset.

Finally back at home, Kayla made a late dinner which they enjoyed over a movie that Charlie and Lucas had picked out.

It didn't take too long for Charlie to fall asleep.

"I think it's time for bed," Lucas whispered as Kayla looked over at Charlie, passed out in Lucas' lap.

"I think so, too," Kayla whispered back.

He carefully untangled himself from Charlie and wrapped him up in a blanket to take him back to the apartment.

"Lucas, I think I'm going to head to bed, too. I'm exhausted," Kayla yawned.

Lucas held Charlie on his shoulder with one arm and hugged her with the other.

"Goodnight," he whispered and kissed her gently on the lips.

"Goodnight," she whispered with a small smile.

He carried Charlie to the door and Kayla walked him out.

"See you tomorrow, Gorgeous," he winked at Kayla.

"Sleep well, Handsome," she teased.

He turned and waved as he walked away.

The June wind still held the slight chill of May on its wings. It blew over them, and he hugged Charlie closer to keep him warm. With one hand, he opened the door to the apartment and climbed the stairs.

Lucas tucked Charlie in as soon as he got in the apartment.

An un-open pack of cigarettes lay on the table next to the bed. Without a second thought, he tossed them in the garbage. He didn't need them anymore, he decided. The pain that had caused him to start was just a memory. He climbed in beside Charlie and fell asleep almost immediately.

EIGHTEEN

CRASH! KAYLA'S EYES FLEW OPEN as the sound of broken glass shattered the silence of the house. Her heart raced as she saw the shadows move. Before she could scream for Lucas a hand covered her mouth. The intruders dragged her off the bed as she kicked and struggled. The hand over her mouth slipped for a moment.

"Lucas!" she cried, desperately.

They forced her up against a wall as she struggled.

"LUCAS!" she screamed.

Lucas was startled awake. At first he thought it was another nightmare. As his eyes adjusted to the darkness, he listened again. In the distance, he could hear sounds coming from the house. Lucas flew out of bed and hastily threw on his pants.

Charlie stirred as Lucas rushed around.

"What are you doing?" Charlie asked groggily.

"I have to check on something. I'll be right back," Lucas started to open the door without thinking.

"Don't leave me by myself!" Charlie cried.

"What am I thinking, leaving the kid by himself?" Lucas muttered out loud.

Lucas grabbed Charlie and quickly ran down the stairs. In his rush, he had forgotten shoes and a shirt.

Lucas sprinted barefoot up the pathway to the house. He stopped himself outside the door and tried to catch his breath. He could hear sounds of a struggle coming from inside. Memories of his past flooded him and adrenaline rushed through his veins. He slipped his phone out of his pocket and dialed the number he had grown up knowing so well.

"9-1-1. What is your emergency?" the calm voice answered after what seemed like an eternity.

"I would like to report a break in at 13 Ambrove Road. My girl-friend is being attacked! Please send help!" Lucas spoke hurriedly.

"Don't take matters into…"

Lucas didn't wait to hear anything more.

With the fierceness and stealth of an angry tiger, Lucas entered the house holding Charlie tightly. In the middle of the living room, he saw Kayla struggling against two dark figures.

Lucas put Charlie down on the stairs out of the way, putting a finger to his lips to make sure Charlie stayed silent.

Charlie curled up in a tight ball, closing his eyes and ears to the horrifying sights and sounds.

Kayla lay flat on the ground as a heavyset figure clothed in black was ripping her hair. A taller, slimmer form was shoving a taser into her side. She screamed in agony as electricity jolted through her body. They hauled her to her feet.

"Where's Lucas?" the heavyset one demanded of Kayla.

"He's not here!" Kayla cried through gasps of pain.

Lucas watched as the heavyset figure punched Kayla and she crumpled to the floor. Enraged, Lucas charged the one who had struck her. The figure fell heavily to the ground as Lucas slammed down on top of him. The masked man groaned under Lucas' punches. He reeked of alcohol. Lucas ripped the mask off. Scott rolled to the side and Lucas pulled away.

"Scott!" Lucas growled angrily as he got to his feet.

Scott launched himself at Lucas' legs, knocking him down.

"Lucas!" Kayla screamed as a second person descended on Lucas.

"Not so tough, now," Erik spat as he kneeled on top of Lucas.

Erik pinned him down as Scott punched him in the head. Spots colored Lucas' vision, temporarily dazing him. Erik hauled him to his feet and shoved his arms up behind his back. Lucas could tell by Erik's blood shot eyes that he was high.

"You've been doing cocaine and smoking weed again, haven't you?" Lucas rasped.

The scent of marijuana swirled hazily as he tried to stay conscious.

"What do you care? You ratted us out!" Scott shouted.

He grabbed the lamp off the end table and smashed it against Lucas' bare chest.

Kayla screeched as the broken glass ripped at Lucas' skin. She could see a large piece of glass glittering in his blood that quickly flooded the floor.

Lucas did his best not to distress Kayla further by crying out, but he could feel the sharp piece of glass in his chest with every jagged breath he took.

"Stop! Leave him alone!" Kayla begged hysterically.

"Take Charlie out of here…" Lucas wheezed.

"No, I'm not leaving you!" Kayla cried, running to hold Charlie close.

Lucas was terrified that Erik and Scott would turn on her, but Scott made no motion toward her. Glass crunched under his boots as he came closer to Lucas. Lucas was quickly losing strength. Erik forced him to a standing position and held him there.

"This is how we felt when you betrayed us by ratting us out to that dirty cop," Erik's raspy smoking voice crackled as Scott took out a small black device from his jacket pocket.

Scott came closer, and Lucas began to struggle against Erik's hold. Grinning, Scott jammed the device into Lucas' stomach. With a flick of his thumb, Scott sent a jolt of electricity shooting through Lucas' body.

As Lucas slumped to the ground, his body jerking from the blast, he lunged weakly toward Scott, knocking him off balance. Falling down on his own taser, Scott groaned and cursed angrily as he writhed in pain.

Kayla couldn't take it anymore. Leaving Charlie at the foot of the stairs, she jumped to her feet and ran at Erik. She shoved him as hard as she could. He tripped and crashed to the floor.

As he scrambled to get up, Kayla grabbed the heavy silver candlestick from the mantle and smashed it into Erik's head. Erik collapsed as blood oozed out onto the rug. Terrified that he would get up and attack, she wielded the candlestick several more times.

Finally, Erik lay still as blood pooled around his head.

With shaking hands, Kayla dropped the candlestick. She quickly looked around for another weapon.

Grabbing the fireplace poker, she snuck up behind Scott, who had recovered from tasing himself, and rammed it toward his back just as Lucas pushed him forcefully.

Kayla recoiled as Scott turned toward her. In horror, she saw that the poker had pierced through to his chest and poked out the other side, the bloody tip just visible below his ribs. Blood began soaking through his shirt. Scott finally lay still.

Heaving deep breaths, Lucas collapsed against the staircase. Blue lights flashed through the living room, sirens blared in the driveway. Kayla stumbled to the door and opened it. Policemen rushed in.

Kayla lifted Charlie from the bottom of the stairs and carried him over to where Lucas lay where they huddled together.

They stayed there for what seemed like forever before one of the police finally came over to talk to them. He knelt down in front of them. Kayla recognized him as her dad's old partner, Terry. He hugged her and placed a hand on Charlie.

"I know you've been through a lot tonight, kids, but I am going to need to talk to both of you. I'll have talk to you first, Kayla, while the paramedics take a look at Lucas," he motioned for her to join him across the hall.

Kayla nodded and followed him over, carrying Charlie with her. Kayla told Terry all about the break-in, and about how Scott and Erik had tried to hurt her.

Finally, the paramedics came. Kayla watched as they went over to Scott and put a finger to his neck.

"Dead," the paramedic pronounced.

A chill came over Kayla when she heard the words. A few moments later, Erik's death was also pronounced.

Kayla felt numb as she watched the paramedics wheel their bodies out on a stretcher.

Finishing up with Terry, she and Charlie went back to sit down next to Lucas. Sweat shone brightly on his forehead and his eyes appeared glazed.

"Are you okay?" Kayla whispered, holding Charlie on her lap with one hand while she stroked Lucas' forehead.

Lucas didn't respond.

"Hurry!" Kayla cried as the paramedics trudged over with heavy bags in their hands.

"Hi, Kayla, my name is Hannah. I remember you when you were a little girl. Your dad and I were good friends," the petite, young, brown-haired paramedic greeted her as she set her bags down.

"He needs to go to the hospital!" Kayla was too upset to respond to her. Couldn't they see Lucas was hurt?

"No, no hospitals…" Lucas rasped, holding up his hand to motion for them to stop.

"You really should go to the hospital, there isn't a lot we can do for you here," Hannah insisted.

"Lucas, please!" Kayla begged.

"No, I'll be fine," Lucas shook his head defiantly.

"Just take him!" Kayla exclaimed, standing so Hannah and her team could move in.

"Kayla, we can't. He has the right to refuse treatment. If he doesn't want to go, there's nothing I can do," Hannah explained gently. Kayla burst into tears, clutching Charlie for comfort. Hannah put a hand on Kayla's back.

"Look, I loved your dad like a brother. I wouldn't be a good friend if I didn't help his family. We'll work on him as much as we can here, okay?" she soothed.

"Thank you," Kayla sniffed.

"Really, I'm fine," Lucas tried to insist.

He didn't trust anyone to take care of him. His whole life he had taken care of his own wounds. After so many beatings, he had learned how to bandage and cover up the cuts.

Hannah turned to Lucas. "You really need to let us help you," Hannah insisted.

The other EMTs spread a blanket out on the floor. Lucas didn't resist when they lifted him onto it. He didn't have strength to fight any longer.

"I'll watch Charlie, you stay with Lucas," Terry instructed Kayla. She held out the boy and Terry carefully lifted Charlie into his arms.

Kayla tenderly guided Lucas' head into her lap. Her fingers could feel the wet stickiness of his blood dribbling down his cheeks.

He winced as Hannah stuck his arm with a needle.

"I'm starting the IV now, Lucas. We'll be able to give you some medication for pain through the IV. In a minute, we're going to take the glass out, but I have to warn you, we don't have all the medication that the hospital would," Hannah warned, fishing in her bag for tweezers.

Lucas could barely hear her. The blood loss and pain made it hard to concentrate. Hannah motioned for the EMTs to help hold Lucas down.

"Okay, Lucas, we'll do this as quickly as possible, okay?" Hannah nodded and the EMTs tightened their grip on Lucas' arms and legs.

She examined Lucas' wounds and grabbed the largest piece of glass with the tweezers.

Every time Hannah slightly inched out the piece of glass, the pain felt like fire burning in his chest, in spite of the sedative. He hissed through his teeth, thrashing against being held down, but the paramedics' grip was too strong.

"Hold still, we're almost done," Hannah encouraged, though she knew it would be longer.

Delicately, she slid the piece of glass out and covered his wound with a mound of gauze until the bleeding lessened.

Five more times she repeated the process until finally, the last piece of glass was out.

Lucas' breath came in shallow gasps.

"Hang on, Honey, we're almost done," Hannah's tone softened as Lucas grew weaker.

She bandaged the wounds and then covered the taser burns in cream.

"I'm going to call Uncle Bobby to come over, okay?" Kayla whispered to Lucas as Hannah finished.

She kissed his forehead and left to make the call.

The EMTs wrapped Lucas in a blanket and laid him on the couch.

"He's still really dehydrated. I'm going to open up another vein and drain a bag in him," Hannah explained as she took his other arm and wrapped a tourniquet around it.

The vein was hard to find. She held his arm and moved the needle around inside until she found the vein.

"Sorry," she apologized as Lucas groaned.

She hung another IV bag and waited with Kayla. Lucas' eyes finally drooped to a close.

"We'll get a statement later, let him rest," Terry instructed Kayla as she worriedly stroked his forehead.

Once Lucas' color had come back and his breathing returned to normal, Hannah and her crew left. Uncle Bobby arrived half an hour later as Terry was helping Kayla clean up.

"I'm going to leave you and Charlie in your Uncle's care, okay? I'll be back in the morning," Terry tipped his hat and left.

Uncle Bobby embraced Kayla and Charlie.

"I'm so sorry," he whispered as Kayla sobbed into his shoulder.

"It was horrible, Uncle. Lucas saved us, but I thought he wasn't going to make it. There was so much blood!" she cried.

Uncle Bobby held her until her shaking calmed. Charlie sat still as stone, never making a sound.

"I think it's time to put Charlie to bed. If you set up a bed on the floor, I'll sleep out here with Charlie and Lucas. You need to rest," Uncle Bobby insisted.

She nodded and wiped her tears. Uncle Bobby held Charlie while she set up a bed for them. She gave him his teddy and tucked him in. Charlie went to sleep without a sound.

"You did the right thing," she whispered to Lucas as she knelt down by his head.

Lucas could only nod.

"Let him rest, Kay. It's been a long night." Uncle Bobby placed a kind hand on Kayla's shoulder.

Lucas' eyes were already closing again. Before she could say goodnight, his eyes shut and his muscles finally relaxed.

"Go to bed, Kayla. I'll take care of him and Charlie tonight," Uncle Bobby coaxed, helping her stand.

Tears streamed down her cheeks and he drew her into a reassuring hug.

"It's going to be okay, Kayla. You did your job. You protected Lucas and Charlie. Your father would have been proud. He spent his whole life protecting people from scum like that."

"But they were still people, and I killed them. I didn't mean to, I was just so angry and scared, I just…" she grew hysterical as she relived the memory.

Uncle Bobby held her tightly and let her cry. He prayed for words of wisdom.

"You did what you had to do. It was only self-defense. What if they had killed Charlie? Or Lucas? They were on drugs. Drugs make people do things they never ever would have done, sometimes it makes them very dangerous people. You did what was right."

Kayla didn't want to hear any of it. She couldn't get the picture of Erik's blood pooling around her feet out of her mind. Their lives were over and it was her fault. She felt as if she could hardly breathe. Uncle Bobby's attempts to comfort her did nothing. Without another word, she went to her room and shut the door.

Uncle Bobby sighed heavily. Tomorrow, he would install video cameras so that Lucas could make sure Kayla was safe when he and Charlie were at the apartment.

He lay down on the makeshift bed and hoped for sleep to come quickly.

With the rising of the sun, came the dawn of another day.

Lucas opened his sore eyes. He lay on the couch for a moment, hoping he had only dreamed about the night before. But the overwhelming pain in his body told him it was real.

The memories came back in a rush. Lucas felt relieved Scott was finally out of his life, but Scott had been his best friend. The thoughts were too much for him to handle. He needed to do something to get his mind off of it.

Lucas forced himself to sit up. Every bone in his body ached. The taser burn on his stomach felt like flames on raw skin that only intensified with his movements. The perfectly white bandages Hannah had wrapped around his wounds were tinged with pink. It made him queasy to look at them for long.

Limping into the kitchen, he found Kayla kneeling on the kitchen floor. Her shoulders shook with her sobs. Lucas slowly forced his sore body into a kneeling position next to her. Sharp stabs of pain shot through his chest as he placed a hand on her back.

She carefully leaned into him as he wrapped his arms around her.

"Shhh," he comforted her, stroking her hair. He winced as her head grazed the bandages.

"I killed them," she whispered the words as if saying them out loud would make it worse.

"You were protecting us," Lucas whispered in her ear.

"What if they send me to jail?"

"Terry won't allow that. He knew your father, remember? They know your situation. Now we're even, though," Lucas whispered.

"Even for what?"

"I saved your life, now you've saved mine. We're even," he smiled as she wiped her tears.

"Actually, I saved you twice. You owe me one more," she smiled a small smile as Lucas laughed.

"How about I give you my life to keep and then we will really be even?"

Lucas lifted her chin so he could look in her eyes. Black was just beginning to appear under her eyes from where Scott had hit her. Lucas traced the bruise lightly with his finger.

"I love you," he whispered, kissing her tenderly.

"I love you, too," Kayla replied softly.

"Okay you two, break it up!"

They both jumped at the sound of Uncle Bobby's voice. He leaned against the kitchen door with his arms crossed, having finished the video cam system install.

"That was very touching, but aren't you supposed to be resting?" Uncle Bobby directed his gaze at Lucas.

"I couldn't sleep," Lucas explained.

"I can see that," Uncle Bobby teased.

Lucas grinned as Kayla blushed.

NINETEEN

"HOLD STILL!" LUCAS TICKLED CHARLIE who was squirming around on the floor.

"Never!" Charlie gasped between breaths.

"Surrender or she dies!" Lucas leapt to his feet and wrapped an arm around Kayla.

"Hey, I'm reading," she protested. Lucas pulled her off the couch and held her close to him.

"Give up, or I'll kidnap her and take her to the pirate ship!"

"Not again!" Kayla shrieked.

"You can have her," Charlie shrugged.

"You're no fun," Lucas sighed, relaxing his grip around her.

"Can the princess go back to reading? She's not feeling very well," Kayla requested as she rested her head on Lucas' arm.

He turned her around to face him.

"Are you okay?" He put a cool hand to her forehead.

"You're not hot. Your forehead I mean…" he smiled as she tried to smack him.

"No, I'm not sick. I just have a really bad headache."

Lucas put his arms behind her and cradled her to his chest.

"That's it! She's mine, Peter Pan! Captain Hook wins again!" Lucas announced.

"I let you win because she's not a good prize," Charlie rolled his eyes and flopped onto his back.

"You're first prize in my book," Lucas whispered for only Kayla to hear.

She smiled and laid her head on his chest.

"This is the third headache in the last couple weeks, Babe. You sure you're okay?" Lucas said quietly as he helped her back to the couch.

"I'll be fine! Why don't you take Charlie outside to play for a while? I just need to rest."

"Anything for the princess." Lucas kissed her forehead and took Charlie outside to play.

Kayla slept for most of the day. Lucas was worried about her. Her headaches had gotten more frequent and intense, and he didn't like the way it knocked her out for the whole day. He decided he would make a doctor's appointment for her soon, even if she didn't want him to.

"What do you want for dinner?" Lucas asked Charlie, lifting him off his shoulders and placing him in his wheelchair.

"Candy?" Charlie suggested eagerly.

"No, you can't have candy for dinner," Lucas rolled his eyes, searching the fridge for leftovers.

"Please? Kayla is sleeping. She will never know. Besides, we had a healthy lunch. I ate an apple dipped in chocolate."

"Actually, it was more like you had chocolate dip with tiny apple pieces," Lucas reminded him, shutting the fridge.

The fridge was looking bare. Kayla had been too sick to do a lot of grocery shopping. Last night, they had used the frozen pizza Kayla had bought for the times she couldn't cook for them.

"Please?" Charlie begged again, pouting in his chair.

"I have a better idea, let's go out to eat!" Lucas proposed.

Charlie's face brightened, then darkened for a moment as his brow furrowed in consideration.

"Okay, but should we wake Kayla? I don't want her to miss coming with us," Charlie wondered.

Lucas debated silently for a moment. If he woke her, she might try to force herself to come with them so Charlie wouldn't be upset. If he didn't wake her, she might wake up alone. She was still shaken up from the break-in, and Lucas didn't want to leave her by herself. Thinking about how to wake her, he drummed his fingers on the table.

"I'll wake her!" Charlie offered, sticking his hand up in the air as if to be called on.

"No," Lucas immediately replied. "She still has bruises left over from the attack, she doesn't need anymore. I'll go wake her. You wait here and play with my phone."

Lucas put his phone on the table where Charlie could bend over and use his nose to browse the apps. Quietly, Lucas tiptoed into the living room and knelt down next to the couch.

"Hey, Babe," he tenderly brushed her hair back from her face. She stirred at his touch.

"We're going out to eat, do you want to come?" Lucas stroked her forehead as her eyes opened.

"Where are we going?" she asked groggily.

"Wherever you want. I'm in the mood for anything, except food I have to cook."

"Isn't that what happens every day?" Kayla smiled as Lucas winked.

"That's what happens when the women are sick. We men have to resort to some cheap restaurant food," Lucas dodged her feeble swipe at him.

"Okay, I'll come, just give me a minute to get ready," she said as she yawned and stretched.

"It's not a beauty contest. No one cares what you look like. Come on, I'm hungry!" Lucas tried to pout like Charlie always did to get his way.

"It will never work, Lucas. We'll be here another hour if you let her in the bathroom," Charlie called from the kitchen.

Lucas laughed as Kayla narrowed her eyes at him.

"Please, Babe, I'm starved," Lucas lay his head down on her shoulder. She pushed him off and sat up.

"Okay, I can be quick. Just one minute," she insisted.

"Nope, we're going now. Cave man hungry!" Lucas growled as he bent down and lifted her over his shoulder.

"Lucas Josiah McMullen, put me down! What if we see somone we know? They're going to think I look awful!" Kayla pounded on his back as he carried her towards the front door.

"It's okay, we'll just tell them you've been drinking," Lucas grinned as Kayla gave up fighting and began to laugh.

"To the diner!" he declared, opening the front door with one hand.

He carried her out to the car and sat her in the front seat.

"I hate you," she mouthed as he shut the car door and went back in for Charlie.

Lucas wheeled Charlie out to the car and buckled him in.

"Where to, Princess?" Lucas started the car and backed out of the driveway.

"Let's go to Bob's. Ruthie always makes me a frosty with extra whipped cream," Charlie suggested, leaning forward so his head was in between Kayla and Lucas.

"I've never heard of Bob's. Is it good?" Lucas questioned.

"No! Everyone knows us! I look awful! You didn't even give me time to change out of my sweat pants. Plus, I still have a fading black eye," Kayla pointed emphatically to the light bruise that still colored the skin under her eye.

"It's not that bad! You can barely even see the green, sort of purple, sort of blue, rainbow-like bruise," Lucas smiled, trying to make her laugh.

She crossed her arms in defiance. Lucas could see she really was upset. He felt bad he hadn't given her a few more minutes.

"I'm sorry, Babe. You look beautiful to me. I don't really care what the diner people think of you, because I think you're the prettiest girl I've ever seen – even in sweatpants, with smudged makeup, and messy hair," he teased.

"I have smudged makeup?" Kayla freaked, slamming the visor down and flipping open the cover over the mirror to peer anxiously at her reflection.

"You're missing the point."

Lucas rolled his eyes as she frantically rubbed at a spot of mascara on her cheek.

Lucas followed the directions of his phone G.P.S. into the gravel parking lot at Bob's. The building was small and had a homey feel to it.

Kayla was still fixing her makeup after Lucas had parked the car and turned it off.

Charlie sighed heavily, resting his head on his lap. Lucas leaned over and snapped the visor shut.

Kayla turned to glare at him, and Lucas held her angry gaze steadily.

"You are beautiful just the way you are right now. You are going to go in there and eat and enjoy yourself," Lucas continued to hold her gaze until she looked down, unable to believe his kind words.

He put a hand under her chin and tilted her head up to face him.

"You are the most beautiful girl I have ever met," Lucas whispered sincerely.

She felt the genuine love in his tone, and kissed him softly.

"I love you," she whispered into his ear.

"Can we go in and eat now?" Charlie impatiently demanded.

Lucas laughed. "Let's go meet the locals!"

Lucas jumped out of the van and wheeled Charlie inside. Kayla trailed behind straightening her sweatshirt and searching for stains on her sweatpants. The tiny bell above the door rang shrilly, announcing their entrance as Lucas pushed the wheelchair through.

"You're here!" A very heavy, old woman shoved herself through the kitchen door, and into the dining area, hurrying toward them.

"Charlie! Come here, my little friend!"

Lucas stepped back as Charlie was crushed into the arms of the large, grey haired woman.

"Hi," Charlie's answer was muffled as her bright purple flowered dress pressed against his mouth. His arms flailed as he attempted to hug her, but he couldn't quite reach all the way around.

"It's been so long since I've seen you!" the woman shrieked, squeezing him tighter.

"Ruthie, it's so good to see you!" Kayla smiled warmly.

"Oh, Kayla, my darling!" Ruthie flung her arms out wide and waddled around Lucas to hug Kayla.

Lucas pressed himself against the glass pastry window as the woman squeezed in the small space between Kayla, Lucas, and the wheelchair.

Charlie leaned over, gasping for air.

"How are you, Honey? I know it's been a rough last couple of months for you," Ruthie empathized as she released Kayla.

"It's been...difficult," Kayla admitted.

"Excuse me, Honey," Ruthie wheezed, reaching over Lucas to grab the menus from the box by the cash register.

Lucas ducked as she leaned in closer to try and reach the box.

"Got 'em!" she announced as her stubby fingers grasped onto the menus and held them in the air.

"This way," she directed, squeezing by Charlie's wheelchair.

"I heard about the break-in. We've all been praying for you down at church. At least you only got one black eye!"

Ruthie led the way to a booth in the back where Charlie's wheelchair wouldn't be disturbed.

"Yes, it was terrifying, but we could have been much more seriously hurt," Kayla agreed. "Thankfully, the families decided not to press charges. The police determined it was a clear case of self-defense. We were so scared that I might be headed to jail!"

"Thank God you guys are okay and safe!" Ruthie said with a sigh of relief. "Here's your usual spot. We've missed seeing you around. You should come to church sometime. Everyone would love to see you. Your father used to come at least once a month."

Kayla's eyes fell to the floor as she remembered. Lucas placed a comforting hand on her shoulder. Ruthie noticed the small exchange.

"I'm sorry, that was insensitive. We miss your father, too. He was a great man. But he also raised a wonderful daughter and son." Ruthie placed their menus down on the table and smiled warmly at them.

"Thank you, Ruthie. We have missed coming here and seeing everyone."

"And I miss my frosty," Charlie added in, reminding her.

Ruthie laughed heartily. "It's good to see some things don't change. I will have Gerry make it special for you. He'll probably bring it out himself. He's missed you!"

Lucas and Kayla slid into the booth as Ruthie delivered the silverware. She took down their drink orders on an old worn pad of paper.

"Okay, thanks, kids. I'll be back to hear more later," she nodded her head at Lucas and winked at Kayla.

Lucas smiled, unsure of what to say.

Kayla assured Lucas, "She just wants to get to know you. You're the first boyfriend I've ever had. It's a big deal in this town."

"Oh, really? I should have taken time to look more dashing today," Lucas laughed.

Ruthie came back with their drinks and set them on the table.

"Now, who's this young man?" Ruthie inquired as Kayla blushed.

"This is Lucas. Lucas, meet Ruthie, our faithful family friend."

Lucas stuck out his hand and was met with Ruthie's iron grip as she shook back.

"Nice to meet you, Lucas. You're not from around these parts, are you? Kayla, you should try our new chili recipe. I know the chili was always your favorite. Gerry tweaked it a little to give it more of a kick," Ruthie suggested as she waited for Lucas to answer.

"No, I'm from the city, ma'am," Lucas replied respectfully.

"Oh, a city boy, huh? How did you meet Kayla? Do you work up here? Charlie, you should try the cake batter pancakes. Gerry thought them up just for you. We know how much you love sugar," Ruthie smiled.

Lucas met Kayla's eyes in silent communication. She shrugged.

Ruthie's watchful eye didn't miss a thing.

"What, you didn't find him in a park drunk or something, did you?" Ruthie joked.

"Something like that," Kayla answered for Lucas who looked chagrined.

"Well, I trust Kayla's judgment. She would never fall in love with just any boy. You must be special," Ruthie winked at Lucas. "Okay, ready to order, kids?"

She took their orders one by one and left hastily to deliver them to the kitchen. A short while later, the food arrived, along with the cook.

When the cook came out, Lucas thought he was the strangest looking man he had ever seen. His blue eyes stood out from his dark skin, and his afro stuck straight out in a million different directions. A comb sat precariously perched right in the midst of the chaos.

"Hi, Charlie, how are you?" The man asked, getting on one knee to be eye level with him.

Startled, Charlie had a CP moment and accidentally punched him in the face.

"Thank you for the one millionth CP whack," Gerry said with a smile.

"That wasn't the millionth, that was probably the ten millionth," Charlie corrected as Gerry rubbed the red spot where Charlie had made his mark.

"Lucas, this is Gerry, Charlie's favorite chef," Kayla introduced.

Lucas waved as Gerry turned to say hello.

"Order up!" someone shouted from the back of the kitchen.

Charlie jumped at the sound and whacked Gerry on the other side of his head. Gerry pretended to fall dramatically to the floor.

"Oh my gosh, are you okay?" Lucas stood up in the booth to examine the lanky man sprawled out on the floor.

Charlie giggled hysterically as Gerry flailed around.

"Get up you old fool," Ruthie laughed as Gerry scrambled to his feet.

"It's okay, Lucas. Gerry is just kidding. Charlie always has CP moments around him. Sometimes Gerry scares him on purpose," Kayla explained, tugging on Lucas' shirt to get him to sit.

"Oh, well, as long as you're all right," Lucas laughed, sitting back down.

"He's fine, the old coot. Now you kids enjoy your meal. We have to get back to business. The dinner crowd is here, and we have to get them all served on time," Ruthie hugged Kayla and Charlie and shook Lucas' hand again.

Gerry gave Charlie a panicked look as Ruthie stepped over him to get back to the kitchen.

"Help me!" he whispered as Charlie tried to muffle his laughing.

"I heard that!" Ruthie yelled over her shoulder as she gathered menus for the customers by the door.

"No, you didn't," Gerry teased, smoothing his hair straight up and re-positioning the comb as he stood to his feet.

"You kids have a nice dinner now. Eat all your healthy chocolate syrup and starch, ya hear? The bill's on us. You kids be sure to have a good night!" Gerry punched Charlie playfully and headed off back toward the kitchen.

"Are you sure about the bill?" Lucas asked, taking out his wallet.

"Never more sure of anything in my life. You take care of them now, Lucas. Drop by soon!" Gerry called back as he pushed open the kitchen door and disappeared.

Lucas stared after him, unsure of what to do.

"Put the wallet away. Gerry is a joker, but not about that," Kayla rubbed Lucas' arm as he slowly put the wallet back in his pocket.

"This is a small town, Lucas. If you're having a bad day, or your dad is the local cop, you get free meals," Kayla explained.

Lucas heard the hint of sadness in Kayla's voice at the mention of her father.

"They must have loved your dad a lot," Lucas whispered.

"They all did. If old Mrs. Willard's fifteenth cat was in a tree, he was up there even before the fireman. Or if the war veteran at the local bar had too much to drink, he would drive him home and listen to his stories. Dad was a wonderful man. He protected this community, but he also loved it…" Kayla's voice trailed off.

Lucas looked to Charlie to make sure he wasn't listening. Charlie glanced up at him from the stack of pancakes he was devouring. With his CP, he normally couldn't feed himself, but with pancakes, it was a different story. He was able to dig his face into the pancake stack and chow down. Chocolate covered his mouth and shirt.

Lucas rolled his eyes, and Charlie happily leaned forward and continued to enjoy his favorite diner meal.

Kayla continued, "Dad was a great cop. He didn't belong in a small town like this, but he stayed for mom and for us. He was always being called off to the city to help when they needed officers on a shift. We were really up a creek with the bills, and he got paid overtime to go. I worried about him every time he left. We needed him so much, especially after mom died. When he died too, I thought I wouldn't be able to go on, but then, there you were." She smiled at Lucas who turned to look at her.

She put a hand on his cheek as he rested his forehead against hers.

"You were there to pick up the pieces. You're so strong. You and Dad were cut out of the same cloth. He grew up in a broken home too," Kayla stroked his cheek.

Lucas closed his eyes.

Memories flashed through his mind - all the broken memories he had pushed so far down inside his heart. He remembered how Mr. Maxwell had taken him back to his house that day and stood up for him. He stood up for him in a way no one ever had, and suddenly Lucas knew it was because he understood. He saw who Lucas really was and he fought for it.

It seemed as if God had been at work all along, even before Kayla and Lucas were born, to bring them to this place in their lives sitting at a diner in the middle of nowhere. God knew that the man whose life was broken from the loss of his wife would one day rescue Lucas, and Lucas in turn would take care of his family.

Tears came to Lucas' eyes as he thought about how great God's plans for them were, but he cried, too, for the suffering that had had to be endured.

Lucas and Kayla seemed frozen for a moment, deep in thought, before they noticed Charlie staring.

"Can I eat my pancakes without having to watch you two cry all over each other?" Charlie sighed, licking chocolate from his lips.

"Come on, Little Man, finish up and let's get you home and into the bath," Lucas laughed, shaking his head at the chocolate mess that covered the table.

They finished their dinner and said their last goodbyes to Ruthie and Gerry.

Lucas drove them home, and Kayla gave Charlie a bath while Lucas picked up the living room and found Charlie's favorite episode of Sesame Street.

After Charlie's bath, Lucas let Charlie cuddle on his lap to watch Sesame Street, as Kayla leaned against Lucas' shoulder. It wasn't long before Charlie's eyes closed, and he relaxed into Lucas' arms. Kayla smiled as Lucas gently shifted Charlie to the living room floor and covered him with a blanket.

"Well, Charlie's sleeping, we can watch anything we want, now," Lucas whispered.

"Okay, how about *Beauty and the Beast*?" Kayla looked up at Lucas hopefully.

"You've watched that three times already in the last two months," Lucas whined, nestling his head into her hair.

"Okay, okay, what about *101 Dalmatians*?" she giggled as his breath tickled the back of her neck.

"Fine," he sighed, resting his head on hers.

"We don't have to…" she pretended to be hugely disappointed.

"I'll watch whatever it is you want to watch, Princess, on one condition," Lucas relented.

"What could you possibly want besides my presence?" Kayla teased.

"Cookies," Lucas grinned.

"Oh alright, Prince Charming. You put the DVD on, and I'll slave over the stove for you," she laughed, beginning to stand.

As she stood, she let out a screech of pain and nearly collapsed. Lucas jumped up and caught her before her knees buckled.

"I've got you," he whispered leaning his forehead on hers.

She buried her aching head into his chest as she tried to catch her breath.

"It's okay," he reminded her, guiding her toward the couch.

"Sit on the couch with me." He grinned to cheer her up as she reluctantly acquiesced.

She sat on his lap, and he covered her with a blanket. She melted into his arms.

To him, her body felt cold and clammy. His heart broke for her. He would do anything to make her comfortable again.

"Do you need anything?" he whispered, kissing her pale forehead.

"Cookies?" she smiled as he laughed softly.

"Cookies it is," he sighed.

She moved off his lap and he stood up. She rested her pounding head on the couch.

"There's Break and Bake in the freezer," she called to him as she heard him rummaging through all the cabinets for ingredients.

"Thanks, Babe," he sighed in relief.

The smell of cookies soon filled the house. Lucas joined Kayla, bringing a plate of chocolaty goodness. He put on *Beauty and the Beast* for her and wrapped her in his arms. Kayla closed her eyes, hoping the pain in her head would go away soon.

TWENTY

"Oh, you're dating Lucas? I dated him once, too. So did all of them," the beautiful girl swept her hand out behind her.

Horrified, Kayla watched as Lucas walked to each one, taking them in his arms. All of them were stunningly beautiful and healthy. A mirror appeared in front of her. Kayla fell to her knees as she saw herself in the mirror. She was the same age, but bald, and hauntingly thin, with a tumor snaking down from her head. The thing began to creep around her neck, choking out all of the memories she had with Lucas and Charlie and replacing her in their lives with these healthy girls and their snide smiles.

"Babe, wake up, it's morning." Lucas tried to gently shake Kayla awake.

She opened her eyes and jumped up from the couch. Lucas stepped back defensively as she whirled around.

"Who's Emily?" Kayla demanded angrily.

"Who?" Lucas asked, bewildered.

"There were all these girls, and she said that you had dated all of them!" Kayla broke down as she remembered staring at herself in the mirror.

"I don't know what you're talking about," Lucas exclaimed, throwing up his hands.

"You could have had any girl you wanted! I really believed you cared for me!" she angrily wiped her tears off her face.

Lucas listened to her babble on and tried desperately to figure out where her anger was coming from.

"I'm so ugly!" She sat down on the couch with her face in her hands.

Something in Lucas finally snapped. He was sick of hearing her talk about herself like she was trash, and he hated that she thought he would prefer to be with someone else.

"Now stop that right now!" he yelled, slamming his fist on the coffee table.

Charlie jumped from his place on the floor as Lucas' voice rose higher.

"Do you really think I'm cheating on you?" Lucas roared at her accusation.

Charlie sat frozen in fear as he watched Lucas' face turn an angry red.

"I don't know, you tell me!" she said, her voice breaking. "It's just… you could have had anyone. I just don't understand why you chose me," Kayla lied.

She couldn't tell Lucas her fears about why her headaches were getting so intense, or what the dream pointed to. He would be crushed, and upset that she had lied. But she couldn't contain her cries as she realized what the dream might mean.

His tone softened as her shoulders shook with sobs.

"No, I would never do that, I promise. You are the only one I have ever loved," he said as he reached out to hug her. "I love you, and I always will," he promised as she leaned into his hug.

"You promise?" she whispered.

"I promise," he responded, hugging her tightly.

Kayla knew that she had to go to the doctor soon and see if what she feared most was true, but for now, she decided, she would just try to enjoy the next couple of days.

Charlie stared at Lucas, a look of terror in his eyes.

"It's okay, Bud. I'm sorry, I didn't mean to scare you." Lucas knelt down and hugged Charlie.

"Well kiss her already, will ya?" Charlie exclaimed as Lucas stood and faced Kayla.

"You watch too many chick flicks," Lucas said rolling his eyes as he leaned in to kiss her.

Charlie ducked as she leaned back.

"There, you happy now?" Lucas asked Charlie.

"Yes! Now I'm hungry!" Charlie said laughing.

"Okay, okay. What do you want, your Royal Highness?" Lucas asked dramatically.

"Ah…food?" Charlie answered.

"How did your sister live with you for five years?" Lucas asked Charlie looking at Kayla.

"Love, joy and peace," Kayla replied, interrupting Charlie.

"I'm not that bad," Charlie said as he leaned forward to lick his foot.

"Gross!" Kayla said gagging.

"Anyway, what do you want for breakfast?" Lucas asked Charlie.

"Sunny-D and cookies!" Charlie answered immediately.

"Okay!" Lucas said laughing.

"Oh boy…" Kayla said shaking her head.

"What?" Lucas asked her.

"You'll see in about an hour…" she sighed. Forty-five minutes later Charlie was on the floor bouncing up and down on his knees.

"Told you," Kayla told Lucas while the two of them were on the couch watching Charlie shout and clap his hands while he bounced.

"Now can I have coffee?" he requested, grinning hugely.

"No, but Lucas can," Kayla said rubbing Lucas' leg.

"Yes, please!" Lucas answered immediately.

"Okay, I'll be right back."

"Hurry! I can't take it much longer!" Lucas said laughing.

"Hey, this is your fault," Kayla reminded him.

"I'm a boy; it's never the boy's fault," Lucas whined.

"Fine, do you ever *not* spoil Charlie?"

"Nope…. Oh wait… Yeah… no. You love me," Lucas said smiling.

"I hate you!" Kayla said rolling her eyes. She came back with the coffee and placed it on the coffee table. Lucas was on the floor wrestling with Charlie.

"My turn!" Kayla shouted, tackling both of them.

"Charlie, stop! You're killing both of us!" Lucas yelled as Charlie climbed over them. Lucas lifted Charlie in the air and whispered something to him.

"What are you doing?" Kayla asked as if she were scared.

Lucas and Charlie tackled her.

"Give me her socks!" Lucas yelled to Charlie. Charlie yanked her socks off and gave them to Lucas. Lucas took the socks and put them in Kayla's mouth.

"Let's tickle her," Lucas whispered to Charlie.

"Okay!" Charlie yelled.

"No!" Kayla screamed in laughter.

After about an hour of Charlie and Lucas torturing Kayla, they all were hungry. Lucas gave Charlie a piggyback ride to the kitchen to eat.

"Can we eat in the tree house, Lucas?" Charlie asked Lucas with big, brown eyes.

"Sure, Kiddo," Lucas answered with the cute smile on his face that Kayla loved.

He pulled a package of Oreos out of the cabinet.

"Hey, guys – I'm really not that hungry anymore and my body hurts." Kayla excused herself and went back to the couch to lie down.

"Okay. No more nightmares though," Lucas made her promise.

"Okay, I promise," she laughed.

"Come get me if you need anything, okay?" Lucas firmly told her.

He didn't want her trying to do too much herself without him around.

"Okay, okay..." She rolled her eyes but smiled back. She watched the two of them prance out the door, and thanked God for Lucas. She knew she didn't deserve him, especially not when he finds out the truth about her health.

Charlie and Lucas ventured out to the tree house.

"I wonder if Daddy is in heaven looking at us right now?" Charlie pondered as they sat together.

Lucas paused, unsure of what to say next. He opened the Oreo package as he thought about how to respond.

"Do you miss your parents?" Lucas asked Charlie, giving him a bite of Oreo.

"Sort of... Wouldn't it be funny if we were on the front of the Oreo packages?" Charlie asked Lucas, switching topics.

Lucas laughed, relieved to not have to try to counsel Charlie without Kayla there.

"That would be funny, but we should remember that the famous people who are on there are just people," Lucas reminded him.

"Why do people make a big deal about famous people if they do what usual people do?" Charlie questioned.

"I honestly don't know Charlie. I really have no idea…" Lucas said, gently wiping Oreo off Charlie's face.

The rest of their conversation was about Charlie and how much he loved cookies. Lucas began to worry about Kayla. As Charlie talked, he wondered if she was all right. She usually never took two naps, or even one, for that matter.

"Why don't we eat more of these back at the house, okay?" Lucas suggested as Charlie finished off a sixth cookie.

"We don't have to. I'm done." Charlie smiled with a mouth full of food, letting cookie spit dribble from both sides of his mouth.

Lucas grimaced, picking Charlie up and holding him out a good distance to avoid being cookie-slimed as they headed back to the house.

"Where've you two been?" Kayla asked in a motherly voice.

Lucas breathed a silent sigh of relief to see her up and walking around.

"Africa!" Charlie answered immediately from the kitchen floor as Lucas wiped Oreo off of Charlie's mouth.

"You guys are so weird," Kayla said to both of them.

"I know. You love us," Lucas said, giving Kayla the cutest smile she'd ever seen.

"I'm bored…." Charlie whined.

"Of course you are," Lucas said rolling his eyes.

"What does that mean?" Charlie asked trying to act insulted.

"You're always bored!" Lucas sighed. "Let's play 'Tickle Kayla'!"

"Do you just love torturing me?" Kayla asked Lucas, trying to look mad.

But when she looked at Lucas, all she could think about was how much she loved him.

"Ow!" Charlie interrupted.

They both looked at Charlie and saw he had lost his balance and had tipped over onto the hard kitchen tile.

Lucas rushed over to him as fast as lightning.

Kayla thought to herself, "What a wonderful boyfriend I have."

"Are you okay?" Lucas asked, worried.

"Lucas, I'm fine. I just fell over," Charlie said, laughing.

Lucas sighed. "Are you sure?"

Charlie laughed. "Yes, Mother…"

"That wasn't motherly," Lucas said, giving Charlie a playful slap on the back of his head.

"Ow!" Charlie said to Lucas, pretending to be in pain so he'd get more sympathy.

"You really think I'll fall for that?" Lucas asked Charlie.

"Of course he does," Kayla interrupted before Charlie could say anything.

"Well, I have CP!" Charlie answered.

Kayla and Lucas looked at him.

"Don't even try that excuse," Lucas exclaimed rolling his eyes at him.

"Why not? I'm not lying," Charlie teased.

Lucas hated it when Charlie said that because he knew he couldn't argue with that.

"You are such a brat," Lucas said smacking him.

"I know. You love me!" Charlie said smacking him back.

"How about Clue Jr.?" Lucas suggested, smiling.

"What's Clue Jr.?" Charlie asked with a confused face.

"You know what Clue Jr. is," Kayla said to Charlie.

"Is it the one where you sink the ships?" Charlie asked again.

"No, that's Battleship!" Kayla answered. "In Clue, you have to figure out who killed a guy, where, and with what."

"Oh. Who would ever kill a guy?" Charlie asked.

"Probably you," Lucas answered with a grin.

"Me? Never…!"

After they finished the game, Charlie was shocked. Lucas won!

"Thank you, Lucas! Finally! Someone who can beat Charlie at a game!" Kayla thought to herself.

"What do you want to do next?" Lucas asked Charlie in a sweet voice.

It was the sweetest voice that Kayla had ever heard in her life. She giggled out loud a little. Thankfully, Lucas didn't hear her.

"Kayla, I love you," Lucas said with his smile that Kayla loved.

When he held her hand, she knew that he meant it.

She blushed, "I love you, too."

They leaned in and kissed.

"I'll never understand big people," Charlie said giggling.

"You will, Bud, give it some time," Lucas said rubbing Charlie's head.

"Let's go on the trampoline!" Kayla squealed.

"Yeah!" Charlie shouted happily.

"Where is it?" Lucas asked.

"In the garage," Kayla answered with a cute grin.

"You mean I have to set it up?" Lucas asked sarcastically.

"Yup," she answered.

Lucas picked up Charlie, and they followed Kayla to the garage. She put two hands on the garage door handle and pulled as hard as she could. It felt like lead.

Lucas saw her having trouble so he put Charlie on the ground and ran over to help. He nudged Kayla out of the way and pulled up on the handles. The door slid up easily.

Kayla looked at Lucas with a sweet smile. "Thank you so much, Lucas."

"No problem! I know how weak you are, so I decided to help," he dodged her smack as he pulled the trampoline out and placed it on the grass.

"Run, Lucas!" Charlie yelled.

Lucas hopped up on the trampoline and jumped away from her. As she struggled to get on, he jumped down to get Charlie. Kayla was waiting for him as he sprang up. He jumped high and came down hard. Kayla wobbled off balance and Charlie flew into the air.

"Yay! Popcorn!" Charlie squealed.

Lucas reached out a hand to steady Kayla because it looked like she was going to fall.

"Hah! Gotcha!" she said, suddenly regaining her balance and tripping him.

Lucas landed flat on the trampoline. She put her foot on his chest and raised her fist in the air.

"Kayla wins!" Charlie announced.

Lucas grinned and pulled her leg out from under her. She landed next to Lucas, laughing.

"Jump, Lucas! I want to go high!" Charlie exclaimed.

Lucas looked into Kayla's eyes for a moment and smiled. She smiled back and smacked him lightly on the cheek.

"That's for calling me weak," she reprimanded. Lucas pretended to fall back as if she had punched him.

"You killed him!" Charlie pretended to cry.

Ignoring the pair of them, Kayla jumped up and hopped over to Charlie.

"It's my turn to play with you! I'm your sister, you know! What? … You like Lucas better?" she teased, jumping lightly so Charlie would go high, but not fall.

"Maybe," Charlie teasingly responded, screaming in delight as she made him fly higher.

Lucas watched Kayla smiling and jumping with her hair flying through the breeze. He thought she was beautiful.

Kayla turned and caught him staring. She smiled and winked at him.

"Got you!" Charlie yelled and grabbed hold of her leg.

She started to fall, and Lucas tried to catch her, but Charlie fell on Lucas' hand. They all landed on each other, laughing.

Charlie kicked his feet trying to get off of his stomach, and Kayla was laughing as she struggled to help. Lucas realized how much he loved both of them. They loved each other so much and were so caring toward one another. Even though Charlie was only five, Lucas knew he cared a lot about his sister. Kayla clearly adored her younger brother, and that was one of the things Lucas loved most about her. She didn't see Charlie's disability; she saw his heart.

Lucas rolled over onto his back and let them have a private sibling moment. While they laughed and teased, Lucas lay staring at the clouds. He started making shapes out of them.

"Look Charlie, it's a bunny!" Lucas suddenly exclaimed, pointing at the sky.

Kayla rolled her eyes as Charlie flopped over on his back to look at clouds, too. The sun was beating down on their faces. Kayla could feel the sweat beginning to drip off her forehead. She watched the boys find cloud animals as she rolled up her sleeves and lay down to tan.

The sun warmed her whole body. It seemed to ease some of the pain. Though she had already had three naps, Kayla felt as if she hadn't slept in days.

"I'll just close my eyes," she thought to herself.

After a few minutes, she fell asleep to the comforting sound of Charlie and Lucas laughing.

Kayla woke up a few hours later. The sun was just setting behind the trees. Her head felt like it was going to split open from the pain.

"I must have been in the sun too long," she said out loud, expecting Lucas to reply.

She looked over to where they had been sitting and realized they were gone. She tried to sit up too quickly and the yard seemed to spin.

On the edge of the trampoline, she tried to regain her balance. After a few minutes, the dizziness faded but didn't stop. She knew she had to go into the house and lie down. Holding one hand to her head, she stood and stumbled towards the house.

Inside, Charlie and Lucas were watching Sesame Street. The program was just ending as Lucas heard a crash in the kitchen. He turned and saw Kayla drop to the floor. Lucas switched the channel to a new program so Charlie wouldn't notice and ran to her side.

"Hey, what's wrong?" he asked, kneeling next to her. She looked up, and he saw her face was bright red from the sun.

"Oh, Kayla, I'm sorry. We shouldn't have left you out there," he apologized as she shook her head.

"No, it's just a headache. I've been getting a lot of them, but I think this one's from the sun," she said in a hoarse tone. "Can I have some water?" she asked, laying her head on the cool tiled floor.

"Yes, let's go to your room, so you can rest, and I'll bring some up," he replied, helping her up.

He followed close behind her as she stumbled to her room. Lucas could hear Charlie singing along with the songs as they walked past him to go upstairs. If he noticed, he didn't show it. Lucas was glad. He hated when Charlie saw his sister upset or sick. Kayla lay down in her bed, and Lucas covered her up.

"I'll get you that water now," he said quietly and she nodded.

He went out to the kitchen, walking past Charlie again.

"Charlie, you okay in there?" he called out as he poured a glass of water.

"Yup, just bored to *death*," Charlie replied.

"I'll be right there, just give me a minute."

"Okay, hurry up because Dora the Explorer just came on!" Charlie answered, wishing they had never created such a weird children's show.

"Why would they even have a monkey speaking Spanish anyway?" Charlie muttered to himself as Lucas passed him on his way to the bathroom.

Lucas put the water down and searched the bathroom for the aloe. He found the green bottle in the medicine cabinet and brought it back to her room.

"Here." He sat down at her bedside and held out the cup.

She sat up a little and the dizziness came back again. She could only manage a couple of sips before she started to lie back down.

"Wait," he requested and gave her some Tylenol to swallow.

She swallowed the pills and got horizontal again. He put the cup of water with a straw next to her bed so she could reach it in the middle of the night. She closed her eyes as her head pounded.

"I'm sorry," he said quietly.

He hated seeing her sick, and he hated that it was his fault for letting her sleep in the sun for so long.

She shook her head again.

"You guys were just being nice and letting me sleep. Charlie has been waking up so early lately, I guess was just tired," she replied, her voice a little clearer.

"Yes, well, I still feel bad," he answered, rubbing the aloe on her forehead.

She winced, "I didn't think I got *that* sunburned."

His gentle fingertips seemed to burn her skin as he rubbed the gel in.

"Ah!" she hissed quietly as Lucas finished up.

"Sorry!" he apologized again, mentally kicking himself for leaving her out there.

"I'm fine, really. It's just a sunburn," Kayla insisted as his worried eyes searched hers.

Finally, the burning numbed as the aloe soaked into her skin. Her eyes started to close as the Tylenol took effect.

"Thanks, Lucas," she whispered before she closed her eyes.

Lucas watched her fall asleep and tiptoed out of the room, shutting the door. He went out into the living room where Charlie was. Charlie looked at him and then looked back at the TV and realized that Dora was still on.

"I am so sorry that you had to watch that," he said quickly, grabbing the remote to turn it off. He needed to get his mind off worrying about Kayla, and he knew another episode of Sesame Street wouldn't help.

"Charlie, want to play a game before dinner?" He asked, turning off the TV.

"Yeah, what game?"

"Whack –a- Mole?"

"Yeah!" Charlie yelled.

Lucas put one finger to his mouth. "Shh, your sister is sleeping."

"At this time of night? She's not a grandma yet!" Charlie laughed.

"She's not feeling so good; I think she is allergic to trampolines," Lucas joked, trying to distract Charlie.

"Oh well, let Grandma sleep. I want to play Whack a Mole!" Charlie cheered.

They played for over an hour. When they finally finished, Lucas was covered in little red welts.

"You know you're supposed to hit the mole. It's not 'Whack a Lucas'," Lucas chided as Charlie hit him again on the hand.

"But this is more fun!" Charlie insisted.

"Okay, time for dinner," Lucas announced, pulling the mallet from Charlie's hand.

Lucas fed him dinner and tucked him into bed at the apartment. Before he lay down, Lucas crept quickly back to the house, baby monitor in hand in case Charlie should wake, to check on Kayla.

She looked more peaceful than before, and he knew the medicine had finally done its job. He felt a little better knowing she wasn't in pain, but he still worried if she would be all right.

He went back to bed and prayed he never had to see her that sick again.

TWENTY-ONE

IN KAYLA'S HEART, SHE KNEW what was happening, but she desperately hoped it wasn't true. She couldn't ignore her symptoms anymore. She needed answers, but she didn't want Lucas to know. He would only worry, and maybe there wasn't anything to worry about, Kayla reasoned with herself.

She made an emergency doctor's appointment with her pediatrician.

The morning of the appointment, she woke up earlier than Lucas or Charlie and snuck out to go to the doctor's office. He took her in right away.

"Good afternoon, Kayla, what seems to be troubling you?" the doctor asked as he took a seat.

"I think the tumor is back."

She tried to contain her emotions, but fear made her tremble.

"Before you get upset, tell me your symptoms and we will complete some tests," the doctor suggested kindly.

She told him all of her symptoms, including the fainting spells and severe headaches.

With each description, the doctor seemed more and more concerned. He sent her to the hospital to have imaging taken immediately.

Kayla wished she had brought Lucas with her. She was terrified. She forced herself to be strong and walked into the imaging lab.

They completed the scans and asked her to have a seat in the waiting room.

Nervously, she locked and unlocked her phone, trying to decide whether or not to call Lucas. She didn't want to hear this news alone, but she didn't want to upset him, either. Before she had a chance to decide, a doctor walked in.

"Kayla, my name is Dr. Beeoko. I am a cancer specialist here. I have examined your scans and I see a large brain tumor. I understand you had one as a child?"

Kayla nodded numbly.

"I wish I could tell you that we can just do surgery and remove it, but unfortunately the tumor has grown too big to be able to safely remove. Our best bet right now is to shrink it with chemotherapy and radiation." He watched for Kayla's reaction.

Her blank stare continued, and he locked eyes with her.

"Do you understand what I'm saying, Kayla? It isn't hopeless, but the survival rates all depend on how each individual does with therapy. I can't tell you at this time how long you will have," he informed her gravely.

As the look of fear and pain registered on her face, Dr. Beeoko wished, as he had many times before, that he had chosen a different practice. He hated seeing suffering in someone so young.

"Do you have family that can support you through this?" he inquired, trying another approach.

"Yes, I do," she replied softly, her mind trying to process Dr. Beeoko's words.

"Well then, here is my number. If you or anyone else in your family has any questions, give me a call. You should schedule your next appointment right away so we can begin treatment," he said, exiting the room and quietly shutting the door.

Kayla sat there dazed for a few moments before she realized what had just happened. She knew she had a choice to make. Should she tell Lucas? Or should she try to handle it on her own? The two options ran through her mind over and over again as she made the long trip home.

TWENTY-TWO

THE NEXT SUNDAY, LUCAS DECIDED to make breakfast in bed for Kayla, so he woke up early to make pancakes, eggs, waffles, and French toast. While he was making breakfast, he heard Charlie waking up, so he went into their room to get him out of bed.

"Morning, Bud," Lucas whispered softly, lifting him out of bed.

"Why are you up?" Charlie asked, groggy-eyed.

"I'm making breakfast," he answered putting Charlie's pants on.

"Can I help?"

"Sure!" Lucas answered, wheeling Charlie into the kitchen. "I was just about to make the waffle batter."

"You know, we have frozen ones," Charlie said laughing.

"But that's cheating!" Lucas exclaimed.

"So? I thought you were a city boy," Charlie shot back.

The door opened and a groggy Kayla let herself in.

"What are you doing here?" Lucas asked, astonished to see her. "We were trying to make breakfast as a surprise for you, but here you are," he smiled.

"Yeah, look! Lucas is gonna make waffles!" Charlie said excitedly.

"You're making breakfast? Why?" Kayla asked rubbing her eyes.

"Because, I love you," Lucas said grinning.

Kayla blushed. "I love you too," she said giving him a sleepy grin back.

"I was going to bring breakfast to you in bed but you woke up too early," Lucas explained.

"Well, let's eat at the table then," Kayla suggested.

"Do you want coffee, Babe?" Lucas asked.

Kayla's eyes suddenly opened wide. "Yes, please."

He gave her a mug and poured the coffee.

"Thank you," Kayla smiled.

"What are we doing today, Charlie?" Kayla asked Charlie.

"Bowling!" Charlie answered excitedly.

"Okay..." Kayla answered, reluctantly.

Lucas knew she hadn't felt well lately and that her energy wasn't good.

"How about we have a boys' day out?" Lucas suggested.

Kayla mouthed "Thank you."

"Yeah!" Charlie yelled.

"But first, we have to eat my wonderful breakfast," Lucas added.

He placed his hands on Charlie's shoulders to keep him from jumping in the wheelchair.

"Bowling! Bowling! *NOW!*" Charlie whined with a cute face.

Lucas couldn't say no. "Fine, but we have to eat these when we get back."

He looked over at Kayla, waiting for her to jump in with her mother voice insisting that they stay and eat. But Kayla was silent and just smiled at Lucas.

"Have fun," she said.

"Thank you," Lucas murmured, worried.

"Charlie, could you watch a quick episode of Sesame Street while I talk to your sister for a minute? Then we'll go. The Bowling Alley doesn't open for awhile anyway."

Charlie pouted, hoping Lucas would change his mind.

"If you're good, we'll get cheese fries," Lucas whispered, pretending Kayla couldn't hear.

"Yes!" Charlie whispered back in excitement.

After wheeling Charlie into the living room and turning on the TV, Lucas went back to the kitchen. Kayla was resting her head on her arms at the table. Lucas put his hand on her back. She lifted her head, and he put his other hand on her forehead.

"You don't have a fever," he said.

She nodded, "Yes, I know, Dr. Lucas."

He didn't smile.

"Are you going to be okay?" he worried.

"Yes, I'll be fine. I used to get migraines a lot as a kid; I just need to rest for today."

"I'll be fine! Really!" she insisted.

He sighed, "I guess I can be away from you for one day..."

She laughed. "Of course you can, but do *NOT* give him too many cheese fries, you will regret it."

Lucas rolled his eyes. "Yes, Mom."

She shook her head. She knew he would find out later what she meant. "You guys go have fun. I'm going to go eat the perfect breakfast you made me."

He smiled and squeezed her hand before heading into the living room to get Charlie.

"It's a boys' day!" Charlie cheered.

Lucas gathered Charlie's things and put them in his backpack. He hung the backpack on the back of the wheelchair and headed out to load Charlie in the van.

"Bye, Sis!" Charlie yelled on their way out the door.

"Bye! Behave!" She yelled back.

She heard Charlie laugh and the door shut. Kayla sat down to eat, but just couldn't, so she set to work clearing some of the dishes.

Outside, Lucas put Charlie in the front seat, putting the wheelchair in the back of the van.

"I'm too young for the front," Charlie said.

"I know, but Kayla's not here to yell at us, so you can do it this time."

"Okay, but if I die, it's your fault."

"You're not going to die," Lucas responded closing the door.

He drove to the bowling alley and parked the car in the handi-capped space.

"Oh no," Lucas realized something at once.

"What?" Charlie asked.

"We forgot the handicapped parking tag."

"Oh, its okay. If they catch us, you'll only have to pay about a thou-sand dollar fine."

"Thanks for your sympathy," Lucas said sarcastically.

"It's fine, let's just go," Charlie said jumping up and down in his seat.

Lucas hauled the wheelchair out of the back of the van. He was so worried about the handicapped tag that he pushed the wheelchair over the curb and tripped. The wheelchair and Lucas toppled over.

"Haha," Charlie laughed from where he was watching in the rear-view mirror.

Lucas picked himself up and tried to get the wheelchair upright again. One of the back wheels had fallen off. Lucas sighed as Charlie burst into laughter.

"Can this day get any worse?" Lucas wondered out loud.

Dragging the wheelchair behind him on the three remaining wheels, he carried Charlie to the bowling alley entrance. Lucas struggled to get Charlie and the wheelchair through the narrow old doorway.

Charlie rolled his eyes. "Uh….door?" he asked, pointing to the automatic handicapped entrance.

"Thank you for telling me that ten minutes later," Lucas muttered under his breath.

"You're welcome," Charlie answered brightly.

Lucas hauled them over to the automatic door and pushed the button. Once inside, he picked one of the lanes that didn't look busy. He set Charlie down and went to work on the wheelchair.

"Hi, excuse me," the attendant interrupted nervously.

"Yes?" Lucas responded tensely as he tried to wiggle the wheel back on the axle.

"We actually have this lane reserved for the nursing home residents; it's kind of their day to bowl. They always use this lane."

"Tell them to use a different one; this is the only one with wheelchair access," Lucas responded sternly as the wheel popped back off the chair.

"Well, we can't really do that," the attendant answered, backing away from Lucas.

"Well you're going to," Lucas responded, shoving the wheel back on. It finally popped into place.

Lucas turned to face the young attendant. The teen seemed to shrink as Lucas stood over him.

"I don't mean to be rude, but this lane is reserved for handicapped use. Please inform the nursing home they will be sharing a lane with us today," Lucas instructed.

The teen pushed his glasses up and wrung his hands as his greasy curls flopped into his face.

"Okay, I suppose..." he answered, walking away.

He went to contact the manager, and Lucas turned back to Charlie.

"Ready?" he asked, his mood changing as Charlie beamed.

"Yes, I am *SO* ready for this! I'm going to beat you!"

"No you're not!" Lucas teased back.

He wheeled Charlie up to the lane and grabbed the metal ball ramp from the wall. Charlie needed it to be able to launch the bowling ball down the lane as much by himself as possible.

"See Charlie? This is so you can bowl by yourself...well, with less help anyway."

"Cool!" Charlie exclaimed. "How does it work?"

"Well, you point this ramp in the direction you want the ball to go and you put the ball on top. Then when you're ready, you push the ball down, and it rolls down the lane."

Lucas grabbed the lightest ball he could find and showed Charlie how it worked.

"Your turn," he said, wheeling him up to the metal ramp.

Lucas set the ball up and Charlie pushed it as hard as he could down the ramp. He got a strike! Lucas wheeled him back and took his turn. He got a gutter ball on both turns.

"You'll get it...maybe..." Charlie tried to encourage.

Lucas set the ball up for Charlie's second turn.

"Helloooo!" a little old lady yelled.

"Here we go," Charlie whispered to Lucas.

The little grandma pushed her walker over to where they were standing. She had on a bright purple vest with polka dot pants and red bowling shoes.

"Aren't you adorable?" she said loudly to Charlie reaching out to pinch his cheeks.

Charlie tried to lean away and accidentally knocked the ball off the ramp and onto Lucas' foot. Lucas hissed through his teeth, trying to smile anyway.

"Yes, he *is* adorable," Lucas smiled, pushing Charlie even closer and locking the wheelchair.

"This will be fun," Lucas thought to himself as he watched the grandma yelling in Charlie's face.

His foot throbbed, but he felt a little better watching Charlie's face.

"He seems very sweet," the grandma said over Charlie's head.

"He is! He's very, *very* sweet!" Lucas said, tapping Charlie's head.

"Poor thing…" she clucked her tongue.

"Are you going to bowl?" she asked in a scratchy high-pitched tone.

Charlie smiled and nodded, hoping she would go away. Lucas was just about to rescue him when the teenage attendant came back over. "Excuse me, ma'am. You ladies are over here today."

Lucas and Charlie breathed a sigh of relief.

"You boys take care now," she said, slowly following her friends over to the other side of the bowling alley.

Lucas doubled over laughing while Charlie glared at him.

"You couldn't just have rescued me before that?"

Lucas smiled, "I hurt my foot! You wouldn't ask an injured man to rescue you, would you?"

"Yes, I would," Charlie laughed. "You should buy me cheese fries, *NOW!*" Charlie begged.

Lucas sighed and limped over to the counter to order. They finished their game and ate two more rounds of fries. Lucas scored 50 points and Charlie got 100. At the end of the last round, Lucas looked over at Charlie who was grinning through a mouth full of fries and cheese.

"I win! That's what you get for what you did to me, today," Charlie teased.

Lucas rolled his eyes. He returned his bowling shoes and paid for the game. As they were leaving, the little old lady called out to them.

"Run!" Charlie whispered.

Lucas wanted to get home to Kayla so he jogged with the wheelchair out the door and to the car. Unfortunately, the rear wheel popped off again.

"Uh…Lucas? Ark…." Charlie said quietly.

"What?" Lucas asked, confused.

"You know…Noah? In the Bible?" Charlie hinted.

"Great….just… great…." responded Lucas, reaching for the backpack with the diapers.

"It's not my fault you let me have three orders of cheese fries with chili," defended Charlie.

When they got home, Kayla was in the kitchen cooking.

"What are you making?" Lucas asked as he dragged Charlie and the broken wheelchair through the door.

Kayla looked at them in shock. "Why are you carrying Charlie and dragging the wheelchair?"

"Don't ask. What are you baking?" he asked again.

"Cookies! You look like you could use one. Long day?" she asked,

Lucas just looked at Charlie.

"Oh I see. Charlie, I told you to behave."

"I did!" he defended. "Lucas is just a sore loser. Even the old lady got a better bowling score."

Lucas shook his head. "I didn't really want her knowing that, Bud."

He carried Charlie to the living room, put him on the couch, and sat next to him, turning on the TV.

"Need any help?" Lucas called to Kayla from the living room.

"No, you had a long day taking care of Charlie. I'll bring in a plate of cookies."

"Okay," Lucas yelled back, putting Charlie on his lap.

A minute later, Kayla came in with a plate of cookies and cups of soda.

"Here you go, Sweetie," Kayla said, smiling sweetly.

"Thank you," Lucas said, giving Charlie a bite of cookie.

She went back out to the kitchen and grabbed her drink.

"What are we watching?" she asked as Lucas put his arm around her.

"Football!" Lucas answered, squeezing her shoulders as she sighed. He knew she hated it.

"Pleeease," he whined, knowing she would give in.

"Fine," she relented.

"I love you," he said grinning.

"Sure, sure," she answered, pretending to be annoyed.

She fed Charlie a couple more cookies while he sat on Lucas' lap cheering for the teams.

"How was your day?" Lucas asked Kayla quietly when Charlie was distracted.

"Okay. The migraine finally went away."

"That's when you decided to make me cookies?" he teased.

"Yes, I knew that would make you happy. And you did make me a beautiful breakfast this morning…and didn't get to eat any of it!"

"Oh – I knew I must have done something right to get cookies *and* a football game," Lucas teased back.

"Hey! Quit talking! I can't hear!" Charlie interrupted.

Kayla ignored him and resumed talking to Lucas.

"Thanks for taking Charlie; I know it meant a lot to him."

Lucas shrugged.

"It was interesting; things tend to go better when you come with us."

Kayla laughed as they both looked at the wheelchair lying on the floor, the broken wheel next to it.

"I can see that."

"Don't worry; I'll fix it after the game."

Charlie, still on Lucas' lap, pressed back so he was between them and cleared his throat.

"I'm trying to watch a game here," he said.

Lucas laughed, tickling Charlie.

"Didn't anyone teach you it's rude to interrupt?" Kayla asked.

"I learned it from you! And besides, why do you care? Were you trying to kiss him?"

"Maybe," Kayla answered, looking into Lucas' eyes.

"Only if she wants me to," he answered.

She blushed and he kissed her.

"Bleh," Charlie responded making a disgusted face and moving away.

"Okay, little boy, I have to fix your wheelchair, so it's Kayla's turn to babysit."

Charlie looked at him in mock horror.

"I am *not* a baby!"

"I wouldn't say that," Kayla answered, standing up.

Charlie looked insulted.

"I am *NOT* a baby!"

Lucas handed him to Kayla and stretched. He brought the wheelchair into the kitchen for more light.

When he got into the kitchen, he laid the chair on its side and looked at it. All he had to do was spin the wheel back on slowly. After finishing, he brought it back to the living room to find that Kayla was fast asleep. Charlie, on the other hand, was looking bored.

"Can we play a game?" Charlie asked Lucas loudly.

Lucas put his finger to his lips to try to get Charlie to be quiet.

"Let me put Kayla in bed first," he whispered softly.

"Okay," Charlie whispered back.

Lucas carried her to bed, kissed her forehead, and quietly shut the door.

When he returned to the living room, Charlie was trying to change the channel with the remote, but with his CP, he couldn't hit the small buttons.

"Need help, Bud?" Lucas asked, trying not to insult him.

"Um…um…yeah…" Charlie answered, his bottom lip quivering as he tried not to cry. "Why can't I do anything by myself?"

Lucas scooped him up and hugged him.

"It's okay, I can't do some of the things you can do." Lucas said, wiping Charlie's tears off his face.

"Like what?" Charlie asked sniffling.

"Like making me laugh," Lucas said, laughing.

Lucas held Charlie for a bit, and he finally fell asleep in Lucas' arms. Setting him down gently on the couch for a moment, Lucas ran up to check on Kayla one more time. She was fast asleep.

"Goodnight, my love," he whispered quietly, kissing her on the forehead.

Lifting Charlie into his arms, Lucas carried him to the apartment and tucked him into bed. Lucas crawled into bed too, hoping Kayla would get better soon.

TWENTY-THREE

THE SEPTEMBER WEEKS WERE PASSING quickly. Muggy Florida summer days were coming to an end and the cooler beach breeze moved in to settle on the little town. Kayla seemed only to get sicker and sicker, though Lucas had tried to keep her out of the sun as much as possible. At first the migraines were only every other day, but as the third week passed, it seemed as if she had one every day. She was sick so often that she decided not to return to school. She wouldn't tell him what was wrong, but he noticed her wincing when she stood or sat or tried to pick up objects. Though she continually assured Lucas that the doctor had told her she was fine, Lucas began to wonder if she really was.

"Charlie, stop dancing in your diaper! Lay back down so I can put your pants on!" Lucas laughed as Charlie shimmied away from him.

On his knees, he swayed back and forth in only his diaper to the Sesame Street theme song.

"Charlie, put your pants on!" Kayla called from the kitchen as she basted the chicken she was cooking.

Lucas gave up and leaned back on his elbows to watch Charlie dance exuberantly along with his favorite characters.

Kayla grunted with effort as she tried to lift the large chicken to put it back in the oven.

Lucas waited, watching her wince. He tried to force himself to let her be. He knew she didn't want him to notice how weak she was becoming, but it was hard for him to watch her struggle.

With great effort, she tried to lift the pan again. Lucas was already on his feet by the time the pain overwhelmed her and she began to drop the pan. With one hand, he grabbed for it, unaware that it was hot. Lucas swore under his breath as he swiftly shoved the pan into the oven and slammed the door.

Tears streamed down Kayla's face as she wet a cloth for Lucas' hand.

"I'm sorry, it just slipped," she blubbered as she pressed the cold cloth into his hands.

"Kay, it's okay. It's just chicken," Lucas reassured, rubbing her back with his good hand.

"It's not okay, I keep dropping everything!" she cried into her hands.

He held her, waiting for her tears to stop.

"I just...I don't know what's wrong. I used to be able to do it just fine, and now my hands just feel so weak."

"It's okay, that's what I'm here for. Super Lucas! Here to rescue cooked chickens and pretty girls everywhere," Lucas put his hands on his hips and pretended to fly.

Kayla wiped her tears as a smile spread across her face.

"That's what I was waiting to see," Lucas smiled as she grinned.

He pulled her close and held her for a moment, pondering his next words. Carefully, he decided he had to ask.

"Do you think maybe you should see a doctor? I feel like this isn't just sun poisoning," Lucas suggested gently.

He felt her tense as she responded.

"I'm fine, Lucas, really. I'm just not feeling so good today."

"That's what you said yesterday, and the day before that," Lucas worried, resting his forehead against hers.

She pulled away and turned back to the stove, "I'm okay...really! Now go play with Charlie, Superman. I'll call you when the chicken's done."

Lucas hesitated for a moment. He knew she wasn't okay, but pushing the issue would only set her off. He had debated all night about what to do, but ended up settling for continuing to wait.

The three ate a late supper together and headed to bed.

Over the next couple of days, Lucas made sure to stay close by her side. He tried not to be overly helpful and upset her, but he also wanted to keep an eye on her. She slept a lot, even during the day. He was worried.

Kayla felt like the pain was attacking her whole body. She grunted, lying down on the couch.

"Lucas?" she called.

Lucas sat next to her with a cup of water. "You okay, Babe?"

"Just in a lot of pain tonight," she explained with a wince as the headache engulfed her whole head.

After she took a sip, she started sobbing from being so overwhelmed. Lucas pulled her in close so he could comfort her. He stroked her hair.

"Can I do anything for you?" he asked.

"Just don't leave me," Kayla groaned, laying her achy head on his shoulder.

"I'm here for you, and always will be," he whispered softly putting a blanket over her.

"Where's Charlie?" she asked.

"In bed, waiting to be tucked in," Lucas responded.

"Are you his PA or his father?" Kayla joked.

"Well…I love him like a…" Lucas then realized what he was going to say.

"A father?" Kayla finished his sentence for him.

"Yes," he smiled, and she grinned.

"Okay, Dad, go tend to Charlie. I'll be okay."

She rubbed Lucas' shoulder.

"Are you sure?" Lucas worried, unsure of what to do.

"Yes, positive. Go ahead," Kayla forced herself to smile, though pain coursed through her.

Lucas sighed and kissed her goodnight. The nights were the worst. He hated leaving her. His mind wandered, thinking about all her pain, as he tucked Charlie in.

"Hey, Lucas?" Charlie waved his hand in front of Lucas' face.

When Lucas didn't respond, Charlie waved harder and accidentally whacked him in the face.

Lucas jolted to reality. "Ow!" he cried, holding his nose.

"Sorry! You looked like you didn't hear me. You were acting like a zombie," Charlie accused.

Lucas rubbed his nose where Charlie had smacked him.

"I was just thinking," he defended.

"Thinking about what?" Charlie pressed as Lucas undressed him.

"Thinking about how Kayla is doing," Lucas answered tiredly.

"Why don't you just marry her? Then you can be with her all the time, and I won't have to smack you," Charlie suggested, smiling.

"Maybe," Lucas agreed as he yawned.

He dressed Charlie in his pajamas and tucked him in. Lucas then got ready for bed and climbed in next to him. He could hear the deep even breaths of Charlie's sleep.

He lay awake staring at the ceiling, Charlie's words echoing in his mind. Why had he never thought of it before? They spent so much time together, and Charlie looked to him as a father already. He could never picture himself spending his life with anyone else. He wanted to be there for her forever, and there was no better way to show her then to buy a ring, he thought.

"God, if this is right, I pray you would give me peace about this. I want to take care of Kayla and Charlie forever. I love the life you have given me. Thank you...for everything," Lucas prayed as his eyes slowly closed.

"Lucas!" Charlie sang out.

"Yes?" Lucas groaned, rolling over onto his back.

"Time for breakfast!" Charlie sang, turning his head to smile at Lucas.

"Just five more minutes," Lucas groggily rolled back over onto his side.

"Let's do something fun today," Charlie suggested, undeterred by Lucas' lack of enthusiasm.

"This *is* fun...sleep *is* fun," Lucas mumbled, lifting his arm up and pointing to himself.

Silence followed and Lucas sighed in relief, happy to get even a couple minutes more of sleep. He felt a slight warm sensation underneath him.

Charlie leaned over and stared into Lucas' face.

"I leaked," he announced.

Suddenly Lucas understood why the bed was warm.

"You peed on me!" he accused, leaping out of bed.

Pee dripped off of his side onto the floor.

"I told you I was awake! I can't hold it after I'm awake," Charlie grinned evilly.

Lucas heaved a heavy sigh.

"You love me, right?," Charlie reminded him as Lucas began to pull all the pillows and blankets off the bed.

"I do love you…but I can't say that I love all this pee," Lucas muttered under his breath as he wiped the pee off him with the dry part of the blanket.

He lifted Charlie and held him away from him at arm's length. The boy was soaked from head to toe.

"Well, we don't have a bath chair here, so you're going to have to take a big boy shower," Lucas told Charlie.

He kicked open the door of the bathroom and turned the water on. Once the water was warm enough, he put on his bathing suit and stepped into the shower with Charlie.

After they finished showering, Lucas dried him off and dressed him for the day. Lucas carried Charlie and the huge laundry basket of urine-soaked bed sheets to Kayla's.

"Morning, Babe. I have a present for you," Lucas jokingly announced as he walked in the front door.

"I don't think I'm quite in the mood for presents," Kayla rubbed her eyes sleepily.

She was still dressed in her pink pajamas with her robe wrapped tightly around her. Lucas frowned. Kayla was always up and ready before him and Charlie. She was almost never cold either, but she stood in the kitchen desperately clutching the thick robe around her as if she couldn't get warm.

Lucas tried to contain his anxiety as he calmly set Charlie down on the floor in front of the TV and turned on the Disney channel.

"I'm going to help Kayla make breakfast, okay, Bud?" Lucas ruffled Charlie's still wet hair and crossed the living room to Kayla.

"Hey, Babe, how are you?" Worry colored his tone as he held her close.

"I think I might have a fever, 'cause I'm freezing," she chattered as she pressed against Lucas.

He took off his sweatshirt and slipped it over her head. She put her arms in and he pulled it down.

"Here, sit," Lucas offered kindly.

He guided her to the couch and helped her lay down. He carefully wrapped a white furry blanket around her.

"How come you take care of me so well?" she asked, clutching the blanket tightly around herself.

"Because you took care of me first," he answered kissing her forehead.

"Now, you lay here, I'll go make breakfast." Lucas fluffed the pillow behind her.

"Okay," she agreed, snuggling deeper into the blanket.

Lucas tried to push away his anxiety, but he couldn't.

Lucas glanced back at Kayla who was still chattering underneath all the blankets. She definitely was *not* fine, he determined. But what could he do? Her stubbornness would win out over his concern – he knew that. If this went on any longer than another couple of weeks, he vowed he would take her to the doctor himself.

Lucas baked cinnamon buns and swirled most of the frosting over Charlie's when they came out of the oven. Out of the fridge, he grabbed a bottle of chocolate syrup. He waited for Kayla to protest as he prepared Charlie's plate with a huge cinnamon bun thickly coated in frosting and chocolate syrup.

But she said nothing, even when Lucas brought it into the living room to eat on the sofa.

"Yay, we're eating breakfast in the living room! Sugar breakfast!" Charlie whooped.

"Well, it's a sick day. We don't want your sister to have to force herself to make anything healthy," Lucas teased Kayla, who normally would have smacked, chased, or tackled him.

But again, she made no response and did not acknowledge Lucas' joke. She merely sat up and pushed the long sleeves of his sweatshirt back.

"Are you okay, sis?" Charlie worried as his sister watched Lucas feed him the first bite without saying a word.

"I'm alright…just tired…and really cold. Can we turn up the heat in here, Lucas?" Kayla held the warm cinnamon bun in her hand, soaking in its heat.

"Here, I'll make you some tea," Lucas offered quickly.

"Can I eat the cinnamon bun by myself?" Charlie requested, already leaning toward the messy breakfast.

"No! You just had a bath!" Lucas answered, lifting the plate away from Charlie.

"Aww," Charlie pouted, disappointed.

"Let me make your sister some tea, and I'll feed the rest to you," Lucas promised.

In the back of the cabinet, he found the cup designed to allow her hands to tuck inside the ceramic handle and get warm as hot water was poured in. He heated the water in the microwave and placed a bag of her favorite green tea in the mug.

"Here, take this," Lucas pressed the cup into her hands.

"Thanks," she responded, eagerly clutching the cup in her hands and leaning her face over the steam rising from the brim.

Lucas watched her closely while he fed Charlie. She seemed awake, but groggy still. Maybe she didn't get enough sleep last night, he reasoned.

"Charlie wants to go out today. Is it okay if I take him to the mall? That way you can rest some more?" Lucas hinted, hoping she would take the offer and rest.

He was sure, though, that she would protest.

"Okay, you guys have fun. Would you mind turning on the TV before you go? I just want to fall asleep to a movie. I hate a quiet house." She had already placed the cup on the coffee table and lay down again.

"Maybe I shouldn't leave you," Lucas reconsidered, but she was already waving him off.

"You two go! You don't need me to have fun. I just need to sleep off this headache. I'll be fine in a few hours. I'll make lunch, so don't waste money eating out," Kayla warned in her scolding tone.

Lucas smiled, relieved to hear her acting motherly again. Maybe it really was just a headache, Lucas reasoned, and cleared the dishes.

He wrapped Charlie in a coat and headed to the mall before the crowds arrived. They found a parking spot right in front of the main entrance.

At nine in the morning, the mall was empty. Only a few bored attendants glanced at them as Lucas wheeled Charlie by.

"What are we doing here, Lucas? I forgot," Charlie's brow furrowed, trying to force himself to remember their conversation from just a few minutes ago.

"I decided you were right."

Lucas wheeled Charlie in front of the jewelry store and stopped.

"I'm always right, but what about this time?" Charlie grinned.

"Charlie Maxwell, I have to ask you a very important grown up question, and you have to answer honestly." Lucas knelt in front of Charlie.

"Okay," Charlie gave him the go ahead, unsure of what Lucas would ask.

"Charlie, I would like to ask your permission to marry your sister," Lucas smiled as Charlie laughed.

"I thought for a minute you were going to ask *me* to marry you. I mean, we do sleep in the same room anyway," Charlie giggled.

Lucas threw back his head laughing at the thought.

"No silly. Remember? You told me last night to just marry her. That way, we can all be together—forever," Lucas reminded.

Charlie looked up at the tiled ceiling, his eyes scrunching as he tried hard to remember.

"Nope, that must have been God. I think I would remember saying that," Charlie responded seriously.

Lucas laughed again, shaking his head.

"It must have been, but either way, we need a ring. I've been saving part of my PA paychecks each week in case we needed something extra."

Lucas started to wheel Charlie into the store.

"Oh, I know, we can make one out of paper...and duct tape!" Charlie suggested excitedly.

"I was thinking more along the lines of a real ring, but you can make her a duct tape one, and we can fool her with that first!" Lucas suggested jokingly.

"Yes! It will be easier than looking at all of these. I don't understand why girls can't just all have the same one," Charlie sighed as the rows of rings glittered under the store lights.

"Be a good sport, and I'll take you for fro-yo afterwards," Lucas promised.

Lucas poured over the rings for an hour, but he refused help from the managers. He wanted to ensure that the ring was special, and from him, not a store suggestion. He couldn't afford much, but he knew Kayla wouldn't want something gaudy to show off. He wanted to pick something that would be meaningful to them.

"How about this one?"

Lucas requested that the manager open the case and the man held it up to show Charlie.

"Perfect! Can we go now?" Charlie asked, taking his finger out of his nose in the hope that it was time to leave.

Lucas examined it in the light.

The simple ring held one small diamond in the center but was beautiful and elegantly crafted.

"This is the one."

Lucas handed the ring back to the manager and paid for it. He had been saving up for awhile. And now he knew why.

"Would you like anything engraved on the inside?" the manager requested stiffly, offended that Lucas had not listened to any of his previous suggestions.

"Together forever," Lucas replied.

TWENTY-FOUR

THE NEXT MORNING, LUCAS WAS still asleep when Charlie got up.

"Lucas, wake up!" Charlie yelled jumping on Lucas.

Lucas moaned. "Can't you sleep in just once?"

"No, it's boring." Charlie said laughing.

Lucas got up to look in the closet for a T-shirt for himself.

"Blue or green?" Lucas asked lifting both shirts up.

"Kayla likes blue better," Charlie advised from the bed.

"Good plan," Lucas answered putting the blue shirt on.

He dressed Charlie for the day and carried him over to Kayla's house. Opening the door, they were greeted with the aroma of breakfast.

Kayla was making three of Charlie's special breakfast sandwiches in the kitchen.

Lucas pretended to fly with Charlie into the kitchen and set him in his chair.

Lucas crossed the kitchen to where Kayla stood over a skillet pushing sausage back and forth. He was happy to see her up and about.

"You're the best," Lucas said to Kayla kissing her cheek.

Kayla looked at him with her cheeks getting red as roses.

"No, I'm not...now go sit at the table while I bring the food over," Kayla said smiling.

"Okay," Lucas said grinning at Kayla's beautiful smile.

She brought over the sandwiches that had the sweetest strawberries he had ever tasted.

"What is this?" Lucas almost drooled as he bit into the strawberry-covered French toast.

"It's Charlie's recipe. He and Mom made it up when Charlie was two. The ingredients are sausage, scrambled eggs, strawberries, bananas, and strawberry cream cheese, in between two pieces of French toast.

"It's really good," Lucas complimented as juice dribbled down his chin.

Kayla got a damp towel from the kitchen and came over to him. She softly put her hand on his shoulder. He slowly looked up and all he could see was her big, brown eyes.

"You know you're beautiful, right?" Lucas asked Kayla when she was done wiping all the strawberries off his face.

She blushed again.

"Hey, I'm hungry! Can someone please feed me?" Charlie asked impatiently.

"Okay, okay," Lucas replied.

Charlie laughed the cutest laugh Lucas had ever heard.

After breakfast, Lucas showered at his apartment while Kayla watched Charlie. She tried hard to focus on the game they were playing, but her head kept swimming. The room seemed to spin and turn as she tried to focus. Her body was exhausted from making breakfast, but she didn't want Lucas to know. She knew he was worried about her, even though he hadn't said anything. He had kept particularly close to her the last couple of weeks and hardly let her do anything by herself. What would he do if he knew?

She quickly pushed the thoughts away as the door opened and Lucas waltzed into the living room. Kayla had given up on the game and was opening a bottle of nail polish as he danced past.

"What are you doing?" Kayla asked, carefully painting her left big toe.

"Nothing, just happy. Do you need help with your toes?" Lucas quickly inquired, noticing Kayla wince when she leaned over to paint her toes.

"You want to?" she asked with a hopeful voice.

"Sure," he said grabbing the pink nail polish.

"Thank you," Kayla said, laughing because the brush was tickling her toes.

"Hold still," Lucas chuckled, holding her toes tighter.

"Sorry, it tickles," Kayla said giggling.

By the time Lucas had finished painting her toes, it was lunchtime.

"You're supposed to paint my toe *nails*, not my feet," Kayla laughed, examining the pink painted streaks.

"Close enough!" Lucas shrugged, dodging her swipe at him.

"Want me to make lunch, Babe?" Lucas asked Kayla as he rubbed lotion on her feet. Kayla rolled her eyes and lifted her paint covered feet out of his grasp.

"No! A five-year-old CP kid had to teach you how to cook waffles! That's just wrong," Kayla said, slapping Lucas' chest.

"What's so wrong about that?" Lucas asked acting insulted.

"Lucas, I'm a girl. I know everything."

"You don't know what I'm going to do now," Lucas taunted.

He grinned evilly and stood up with his hands outstretched.

"Tickle her!" Charlie said jumping up and down from his kneeling position on the floor.

"NOOOO!" Kayla screamed, belly laughing.

Lucas adored her laugh. To him, it sounded like an angel singing.

"Okay, okay…uncle!"

Kayla was in tears from laughing so hard.

Lucas paused and let her catch her breath. He hovered over her, waiting until she could breathe normally.

"Please, please don't!" she begged laughing as Lucas attacked again.

"What say ye, Captain Charlie? Should we let her walk the plank instead?" Lucas' pirate voice made Kayla laugh harder though Lucas had stopped tickling her.

"Walk the plank to the kitchen! I'm starving!" Charlie commanded.

"You heard the boy, time for plank walking and sandwich making."

Lucas offered her a hand up and pulled her to her feet.

"What if I don't want to walk your plank?" Kayla stood still.

"Then it's back to the brig with ye," Lucas threatened, leaning in close and touching his forehead to hers.

"Come on, Kayla! You HAVE to walk the plank and go make sandwiches!" Charlie whined.

"You heard the boy! Off with ye!"

Lucas kissed her cheek quickly and gently pushed her toward the kitchen.

Kayla rolled her eyes and complied.

Lucas put Charlie on his lap on the couch and turned on Sesame Street.

"I would've never thought that I would be watching Sesame Street with a five year old and actually enjoy it," Lucas thought to himself as he sang along with the Elmo's World theme song.

A few minutes later, Kayla came out with two sandwiches consisting of a slice of ham, bologna, turkey, American cheese, and a pickle on the side.

"Thanks, sweetie," Lucas said, grabbing the two plates for him and Charlie.

Kayla sank heavily down on the couch. She held a damp, wet towel to her head.

Lucas looked at Kayla. Her skin was gray.

"Babe, what's wrong?" Lucas worried.

Kayla looked at him for a moment. Her body crumpled in pain.

"I'm taking you to the hospital," Lucas announced decidedly.

He quickly buckled Charlie in his wheelchair and loaded him in the van. Running back inside, he found Kayla slumped over on the couch.

"Wake up, Kayla, wake up!" Lucas shook her.

She moaned and tried to open her eyes.

"Babe, I'm going to carry you out to the car, okay?"

Lucas gently carried her to the van. He reclined the front seat and buckled the seatbelt. Starting the car, Lucas tore down the street. The speed limit meant nothing to him. All he cared about was getting Kayla to the hospital.

"9-1-1, what is your emergency?"

"I'm headed to Mercy Medical Hospital with my girlfriend. She passed out and she's breathing, but just barely. Her skin is pale and she keeps fading in and out of consciousness. I'll be at the ER in about fifteen minutes."

The operator took down more of Kayla's information and promised to inform the hospital.

The medical staff was waiting for them at the door when they arrived. Lucas sat in the waiting room and tried to entertain Charlie by letting him play apps on Lucas' phone.

Lucas and Charlie waited anxiously as the hours passed.

Finally, a nurse appeared and asked them to follow her. She brought them to Kayla, who was resting comfortably.

"What's wrong?" Lucas whispered in Kayla's ear.

"I'll tell you when we get home," Kayla answered. "They are going to discharge me in a few minutes."

Lucas tried to contain his questions as he loaded Charlie in the van. He felt like he was going to explode.

Kayla leaned heavily against the van looking more and more upset with every passing moment.

"What's wrong?" Lucas mouthed to Kayla as he pushed the button for the ramp to go up and the door to shut.

Kayla couldn't take it anymore. She fell to her knees, sobbing.

"Charlie should know too!" she cried quietly, not wanting Charlie to hear.

"Know what?" Lucas asked, rubbing her back to try to comfort her.

Continuing to sob, Kayla remained silent.

"What?" Lucas demanded, losing patience.

"If I tell you, you'll dump me!" she groaned.

Lucas wrapped his arms around her. "I would never do that."

"Really?" Kayla asked, teary-eyed.

"Of course not," Lucas insisted. "Now please tell me what's going on!"

"I…uh…there's something that I haven't told you about my child-hood…" Kayla mumbled.

"What?" Lucas asked quietly.

"When I was five, I had a brain tumor. On my tenth birthday, it was declared healed. Now it's back and I don't know how long I have. It's inoperable. I've put off starting treatment because I didn't want to tell you. The doctor doesn't even know if the treatments will work…" Kayla blurted, starting to sob again.

Lucas was in shock. What would he do without her? He'd have to take care of Charlie by himself, he thought, a tear rolling down his cheek. He felt like someone had thrown him off a ship and into icy cold waters. Lucas clutched his chest as if his heart would explode. He took a deep breath.

"Let's just get in the car, and we'll talk about it at home, okay?" Lucas encouraged, glancing around at the people in the parking lot who were beginning to stare.

Kayla nodded and let Lucas help her into the van.

They traveled home in complete silence. It was as if even Charlie sensed that something was wrong.

Finally, they arrived at home. Lucas felt like the drive had taken forever. He didn't recall the ride being that long ever before. As soon as he had parked, Kayla ran inside sobbing while Lucas unloaded Charlie.

"Why is Kayla so upset?" Charlie asked curiously.

Lucas paused. How could he explain this to a five-year-old kid? He knelt next to the wheelchair so that he could be eye to eye with Charlie.

"First of all, I love you. You know that, right?" Lucas asked Charlie, trying to hold back the tears by squinting.

"Yeah," Charlie responded, wondering why Lucas was so serious.

"I'll tell him inside, Lucas," Kayla insisted from the front porch.

Lucas got Charlie into the house and sat him down on the couch.

Kayla slowly sat down next to Charlie as Lucas sat on the other side of him. She put her hand on Charlie's and held it for a minute in silence.

"Charlie, you know how, when you get sick, Lucas or I go to the pharmacy and pick up medicine, and you get better the next day?" Kayla asked Charlie, putting him on her lap.

"Yup," Charlie answered as he was playing with her hair.

"Well, I'm sick, and I won't be getting better," Kayla said to Charlie, putting her fingers through his hair.

Charlie had a puzzled look on his face. "What do you mean?"

"I'm going to die soon," Kayla said firmly.

Charlie's little body tensed as he began to cry.

Kayla helped him onto the floor and lay down next to him to hold him for a bit.

"Don't worry...Lucas will take good care of you," Kayla assured Charlie, looking up at Lucas.

Lucas knew what she wanted.

"I will," Lucas promised.

"Just don't eat too much candy," Kayla demanded, smiling and trying to make Charlie laugh.

It worked for a minute or two, but the five-year-old's cute smile soon dissolved.

"I'll get something to eat," Lucas said getting out of the chair while Kayla continued to hold Charlie to calm him.

Kayla tried to think what she could do to calm him down. S'mores! They could make s'mores! She went into the pantry and came out with marshmallows, chocolate, graham crackers, and a candle.

"Let's have a little party on the porch!"

Trying hard to pretend to be upbeat, Kayla carried Charlie to the porch. She lit the candle, hoping it would cheer Charlie up.

"Lucas?" Kayla called.

"Yeah?" he yelled back from the kitchen.

"We're having s'mores for dinner."

"What?" Lucas asked, dropping the plate he held in his hand.

"Yup!" Kayla exclaimed as both Kayla and Charlie heard a crashing noise.

"Oops," Lucas said to himself quietly.

"*LUCAS?*" Kayla shouted, running to the kitchen.

Lucas was already bending down to clean up the mess when she got there.

"It's okay, Babe, it was just a plate," Lucas reassured her.

"Are you hurt?" she fretted.

He laughed, "No, but I broke all your other man-eating plates. This was the last one."

She half smiled and smacked him. "Don't make fun of me. I was scared you were hurt."

He stood and dumped the dustpan of glass into the garbage. He moved the broom aside and took her in his arms.

"The only thing that can hurt me is to know that you're hurting," he whispered holding her tightly.

A high-pitched wail stopped both their hearts as they remembered Charlie was on the porch.

Kayla ran out first but Lucas was right behind her. Kayla's mouth opened in shock as she saw orange flames beginning to spread from the candle tipped over on its side.

"Lucas!" she yelled just as he came up behind her and saw the flames.

Charlie had fallen to the last step of the porch, crying and calling for Lucas.

Lucas didn't waste any time. He jumped over the growing flames and picked up Charlie from the ground, setting him on the lawn far away from the fire. Kayla ran to stay with Charlie while Lucas went to get the garden hose. Turning it on, he walked up the porch steps swinging it from side to side. The flames quickly went out. All that remained was black streaks revealing the destructive path the fire would have taken.

Lucas dropped the hose and went to Charlie who was lying in the grass still whimpering. Lucas picked him up and held him close.

"It's okay, the fire's out. It can't hurt you now," he soothed as Charlie clung to his shirt.

He carried him back up the steps and Kayla followed. She didn't notice the puddle where Lucas had just put the fire out, and she lost her balance. Lucas quickly put his free hand out and caught her.

"Thanks, Superman," she said as he pulled her close.

"Anytime," he replied grinning.

He set her back on her feet without letting go of her waist.

"Let go!" She teased, attempting to get away. His arm was iron strong around her.

"Come on," she laughed before giving in.

"Nope," he said, pulling her closer. She gave in and looked up at him.

"I love you," Kayla whispered, leaning in to kiss him.

He kissed her and smiled.

"Okay, you can go," he said.

"Nope," she responded, gazing into his blue eyes.

"I'm sorry," Charlie whimpered, interrupting them. "I didn't mean to start a fire; I just wanted to move the candle away from me. I was worried I would catch fire."

Kayla let go of Lucas and took Charlie into her arms.

"It's okay, what matters is that you're safe," she said, carrying him into the house.

Lucas and Charlie watched a cartoon while Kayla heated up leftovers in the microwave, deciding to save the s'mores for another time.

They ate dinner and watched a marathon of Barney until Charlie was calmed down enough to sleep.

"Come on, Little Buddy, time for bed," Lucas said, as Charlie's eyes were closing.

Charlie let Lucas pick him up without protest.

"I'll turn the lights off and lock the doors when you guys leave," Kayla said quietly, and got up from the couch.

The words they couldn't say hung between them, pressing heavily on them.

Lucas hugged and kissed her goodnight.

He carried Charlie to the apartment and tucked him in. He himself got ready for bed about fifteen minutes later. He lay in bed for about five minutes before he drifted off to sleep.

TWENTY-FIVE

LUCAS WOKE UP WITH A start around two in the morning. Unsure of what woke him, he sat up. He was just about to go back to sleep when he heard Kayla crying on the video monitor. Carefully, he pushed back the covers and climbed over Charlie. He put on a pair of sweats and a shirt and tiptoed across the yard to the house.

Quiet worship music was softly playing in the living room. Lucas' heart broke as he listened to his beautiful love crying out to God for her life.

"I can't do this, God," she whispered desperately, beginning to sob.

He knocked quietly on the door. Her light footsteps tread quickly across the floor and she let him in. He entered and shut the door as she collapsed on the floor again by the couch. Lucas went to her side and knelt beside her. He touched her back gently and she leaned into his shoulder.

He wrapped his arms around her. Her tears fell on his shirt as he rocked her and prayed. It was clear that she had been down there for a while. He let his prayers drift over her as he held her close. Fifteen minutes later, she was fast asleep.

"God, why this, why now?" Lucas demanded, tears pouring from his eyes.

It didn't seem fair; they had suffered so much already. How could God allow her to have cancer too?

"I don't understand, God, but You have gotten us this far. You brought me out of the darkest place in my life and I believe You can pull us through this one. Just please don't let her suffer, Father," Lucas cried out into the silence.

For a few moments more, he held her there until he was sure she was asleep. He turned off the music and delivered her to bed. Lovingly, he tucked the blankets in around her and put her cell phone next to her head in case she needed him.

With one last prayer, he turned out the lights, locked up, and walked back to his apartment, going straight to bed.

When he hopped into bed, he noticed Charlie tossing and turning.

"Another nightmare," he thought to himself, putting his arm around Charlie to comfort him because he knew Charlie would wake up crying.

Sure enough, thirty seconds later, Charlie woke up crying.

Lucas pulled Charlie closer. "I'm here. It's okay."

Charlie rolled over, accepting his comfort and quickly fell back to sleep.

Lucas, on the other hand, had trouble falling asleep. He read his Bible and prayed for a while. It felt like hours until he finally fell asleep, shortly before morning.

He woke up to Charlie jumping on him, giggling.

"Of course you want to get up this early," Lucas mumbled, wiping the sleep from his bleary eyes.

He rolled out of bed and searched in the closet for some clothes for both of them. They got dressed, and he wheeled Charlie to Kayla's for breakfast. Unlocking the door with his key, they slipped in.

The lights were still off from when he had turned them off the night before. It looked as if Kayla hadn't stirred. Lucas swallowed hard as he stepped over the place where she had lay sobbing just a few hours before. He had to put on a brave face for Charlie.

"What will Sleeping Beauty want for breakfast, do you think?" Lucas mumbled to Charlie, laughing.

"Gee, I don't know. It changes every day," Charlie said giggling.

"Well, let's start making a pattern," Lucas said exaggeratingly serious.

"We should," Charlie laughed bouncing in his chair.

"Calm down! You'll break your chair again. It was hard enough to fix it once! I really don't want to fix it again," Lucas said, getting out pancake mix and starting the stove.

"Why not? It was really fun last time!"

"For who?"

"Me, of course," Charlie said reaching over for a knife on the table.

"Oh no, no, no!" Lucas chanted running over to Charlie and quickly grabbing the knife from his hand.

"Why not?" Charlie asked trying to look like he was crying.

"I don't want you to accidentally stab yourself," Lucas laughed rolling his eyes.

Abruptly, he stopped laughing as Kayla's door creaked open. Kayla shuffled into the kitchen with her dark hair curlier than ever. Lucas had to admit that she was more beautiful without makeup.

Kayla saw Lucas and Charlie fighting about something but didn't know what.

"Charlie, listen to Lucas," Kayla said walking to the table and not even looking at them.

"How did you know what I was doing?" Charlie asked Kayla.

"Because I'm a woman. I know everything," Kayla remarked.

"Whatever," Charlie said rolling his eyes as Lucas brought the food over.

"Finally! I'm starving!" Charlie said dramatically.

"Yeah, yeah, yeah, whatever…" Lucas said rolling his eyes as he put the plates on the table.

Lucas sat down at the table to cut up the pancakes so it was easier to feed Charlie.

"Don't kill me with that fork!" Charlie said laughing, backing away from the fork coming toward his mouth.

"Just eat the food," Lucas said jokingly, cramming pancake into Charlie's mouth.

"Yes, *Father*," Charlie said laughing as pancakes spilled out of his mouth.

"Someday, when we have kids, will you spoil them too, Lucas?" Kayla smiled.

"Maybe, maybe not," Lucas responded as he kissed her. "New perfume?" Lucas asked as he gave Charlie another bite.

Kayla blushed. "You like it?"

Lucas lightly pushed her hair behind her ear.

"I love it," he said with his sweet smile kissing her again.

"Gag!" Charlie yelled putting his pointer finger down his throat.

"You know, when you find a girl when you're older, …" Kayla paused. "I'll be gone by then," she thought to herself.

"… Lucas will make fun of you!," she rephrased so she wouldn't upset Charlie.

Lucas knew she was about to cry. He stood up and walked over to her, putting his arms around her.

Kayla dug her face in Lucas' shirt so Charlie wouldn't see any of her tears. After a minute or two, she backed away from Lucas and ran to her room.

"How about we go to our place so I can pick out a new shirt?" Lucas tried to cover, looking at his tear-streaked shirt.

"Yeah!" Charlie happily yelled, reaching his arms to grasp Lucas' neck.

After a shirt change, the two boys went back to the house and into the kitchen where Kayla was washing some dishes.

Lucas parked Charlie and his wheelchair in the doorway and walked over to help her. They had their backs to Charlie so he wouldn't notice anything unusual.

"Are you okay?" Lucas mumbled in Kayla's ear.

"Yeah, just in a lot of pain," she said wiping a tear from her eye before it rolled down her cheek. The tears kept wanting to drop, but Lucas stood there just wiping them away with his thumbs, trying to think of how he could possibly comfort her.

After a while, he decided just to hold her.

"Why do you love me? I'm the ugliest seventeen-year-old ever! " Kayla whispered looking at her reflection in the kitchen window.

Lucas grabbed her arm and drew her close.

"Now look at me!" he sternly whispered back, gently turning her face toward him so they were eye to eye...

"You're still beautiful to me, and you always will be," he said softly and leaned into kiss her.

The kiss was more meaningful for Lucas this time. How much longer would he be able to do that?

"I love you so much," Kayla whispered, slowly combing Lucas' smooth, brown hair with her fingers.

Lucas felt a tear run down his cheek. It felt like all the memories he had with her were in that tear, and soon it would drop to the floor and disappear.

"I have to be strong in the Lord, and trust Him now," he thought to himself, holding her closer.

That night, Lucas decided to take them out for dinner at Friendly's. The night was damp and chilly. Lucas bundled up Charlie, and everyone piled into the van.

When they got to the restaurant, they had to wait for half an hour in a line that snaked outside. The wind felt brisk on Kayla's skin. She shivered and her teeth chattered. Noticing her chill, Lucas unzipped his jacket and quickly took it off, wrapping it around her. "Thanks, but won't you be cold?" Kayla asked, concerned.

"As long as you're comfortable, I'm happy," Lucas answered, smiling.

"Thank you," she replied.

When they were finally seated, Lucas noticed one of his mom's boyfriends in a nearby booth. Of course, he was with another woman.

In his old life, if anyone had asked Lucas about all of his mother's boyfriends, he would have responded bitterly. Although one of them was nice, most of them abused Lucas. But now, as he noticed the man in the booth, the bitterness wasn't there. God was healing his heart.

Lucas was thankful that he had met Kayla and Charlie and that his life wasn't like that anymore.

They ordered their food. Finally, after a while, the waitress showed up with their order.

Charlie spotted green beans on his plate. He gazed at the beans and whined. "Do I have to eat those?"

"Of course not, they're gross," Lucas laughed. He started scraping the beans off his plate.

"No way, Charlie! You need to eat at least some of those beans!"

"Poor kid. You shouldn't make him eat those," Lucas whispered.

"Thank you, Lucas," Charlie said, happy that Lucas agreed with him.

Kayla rolled her eyes. "What am I gonna do with you two?" "Just hide them in his potatoes!"

Lucas smiled, gave her a loving kiss, and then leaned back.

"Do you two ever *not* kiss?" Charlie asked rolling his eyes.

"Hey, if you can wake me up at six every morning, I can kiss your sis once in a while," Lucas retorted, still lost in Kayla's sparkly, brown eyes.

Before they left, they looked out the restaurant window. It was raining pretty hard. They raced for the van as quickly as possible.

By the time they got home, the rain had turned into a huge thunderstorm.

Just as Lucas put him on the floor, he noticed Charlie was trembling and then started crying.

"What's wrong with Charlie?" Lucas asked Kayla in the kitchen.

"He's afraid of thunder," Kayla said rubbing her head to try to relieve the headache.

Lucas thought for a minute. He had a perfect idea.

"S'mores!" he yelled out as he raced to the pantry.

"Yay!" Charlie yelled as he immediately stopped crying.

"Okay, but no fires," Kayla warned.

"It wasn't MY fault! You put the candles too close to me, remember?" Charlie responded.

"He does have a point," Lucas answered, coming out of the pantry with the marshmallows.

Kayla smiled. "Oh, so it's all MY fault, huh? Lucas, you're supposed to be on my side!"

"Well, you know, sometimes we boys have to stick together," Lucas said walking closer to Charlie.

"Guess you boys won't be getting any chocolate then." She pulled the candy from behind her back.

Lucas grinned. "Oh yeah?"

She started to back toward the door as Lucas picked up Charlie.

"Get her!" Charlie yelled throwing a fist in the air.

Lucas held Charlie tightly, and Kayla squealed and ran for the door. Lucas chased her out onto the porch.

"Hand it over, and no one gets wet," Lucas smiled, reaching for the chocolate.

"Oh you think I'm going to give in that easily?"

"Wouldn't want your clothes dirty," Lucas responded. "Hand it over."

He stepped toward her, and she took off laughing into the pouring rain, the thunderstorm having passed.

"After her!" Charlie screamed.

Lucas tried to hold Charlie and run, but he couldn't catch Kayla.

"You get her, I'll wait here. We have to have the chocolate!" Charlie yelled.

Lucas raced him back to the porch.

Kayla stood a few feet away. "What's the matter, boys? Wow, this chocolate is delicious!"

She took a bite and waved it.

Lucas set Charlie down, and Kayla took off running again. He gave her a head start and then burst into a run. He caught up easily, but slowed down to gently grab her.

"Gotcha!" he announced triumphantly, pulling her close to him.

"Okay, okay, you win," she said laughing.

He reached for the chocolate.

"Just kidding," she giggled clutching it in her hands.

He wrapped his arms around her and buried his face in her rain-soaked hair. He liked the way she smelled in the rain.

"Give it to me," he whispered persuasively.

"Nope," she smiled.

He let her go, and she turned to face him.

"Give up?" she questioned, her eyes lighting with mischief.

"I didn't want to hurt you." He touched her cheek.

She looked up into his deep blue eyes and smiled widely.

"I love you Lucas Josiah," she whispered as he leaned in close.

"I love you too."

The rain drizzled down Lucas' face from his hair. He kissed her gently and put his forehead on hers.

She smiled and opened her mouth to say something sweet just as he grabbed the chocolate out of her hands.

"I win!" he shouted holding them up for a cheering Charlie to see.

He leaned down and lifted Kayla over his shoulder. Laughing, she pounded his back as he carried her over to Charlie.

"What should we do with the prisoner?" he asked Charlie.

"Not kiss her anymore!" Charlie giggled.

"It's not supposed to be a punishment for me," Lucas laughed setting Kayla on her feet.

"Maybe it should be," she answered reaching out to smack him.

He dodged and pretended to look horrified.

"Please, please, I'll do anything," he pretended to plead.

"Kiss me again and I'll think about it." She crossed her arms, smiling.

"As you wish, Princess." He leaned down and she uncrossed her arms.

He wrapped his arms around her and lifted her off her feet so she could reach him. She draped her arms around his neck.

Charlie covered his eyes. "That's not a good punishment for chocolate stealers!"

They ignored him.

Lucas liked how soft her skin felt in the rain.

"Better?" he asked, smiling.

"Much better," she whispered putting her nose on his cheek.

He held her there for a moment, letting the rain wash away their fears. For now, she was his. He knew he would lock up these moments forever in his heart - even after forever stopped. Tears filled his eyes as he laid his head on her shoulder.

"You're so beautiful," he whispered in her ear.

"I'm not going anywhere yet, Lucas. We still have now. We still have today," she whispered, knowing what was going through his mind.

He nodded, leaning down to set her on her feet. She ran her fingers through his wet hair and rested a hand on his cheek. He took her hand, and they turned to face Charlie who looked irritated.

"Can we get to the fun part now?"

Kayla laughed and wiped her tears. "Sure, we can."

They went back inside and changed their clothes.

Lucas let Kayla wear his sweatshirt while they all sat by the candle in the kitchen and ate their s'mores.

Lucas put Charlie to bed in the spare room so he and Kayla could hang out a while at the house.

He returned to the living room to find Kayla stretched out on the couch.

"How are you?" Lucas tenderly asked as he sat on the couch right by her feet.

"I have a migraine. I think I need that pain medicine the doctor gave me," Kayla moaned, blocking the light from the ceiling above her.

Lucas dimmed the lights for her.

"Are you hungry, Babe? You haven't much today." Lucas knelt next to her and rubbed her forehead soothingly.

"No, I can't, I feel sick."

"Maybe you should eat something more," he insisted.

She shook her head in response as her eyes fluttered closed.

"You're burning up," Lucas noted with concern.

"Really? I'm freezing," she shuddered as a chill ran through her.

"I'll get you a blanket. I'll make some soup that I want you to try, okay?"

Lucas kissed her forehead and left her side. He jogged up the stairs and grabbed a couple of blankets from the closet, and the pain medicine from the medicine cabinet. He carried the blankets downstairs and threw them on the floor by the couch.

The soup he had put on to simmer earlier was dangerously close to bubbling over as he quickly turned the heat down under it. Spooning a small amount of soup into a bowl for her, he wondered if he should call Dr. Beeoko. The clock on the microwave read eleven-thirty. It was much too late to call him, but Lucas wouldn't leave without knowing she was okay.

He brought everything into the living room and set it on the coffee table.

"Come on, Babe, I'll fire up the gas fireplace for you," Lucas cajoled her.

Despite her protests, he lifted her into his arms and carried her over to the fireplace. He carefully placed her on the blanket he had spread out and sat behind her to support her. As she lay against him, he reached behind them and took the bowl and medicine off the coffee table. Her shivering slowed as the warmth of the low fire enveloped them.

"Better?" he questioned as she rested her head on his chest.

"Yes, thanks," she whispered.

"Good. Now eat," he requested firmly.

"You're so pushy," she complained.

"Mm-hmm," he agreed pushing the bowl toward her, smiling.

She sighed.

"Please? I made it myself," he pleaded as he laid his head on top of hers and wrapped his arms around her.

"You didn't even burn the house down. I'm proud of you."

"Please, I can cook," Lucas retorted.

"This is out of a can, isn't it?"

"Maybe, but it took a lot of work to get the can open and put it in the pan and turn the stove on. I even put water in it. So you should appreciate it, Ms. Stubborn."

"I do appreciate it," Kayla responded sincerely, turning her face up towards his.

"Good. Now eat," he kissed her lightly and held the bowl up for her.

Lucas grinned. Kayla finally relented and took the bowl from him. He waited patiently for her as she sipped it.

"Here, take these also." He handed her the pain medication.

"Are these the pills you kill me with so you don't have to listen to my whining?" she questioned, her brow raised.

"No, these are the pills Charlie gave me to kill you so he can have me all to himself."

"Oh, I see. Well, anything to make him happy."

Kayla took the pills with the drink of water Lucas provided.

"Seeing you better would make him happiest," Lucas whispered, holding her tighter as she put the empty bowl back on the floor.

"I wish I could give him that."

Kayla snuggled closer to Lucas and he tucked the blanket tighter around her.

"We will get through this," Lucas promised as he ran his fingers through her hair.

"I hope so," she whispered, fighting back tears.

"We will," Lucas encouraged, pulling her closer as the tears spilled over.

"What if we can't? What if..."

"Don't! Don't say it," Lucas interrupted.

He couldn't bear to hear the words she was about to say next.

"I'm serious, Lucas. What if I don't make it? What if I can't hold on?"

Lucas clamped a firm hand over her mouth.

"Don't say it again," Lucas reprimanded.

Kayla shoved his hand away and struggled to her feet. Lucas stood and tried to pull her into his arms.

"Babe, I'm sorry, it's just I…"

"No, Lucas. You didn't hear the doctor. The treatments may not work. I could really die. I'll be dead, gone, not here – I won't be alive to see Charlie grow up or to get married. Everything could be over!"

Pain ripped through Lucas. Her words cut through him like a knife. Kayla burst into tears, but Lucas couldn't find the strength to comfort her. The pain of hearing the words out loud was too much to bear.

He bolted upstairs and delicately but quickly picked Charlie up and ran out the door. Lucas didn't stop running until he reached the apartment.

"I didn't say goodnight to Kayla," Charlie mumbled groggily as Lucas laid him in his bed.

"I'm sorry, Bud. You can tell her how much you love her tomorrow."

"What if she won't be there tomorrow?" Charlie looked up at Lucas, fear written on his face.

"She will be," Lucas choked, pulling up Charlie's blankets.

"She will be," he whispered to himself as he collapsed on the floor of the living room and sobbed.

TWENTY-SIX

KAYLA JOLTED AWAKE FROM WHERE she had collapsed in the living room when Lucas had run out. Her heart was broken in a million pieces thinking about Lucas, Charlie, and the life they might now have to live without her.

"Let's just get it over with now!" she shrieked.

She stumbled into the kitchen and ripped open the knife drawer, reaching in for the sharpest knife she could find.

Now hysterical, she put the knife to her wrist, beginning to pierce her skin.

Her extreme distress quickly woke Lucas as the video cam echoed her cries.

Lucas dashed to the house, knowing he could hear Charlie on the baby monitor if he awoke.

"Kayla?" Lucas' firm voice filled the whole house.

The kitchen lights lit the dark. Horrified, Lucas watched as Kayla dropped a bloody knife onto the counter. He tore across the kitchen and locked his arms around her waist, trapping her arms at her sides.

"Let me go!" she bawled, as tears streamed down her face.

"Don't!" Lucas said firmly, carrying her away from the knife.

He pulled her down on the kitchen floor with him and held her tightly.

Blood began trickle down her arm. Lucas quickly took off his sweatshirt to wrap the cut on her wrist. All he cared about was saving her.

"Why?" she sobbed, finally giving in and slouching against the cabinets.

Lucas relaxed his hold as she collapsed.

"Because Charlie and I love you so much," he soothed, pushing back the few bangs covering her moist eyes. "God has a plan for you here on Earth, and it's not suicide," Lucas whispered comfortingly, as he held her on the floor.

He tried not to shake as he thought of what could have happened if he hadn't come.

"I'm just a burden on you," she cried, trying to take a deep breath.

"You are not a burden, Kayla Rose Maxwell," he reprimanded.

"I'm so sorry!" she wailed.

"It's okay," he quieted her as she sobbed into his sweatshirt.

Lucas glanced up at the counter. The bloody knife lay where she had dropped it. He tried hard not to throw up as his stomach churned.

"Let's go into the living room and sit, okay?" he suggested, desperately trying to get her out of the room.

She nodded.

He stood and carried her into the living room, placing her on the couch as he grabbed a blanket and draped it around her shoulders.

She laid her head on his chest, breathing in his scent. The smell of him brought back so many memories from the past year. The pain of all that she had been through had hit her hard, but Lucas was always there to help heal it. She wished she hadn't had to go through all the pain, but erasing all of it would erase all the good memories, too.

She looked up into Lucas' big blue eyes as he watched her anxiously. She knew then she wouldn't trade those memories for anything. Her whole life had been filled with pain. Between her mom dying, Charlie's difficult disability, her father's murder, and finding out about a new tumor, Kayla felt as though her world had come to an end.

God had always been faithful to carry her through, but it was as if God knew she couldn't do the rest of it alone. She knew He sent her Lucas to help her get through, and she couldn't believe that, in a moment, she had almost ruined all of it.

"You okay?" he asked the trembling girl.

All she could do was nod to him.

He pressed her head close to his chest and kissed her hair.

"Jesus, help her," he prayed, choking back tears as he replayed the scene of finding her.

Peace filled Kayla as she heard Lucas' whispered prayer. God had come to rescue her again. Her desire to die began to disappear as it was replaced with God's love once more.

Lucas felt her ragged breaths begin to slow as she calmed. Her eyes were fluttering closed.

"Will you be okay if I go back with Charlie?" Lucas asked.

Again, all she could do was nod. She was asleep before he could say anything else. Quietly, he crept into the bathroom and found gauze and bandages.

While she slept, he unwrapped the sweatshirt and examined the wound. It hadn't been very deep, he sighed in relief. But it was jagged and still sluggishly bleeding.

He wrapped it in a bandage and swathed it in gauze. Lucas wondered if he should bring Charlie over to sleep so she would not have to be alone, but it would be horrible for Charlie to see Kayla like this.

Lucas set up the video cam and slipped quietly out the door. He knew that for the rest of his life, he would never forget the memory of almost being too late to save his best friend. He determined to watch her more closely.

The next morning, Lucas was overwhelmed by guilt for how horrific he had been to Kayla the night before. He felt responsible for pushing her over the edge.

"Lucas?" he heard Charlie mumble as he woke up.

"Yeah, Buddy?" he answered crawling on the bed closer to Charlie.

"Can I get up now?"

"Of course, Bud." Lucas grinned, kneeling over him. "We need to see Kayla right away this morning."

Charlie looked anxious. "Are you guys fighting?"

"Of course not, Buddy," he picked up Charlie. "But even people who love each other argue sometimes."

"But if you love each other, why do you argue?"

"Because we love each other."

"So…you don't love me?" Charlie began to cry.

"No, Buddy. I do love you, but in a brotherly way," Lucas reassured him as he held Charlie in his arms.

They got ready and headed to the house. They found Kayla sobbing at the table. Lucas tenderly put his hand on her shoulder.

"I'm sorry." Lucas quietly apologized.

Kayla looked up at him red-eyed.

"I'm sorry, too," she answered, moving in close to him."

He drew her to his chest and held her tight. "This is going to be a long road, Kayla, but I am going to walk it with you. You will never be alone in this. I love you."

"I love you, too, Lucas," tears began to fill her eyes again as she pressed her cheek against his shirt. She could feel his muscles tense as he drew back.

"Promise me, Kayla, that you will fight. If you give up, like you tried to last night, your heart will die long before your body, and I can't bear that. Promise me!" Lucas gripped her shoulders with a fierce intensity.

"I'll try, but I'm scared, Lucas…I'm terrified," Kayla confessed, clasping onto his shirt with her fists.

"I'm scared too, Baby, but we'll get through this, together." Lucas' voice dropped to a hoarse whisper as he struggled to control the conflicting emotions in his heart.

"Forever," she agreed as he pulled her close again.

The ring in his pocket felt like it was burning with the words he had engraved inside the band. Would he ever be able to give it to her?

TWENTY-SEVEN

THE NEXT FEW WEEKS WERE a haze for Lucas. When Kayla wasn't at the hospital doing chemo, they tried to forget that she was sick, but they couldn't. She tried hard not to be irritated with him for keeping her so close all the time, but he knew she was. They tried to keep things normal – fun even – when their time wasn't taken up by hospital visits.

Lucas knew he had to keep things happy for Charlie. They couldn't give up! Instead, he tried to keep them all busy.

Between hospital visits, they went to the park, had picnics, spent long nights out at the campfire, and when he could think of nothing else to numb his mind, he went out and worked on making a railing for the tree house.

Kayla was terrified, but she tried not to show it. Her symptoms kept worsening, even though she was receiving treatment. She wasn't sure how long she could keep Lucas from knowing how bad it really was. She played along, trying to forget, but she knew that neither of them could.

Lucas thought more and more about Charlie's suggestion to ask Kayla to marry him. He wanted them to be together as long as they could, and in every way they could. He couldn't bear the thought of her never having a wedding day.

It was now or never, he decided.

"Babe? You awake?"

Kayla heard Lucas call her, and she opened her eyes. Sunlight streamed in through the window and he sat on the bed.

"Now I am," she mumbled, rubbing her eyes.

He laughed gently. "Good, I have something I want to show you."

He pulled back the covers and she shivered.

"Let me guess, you spilled something on the kitchen floor and you want me to clean it up," she mumbled, rolling over.

He leaned down and kissed her on the forehead. "Nope, come on."

He reached down and scooped her into his arms. Curling into his body for warmth, she let him carry her outside.

She squinted in the fading sunlight.

"Why are we outside?" she wondered.

Lucas just smiled. "You'll see."

She laid her head on his chest and closed her eyes.

As they came over the hill, he nodded to Charlie who was kneeling on a blanket in the gazebo.

"Surprise!" Charlie yelled excitedly.

The gazebo was decorated in pretty shells that formed the shape of a heart.

"Why is Charlie so excited?" she asked, lifting her head.

He laughed and carried her into the gazebo at the center of the heart. Gently, he set her on her feet. Still sick from the hospital, she stumbled slightly; he caught her before she collapsed and helped her sit.

Lucas took her hand.

"First of all, I love you."

"Babe, I know – you tell me twenty-four seven," she laughed.

"No, I mean it, I want to spend the rest of my life with you," he said as he knelt down on one knee.

Kayla eyes widened.

Charlie squealed in excitement as Lucas carefully lifted a small basket from the floor onto his knee. He opened the top of the basket and handed it to Kayla.

As she opened it, she saw the bright blue, yellow, and red butterflies fly out of the basket. She smiled as they flew around the gazebo,

"Lucas…" she started to say, awed.

She peeked into the box.

"Go ahead," Charlie encouraged, trying hard not to giggle nervously.

"What is this?" Kayla asked curiously as she pulled out a small oval ring made of duct tape and string.

"Will you be my sister forever?" Charlie asked, laughing as Kayla hugged her little brother.

Lucas chuckled, and took her hand in his.

She caught her breath as Lucas reached deeper in and pulled out the ring. He showed her the writing on the inside and tears filled her eyes.

"Kayla Rose Maxwell…"

He called her by her full name and she turned bright red as he turned his full attention on her. His deep blue eyes held her gaze as he spoke carefully.

"Will you marry me?"

Charlie yelled in excitement as Kayla tackled him to the ground, kissing him.

"I'm guessing that's a yes?" Lucas chuckled.

"Yes!" she laughed.

"Kayla?" Charlie asked with a scared look on his face.

"Yeah?" Kayla asked wiping away her tears of joy.

"Will you still take care of me?" Charlie asked, preparing himself not to cry.

Lucas rolled his eyes and chuckled.

"Of course we'll take care of you!" Kayla laughed, combing his hair with her fingers.

"On one condition," Lucas firmly interrupted.

Charlie looked a little scared. "What?"

"Would you be my best man?"

Kayla added to that, "Would you also walk me down the aisle?"

Charlie thought about it. "Can you *wheel* me down the aisle?"

"Of course," Kayla chuckled.

"We need to get you a tux. Would you mind if it matched mine?" Lucas asked getting to his feet and putting Charlie on his shoulders.

"Sure, but what's a tux?"

"It's like a suit you wear for Easter," Kayla answered, looking up at Charlie as Lucas helped her to her feet.

"Okay!"

They began to walk back.

Kayla's heart felt heavy. She had always envisioned her life to be so much different than this. She wanted to spend forever with Lucas, and her forever was turning out to be much shorter then she thought.

As if he could read her mind, Lucas slipped his arm around her and pulled her in close. She knew the road ahead would be a long one, but with Lucas, she felt as if she could do anything.

The next couple of weeks were spent discussing the wedding and doing fun things. Even the discomfort of chemo couldn't dull her excitement, and it seemed to make everything happy again. For awhile at least.

TWENTY-EIGHT

After another late night, Lucas and Charlie slept in until late morning. As usual, Charlie woke up first and hopped onto Lucas to wake him up. Lucas rolled over and put the pillow over his head.

"Nooooo!! Go back to sleep!" he groaned.

Charlie scooted closer and pulled the pillow off of his head. Lucas had already fallen back to sleep. Charlie passed gas really loudly and tried hard not to laugh. It was loud enough for Kayla to hear him as she pushed open the door to the apartment and let herself in.

"Charlie!" she scolded from the hall.

"Ugh, Charlie," Lucas said covering his nose with his blanket.

"That's for not getting up. Come on, I want to go to the beach!" Charlie whined dramatically.

Lucas glared at him, clearly not pleased at how Charlie woke him up.

"We were just there last night." Kayla sighed in exhaustion.

"I have an idea, let's play hide and go *sleep*," Lucas said, his nose still under the blanket muffling his voice.

"Nope," Charlie exclaimed, pulling the blanket off.

"Pleeease!" Lucas begged, burying his face in the sheets.

Kayla leaned over to open the window next to them.

"Let's get some fresh air in here," she said, trying not to breathe.

"What did we feed you last night?" Lucas moaned.

Kayla waved her arms since the smell still lingered.

Charlie burst into fits of laughter. "Now I know exactly how to wake you up!"

"Sometimes, Charlie, you drive me crazy," Lucas mumbled as he burrowed under the blankets.

Charlie smiled.

"Well, it is a nice day to go swimming. I guess we have been to the lake a lot these last couple of days. You really want to go to the beach?"

"If I didn't want to, why would I ask you?" Charlie said sarcastically.

Lucas grabbed Charlie and tickled him.

"You better watch that attitude or I'm going to tickle it out of you," he laughed.

"That'll never work! You know I'm not ticklish!" Charlie said between breaths.

"Really, Charlie? I've known you for almost a year now," Lucas teased.

"Are we tickling Charlie?" Kayla grinned evilly.

"No, we're going to the beach!" Charlie yelled as Lucas stopped tickling to let him speak.

"Hmmm, I like this better," she said jumping onto the bed.

"No!"

Charlie laughed and tried to get away, but Kayla had him around the waist.

"Hey, don't tickle my beach buddy," Lucas grinned, grabbing a pillow.

"He's my brother," Kayla said, pulling Charlie closer. "I can do whatever I want."

She pretended to trap Charlie, trying not to wince as his wild arms and legs hit her side.

Lucas noticed almost immediately, and picked Charlie up.

"We have to do Kayla's chemo first, and then we can go to the beach, okay?" Lucas informed Charlie, whose little face fell ever so slightly.

"We could skip the chemo," Kayla offered.

She hated being the reason Charlie's enthusiasm was dulled.

"No, we have to go to the hospital, Kayla. You can't just cancel last-minute," Lucas chided, touching her shoulder.

She looked up at him pleadingly. Every time she went, she seemed to get even sicker.

Lucas touched her shoulder, assuring her wordlessly that it would be okay.

Kayla rose slowly and went to the kitchen to prepare breakfast as Lucas readied Charlie.

They drove to the hospital in silence. Noiseless tears streamed down Kayla's cheeks, and Lucas steeled himself not to turn around and head for the beach instead. She had to get treatment. It was the only way, he thought.

But her tears tore at his heart. He wished they didn't have to go. He wished they could just enjoy the day like every other couple, but they couldn't and he knew he had to be strong.

The boys walked her to the chemo room and then went to the waiting room where Charlie was more comfortable.

For two hours, Lucas sang every song he knew, danced every dance he could remember from Charlie's favorite shows, and tried to do anything to keep him entertained. After what seemed like forever, the nurse finally told them Kayla was released.

A few minutes passed, and Kayla didn't appear.

"Come on, Bud, let's go find your sister," Lucas lifted Charlie from the floor where he was playing, put him in his wheelchair, and they went to find Kayla.

Lucas heard her before he saw her.

"Nurse, would you watch Charlie for a moment, please, while I…" Lucas didn't finish his sentence. He only nodded his head in the direction of Kayla's crying.

The nurse nodded in understanding.

"Want to see the new pictures we put up?" The nurse talked soothingly to Charlie and took him down the hall.

"Kayla?" Lucas called tentatively. He found her in a small room off the chemo room, sitting in a chair, her knees clutched to her chest.

"Hey, Baby," he crooned, sitting at the foot of the bed.

She looked miserable. The skin under her eyes was a dark purple, and her hair seemed to have little patches of bare spots he hadn't noticed before.

She didn't answer; she just shivered in the tiny gown that didn't cover most of her body.

Lucas took off his jacket and covered her with it. She was leaning over a small bowl, and Lucas rubbed her back as she vomited.

"It's okay, Baby…" Lucas began to cry, clutching her closer as her body finally relaxed. "It's gonna be okay," Lucas soothed, choking back sobs as he rocked her.

The nurse who had been watching the scene wiped away a tear. They stayed there together for a few long moments, as Lucas' sobs turned to quiet tears.

"Can we go home?" Kayla's voice was only a hoarse whisper.

"Yes, Baby, let's go home," Lucas sniffed, wiping his nose with the back of his hand.

Lucas went to get Charlie and tell the nurse they were ready to leave.

The nurse helped Kayla get dressed and then escorted the trio to the van.

"Will you guys be all right?" the nurse asked worriedly.

"Ask me when this is all over," Lucas thought to himself as he climbed into the van.

Though Charlie protested, Lucas insisted they go home. Kayla was so exhausted that she could barely make it from the car to the couch where she finally collapsed. Lucas covered her with a blanket and tucked it tight around her.

"Can we eat?" Charlie asked in a cheerful voice.

Charlie knew his sister was sick, but he thought everyone went to the hospital sometimes. Maybe his sister just went more than other people.

"Sure, what do you want?" Lucas asked Charlie, trying to keep a smile on his face, but inside, he was so worried about Kayla.

"What would I do without her?" he thought trying not to cry in front of Charlie.

Lucas made all three of them a late lunch, but only he and Charlie ate it. Kayla didn't stir all day, even when they played video games. Lucas kept checking her breathing when Charlie wasn't looking.

They watched a movie late into the night. Lucas didn't want to leave Kayla's side, but he knew he would have to put Charlie to bed eventually.

"Can we go to bed?" Charlie asked around midnight.

Lucas rubbed his groggy eyes.

"Sure kid," Lucas responded, walking over to scoop him up from the floor. He didn't want to disturb Kayla, but he was terrified of leaving her. Lucas paused, unsure of what to do.

"How 'bout put her on the computer, so we can watch her all night?" Charlie suggested, seeing Lucas' worried face.

"Charlie, how did you get to be so smart?" Lucas teased, though he thought the idea was brilliant.

"Not from my P.A.!" Charlie grinned up at Lucas who laughed.

He grabbed both laptops and set up the video chat. Once he had it centered on her, he took his back to the apartment with him and Charlie.

Tucking Charlie in, he placed the screen on a stand by the bed. Lucas fell asleep staring at the screen of his precious girl suffering.

The following morning, they got up and both realized that Kayla wasn't up yet, which was strange, because even they had slept later that morning. It was ten o'clock and she was still not up.

Getting worried, they dressed and went to the house to check on her. When they entered, they heard her crying in the bathroom. Lucas ran into the bathroom to see what was wrong.

"What's wrong?"

The new medicine was making her skin a bright splotchy red, and she couldn't help staring at the red spots covering her face.

"I'm ugly!" Kayla cried out, putting her hands up to hide her face.

Lucas swept her into his arms.

"What do you mean? You're beautiful," Lucas reassured her, and he meant it.

He held her tightly until she stopped crying a few moments later.

"Come on, let's get something to eat. You haven't eaten anything since yesterday," Lucas coaxed.

She nodded, wiping her tears and following him out to the kitchen.

"I'm hungry," Lucas said rubbing his stomach as he sat next to Charlie at the table.

Kayla poured herself some iced tea.

"Do you feel up to making me a sandwich like the one you made yesterday?" Lucas pleaded.

Maybe she would feel better doing normal things. If he tried to take over everything for her, he knew she would be upset.

"A Reuben?" Kayla asked.

"Yes, please!"

"Me too!" Charlie chimed.

"Two Ruebens, coming up!" she said.

In a short time, Kayla brought the sandwiches to the table along with glasses of root beer with ice cubes and a straw in each.

"For the two best boys in the whole world," Kayla announced.

"I think you mean *men*," Lucas teasingly chided.

"No, I meant *boys*," Kayla giggled as she sat down at the table with them.

They spent the day quietly. Lucas knew Kayla was still feeling very sick, though she refused to talk about it. She made homemade wings for them to eat during the football game. It exhausted her. Propped against Lucas' shoulder, she tried to keep her eyes open, but she couldn't. The ache was too much.

By the time the game ended, it was eleven o'clock. Kayla and Charlie were fast asleep.

"I'll bring Kayla to bed first, then Charlie," Lucas whispered to himself.

Once in her room, he put her to bed, and kissed her cheek good night. Returning to the living room, he turned off the TV and brought Charlie back to the apartment.

As Lucas was brushing his teeth, he heard Charlie call his name. He quietly walked toward Charlie's side of the bed and sat down on the edge. Charlie's hand was reaching for Lucas' face.

"What's wrong, Bud?" Lucas asked, sitting Charlie up on the bed.

"Another nightmare," Charlie moaned leaning into Lucas' chest for comfort.

Lucas put his arm around him accepting the hug. He held Charlie until he fell fast asleep again. Then he got himself ready for bed.

Though he had comforted Charlie through his nightmares, there was no one to calm his own fears.

The next morning, Kayla had a terrible migraine. She joined Lucas and Charlie in the kitchen.

Lucas could tell she was in severe pain. He knew she didn't want to upset Charlie, so she was fighting back the tears.

"Are you okay?" Lucas motioned with his lips.

Kayla's lip quivered as she shook her head.

"A headache?" Lucas asked, whispering so Charlie wouldn't hear.

Kayla gave a quick nod.

"Want me to get your pain meds?" Lucas asked hugging her to comfort her.

"Yes please – hurry though, it's getting worse," Kayla said beginning to cry.

"Wait, Lucas? I might need to go to the hospital…" Kayla collapsed in the living room as a burst of pain shot through her head.

Lucas quickly grabbed Charlie and hurriedly wheeled him to the van. When he finally got Charlie loaded in, he rushed back into the house to get Kayla. She was very weak. He picked her up and ran to the van.

The ER took Kayla in right away.

Lucas could barely wait long enough to park before he pushed Charlie at a run into the back room to be with her.

"I don't want Kayla to die," Charlie cried clutching Lucas' neck.

Lucas rocked him back and forth while a nurse drew Kayla's blood. Lucas looked at Charlie trying not to choke up.

"Now, remember, I'll still take care of you no matter what. You will never be alone, Charlie. God is with us, and you don't have to be afraid," he soothed.

Dr. Beeoko briskly entered the room. "Hi, Lucas," he greeted.

Lucas looked at him expectantly, waiting to hear the horrifying news.

"Kayla will be okay today, it's just a bad reaction to the chemo. We will give her some pain meds, keep her under watch for a couple of days, and send her home."

Dr. Beeoko read the fear in Lucas' eyes and his tone softened. "She isn't going to die today, and she will be okay for now. You're doing a great job, Lucas. She looks as healthy as she can be at this point in her illness," he put a hand on Lucas' shoulder.

The anger that burned inside Lucas scared him. How did this doctor know anything about what healthy looked like? Whatever healthy was, it wasn't his beautiful girl lying in a hospital bed wrapped in tubes and plastic. It wasn't her thinning hair or how the cancer was robbing her of her strength or her life. The tumor was making her sicker. She threw up constantly. They kept a bucket near her all the time now. Lucas couldn't stand the look or smell of it.

Charlie looked scared, even though he wouldn't admit it. He lay on Lucas' chest in the waiting room while Lucas read quietly to him.

"Lucas?" Charlie interrupted him, starting to cry.

"Yeah, Bud?" Lucas put the book down and looked into Charlie's teary eyes.

"Did you mean it when you said you'll still love and take care of me, even if Kayla dies?" Charlie asked.

Lucas held Charlie tighter and closer, beginning to cry himself.

"Of course I will, Bud." Lucas said pulling Charlie in for more comfort.

"You promise?" Charlie asked digging his face in Lucas' shirt, trying to remember all the good memories he had of his life with his sister.

"Of course I will, Bud." Lucas said in tears kissing Charlie's head.

When Lucas looked up, he saw the doctor coming down the long, sterile hallway toward them, looking very serious. It only took the doctor about thirty seconds to approach them, but for Lucas, it felt like forever.

"What's wrong, Doctor?" Lucas asked trying not to panic.

"I wish I had better news," the doctor said with a heavy sigh.

Lucas looked down slowly shaking his head. "How long?"

"Today's scans are indicating that the chemo really isn't working like we hoped. The tumor continues to grow. Perhaps two to three months?"

Lucas struggled to catch his breath, soaking in the devastating news he had just heard. He hugged Charlie tight.

"Can we see her?" Lucas asked quietly, putting Charlie gently in his chair.

"Of course," the doctor said pointing them to the room where Kayla was.

Lucas cautiously pushed Charlie into her room in case she had fallen asleep.

"Hey, trouble makers," Kayla said grinning weakly.

"Hey, Babe," Lucas said kissing her.

"Charlie, I've missed you so much! Come here!" she laughed, reaching her arms out as she waited for Lucas to put him on the bed next to her. Kayla wrapped her arms around him and sighed as she started tickling him.

"You and Lucas are going to have so much fun." Kayla tried to lighten the mood and enjoy the all the moments that were left with her little brother.

"They won't be as fun without you, though," Charlie said digging his face into her hair.

"Hey, I'm not fun enough for you now?" Lucas said making all three of them laugh.

A few hours passed pleasantly as they cracked stupid jokes and laughed together.

"Come on, Buddy, it's getting late," Lucas said lifting Charlie out of the bed and into his chair.

"Goodnight, boys," Kayla grinned.

"Night," Lucas whispered as he kissed her lips flavored with strawberry lip gloss.

On their way home, they stopped to get food.

"What do you want?" Lucas asked Charlie as he studied the drive-thru menu.

Looking out the window, Charlie answered, "I want my sister back."

"Me too, Bud, me too," Lucas said patting Charlie's head.

They ordered their food and drove home in silence to eat.

"I have an idea!"

Lucas ran into their room. He came out with a big piece of paper and a box of markers.

"Let's make a sign for Kayla to cheer her up," Lucas suggested.

Sitting on the floor, Lucas guided Charlie's hand with the marker to make words and pictures. Next, Lucas let Charlie glue glitter onto the card.

After an hour, they were done. Of course, half of the glitter was on Lucas' shirt, but as long as it brought Charlie joy, Lucas didn't mind at all. DaVinci couldn't have done better himself, and as long as it gave Kayla a smile, Lucas would do just about anything.

"Okay, Buddy, time for bed," Lucas said scooping Charlie up and giving him a raspberry on his stomach.

"But I'm too hyper now!" Charlie giggled.

"We can change that," Lucas whispered, putting Charlie over his head while running around and making rocket ship noises.

Charlie laughed like never before. They did this for about ten minutes, until Charlie was ready for sleep. Lucas quietly put him to bed.

But before he went to bed himself, he remembered that he had a six-pack, a pack of cigarettes and a box of matches that he had hid when he moved in a few months back. He thought about the smokes, the beer, then Charlie.

"Just one cigarette and a beer - I can't be this depressed about Kayla," he thought to himself, gagging on the smoke and taking a swig from one of the beer cans.

"Lucas," a strange voice called. And again, "Lucas." Lucas checked on Charlie, but he was fast asleep.

"Who's there?" he whispered, gazing through the darkness of the room.

"I'm called The Great I AM. I am called The Messiah. Do you really want to do that in front of Charlie? What would Kayla say to you right now?"

Without hesitation, Lucas gathered up the beer and smokes and ran outside, dumping them in the garbage can. He quickly ran back to the apartment, got into bed and held Charlie to comfort himself this time.

Charlie slowly woke up.

"Are you okay?" Charlie moaned rubbing his tired eyes.

"Yeah, Bud, just go back to sleep," Lucas whispered pulling Charlie closer to him and rubbing his head as he hummed a lullaby.

The next morning, Lucas gathered all of Kayla's favorite things to bring to her in the hospital.

While Charlie watched Sesame Street, Lucas went into her room to find her slippers.

The room smelled like her perfume. Tears came to his eyes as he turned the corner and saw her wall covered in pictures. They were pictures of the two them together – and of Charlie. He knew she took a lot of pictures, but he never knew what she did with them. Each picture he remembered perfectly – the smells, sounds, and plans of the day.

"These are all I'm going to have left of her someday," Lucas thought to himself.

He dropped to his knees in front of a picture he had taken of her. The sun was setting behind her and her smiled filled the picture the way she had filled his life. Sunlight streamed in through the windows and he cried out to God for her.

"I don't know why this is happening, but I am going to trust You. I am terrified of living without her, but I know You are good. If there's any way You could heal her, please, please…" his voice cracked as he sobbed.

He lay there for a while, feeling the peace of God calm him down a little.

"Lucas?" he heard Charlie call.

Lucas stood and went to see what Charlie needed.

"Can we go see Kayla now?" Charlie asked as Lucas came around the corner.

"Sure, Buddy."

"Did you find the slippers?" Charlie asked.

Lucas doubled back and grabbed them out of her closet.

"Yep, let's go," Lucas said, settling Charlie into his wheelchair.

He carried all of Kayla's things outside to the car and brought the sign as well.

After loading Charlie into the van, he got in the front seat.

TWENTY-NINE

THE RIDE OVER WAS ODDLY quiet. Charlie was scared for his sister. He didn't feel like joking today, which was good, because Lucas barely had the strength to hold himself together, let alone be strong for Charlie.

They shuffled into the hospital and Lucas stopped at the gift shop to buy her some flowers.

"Oh those are pretty," the store clerk remarked.

Lucas nodded numbly pulling out his wallet.

"You must be buying them for someone special," the lady continued.

Lucas nodded again, his shaking hands almost dropping the money.

There was an awkward silence for a moment.

The lady smiled, "Who is it?" she pressed, just as Lucas dropped the wallet on the ground.

"My dying girlfriend," he responded brusquely, too frustrated to care.

The lady looked taken aback, and he barely managed to put the money on the table before he took Charlie and stalked away.

As they took the elevator up to the eighth floor, Lucas tried to control his anxiety. Would they have told him if she had died in the night? Would he walk in to find her struggling to breathe? The questions running through his mind were almost too much for him to handle.

Terrified and nearly running to her room, they entered and peeked slowly around the corner.

Relief flooded through him when he saw her sitting up. Some of her color had returned. Even though she still had IV's in both arms, she looked better. Most of the other tubes had been removed.

She smiled widely when they entered.

Charlie, strapped in his chair, reached for his sister. Lucas unbuckled him and placed him on her bed.

Kayla wrapped her arms around Charlie and held him for a moment. "I'm okay, Honey," she soothed as Charlie began to cry.

Lucas held on to him so he wouldn't fall off the bed, but didn't say anything.

She met his eyes and he held her gaze. Worry clouded his eyes, and she reached for him.

Still keeping a hand on Charlie, he leaned over and hugged her. As soon as she was in his arms, he relaxed. She was alive - frail and still in pain, but alive. He stroked her hair with a shaking hand as she pressed her head into his chest.

Even with his gentle touch, some of her hair fell out and clung to his fingers. He pulled his hand away and she cried.

"It won't stop falling out, Lucas. They said it will just get worse," she cried into his shoulder.

He let the long black pieces fall to the floor and put a hand under her chin.

"You will always be beautiful to me," he whispered, kissing her lightly.

She smiled, "I don't deserve you, Lucas," she whispered back.

"No, I don't deserve you," Lucas said softly, kissing her again.

Charlie was quiet for once.

Kayla noticed and looked down at him. "What, you're okay with us kissing now?" Kayla teased, trying to make him smile.

"If it makes you feel better…" Charlie said, tears rolling down his little cheeks.

Lucas ruffled his hair.

"I guess we can eat green beans for dinner tonight. That will make her feel better," he joked.

Kayla and Charlie laughed.

"Don't take it too far," Charlie smiled.

A nurse came bustling in.

"Good morning! Ready to take those out, Hon?, the nurse asked, pointing at the IV. The doctor said you could go home,"

Kayla nodded and the nurse disconnected the tubing and slid out the IV. Lucas held the gauze on her arm so the nurse could bandage it.

"There we go. The doctor will be in in a few minutes and then you can go home," she said, patting Kayla's hand.

"Thank you," Kayla said to her.

"No problem. You go home and rest." She stood up and put a hand on Lucas' shoulder.

"You're doing a great job," she said, patting his back.

Lucas just nodded as she left.

"I think she likes you," Kayla smiled.

Lucas grinned, "Who doesn't?"

Kayla smacked his arm lightly and laughed. Dr. Beeoko entered a few minutes later.

"Ready to go home?" he asked, smiling.

"Yes, thank you," Kayla said, relieved.

"I know you'll be sorry to not eat hospital food tonight," he joked.

Kayla laughed, "I'm sure Lucas can manage something that might taste similar."

The doctor laughed politely. "I'm sure he can. Lucas, I would actually like to see you outside for a moment if that's all right."

Lucas nodded and followed the doctor out of the room as Kayla wrapped her arm around Charlie to keep him securely on the bed.

"What's wrong?" he asked anxiously, his heart racing.

"Nothing is wrong right now. She is stable, but she is going to have to be more careful. I think we should increase chemo treatments to see if we can at least slow it down."

Lucas thought of Kayla throwing up, her face pale and covered in sweat and he winced.

"Will more really help at this point?" He swallowed the lump in his throat and tried to make his voice firm.

"Yes, if you want more time," he said quietly.

Lucas felt as if his knees might give way underneath him. He nodded.

"You're doing a great job, Son. Not many people could take care of her the way you do. She is doing so well because you are taking such good care of her. Keep it up, and I'll see you next week for increased chemo."

Lucas could only nod, and the doctor left. He turned and slowly walked back into the room.

"What did he say?" Kayla asked anxiously.

Lucas forced himself to sound confident. "He said you're doing well," Lucas announced, smiling for Charlie.

Kayla met his eyes and he looked away. She knew the news wasn't good.

"See, you're doing better. You can go home," Charlie tried to comfort his sister.

She smiled and patted him on the back. Lucas held back his tears and went to her side. He picked up Charlie and waited as Kayla slowly swung her legs over the side of the bed.

"I can help," he offered, buckling Charlie into his wheelchair.

Watching her struggle to stand was painful for him.

"No, I got it," she tried to sound confident as her voice and body shook with effort.

She pushed off the railing and stumbled forward as her knees gave way.

Lucas caught her just before she hit the floor and helped her sit back down on the bed.

"I'm sorry." She started to cry.

Lucas quickly strode into the hallway. "Can I get a wheelchair for my girlfriend, please?" he called to the nurses at the nurses' station.

The nurse arrived with a wheelchair. Lucas' eyes met hers then glanced back to where Kayla was sobbing. The nurse nodded and knelt down in front of Charlie.

"You know what? We have a really cool room just for kids down the hall. Would you like to see it? It has snacks and a TV," he heard the nurse say as she shut the door.

The whitewashed walls echoed her quiet cries. Lucas knew he had to try and ease her pain. What could he say? What could anyone say in the face of such suffering? His mind went through a million different words, as he lightly placed a hand on her back.

"Just leave!" she cried.

Lucas crawled into bed next to her.

She hid her face in her hands, sobbing.

Lucas put an arm around her. "Come here," he whispered.

Her strength gave way and she let him pull her into his lap. She turned and buried her head in his chest.

He just held her more tightly.

She could feel his tears soak her hair as he wept for her.

Caressing her cheek, he gently put his lips on her forehead and kissed her.

"I love you," he whispered.

She tilted her head up and kissed him as the tears continued to roll down her cheeks.

"I love you, too."

He rested his forehead on hers and gently wiped away her tears.

"We are going to make it through this," he said supportively. "I will love you forever – for as long as forever lasts."

Slowly, her sobs turned to tears, and her body gradually relaxed. After a few more minutes, she felt she was strong enough to get ready to go.

"We have to get Charlie," she said, her voice hoarse.

"He's down the hall. We can go get him if you're ready?" he asked.

She nodded, sitting up.

Getting off the bed, he pulled the wheelchair over. She swung her legs over the side of the bed and he lifted her into his arms, kissing her once more before gently lowering her into the wheelchair.

He pushed her out into the hallway and down to the waiting room where Charlie was eating Oreos.

"Are you ready?" Lucas asked Charlie.

"Yeah, but won't it be hard to push two chairs?" Charlie asked laughing.

Lucas thought about it.

"Can you help me?" he requested, looking at one of the nurses standing with Charlie.

"Sure," she smiled.

They got Kayla into the car first, then Lucas loaded Charlie in.

Lucas thanked the nurse then got into the driver's seat.

"So, what are we doing tonight?" Kayla asked Lucas.

"Well, Charlie and I are working on a surprise for you, and it will be ready late tonight."

"Oh no, what are you doing to me this time? Am I going to walk in the house and find peanut butter on the walls?"

"No, I think you'll like this surprise," Lucas laughed touching her shoulder.

"Oh, I can't wait," Kayla mumbled, half-excited and half-nervous.

They got home an hour later because of the rush hour traffic.

When they arrived, Lucas carried Kayla into the house and then ran quickly back outside.

"Babe, where are you going?" Kayla asked sitting up on the couch.

"Uh…getting Charlie. We'll be back in an hour!" Lucas yelled running out the door.

"I love Lucas, but he's so weird sometimes," Kayla thought to herself as she drifted off to sleep.

THIRTY

THE INCREASED CHEMO TREATMENTS WERE hard on Kayla. Lucas never left her side. She loved him so much, but she was beginning to worry about him. She hated letting him see her cry all the time.

That night, the evening of the third chemo treatment of the week, they were all home watching a movie. She excused herself to be alone for a bit. She needed to think and cry, and she didn't want either of them around to hear it.

"I'm going for a walk, it's really hot in here," she lied.

"Okay, have fun!" Charlie piped, his eyes never moving from the screen.

Lucas grabbed her hand as she walked away, stopping her.

"You sure you'll be okay?" he questioned, keeping his voice down so Charlie couldn't hear.

She nodded and forced a smile.

Reluctantly Lucas let her go. "I'm right here if you need me," he reminded her.

She nodded again, unable to speak. Half an hour passed and Charlie had fallen fast asleep. Lucas grew more worried about her as the credits rolled. He shut the TV off, ready to go look for her, when he thought he heard Kayla in the distance.

Carefully, he slid the door open from the kitchen to the back porch. Her cries grew slightly louder as he went out into the yard. Following the sounds, he finally located her out in the tree house. He quietly walked up the wooden ramp and, seeing her, slowly sat down next to her.

"What's wrong, Babe?" he asked softly.

Kayla threw herself into Lucas' arms. "I can't do this, Lucas. I promised myself after Mom died, that I would take care of Charlie. With Dad gone, Charlie will have no one to look after him," she said, weeping into his shirt.

Lucas pushed her away and glared at her. "First of all, don't talk like that. Secondly, you think I'm just going to leave Charlie by himself?"

Kayla looked up at him brushing the tears off her face. "Will you?"

"Absolutely not! I love you, and Charlie, and that will never change!" Lucas said adamantly, pulling her closer to him.

More tears followed.

"I love you," he said again, more tenderly this time.

Sniffling, she looked up at him. "I love you, too. Oh, and by the way, Lucas?"

"Yeah?"

"Thanks – for being so good to Charlie. He really needed it. You know, after Dad died…"

"You don't have to thank me. I know how hard it's been."

His lips gently touched hers.

Suddenly, they were interrupted by the sound of Charlie screaming back at the house.

Lucas raced back and found Charlie crying hysterically, his head bleeding from a fall on the raised edge of the fireplace.

Kayla ran in behind him.

Lucas turned and caught her.

"Turn around, go back outside. I'll handle it," Lucas said, his heart racing.

Kayla read the fear in his eyes. "No, I have to know what happened," she cried pushing past Lucas.

She gasped when she saw the blood.

Charlie sobbed as blood trickled down his neck.

Kayla cradled him in her arms, rocking him back and forth and rubbing his back.

"It's okay," she soothed.

His sobs quieted as Lucas came back in with paper towels and bandages.

Blood trickled down Kayla's leg as Charlie's head continued to bleed.

"Hey, Bud, what happened?" Lucas knelt down and smoothed Charlie's hair back.

"I fell," Charlie whimpered.

Lucas hated seeing Charlie in pain. He lightly put pressure on the wound with the damp towel.

"It's okay, I'm here," Lucas whispered, lightly kissing his head.

Charlie pulled away and looked at Lucas, his tears suddenly turning into laughter.

"Your hands are bloody."

"Um, excuse me, this is your fault," Lucas chuckled showing his blood-spotted hands to Charlie and Kayla.

"Hold on Superman, I'll go get more paper towels," Kayla said, heading for the kitchen, her weakened body struggling with all the commotion.

"Got them," she said as she returned.

"Thank you, Superwoman," Lucas said with a grin on his face.

"Are you almost done? I'm starving, and I think you're breaking my neck," Charlie moaned.

"Almost, Buddy. You're doing great!" Lucas smiled.

With a big bear hug and a belly raspberry, Kayla announced, "You stopped bleeding!"

"Okay back to bed, Bud – this time, in your actual bed!" Lucas said clapping his hands and scooping up Charlie to buckle him into his chair.

"Yay!" Charlie yelled. "Can we do the rocket ship?"

"Absolutely! Ready, Rodger?" Lucas asked. "We're off in three, two, one, *BLAST OFF*!" Lucas yelled as he made rocket noises.

He lifted Charlie into the air and zoomed back to the apartment, gently landing him in the bed. Charlie giggled, and Lucas tickled him. Kayla had followed them over and watched them fooling around with a huge smile on her face.

For a moment, she almost forgot she was sick. She took a step toward Lucas, and the room seemed to spin. Pain shot through her body, and she almost collapsed. She grabbed the dresser to regain her balance.

"I think I'm going to lie down, too."

Kayla put a hand to her head and hoped the spinning would stop soon.

Lucas helped her stand. "Think you will make it down the stairs?" he worried as she swayed on her feet.

"I've got it, Superman," she smiled weakly.

He laughed and kissed her. "Good night, beautiful," he whispered.

"Night, Handsome," she whispered back and turned.

He watched her to make sure she made it to the stairs okay. He knew she would call for him if she needed him.

He turned back to Charlie whose eyes were already closing. Turning off the light, he climbed in next to him.

"Goodnight, Dad," Charlie whispered before turning over to go to sleep.

Stunned, Lucas didn't respond.

Almost immediately, Charlie's breaths became slow and deep, letting Lucas know he was soundly asleep.

Lucas lay on his back and stared at the ceiling. He thought about what Charlie had said. Lucas really *was* like his dad.

It never really hit Lucas until now. He thought of everything he had to do to take care of Kayla, and how much she depended on him. He never really stopped to think about how much responsibility was on his shoulders.

How would he handle her death? The pain of that thought felt like an anvil crushing his chest. It was hard to breathe, thinking of her gone.

How would he support Charlie? Could the uncle really care for them for the rest of their lives?

He thought of Kayla, of her beautiful smile. He couldn't wait to see her face on their wedding day…if she made it that long! The wedding had to be soon!

He had never even been to a wedding! How would he pull together one that would be amazing enough for such a wonderful girl? The engagement was hard enough. He wasn't a very romantic person. Loving her came easily, but a wedding?

He hoped Charlie would have some good ideas. Parties weren't really his thing. He knew he had to invite family – crazy Aunt and Uncle included. It might be the last time they saw her.

What about flowers? What kind of flowers do you need for a wedding? He didn't know anything about flowers.

Lucas rubbed his forehead where he was starting to get a headache. Maybe they should just elope? He knew she deserved better though. He wanted her to have the wedding of her dreams.

Doubt crept in. He just didn't feel as if he was good enough for her. She deserved someone who was better at handling things, someone who could be strong for her even at the very end. He wasn't sure if he could do it. Tears formed as he began to think about it.

"God, You have to give me strength. I can't do this," he whispered into the darkness as he began to cry. He spent the rest of the night crying and praying to God for help.

"Lucas!" Charlie jumped on Lucas to wake him up.

Lucas' eyes flew open.

"What time is it?" Lucas moaned as Charlie pulled the blankets off.

"It's nine o' clock. That's why I think there's something wrong with Kayla. We never sleep until nine," Charlie cried. "You have to make sure she's okay!"

Lucas was already out of bed and putting his clothes on.

"I'm sure she's fine," he lied as he pulled his pants on quickly.

His heart felt like it was beating out of his chest. He put on a t-shirt and scooped Charlie off of the bed. They ran downstairs and across the sidewalk into the house. Lucas placed Charlie on the floor near the TV.

"You watch cartoons, I'll check on your sister. I'm sure she's all right." Lucas fought to keep his voice steady as he held the remote in shaking hands.

Finally, he managed to force his fingers to push the right channel for cartoons. Dropping the remote as Arthur came on, he hurried to Kayla's room. He knocked, anxiously waiting for her annoyed voice to tell him to give her a second to finish her makeup. The seconds seemed like hours as he waited. There was no answer. He knocked again, wishing he would hear her usual complaining about how impatient he was. All he could hear was silence.

Taking a deep breath, he pushed open the door. She didn't look dead, but then again, he wasn't sure what a dead person looked like. He tiptoed to her side, watching for any signs of life. Creeping closer, he reached out and touched her.

"Kayla?" he called quietly.

Her eyes fluttered open. He was never so happy to see her beautiful brown eyes looking at him. He let out a sigh of relief. She reached out her hand and he took it in his.

"What's wrong?" she inquired, her voice hoarse.

He shook his head. He didn't want to tell her what he was afraid of – what he thought when she didn't answer.

"I just can't help staring at you," he smiled.

She rolled her eyes. "I'm a mess," she responded, her voice crackly.

He shook his head again. "You are the most beautiful in the morning before you do your makeup and…"

"…And without a shower?" she interrupted, her eyebrow raised.

He laughed. "*And* without a shower. That hairdo is in style, you know."

He reached out a hand and ruffled her sparse hair. A few strands fell onto the pillow beneath her head. Lucas tried to ignore it. "There, much better."

She pulled his hand to her face. "I'm sorry, Lucas. I'm just too tired to do anything today," she sighed, her eyes closing.

His smile faded as he realized she was feeling like giving up.

"Come on, Babe, you got to get up. We don't have to do anything. We can just hang out here today. I'll even make you breakfast, but I *really* think you should come down and be with us – you'll feel better," Lucas encouraged, picking up a brush off the nightstand.

She nodded and he pulled back the covers so she could sit up. She started to sit up, but coughs began to rack her body. She wrapped her arms around her stomach.

Lucas handed her a tissue and she held it over her face as she coughed up blood. He gently rubbed her shoulder as she tried to catch her breath.

She took slow deep breaths as the coughing finally subsided. Once again, she began to cry. Once again, he pulled her close.

"It's okay," he said softly, rubbing her back.

"I'm sorry," she sighed, laying her head on his chest.

He kissed the top of her head. "You have absolutely nothing to apologize for," he said firmly.

"I wish I could be a different person. I hate being sick all the time," she cried, her words muffled by his t-shirt.

"There is no one who could be as amazing as you are to me, Kayla. I don't care if you have pink polka dotted spots, you are *still* my girl."

She laughed weakly.

"What about purple polka dotted spots?" she sniffed.

"Then I would just have to disown you." He pretended to be serious, and she smacked him lightly.

His face broke into a smile.

"Come on, I'll make breakfast to keep those purple polka dots away."

"I would think that would *give* me purple polka dots," she teased, smiling.

He pretended to be offended.

"Well then, I'll just let you and your pink polka dots get ready."

He stood and left her to get dressed.

"Is she okay?" Charlie demanded as soon as Lucas walked into the living room.

"Just a little sick, that's all. What do you want for breakfast?" Lucas asked donning an apron in the kitchen.

Charlie rolled his eyes, "Anything but your pancakes, Lucas."

"I told you, those were Canadian pancakes I made last time. They were supposed to be runny."

"And burnt," Charlie added.

"Yeah, yeah," Lucas responded, pulling out eggs and bacon from the fridge.

"I hate eggs," Charlie yelled from the living room.

Lucas put a hand on his hip. "You will eat it and like it," he said loudly, imitating Kayla.

"I heard that!" Kayla called from her room.

Charlie laughed.

"Chocolate covered Pop tarts it is," Lucas sighed.

Charlie cheered.

"No!" Kayla called from her room.

Lucas laughed, putting a Pop tart in the toaster. "Love you, honey," he called, melting the chocolate for Charlie.

"Don't forget the sprinkles!" Charlie called.

"Absolutely not!" Kayla poked her head out of her bedroom.

"Of course! You can't have chocolate covered Pop tarts without sprinkles! Duh!" Lucas responded.

"Lucas!" Kayla warned coming out of her room. "I hate you!"

She tried to keep a straight face as she came into the kitchen where Lucas was pouring chocolate over two Pop tarts.

"What? This is healthy," Lucas defended, looking at the box.

"See? It says blueberry! That's a fruit! So, hah!" Lucas held up the box.

Kayla reached out to take it from him, and he pulled it away.

"You know, most girls with cancer just wake up and are given everything they want. I have to put up with *you*," she smiled.

"You *can* have whatever you want," Lucas smiled.

"Except the Pop tarts!" Charlie called.

Lucas wrapped his arms around her as she reached to take the box. He held it above her head with one hand and kissed her. Dipping a finger in the chocolate sauce of Charlie's Pop tart, he smeared it on her lip.

"Here, you could use some calcium."

She rolled her eyes and licked the chocolate off her lip.

Lucas released her and went to get Charlie.

"You want eggs, Babe?" he asked as he came back in with Charlie.

"I'm not that hungry," Kayla said, holding her stomach.

"You have to eat something," Lucas insisted.

She shook her head. "I can't, I'll throw up."

"No you won't. You're not allowed."

She sighed.

He smiled. "In girl language, Charlie, that's a yes," Lucas said, cracking an egg into the bowl.

"Oh! Then can I have a million dollars?" Charlie asked.

Kayla sat down and put her head in her hands.

"She didn't sigh, so no dice, Bud. Try again later."

"Darn," Charlie responded.

"Just eat your Pop tart," Kayla retorted, putting a piece in his mouth.

"Yes, Mom," he rolled his eyes.

Lucas saw Kayla grimacing in pain.

"You okay, Babe?" Lucas asked rubbing Kayla's back.

"I don't understand how and why you stay with me! You have to do so much for me! I'm so sick, and I look terrible! You need to just leave me! You deserve better!" Kayla cried, pressing her face into her hands.

Lucas slammed his hand onto the table. He was at his breaking point. If she didn't start fighting for herself, they would lose her.

"You do not talk like that! You're beautiful to me, and I love you!" Lucas fumed, clenching his hands into fists.

Standing, Kayla wrapped her arms around his neck, trying to calm his sudden anger.

"I love you, too," she whispered, tightening her grip.

Lucas lifted her off her feet and held her in his arms for a long moment. Then gently putting her back on her feet, he kissed her hand softly and directed her to lie down on the couch until breakfast was ready.

"Are we ready for eggs, then?" Lucas asked, grinning at Charlie.

"I hate eggs," Charlie mumbled, his head down.

"What's wrong, Bud?" Lucas asked, slowly walking toward Charlie.

"My dad died. And now my sister might die. What happens then? I'll be all alone! Lucas, I'm scared!"

Lucas quickly unbuckled him and pulled him to his chest.

"I know, Charlie. I can see why you're scared. But I am here for you, Buddy. I will always be here for you." Lucas spoke in Charlie's ear.

Kayla walked into the kitchen rolling her hair into a bun. "What did I miss?" Kayla asked curiously.

Lucas looked at Kayla, then glanced down at Charlie.

"We were just talking," Lucas answered, pulling Charlie's head closer to his chest.

Lucas knew that when he did that to Charlie, Charlie felt assured of his love for him. Charlie's strong feelings would be their secret.

After breakfast, Lucas quietly puttered around fixing a couple of squeaky doors and a leaking pipe. He tried to keep his mind as busy as he could, while Kayla spent time with Charlie in the living room. Lucas figured they needed some sibling bond time, and the house needed a bit of work.

He worked into the evening, finally finishing the house repairs. He was exhausted. Entering the living room, he saw Kayla asleep on the floor, and Charlie on his knees next to her. Lucas scooped him up and sat down on the couch.

"Dinner?" Lucas asked Charlie.

"Yeah!" Charlie said loudly.

Kayla awoke as Charlie cheered. "What are we doing?" she asked sleepily.

"I'm making dinner," Lucas announced proudly, heading for the kitchen.

After putting on Dragon Tales for Charlie, Kayla left her place on the floor to follow Lucas.

"What's for dinner, my prince?" Kayla asked, leaning her forehead on his as he bent down to meet her.

"What do you want, my princess?" Lucas asked as he kissed her.

"Something yummy…like you…" Kayla teased.

"So corn dogs it is!" Lucas said, quickly turning toward the freezer. Kayla laughed. "*NOOO!*"

"You *said* anything…" Lucas retorted.

"*I* know! How 'bout *YOU* make *ME* a sandwich!" Kayla giggled, gently slapping Lucas' cheek.

"Do you want one?" Lucas said becoming more serious.

"No, it's okay. Whatever you want to make is fine – even corn dogs," Kayla relented as she made her way back to the living room.

"Men," she mumbled, shaking her head and shutting her heavy eyes.

She opened them a minute later – or so she thought.

"Lucas? Charlie?" she called out.

Her mother's antique clock struck one exactly. Could it really be that late? And where were Lucas and Charlie?

Quickly realizing that she was alone in the house, she crossed the yard to the apartment and quietly opened the door. She tiptoed to Lucas' and Charlie's room and peeked in the door.

What she saw melted her heart. Charlie was fast asleep on Lucas' shoulder, their heads touching. She quietly walked toward the bed and brushed Lucas' hair behind his ear, kissing his cheek.

"Goodnight," Kayla whispered as she walked out, shutting the door behind her.

THIRTY-ONE

LUCAS HEARD CHARLIE GIGGLING.

"Come on sleepy head, time to get up." Giggling, Charlie jumped onto Lucas' back.

Lucas decided to have some fun with Charlie and play along with it. He slowly crawled under the covers.

"I'm going to get you," he said to Charlie, tickling his stomach.

"Stop! That tickles!" Charlie burst into laughter.

"Good! That's what you get for waking me up so early every morning," Lucas chuckled, getting out of bed.

"Hey! Don't forget about me!," Charlie chirped.

"Oh, I just decided to leave you in bed all day, and Kayla and I will have fun without you," Lucas joked, looking through his dresser for clothes.

"Well, then, you're fired!" Charlie said trying to roll out of bed.

Lucas was laughing so hard he doubled over. "I would love to see you get out of bed by yourself!"

"Just get me up," Charlie demanded trying to keep a straight face. "Please and thank you?"

"*NOW!*" Then quietly, Charlie said, "Please?"

Lucas picked Charlie up off the bed. "It's a good thing I love you!"

"I know, having an annoying brother is tough. Especially the older ones…" Charlie giggled as Lucas was placing him into the chair.

"You little brat!" Lucas teased, tickling Charlie.

Pointing his finger at the door, Charlie barked, "Time for Kayla and the kitchen!"

When they arrived at the kitchen, Kayla was teary-eyed at the table sipping on her coffee.

"Lucas?" Charlie whispered so Kayla wouldn't hear them.

"Yes, Bud?"

"Why do girls cry *ALL* the time?" Charlie asked dramatically.

"Well, that's their job."

"What?" Charlie looked confused.

"In a relationship, their job is to cry and our job is to comfort them. Look, I'll show you," Lucas quietly said walking over to her.

He slowly placed his hand on hers, gently rubbing her arm.

"It's okay, I'm here," he assured.

Charlie watched as Kayla jumped up. She collapsed into Lucas' strong arms.

"I can't do this, Lucas! I feel like I'm abandoning you here with Charlie!"

Lucas glared at her, partly in anger and partly in frustration.

"Please don't talk like that, Kayla!"

" It's true!" she yelled loudly.

"This isn't your fault, Kayla. None of it is," Lucas spoke softly to her, cupping her face in his hands.

She finally calmed down and gave Lucas a weak smile, slowly running her fingers through his hair.

"I love you so much," he whispered, pulling her closer.

Unbelievably, Charlie had fallen fast asleep in his chair.

"Wow, are we that boring?" Lucas asked Kayla as they looked at Charlie.

"I guess so! No wonder it was so quiet," Kayla whispered back to him, giggling. "Did he not sleep well?"

Lucas shrugged. "Too many late nights, I guess...now what?"

"Oh loving, dearest fiance?" Kayla flirted, wrapping her arms around him.

"Oh, no...what?" Lucas responded reluctantly.

Kayla batted her eyelashes at him. "Would you watch a chick flick with me?"

He hated when she batted her eyelashes because he couldn't say no to those eyes.

"Fine, but only if you promise not to cry," he said with a sigh.

"Why can't I cry?" Kayla teased.

"Because it makes me upset when you're not happy," Lucas blushingly admitted.

"Really?"

Lucas rubbed the back of his neck. "Yeah."

"Well, now I know how to get my way," she said as she skipped to the living room with Lucas in tow.

"Now I know where Charlie got his sense of humor," Lucas thought to himself.

It took a while, but they picked out a movie

Kayla lay down on the couch. Putting her feet on his lap, Lucas started rubbing them.

"What are you doing?" a confused Kayla asked, pulling her feet away.

"Don't you like your feet rubbed?"

"Yeah, but you hate that, I thought."

"Well, then, give me your feet," Lucas demanded, picking up her feet and placing them across his lap once again.

He rubbed them through the whole movie.

Of course, after the movie, Kayla was balling her eyes out.

Lucas grinned. "I told you not to do that," he said, giving her a tissue and a kiss on her forehead.

Charlie began to stir from where they had placed him to sleep on the floor. "Lucas?"

"Right here, Little Buddy," Lucas replied, getting up off the couch.

"Morning, Sleeping Beauty," Lucas teased as he scooped Charlie up.

Charlie reached up to latch his arms around Lucas' neck. "I am *not* a girl!"

Lucas laughed. "Did you have a good nap?"

"I guess...I'm hungry though," Charlie said grasping more tightly onto Lucas' neck to make himself feel more secure.

Lucas sat Charlie next to Kayla.

"It's about time you woke up," Kayla said tickling his stomach.

"Stop! That tickles!" Charlie slurred the words together because he was laughing so hard.

"I think that means tickle me some more! Lucas, want to help me?" Kayla asked pinning Charlie down.

"With pleasure!" Lucas laughed as he began to tickle Charlie's feet.

"This is illegal!" Charlie screamed in laughter.

"I really don't think tickling my little brother is a crime," Lucas chuckled and then quickly realized what he had just said.

"You okay?" she mouthed to Lucas so Charlie wouldn't know what was going on.

Lucas nodded slowly and then smiled at the realization that Charlie really was like a brother to him – the brother he had never had.

All of a sudden, Kayla got another migraine. The pain felt like bricks pounding on her head. She fell back against the couch, the pain was so dreadful.

Charlie hated seeing what was happening to his sister that he loved so much. Leaning over, he gave her a hug.

Lucas didn't know what to do. How could he help when she was in such severe pain?

"What can I do for you?" Lucas asked pulling her in closer for more comfort.

"Sing to me, please!" Kayla whimpered, curling up in Lucas' arms.

He only knew one song by heart so he gave it a go. When Lucas started singing, Kayla's pain level seemed to go down. After he was done, Lucas held her for a few more minutes in silence, and then rubbed her back as she calmed down.

"Are you ever going to make me mad?" Kayla asked Lucas, burying her face into his shirt.

"Why? Do you want me to?" Lucas asked as he stroked her cheek.

"No, you're just the perfect guy and I'm…"

Lucas interrupted, gently putting his finger over her quivering lips.

"And you're the perfect, beautiful princess," he whispered.

Kayla loved but hated those comments he made to her because she loved that Lucas said those things, but she still thought he deserved better.

"I love you…so much…" Lucas said.

Charlie sighed, tipping himself over onto a cushion at the end of the couch.

He slid himself carefully onto the floor. "Can I watch TV?" Charlie asked both of them, getting onto his knees.

"Absolutely not, it's illegal," Lucas said picking up the remote from the coffee table to turn on cartoons.

Charlie looked insulted.

"What? I can't watch TV?".

Lucas laughed. "Yeah…. I think that's a no."

"Men," Kayla rolled her eyes and played with one of the sofa cushions.

"You love us," Lucas said, turning on the TV and picking up Charlie with one hand. "Here, sit on my lap."

Kayla giggled, "You're so strong, Superman!" She crawled over to them and put her head on Lucas' shoulder.

"Why, thank you," he replied putting his arm around her.

"What will you do when Charlie gets bigger and heavier?" Kayla asked.

Lucas thought about it for a minute. "Well, I guess I'll have to lift more weights, then. Thankfully, that won't be for a while…I hope!"

He laughed, throwing Charlie in the air and then catching him.

Kayla reached out her arms and Lucas passed Charlie to her. "Why can't you stay little and cute?"

Kayla gave him a bear hug. She wanted to try to remember moments like these and treasure them until her last breaths.

"Because I can't beat up Lucas if I stay small like this," Charlie retorted, giggling.

Kayla laughed. "I bet you can beat him up, now!" She winked at Lucas.

"Is that a bet?" Lucas asked Charlie, crawling on his elbows toward him.

"Yup," Kayla answered for Charlie. Kayla nudged Charlie closer to him. "Get him!"

Charlie tackled Lucas as Lucas pretended to fall down and fight back. After wrestling for a while, Lucas played dead.

"Victory!" Kayla yelled, picking up Charlie.

They played for a few more hours and – for the first time in a long time – put Charlie to bed early.

Lucas put Charlie on his shoulders. "Come on, Buddy, let's go to bed."

"Night, Buddy," Kayla said going up on her tiptoes to kiss him.

"And what about me? I don't get a kiss goodnight?" Lucas asked, pouting.

Kayla shook her head.

Lucas pretended to cry.

Kayla knew he was joking, but it still moved her. "Fine, I guess so. But just because you're my boyfriend and I love you," Kayla relented, kissing him.

"Yay! Now I'm happy! Goodnight," Lucas said, rocketing Charlie over to the apartment and up the stairs.

The night always seemed so much worse to Kayla, especially lately. Once Lucas and Charlie went to bed, there was nothing for her to do except feel the pain. She used to be able to read or write in her journal, but nothing seemed to ease it tonight. Her back hurt so badly, she couldn't sit up to read, and she had nothing to write. All she wanted to do was cry as the pain seemed to take over every part of her.

Pushing off the blankets, she stumbled to the living room and fell onto the couch. She turned the TV on, and curled up in a ball with her knees pulled to her chest. Waves of heat washed over her and she felt like she was going to throw up. Each breath she took was painful as she tried to manage the nausea. Tears streamed down her face as she clutched her arms around her stomach.

Lucas was awakened by the sound of the TV coming across the computer monitor at the house. He opened sleepy eyes and looked at the computer screen that should have shown Kayla sleeping.

It was almost two in the morning. Did I forget to turn the TV off? He wondered to himself, drifting back to sleep. Then he heard her quiet cries over the hum of the TV and he rolled out of bed. He put on some clothes and ran down the stairs and across the yard.

"Babe, you okay?" he called softly as he entered the house.

She closed her eyes. "Just go away!" she cried.

He saw her holding her stomach and went in the kitchen to get a bowl. He wet a dishtowel.

"It's okay," he said gently, coming to kneel beside her.

"Go away!" she sobbed, trying to push him away from her.

He ignored her weak attempts and helped her sit up. She was burning up. He put the cool cloth on her head and wiped her face.

"It's going to be okay," he soothed.

She threw up into the bowl until finally she collapsed.

Lucas dumped it outside and rinsed the bowl off underneath the hose so she wouldn't have to see it. Coming back in, he poured her some ginger ale and put a straw in it. He went back into the living room and pulled up a chair.

"Here, drink," he directed, pressing the cup into her hands.

Shaking, she took a couple of sips.

"A little more," he encouraged, wrapping his hands around hers to steady it.

Obediently, she sipped a few more times.

"Good," he affirmed, taking the cup from her hand.

She settled herself back down on the couch, clutching his hand in hers.

"Do you want to go back to sleep?"

She shook her head. "No, I can't sleep. You can go back to bed though."

She tried to deny his offer of comfort as Lucas put an arm around her and drew her close.

"Nice try," he grinned. "Why can't you sleep?"

"Too much pain…" She barely was able to form an answer to his question as her lungs contracted sharply.

"Want to watch *Beauty and the Beast* until you fall asleep?" Lucas offered.

"What about Charlie?" Kayla forced herself to ask.

"He'll be fine. I put the baby monitor on so we can hear him if he wakes up," Lucas responded.

Kayla sat up and curled her knees into her chest while Lucas popped in the DVD.

"Can you sit with me?" Kayla moaned.

"No. What do you think, that I love you or something?" he asked jokingly as he sat down and wrapped an arm around her.

"Well, the cuddling does give it away," Kayla giggled, laying her head on his shoulder.

"Darn it!" Lucas snapped his fingers acting disappointed.

She shifted herself so she could be as close to him as possible.

"I'm assuming this snuggling means you love me too? Or do you just do this to me because I'm lucky?" he asked, wrapping his arms around her.

"You're not lucky," she said, glancing down.

"Yes, I am," he corrected her, kissing the top of her head.

Lucas wanted to make sure that this girl, the love of his life, knew that he loved her, and would always love her.

"I'm cold," she shivered.

"Here."

He grabbed a blanket from the side of the couch and spread it over her with his free hand.

She could feel the pain easing as sleep drew her closer. "Thanks," she whispered as she fell asleep.

He kissed her forehead and watched her drift off. He spent time praying as he held her hand. He cried out to God again for her life, until his eyes began to close as well.

Turning off the TV and shutting off the lights, Lucas checked the laptop to be sure it was on so he could keep an eye on Kayla, and then he went back to the apartment. He prayed until he fell asleep.

Within minutes, Charlie woke him.

"Lucas?" Charlie whispered nudging Lucas' back.

Lucas opened his eyes and rolled over onto his side.

"You okay, Bud?" he asked, rubbing Charlie's cheek with his thumb.

"I had a nightmare," Charlie cried softly.

Lucas pulled Charlie close to comfort him. "It was just a dream. I'm right here."

Charlie accepted the comfort and slowly shut his eyes.

Lucas fell right back to sleep as soon as his head hit the pillow.

The next morning, Lucas brought Charlie over to the house. Upon entering, they found Kayla in front of the oven crying.

He wrapped his arms around her. "Are you okay?" he asked.

"I was just trying to cut the pineapple and my hands were shaking so badly, my hand slipped," she sniffed, holding back the tears.

"Oh, is that all?" he teased. "Come here."

She approached him obediently.

"I love you," Lucas gently spoke into her ear as he hugged her.

"Do you know any words other than those three?" Kayla giggled.

"Not when I see you," he grinned.

"You're lying!" She slapped his cheek playfully, her face turning rose red.

Lucas laughed. "No, it's true, though."

He held her hand on his cheek so he could feel it and remember it. One day she won't be in pain anymore. She'll be with her mother and father again. But she'd be gone from him forever.

"Yeah right," she said.

"How can I lie to those pretty brown angel eyes?" he asked, letting go of her hand.

The hand slowly dropped onto the table. To Lucas it felt like her hand was her life, and soon, he would have to let her go, too.

Kayla saw a tear roll down Lucas' cheek. Tenderly, she wiped it away with the back of her hand.

"Time to get ready to go for chemo," Lucas quickly changed the subject.

She sighed and leaned her head against his chest. "Do I have to go? Can't we just tell him I died?"

Lucas' mouth opened in horror.

"I was just kidding," she squeezed his hand as the color returned to his face.

"It's not funny," he whispered looking away from her gaze.

"I know, I'm sorry. I'll go, but what if it just keeps making me sicker and doesn't do anything?"

Lucas kissed the back of her hand. "Then we will decide what to do from there."

She nodded. "I'm going to change."

She stood and went into her room.

Charlie went back to watching Sesame Street. Lucas sat on the couch as they waited for Kayla, but he was so tired, his eyes closed and he slept. He woke to her gently shaking his shoulder.

"Wake up, Babe," she whispered.

His eyes flew open.

"I'm sorry Kay, I was just tired," he apologized sitting up.

"No it's fine, I know you stayed up late last night. I wish I could be a good girlfriend and just let you sleep in." She ran a hand through his hair.

He shook his head. "You're the best girlfriend I could ever ask for."

She laughed and hit him lightly on the shoulder. "You are one lucky guy."

"Yep," he agreed and kissed her.

"Ready, Charlie?"

They looked down at Charlie who was fast asleep on the floor. Loading the wheelchair in the back, Lucas scooped him up and carried him to the van.

They drove to the hospital in silence. Kayla was nervous, and Lucas was worried for her. They had been warned that the side effects of this new chemo could be severe. He thought that what she was going through now was severe enough. He couldn't begin to imagine what it would be like for her to get worse.

Every step down the hospital corridor felt heavy to Kayla. Millions of questions ran through her mind, but the worst – the scariest – was what if this treatment did nothing? What if she was just sent home to die? How could she watch herself waste away to nothing?

Lucas seemed to sense her worry and he squeezed her hand as Charlie slept on his shoulder.

They rode the elevator up to the eighth floor. A nurse prepped Kayla as they waited for the doctor to arrive.

"Okay, down to business," Dr. Beeoko said after he had greeted everyone. "We'll put an IV in and continue to do the chemo that way, but you might need a port – a way to more easily access your bloodstream if your veins are not cooperative."

He put a hand on her shoulder as she bravely nodded. The nurse came in with the medical cart. Kayla closed her eyes as the nurse started the IV.

"Okay, we are going to go ahead and start treatment."

Kayla nodded, steeling herself not to cry, not to throw up. She just wanted to get it over with.

Almost instantly, the medicine began to take effect and her stomach clenched. The aid held a bucket for her and Lucas rubbed her back with his free hand. Charlie covered his eyes and hid in Lucas' shoulder.

Deciding Charlie needed to get out of there, Lucas took him out to the van for the wheelchair. They got a snack for Charlie at the hospital cafeteria and headed back for the eighth floor waiting area.

Lucas did his best to entertain Charlie, but inside he cried as Kayla suffered. He had to hold himself back from running into that room and ripping the IV out – from taking her far away. He knew it would do no good. The chemo was going to help her…wasn't it?

After what felt like days, the nurse came in to get them. "All done," she said gently.

The boys warily entered Kayla's room. A nurse was patting Kayla's shoulder.

Lucas quickly went over and hugged Kayla carefully. She slumped against him, her body drained of strength.

"Could you get us a wheelchair?" Lucas asked the nurse.

She nodded, herself almost teary-eyed at the scene. There was so much love mixed in with so much pain. She could see the responsibility Lucas bore – the weight of Kayla's pain on his shoulders.

"Anything you need, just ask," the nurse told Lucas as she brought the wheelchair in.

"Thank you, I appreciate it," he said, standing.

She clasped his shoulder. "You're doing great, kid, keep it up. Things will get better."

Lucas nodded numbly, wishing it were true. He helped Kayla into the wheelchair. Her face was pale, her eyes bloodshot.

"Make sure she drinks lots of fluids," the nurse instructed as she helped them out to the van.

"I will. Thanks." Lucas answered.

He put Charlie in first and lifted Kayla in after him. He knew Kayla wanted to help herself – that she hated for him to have to help her with everything – but he also knew her arms and legs felt like lead to her. Her strength was gone.

Lucas turned toward the nurse. "Could we…I mean…I know you don't usually allow it…but could we borrow the wheelchair? We'll return it when we come for the next treatment. We just don't have anything else to use right now."

The nurse, now familiar with Kayla and Lucas, did not even hesitate. "Of course you can! I'll let someone know. And the next time you come, we'll look into getting Kayla one of her own if it's an ongoing need."

Lucas hugged the kind nurse and loaded the second wheelchair in the van. He climbed in.

Knowing it was risky because she had been through so much that morning, Lucas had to do something to cheer her up. He had to see her smile again – if that were even possible.

He drove for half an hour to the place he knew she loved. In a sleepy little nearby town stood a butterfly conservatory. He knew she had always wanted to see it with him. She talked about it all the time.

He pulled in and parked the car.

"Where are we?" Charlie wondered aloud, looking around at all the flowers.

"The butterfly conservatory," Lucas responded, lifting Kayla from the car and placing her into the waiting wheelchair.

"We are?" she whispered, smiling.

"Yep, come on, it's warmer in there."

She nodded as chills ran through her. He took off his jacket and laid it across her. Charlie reached out his arms and Lucas scooped him up. He carefully strapped both Kayla and Charlie in the chair together, paid their entry fee, and wheeled them in.

The humid air warmed her freezing body instantly as the sound of birds whistling and the smell of flowers filled the air.

"It's beautiful," she whispered as butterflies flitted around her.

One came to rest on her shirt and she grinned.

"There's what I came to see," Lucas whispered kissing her forehead.

He wheeled them carefully through the walkways as Charlie clung to Kayla's neck. The butterflies scared him.

"It's okay, Buddy," Lucas laughed. "It's just a bug with wings."

"*Big* wings," Charlie whispered, clinging closer to Kayla.

One of the butterflies landed on Charlie's head.

"See? They don't bite."

Charlie started to cry.

"What's wrong?"

"It peed on me!"

Lucas and Kayla both laughed.

Lucas hugged Charlie. "You want to leave, Buddy?"

Charlie sniffed.

"I'll take that as a yes. Kayla, are you done, Babe?"

She nodded. "Yeah, I'm not feeling so good. I'm a little thirsty."

"Come on, then, so no more butterflies pee on Charlie."

He wheeled them out front. They went to the little café next door and ordered lunch.

"Lucas," Kayla spoke weakly.

Lucas knelt down so he could hear her.

"I love you," she said and kissed him.

"You're beautiful," he whispered back.

She looked down.

He reached out and put a gentle hand underneath her chin. He tilted her head up to look at him.

"You are," he insisted, gazing into her eyes.

"Lucas, I was almost throwing up on you. You deserve so much more than this," she mumbled, tears beginning to form as she shivered.

Lucas took off his sweatshirt. He put it over her head and helped her slip her arms through.

The sweatshirt was several sizes too big for her, but it made her feel safe and warm. She could smell his cologne – it smelled like him. Her muscles relaxed and the nausea seemed to lessen as her shivering stopped.

The waitress brought the food to their table.

Kayla looked at the food and felt sick to her stomach. Lucas put Charlie on his lap and pushed the fries toward her. She shook her head.

"I can't, I'm going to be sick."

Lucas shook his head. "You have to. You haven't eaten all day."

"I don't want to throw up again. I'll be okay – I'm not hungry," Kayla insisted.

"You at least have to drink something."

"I don't want to," she replied, holding her stomach.

Lucas stood. "I'll get you a hot chocolate. Can you drink that?"

Kayla shook her head.

"You have to – doctor's orders. I'll make them put extra chocolate in it. Come on Charlie, we are going to get your sister a hot chocolate."

"Can I have one too?" Charlie asked, clapping his hands.

"Yes, but only because you were so brave with all those scary butterflies."

"And it peed on me!" Charlie exclaimed.

Lucas laughed and went to the counter.

Out of his sight, Kayla laid her head on the table. The cool tabletop seemed to make her stomach feel better. She was cold and hot all at the same time. She felt so tired. She wasn't sure that she had ever been this tired in her whole life. It was as if someone had sucked the life out of her body and she was just breathing, existing. Even the breathing was painful. Her ribs hurt from throwing up. She started to close her eyes.

"Babe, wake up! Come on, you have to drink."

She opened her eyes to his deep blue eyes anxiously watching her. Slowly she sat back up. He pushed the cup into her hands and helped her sip it. She could feel her stomach turn.

"It's going to be okay," he soothed, holding the cup to her lips.

He shifted Charlie to his other knee as he tried to coax her along.

Listening to his gentle voice, she drank as much as she could before the pain and exhaustion pulled her toward sleep.

"It's okay, Babe, you can sleep now," he whispered, touching her face. He got them out to the car and helped her in. She was asleep almost at once.

Having asked the waitress to put their food in "to go" bags, he loaded the food and Charlie in the van next and took everyone home.

At the house, he took Charlie in first and put him on the floor in front of the TV.

"Barney!" Charlie cheered as Lucas turned the volume up.

He rushed out the door to go get Kayla. Kayla was in the front seat with her head on the dashboard.

"You okay?" Lucas asked Kayla, rubbing her back.

Her sadness was very deep.

"I can't do this! You and Charlie need to do something! He's five years old – he can't see me as I get worse!" she cried.

Lucas looked at her and tried not to break down. "Kayla, listen. As hard as it is, Charlie needs to spend as much time as he can with you before you get really bad," he said, his eyes filling with tears.

"But it's so hard!" Kayla whimpered the tears falling freely now.

"I know. It's okay to cry..." Lucas whispered, holding her as he kissed the top of her head.

She sobbed into his shoulder as she breathed in his cologne. That smell always comforted her for some odd reason. She didn't know why, but it did.

As Lucas helped Kayla into the house, they heard Charlie moaning in front of the TV.

"What's wrong, Bud?" Lucas asked, re-entering the living room and squatting next to him.

"I can't do this dance," Charlie whined, tipping himself into Lucas' arms.

"I'll help you," Lucas said getting Charlie off up the floor.

Lucas wrapped his arms around Charlie's waist as Charlie grabbed onto Lucas' neck. They laughed together, waltzing around in circles.

"See? You *can* do this dance," Lucas encouraged.

Kayla joined them in the living room, wiping her tears and giggling at Lucas from the doorframe.

"So…you can dance?"

"I guess…if you say so," Lucas said embarrassed.

"So you're dancing with me at the wedding?" Kayla asked slowly walking over to him.

"Of course, I'll dance with you at the wedding," Lucas said, blushing.

Charlie cheered. "Yes, I don't have to dance!"

Kayla interrupted him, pointing. "Whoa, whoa, whoa! You are dancing with me, Charlie, whether you like it or not!"

"No, he's dancing with me!" Lucas interrupted, pulling Charlie close to him.

"No, me!" Kayla yelled, playfully pulling Charlie closer to her.

"Men first!" Lucas yelled, pulling him back.

"Ladies first!" Kayla laughed.

Charlie gave a heavy sigh. "Fine, I guess I'll dance at your wedding."

"Victory!" Kayla squealed, giving Lucas a high-five.

"Oh, you'll be fine," Lucas encouraged Charlie, holding out his arms.

Charlie crawled over to Lucas as Lucas put him on his lap. "But I can't dance!"

Lucas nodded his head to reassure him. "Don't worry, Charlie. I'll just hold you and spin you around. We'll have fun!" he said lifting Charlie up into the air.

"Okay…" Charlie burst into laughter.

THIRTY-TWO

As Charlie and Lucas played, Kayla thought more about her wedding.

"Can we get a dress, babe?" Kayla asked excitedly.

"Absolutely! On one condition…" Lucas demanded.

Kayla got nervous. "What?"

"You can't call yourself ugly ever again, okay?" Lucas asked firmly as he held her gaze.

Kayla looked down, shame washing over her. "But it's true, though."

"Kayla Rose Maxwell, do not talk like that! Let's go dress shopping!" Lucas suggested trying to cheer her up.

"But, we don't have any money," Kayla groaned.

Lucas smiled at her.

"I have some. I've been saving up for a while."

Kayla looked at him in shock. "How much?"

"About three thousand."

She looked away, her smile fading. "I can't take your money."

"Yes, you can, and you will," he said firmly.

"So, let's go shopping! Ready, Char?"

Charlie nodded. "Yup."

Lucas loaded Charlie into the van first, and then walked Kayla out.

"I can do it," she moaned, pulling out of Lucas' arms.

As soon as he let go of her, she almost fell onto the pavement. Quickly, he grasped her elbow and helped her regain her balance just in time.

"I've got you," he assured. "Just let me put you in."

Lucas scooped her up. She laid her head on his shoulder and he kissed her forehead. He climbed in the van and pulled out his phone.

"What are you doing?" she wondered aloud, watching him.

"I'm looking up dress shops. I have no idea where they are."

She laughed, "I know, silly. We could go to the bridal shop down the street."

Lucas turned to look at her. "But, I want it to be special for you."

She touched his cheek. "I'm marrying you! It already is special."

He caressed her cheek. "How did I ever find a girl like you?"

"*You* didn't find *me. I* found *you*," she smiled, as he turned the car on.

"You did not! I found you in the middle of the city at two in the morning. *I* found *you* first."

"No, I asked you for directions. If I hadn't asked, we would have never known each other. *I* found *you*! So ha!"

Lucas pretended to glare at her. "I would have rescued you anyway. You sounded like a terrified kitten."

Kayla pretended to be insulted then retorted, "At least I didn't look homeless."

"That is true…" Charlie piped up from the back. "I told her not to take the homeless man home, but she never listens to me."

"I'm glad she didn't," Lucas smiled.

"I'm sorry I scared you that day, Charlie."

"It's okay, I wasn't that scared. Kayla always talks to strange boys," he commented.

"Oh, really?" Lucas winked, watching Kayla blush.

"Don't worry, Lucas. I've never dated anyone before you."

Lucas chuckled. "Well, you're mine now. Finders keepers."

"Well, that would make you mine," Kayla replied taking his hand.

Charlie rolled his eyes.

They all laughed.

A few minutes later Lucas pulled into the bridal shop. He glanced at Kayla and noticed how pale she looked all of a sudden.

"Are you up for this, Babe?" he asked her.

"Yeah, I'm okay," she replied weakly.

Lucas got Charlie out first and then helped Kayla.

Kayla looked around at the dresses in awe. They were beautiful and dazzling.

Lucas watched her smile. He loved seeing her so happy. For a moment, he chose to ignore the sickness. Right now, they were just dress shopping for the love of his life. He hung back as the saleswoman measured her to find the perfect size.

"Who's the lucky man?" the woman asked as she measured.

Kayla glanced over at Lucas. "Lucas – and that's my little brother, Charlie."

"Is there any food here?" Charlie asked.

The saleswoman laughed. "There is across the street. I'm sure if you behave, your sister will take you."

Charlie sighed, "Yeah, but this will take all day. I'm *starved*!"

Lucas tickled him. "This is for your sister, not you, but while she's looking, maybe you can pick out your best man's suit."

"Okay!" Charlie agreed.

"You go take care of Charlie, I'll take care of Kayla," the woman suggested, ushering Kayla toward the dresses.

Lucas smiled and waved. They looked through the suits and picked out one quickly.

"This looks good," Lucas said.

Charlie made a face. "That's for old people."

Lucas laughed. "Well then, what do you think we should wear?"

"Sweatpants and a t-shirt?" Charlie suggested.

"There's no way your sister will let you do that!" he responded.

Charlie was not pleased with the idea of wearing a suit. "I'll wear it, just make sure I have a t-shirt underneath so when she's not looking I can take it off."

Lucas chuckled. "Okay, but don't tell her I agreed to this…"

Charlie pretended to zip his lips and throw away the key.

"Let's give this to the desk and find your sister."

"Okay," Charlie agreed.

"She's probably not even close to done."

They went to the room where she was trying on dresses.

"Kayla? It's us. How are you doing?" he asked before coming around the corner.

"I'm sure you would love to see what your beautiful bride has picked," the saleswoman called out.

Lucas and Charlie came around the corner. Kayla stood beaming in the middle of the room. Tears filled his eyes as he watched her twirl in a circle. Her beauty took his breath away.

"Do you like?" she asked, when he didn't say anything.

He wiped away a tear and held his arms out. She ran to him, and he caught her in a hug.

"I love it," he whispered.

She started to cry as he kissed her head.

"I love you," she replied, burying her face in his chest.

"I love you, too – forever."

Charlie rolled his eyes again. "Can we eat now?"

Lucas chuckled and wiped his eyes. "Of course. Let's let Kayla get changed, and we'll pay for the dress."

"Thank you so much," he said to the saleswoman.

"You're very welcome," she sniffed, wiping her own tears. "I hope you have a very happy long life together."

Lucas locked the sadness away in his heart. "Thank you," he managed as he took Charlie to the waiting room.

Kayla came out with the dress in a bag.

"Ready?" she asked beaming with joy.

"Yes!" Charlie sighed in relief.

After getting a snack for Charlie, they headed home.

Kayla gazed out the window with tears of joy, thanking God for Lucas and Charlie, and what a blessing they were to her. She felt like the luckiest girl on earth.

Lucas noticed Kayla's tears out of the corner of his own teary eyes. He wondered what he would be like as a husband, if he was good enough for her.

He reached his hand out for hers. "I love you...so much..." he said, lightly rubbing her hand with his thumb.

He decided to finally ask her a question he'd wanted to ask her for a while now.

"Babe?"

"Yes, Hon?" Kayla answered with a grin.

"Do you think I'm good enough for you?"

Kayla gave him a blank stare and then burst into laughter. "Number one, that's my line. And number two, you're like...the best boyfriend ever." She gently slapped his cheek.

"I try..." He laughed and then got serious. "You mean it?"

"Yes, what other boyfriend would get up at seven in the morning and take care of my annoying little brother?"

Lucas paused for a minute to think. "You do have a point, there," he said, pulling into the driveway.

"I heard that!" Charlie yelled from the backseat.

"We love you, Bud," Lucas said looking in the mirror to see if Charlie was okay.

"Yeah, yeah, yeah…" Charlie mumbled rolling his eyes.

"We're home!" Lucas announced.

"Food?" Charlie asked optimistically.

"Yes, Bud. Food," Lucas answered as Charlie clasped onto Lucas' neck.

"Candy?" Charlie asked, getting a better grip on Lucas.

"Yes but shhh! We don't want Kayla knowing," Lucas whispered putting his finger on Charlie's mouth.

Neither of them could stop laughing.

Kayla put her hands on her hips. "What's so funny?"

"Quick, get inside before she does!" Charlie yelled, tugging on Lucas' shirt and pointing to the front door.

"I'm going to get you!" she screamed as she chased them into the house.

"No, you're not!" Lucas yelled back.

He flung open the screen door and ran into the living room.

Kayla followed them and gently tackled them to the floor.

"Gotcha!" she yelled pinning Lucas' wrists to the ground.

"Get her, Charlie!" Lucas giggled as he tried to push Kayla off of him.

Charlie smiled evilly. "No, I think I'll help Kayla this time," he said, launching himself into Lucas' stomach.

"No!" Lucas laughed so hard he snorted. He could barely get out his words. "It's illegal to tickle your future husband!"

Kayla paused for a minute. "You do it to me," she giggled, kissing his cheek that was red from laughing so hard.

Lucas chuckled. "Yeah, but you have the cutest laugh. I don't."

"Whatever! Where did I find you, anyway, at the perfect boyfriend shop?" Kayla asked while Lucas helped her up.

Charlie whacked her arm gently. "No, I found him. Actually, I found him on a bench in the park, remember? *I* did, not *you*."

"Well, thank you, Charlie," Kayla rubbed Charlie's head.

"I know, I'm amazing," Charlie grinned his cutest for her.

"Wow, I'm lucky! I don't get one but two of the sweetest people on earth," Lucas said wrestling Charlie.

Charlie stopped for a minute. "So, I'm sweet?"

"Well, let's just say, MOST of the time you are!" Lucas tickled Charlie's stomach.

Kayla could see the glint in Charlie's eyes. He was ready to jump on Lucas to wrestle. So, she scooped him up and tossed him onto Lucas' chest.

Lucas, of course, played along, letting Charlie feel like the victor in this match. "For some odd reason it feels like you and your sister love to gang up on me!" Lucas panted.

Kayla smiled. "Yup! And by the way, did you know we had five PA's before you? Most of them quit the first year or got fired from walking out," she said laughing, patting Lucas' shoulder.

"Thank you for telling me this *after* I took the position."

"No problem!" she smiled, patting his head.

"Ha. Ha." He exaggerated, looking up at her bright, cheerful smile.

"I guess I love you just a little…" Lucas laughed, gently wrapping his hand around hers.

"Just a little?" she questioned, scooting closer to him.

"Okay, maybe a lot…" Lucas said as he plopped his arm around her neck.

"That's more like it!" she squealed and kissed him.

Charlie covered his eyes. "Are you two kissing AGAIN?"

Lucas laughed and started up another wrestling match with Charlie. But, Charlie suddenly turned, pinning Lucas to the floor.

"You really think you're stronger than me, Charlie?", Lucas joked.

"Well, he did beat you in the wrestling match, didn't he?" Kayla commented.

"Hush! You're my girlfriend! You're supposed to be on *my* team!" Lucas yelled putting his hand over her mouth.

"Two against one!" Charlie cheered.

Kayla acted insulted. "Not fair! I don't have a partner like you two do," she whined dramatically.

"The bride should have whatever she wants," Lucas said to Charlie, moving to put his arm around Kayla.

Kayla laid her head on Lucas' shoulder. "The bride already has what she wants," she said, taking his hand.

Lucas held her hand and kissed the top of her head. He cradled her in his arms.

Charlie pretended to fall down on the floor and gag. "Hey! You two are getting mushy again! What about me? I'm hungry!"

Lucas laughed and stood. "I'll go make you something to eat. You play with your sister."

Kayla crawled over and began tickling Charlie.

Lucas smiled to himself as he walked into the kitchen. Their laughs were his favorite sound in the world. He made spaghetti and meatballs for them as they played in the other room.

Kayla held Charlie on her lap while they watched Barney. She laid her head on Charlie's and listened to Lucas hum to himself as he made dinner.

"Nice song." Kayla giggled out loud to Lucas.

Lucas laughed dryly. "Babe, I know you love me, but you don't have to lie."

"No, it's good, keep going," she encouraged him, rocking Charlie and kissing his head.

"Should I, Charlie?" he asked, glancing over at him.

"I like your voice," Charlie encouraged.

Lucas chuckled. "And that's the first lie I've ever heard you tell!"

Kayla shook her head. "Charlie's right, though! I'm your sick girl-friend, and I want you to sing. Right now!" Kayla demanded.

Lucas immediately changed the subject as fast as he could. "Food's ready…. I hope…"

"Fine. But you're singing at the wedding, right?"

"Yes, but only for you, though," Lucas mumbled slowly looking up at her.

"Yes! I win!" She cheered, kissing Lucas' cheek.

"I'm SO hungry!" Charlie whined dramatically.

"Okay, okay, I'm coming," Lucas chuckled as he placed the food on the counter.

"Want some, Babe?"

Kayla cringed turning the other way. "I can't eat anything."

"What did the doctor say?" Lucas asked with a firm look on his face.

Kayla sighed heavily, then answered him. "Eat normal meals even if you don't want to."

"Very good. Now eat," Lucas demanded, putting the plate in front of her with a polite grin.

"Fine," Kayla mumbled pulling the plate towards her.

"Ready, Bud?" Lucas asked Charlie as he put him in his wheelchair.

"Finally!" Charlie responded, pretending to faint.

After dinner, they watched TV for an hour.

"Can we go to bed?" Charlie asked sleepily as he began to doze off in Lucas' arms.

"Of course, little Buddy," Lucas grinned as he gently picked up the exhausted little boy.

"Night, Kay." He smiled at her as they headed for the apartment and bed.

"Night boys."

Kayla was pretty exhausted herself, but her appetite kicked in a little, so she decided to have a little ice cream. After the ice cream, she was even more tired. She was beginning to feel the pain streaming from the top of her head down to her achy heels. Biting her quivering lip, she tried to keep from making any noise on the webcam that would wake the boys. Her trembling legs were barely strong enough to hold her as she stumbled down the hall to her room. She had trouble even turning the knob on the bedroom door. Kayla wished that someday things would be better. She wished she were a different person, living a different life. But then, of course, she would never have met Lucas. She wouldn't change that for the world, but she wished that she could stay longer, live longer. The pain of not being there for all the special moments the three of them would share hurt her more than the physical pain she was in. She tried not to think about it as sleep consumed her.

Lucas jolted awake from a deep sleep. He quietly leaned over and checked the computer monitor. He could hear Kayla moaning. Carefully getting out of bed so as not to wake Charlie, he quickly ran to the house.

"What's wrong, Babe?" he whispered, pulling Kayla close.

"My whole body hurts – I can't sleep!" she cried, reaching for Lucas' hand.

Kayla shivered beneath the blankets, trying to stay warm.

"It's okay," Lucas reassured.

"It's so hard not to scream sometimes," she said through clenched teeth as she buried her face in his chest.

He held her more tightly, frowning as he noticed how thin she had become.

"Go ahead, cry," he whispered in her ear.

"It's so hard not to! I'm so sorry!" She hugged him tighter as tears streamed down her face.

"It's okay," he repeated himself.

He didn't know what to say anymore.

"I love you," Kayla quivered.

"I love you more," he whispered, smiling.

Lucas watched as her teardrops became tear waterfalls.

Kayla felt Lucas' feelings for her as strong as his strong arms holding her shivering body.

"I've got you," he reminded her.

"I'm fine now," she insisted.

"You're not," he interrupted pulling her close again.

"It's so hard not to cry in front of Charlie," she wept.

"Just sleep," Lucas suggested, coaxing her back to the sleep he knew she so desperately needed.

After a few moments, her tears gave way to quiet breathing and sleep overcame her again. Lucas gently rubbed her shoulder.

He desperately wished he could help Kayla. He thought his proposal would make things better for her, but at times it seemed to only make it worse. Occasionally, he noticed that it seemed that her engagement ring reminded her that she wouldn't live forever with him. His observations were correct. Kayla was convinced that she might not even make it a few days past the wedding. She tried hard to hide her dismay from Lucas, but he always seemed to notice.

The next day passed quietly.

Lucas settled Charlie in for an afternoon nap and then went into the living room to check on Kayla. He found her curled up on the couch moaning.

"How you doin, Baby?" Lucas asked tenderly, taking a seat next to her.

"I'm fine." She said in a short tone.

Lucas wrapped his arms around her. "No, you're not."

She sighed. "I'm just tired of being in pain all the time."

"I know," he agreed.

Kayla's eyes shut as she tried to get comfortable.

Lucas reached for the blanket on the back of the couch and delicately draped it over her.

Her eyes flapped open as Lucas slowly sat next to her. "You know you don't have to sit with me if you have something else you need to do?"

"I know," Lucas clarified, moving closer, "But I want to."

"But, Lucas, you do so much for me. All the time, you're doing things for me. I feel so bad."

"That's a guy's job. My job is to spoil you." Lucas smiled, gently kissing her.

Kayla sat up and hugged him tightly. "Well, thank you," she whispered, lying back down.

Lucas stroked her arm.

Kayla closed her eyes, enjoying Lucas' comforting presence. She loved that she had found "the one" that all girls talk about: her "forever love", her "prince". She'd never had someone appreciate her so much. Whenever he touched her, something flowed through her body. She couldn't describe the feeling, but yet it was comfortable.

Kayla started to get up to get some water.

"Let me get it," Lucas offered, jumping up.

"There you go again," she shook her head, "Always spoiling me."

They suddenly heard a small voice from upstairs. Charlie had woken up from his nap.

"Lucas?" Charlie called from his old room.

"Well, I guess the prince is up," Lucas announced.

He headed up the stairs. Kayla slowly followed behind him.

When Charlie saw both Lucas and his sister come in, he joked, "Hey, Lucas! Do you need my sister's help to pick me up now?"

Lucas reached down and pretended to need Kayla's help getting him out, letting out a groan as he lifted Charlie.

Kayla started to help. "Oh, my gosh, he *IS* heavy!" She pretended to agree, grunting as they lifted Charlie.

"It's all those chocolate pop tarts you feed him while I'm sleeping," Kayla accused playfully.

"Who me?" Lucas looked at her impishly and winked.

He easily picked up Charlie and headed downstairs with him.

"Maybe I'm eating too many vegetables, Kayla," Charlie pointed out.

Kayla laughed. "Yeah, right. If anything, you need to eat MORE vegetables!"

They spent the rest of the evening playing games together. Lucas was terribly worried about Kayla, but he tried hard not to let it show. He knew she thought she could hide it from him, but she didn't know he was always watching her. Her sobs broke his heart. He would do whatever he could to comfort her, he determined.

THIRTY-THREE

LUCAS AWOKE TO CHARLIE SOBBING in his own pillow. He tried to figure out what was going on as he rubbed his eyes.

Charlie tossed from side to side trying not to wake Lucas. He couldn't stop thinking about his sister, his best friend. He loved Lucas, but he couldn't bear to think of losing the only one left in his family. He kept reminding himself that Lucas would always take care of him, but still he was terrified of being alone.

Lucas rolled over to Charlie, his hand grazing the pillow now damp from Charlie's tears.

"You awake?" Lucas whispered to Charlie.

Charlie sniffed and rolled over to face him. Lucas felt tears spring to his own eyes as Charlie began to sob. He reached his arms out and hugged Charlie close.

"It's okay, Buddy?" Lucas mumbled, gazing through the deep darkness.

"I don't want Kayla to die," Charlie cried as he buried his face in Lucas' chest.

For a moment, Charlie got quiet. Lucas could hear the crickets chirping as the breeze sifted through the window.

Charlie sniffed, trying not to burst into tears again.

"It'll be okay," Lucas reassured, clutching Charlie closer to him.

"I know the perfect thing for you."

Lucas smiled as he pushed back the quilts and sat up. He felt around in the dark for his t-shirt that he left on the floor.

"Where did it go?" he mumbled to himself as he stumbled around in the dark.

All of a sudden, he let out a screech as a sharp plastic object pierced his foot. "Charlie, I told you to put that toy hammer away!"

Charlie laughed, "But Lucas. I can't do that kind of stuff. You have to help me put stuff away."

"Oh yeah?" Lucas replied. He attempted to sit back down on the bed, but in the dark, he missed and crashed to the floor.

"Ugh," Lucas groaned on the floor.

Charlie laughed and then asked, "Are you okay?"

"Oh, just peachy," Lucas replied.

His fingertips touched the collar of his t-shirt that had somehow traveled underneath the bed.

"How did it get under the bed?" he muttered as he stood.

He pulled the shirt on over his head and reached for Charlie. "Let's go over to the kitchen for a little mid-night snack! Maybe that will cheer you up!" Charlie kneeled on the bed to make it easier for Lucas to wrap his arms around Charlie's waist.

Together, they crossed the lawn in the dark to the house. Lucas tiptoed to the kitchen, putting Charlie on his shoulders as he opened the refrigerator.

"How about chocolate milk?", he whispered.

"Yeah!" Charlie whispered with excitement.

Lucas got the milk out and then opened up the cabinet for the cocoa powder. He paused for a moment and looked up at Charlie with a solemn expression.

"You know, you can't tell your sister about this. It has to be our secret," Lucas said as Charlie smiled.

Lucas poured the ice-cold milk into Charlie's cup. He dug the spoon into the cocoa powder and dumped a heaping teaspoon into the milk.

"More chocolate!" Charlie cheered.

"Shhh, you're going to wake Kayla," Lucas whispered, dumping in a bunch more chocolate.

He lifted Charlie, who was quietly celebrating, off his shoulders and set him on a chair. Charlie drank the milk faster than Lucas had ever seen before.

"Are you happy, King Charlie?" Lucas asked. Charlie slurped the last of the milk.

"Yes, I am," Charlie nodded in glee.

"Good! Let's go back to bed," Lucas said kindly but firmly.

The next morning he awoke to Kayla nudging him. He groggily opened his eyes and found that she was dressed like they were going somewhere.

"You okay?" he moaned trying to wake up.

"Yeah, I have chemo this morning, remember?"

"Oh, I must have forgotten…" Lucas thought to himself.

"I'm sorry, Babe." He apologized and rolled over to wake up Charlie.

"It's okay, I'll get the car started."

"Okay, don't worry about breakfast. We can get something on the way," Lucas called as she walked out the door.

She turned and smiled. "I love you."

He grinned as she spun around and headed outside.

"Ready, Bud?" Lucas asked Charlie as he pulled the blankets back and saw that Charlie was soaked. Charlie arched his back so Lucas could slide the soggy bed sheets out from under him. "I'm hungry, he yawned."

"I know. We're going to get food on the way to the hospital," Lucas responded, quickly changing his diaper.

"For what?" Charlie mumbled as Lucas tugged Charlie's legs through the legs of his pants.

"To bring Kayla to her chemo appointment," Lucas answered.

"Remember the first time you changed me and almost broke my leg?" Charlie teased.

Lucas sighed and laughed. "No fair, that was the first time I had to change you."

"Whatever, just get me in the van so we can get food," Charlie demanded, wrapping his arms around Lucas' neck so Lucas could put him in the wheelchair.

Kayla was back from starting the car. The short trip to the car and back had tired her out. "I'll help you to the van after I get Charlie in," Lucas said, touching her pale cheek.

He left to load Charlie in and returned inside for Kayla as promised.

"What's wrong?" Lucas asked.

"I just want us to be a happy family again," Kayla softly whimpered as Lucas guided her outside.

"What are you talking about? We've always been a happy family, and always will be," he reminded her as he helped her into the front seat.

She winced in pain and the world around her started to spin.

Suddenly she felt his cool hands on her face.

"Stay with me…you're okay…" Lucas tried to soothe.

Her eyes closed then fluttered open again.

"Kayla? Babe?"

"I'm okay, just dizzy," she responded, resting her head in his hands.

He wrapped her in his arms and held her. "We need to head to the hospital, are you going to be okay?"

She nodded weakly. Slowly he let go of her.

"I'm okay, really," she insisted as he stood anxiously watching her.

Lucas didn't move.

"Babe, I just need some coffee, that's all. I'll be fine."

"You aren't fine, Kayla. None of this is fine," he muttered, trying desperately to hide his anger.

The heartbreaking pain he felt was quickly turning into a monstrous rage inside his heart. He shut the door and silently walked to the driver's side, pausing for a moment to beg God for strength before opening the door. In that moment, he felt peace flood his heart. He took a deep breath and opened the door.

"I'm sorry," Kayla apologized with her head in her hands. "I know me being sick is destroying you, and I wish I could stop it."

He touched her shoulder then tenderly drew her hand away from her face. Squeezing her hand in his, Lucas waited for her to look at him.

"We are going to get through this together," he promised, his blue eyes intently peering into hers.

"I love you," she whispered.

He let go of her hand and started the car. "I know," he smiled.

She hit him lightly on the shoulder.

"I love you too," he responded.

"That's better," she grinned, wiping her tears.

"Can I get a donut, now?" Charlie piped in from the backseat.

"It's too early for smoochey lovey stuff, and I'm hungry!" Charlie sighed.

"Yes! You may get any donut you like," Lucas offered.

"Can I get coffee?"

"*NO!*" Lucas and Kayla responded in unison.

Lucas drove through the back roads to get to Bob's diner. He pulled in front and left the car running.

"I'll be right back," he called over his shoulder as he hopped out.

He jogged inside.

"Morning, Lucas," chirped the cheery little old lady behind the counter.

"Hi, Ruthie," Lucas smiled.

"Can I have two coffees and a donut for Charlie?" Lucas asked, grabbing chocolate milk from the small fridge on the counter.

"Are you out running today? You sound out of breath," Ruthie remarked as she made the coffee.

"No, we're late for Kayla's chemo. I overslept," Lucas replied, opening a straw for Charlie.

"That's because you have so much to do for that young man. You're doing a fine job. Here – the coffees are on me," Ruthie smiled and handed him the cups.

"Aw, Ruthie, you don't have to do th...."

"No, no," she interrupted, "It's the least I can do. Here, take the donut too. Run along now," she shooed him with her hands.

"Thanks!" He leaned over the counter and gave her a hug.

"You're welcome. Tell Kayla I'm praying for her," Ruthie said as Lucas ducked out the door.

"Will do!" Lucas promised over his shoulder as he hurried outside to the van.

Holding everything in one hand, he carefully opened the door.

"Ruthie says she's praying for you," Lucas told Kayla as he climbed in.

"Aw, she's so sweet," Kayla replied, taking the coffees so Lucas could buckle his seatbelt.

"I know! She paid for the coffees," Lucas related.

"I'll have to thank her later," Kayla vowed as she sipped the coffee.

"Here, Charlie, hold this. I'll feed the donut to you when we get to the hospital." Lucas tossed the bag onto Charlie's lap.

"I have CP, I can't hold this," Charlie answered dryly.

"Oh, because the donut is *SO* heavy," Lucas teased, rolling his eyes.

Lucas carefully pulled out of the parking lot and drove to the hospital.

Kayla made a face as they pulled in.

"You're almost done with treatments, then we leave…" Lucas said, noticing her expression.

"Leave?" Kayla echoed. "Are we going somewhere?"

"On our honeymoon," Lucas smiled.

Kayla blushed.

Lucas leaned over and kissed the top of her head. "Come on, Beautiful," he coaxed. "Just get through this morning, one step at a time."

She nodded and climbed out.

Lucas unbuckled Charlie and carried him in.

"We'll be right here when you're done," Lucas promised as the elevator opened.

Kayla nodded again, trying not to cry.

Lucas hugged her and let her go. "Come on, Charlie," he said, trying to hide his pain. "Let's go eat that donut."

He carried Charlie to the child play center and fed him there.

"Okay, you hang out and watch TV. I'm going over there to make a phone call," Lucas instructed as he carefully set Charlie on his knees on the floor.

"Okay," Charlie agreed.

Lucas nervously walked over to the other side of the room and dialed Uncle Bobby with shaking fingers. He knew he was making perhaps the most important decision of his life. He prayed as the phone rang, and once again, he felt that overwhelming peace.

A million memories flashed through his mind as the phone rang. He could see her smile, the way her hair blew in the wind, her adorable laugh, the way she loved him, her kindness toward Charlie – he loved everything about her. He knew if he ever did anything right in his life, it was deciding to help her that long-ago night. How close he had been to walking away!

Lucas knew in his heart it was God that turned him around – God who rescued him from his dark world. God not only rescued him, but gave him Kayla and Charlie. It was all Lucas could do to keep from falling on his knees there in the hospital playroom. He was in the middle of pouring out his gratitude to God when Uncle Bobby finally picked up.

"Hello?" Uncle Bobby answered.

Lucas tried to pull himself together.

"Lucas? Are you there?" Uncle Bobby sounded confused.

Lucas swallowed hard as tears began to fill his eyes. "Uncle Bobby, I need you to do me a favor."

THIRTY-FOUR

KAYLA CAME OUT FROM THE treatment room searching for only one face. He stood there at the end of the hall. She could barely make herself walk toward him. She felt as though she had no strength left.

Lucas crossed the hall toward her, carrying Charlie. As she leaned against the wall for support, he rushed to her side.

"Hey, Babe." He touched her shoulder as she rested on the wall.

"You okay?" he worried.

She shook her head.

"Can we get a wheelchair over here, please?" Lucas called to the few nurses standing by the nurses' station.

One of them rushed to their aid, and he stepped back as she helped Kayla into the chair. The nurse took her pulse and felt her forehead.

"Lucas?" he heard his name called and turned.

The doctor motioned him over.

"I'll keep an eye on them," the nurse promised.

Lucas didn't think to thank her. His pulse was pounding like a hammer in his ears. He set Charlie back down in the waiting area and glanced back at Kayla who was watching intently.

The doctor's face was tense. He grasped Lucas' shoulder and spoke in a quiet voice. "Lucas, she isn't doing well. I think she should come into the hospital for more intense treatments."

Lucas' chest tightened into a knot, and he barely could force himself to form words.

"You mean stay? Stay here at the hospital? But why? I thought she was doing better?"

The doctor was already shaking his head. "She isn't doing well, Lucas. She may not have much time left if she stays at home. Here, we might be able to give her more powerful, concentrated treatments that will slow it down."

Lucas felt far away. The doctor's words echoed through his mind, but he couldn't make himself believe them.

The doctor squeezed his shoulder. "I will give you tonight to talk to her about it. Let me know your decision in the morning."

Lucas forced himself to nod.

The doctor patted him on the back and left him standing there.

Lucas heard Charlie call his name. He forced his numb legs to move toward him.

The nurse stood and addressed him. "I think she's just weak from today's treatment. Are you okay to get her home?"

Lucas nodded. "Can you just help me get her to the van?" he asked, attempting to steady his shaking voice.

"Of course," the nurse assured with a hand on his shoulder.

Two aides helped Lucas get Kayla and Charlie into the van.

"Do you have any family who can help you?" they asked as they watched Lucas struggle to lift Kayla, who was still in a weakened state, into the van.

"No, we don't," Lucas replied. "We'll be fine. Thank you so much," Lucas told them gratefully.

"You're sure we can't call anyone for you?" the aide worried.

"I really don't think you should be doing this alone."

Lucas turned to the aid. "I've been doing this for quite a while."

He slammed the door shut and grabbed Kayla's things.

"Where's your family?" the aide pressed with a firm hand on his shoulder. "They're dead," he responded dryly. He just didn't have it in him to explain. He was starting to feel angry about it all.

The aide dropped her hand and stepped back. Lucas threw the bag into the back of the van. Looking in the rearview mirror, Lucas observed that the aide maintained her shocked expression as they drove away. He gripped the steering wheel so tightly that his knuckles were white.

Kayla noticed his cheeks turning red. She had never seen him so upset during their relationship.

"What's wrong?" Kayla inquired as she placed her hand on his shoulder to comfort him.

"Nothing, Babe, I'm fine," Lucas forced himself to respond coolly. He didn't want her to get upset.

"You're lying." She said perceptively as she stroked the side of his face.

"I'm just thinking about a lot of things, that's all, and I've had enough of hospitals for today," he assured her. "Hey! I have a surprise for you." He tried to sound enthusiastic.

"What?"

"Uncle Bobby is coming tonight."

"Oh, that's good," she sighed.

She knew Lucas wasn't okay, but her body ached and she felt so tired. She couldn't keep her eyes open. She fell asleep holding his hand.

Lucas drove home and pulled in the driveway. Charlie, too, was quiet. It was as if he could feel that something was wrong. Lucas didn't have any energy left to try and cheer him up. He carried him inside and put him on the floor to watch TV.

"I'll make lunch in a minute, okay?" Lucas promised.

Charlie didn't respond. He hated seeing his sister so sick and Lucas so upset.

Lucas trudged back outside. The gray clouds cast their sorrow over the desperate scene. Lucas didn't know how to tell her the wonderful news of the wedding he had planned at the same time he had to tell her the doctor's terrible news that she wasn't getting better – that she had to go back into the hospital. She had to do whatever it took to get better. He would not let her come home just to die, he vowed, as he opened the passenger side door.

She was curled up in the van seat, which was tipped all the way back. Dark circles colored the skin under her eyes. Tears came as he stroked what was left of her hair. Her beautiful black hair fell easily from her head in several strands at his delicate touch.

"I love you," he whispered, the tears falling freely now.

Lucas had no more strength left, and the flood of emotions he felt inside overtook him. He covered his face and tried to contain the sobs.

Tires crunched on gravel behind him, and he heard a door slam. He didn't care who it was, he couldn't hold on any longer. In an instant, a hand was laid on his shoulder and strong arms wrapped around him.

"It's okay," Uncle Bobby soothed.

He sobbed and sobbed. He sobbed for all the nights he would never see Kayla smile or hold her hand. He sobbed for Charlie. He sobbed because he wanted so badly to give her a beautiful life, and he sobbed because it was all on his shoulders and his heart was too overwhelmed to bear it all.

Holding Lucas tight, Uncle Bobby prayed out loud and just let him cry. It was the only thing he felt like he could do. He couldn't bear to look at his beautiful niece so sick and depressed. He couldn't imagine how Lucas was handling it. He knew they needed him now more than ever.

Uncle Bobby continued to pray until Lucas finally felt himself calm. That all-encompassing peace flooded him again. Though he knew what her fate was likely to be, he knew God was still holding them.

He wiped his eyes, and went inside to check on Charlie and to make lunch.

Outside, Uncle Bobby carefully lifted Kayla from the car and brought her inside. He laid her on the couch and knelt beside her as her eyes opened.

"Hey," Uncle Bobby smiled.

"Hi," she whispered, her voice hoarse.

"How's my beautiful niece?" he whispered, stroking her forehead.

"Not so good," she whispered back weakly.

"I know, Hon, I know," Uncle Bobby responded, touching her cheek.

"Where's Lucas?" Kayla tried to sit up and look around.

Uncle Bobby delicately pushed her back down.

"You need your rest. He's fine. He's in the kitchen making lunch for us."

"Charlie?" she called. "Are you okay?"

"Yeah, I'm fine. Just hungry," he replied.

Uncle Bobby chuckled. "Sounds like a healthy young man to me! I'm going to help Lucas. I'll be right back."

Lucas handed Charlie's plate to Uncle Bobby. He also took Kayla's and brought it in to her.

"Come on, Charlie, let's eat!" Uncle Bobby encouraged as he sat Charlie on his lap.

Lucas helped Kayla sit up. She leaned against him as she tried to eat. She couldn't manage much.

"There's something Uncle Bobby and I have to tell you," Lucas said, helping her take a bite of her sandwich.

"What's wrong?" Kayla anxiously asked shifting herself into a sitting position.

Lucas put on a fake serious face. "Well, let's just say that in two weeks, you'll be a wife," he then said with a huge smile.

"*WHAT??!?*" Kayla screamed, bursting into tears of joy.

"I love you, Kayla, and I want you to know that you're beautiful, and however much time we have left with each other, we'll make all happy memories," Lucas said, choking up and cupping her face with his trembling hands.

Kayla saw the joy, but she also saw a flicker of hesitancy.

"I'm getting sicker, aren't I? That's what you were talking to the doctor about," Kayla spoke softly.

Lucas couldn't speak the words. She leaned into him and he wrapped her in his arms.

"He said you have to go stay at the hospital for awhile. If you stay there, he might be able to use a more intense treatment that would give us more time." Lucas tried to steady his shaking voice.

Kayla sobbed into his chest as he held her tighter.

"You won't have to do the wedding there. Uncle Bobby has already set up a place," Lucas soothed. "So…are you okay with that?" Lucas asked, holding her trembling body.

"Yes, but I've lost so much weight from the cancer. What about the dress?"

"You'll look perfect, whatever you wear," Lucas interrupted, putting his finger on her lips. "I love you, Kayla," he added, kissing her forehead.

"I love you, too!" she cried.

"Do you ever *not* cry?" Lucas teased.

She took his hand and held tightly. She wasn't in the mood for teasing. Her heart felt like it was caving in.

"If you do decide to go back for the intensive treatment, when do you have to get her back to the hospital?" Uncle Bobby questioned, bear-hugging Charlie.

"Tomorrow," Lucas sighed.

"Well, why don't we order out for dinner tonight? I'll stay and help you get thinking through the wedding plans," Uncle Bobby offered, trying to sound enthusiastic for Charlie.

Even Charlie was miserable. "I'll miss my sister," he started to cry.

"You'll be with us, Charlie. We won't leave you alone," Lucas soothed, rubbing his back.

"Come on, we have a wedding to prepare for," Uncle Bobby encouraged.

Kayla's eyes were closing. Her body was so debilitated.

"Let me put you to bed," Lucas suggested, lifting her into his arms.

He carried her to her room and delicately put her on the bed. Covering her, he kissed her forehead again and slipped quietly out of her room, shutting the door behind him.

Uncle Bobby was cleaning up dishes from lunch when Lucas came back downstairs.

Charlie was kneeling on the floor watching yet another episode of Sesame Street.

"Hey, Big Guy," Lucas called, slumping onto the floor next to him.

Charlie laid his head on Lucas' shoulder. Little tears pooled in his eyes.

"I don't want my sister to die," he moaned quietly.

Lucas lifted him into his lap and rocked him slowly. "We will all be with Jesus and Kayla someday in Heaven. We just have to live for a little while without her," Lucas quieted him.

"I don't want to!" Charlie sobbed.

Lucas just held Charlie tight, crying out to God on behalf of this family – *his* family. Lucas rocked him there for a long time before he finally calmed.

"Come on, Big Guy, wedding plans," Lucas reminded, trying to distract and excite him.

Charlie sniffed and Lucas wiped his nose for him.

"Okay…" Charlie agreed reluctantly. "It has to be pretty for her," he added.

"It will be the prettiest wedding you've ever seen," Uncle Bobby promised, joining them.

"Who's going to be there?" Charlie wondered. "The only family I have are crazy," he pointed out, thinking about his aunt and uncle.

Lucas laughed for the first time that day.

"Well, that's why it's just going to be me, you, and Kayla. And Uncle Bobby is going to marry us," Lucas responded.

Charlie looked confused. "He's gonna *marry* them? I thought Uncle Bobby was already married?"

"He is, silly," chuckled Lucas. "He's going to perform the ceremony for us, is what I meant!"

"Oh! Phew, I was worried there for a minute!" Charlie said sounding relieved. "Who's going to help Kayla with the dress?"

"I really hadn't thought about that…" Lucas pondered for a moment.

"Ruthie!" Charlie exclaimed after a few moments.

Uncle Bobby's eyebrow went up quizzically. "Who's Ruthie?"

Lucas laughed. "Perfect!"

"Yay!" Charlie exclaimed, clapping his hands together as best he could with his CP coordination.

"Who's Ruthie?" Uncle Bobby asked again, exasperated.

"She's our favorite waitress at Bob's Diner. She's really nice," Charlie smiled.

"You don't want any family, but you want your favorite waitress?" Uncle Bobby started to laugh, too.

"She's kind of like a loving old grandmother. She knows about Kayla's sickness. Last week she even sent soup over," Lucas explained.

"Well then, Lucas, Kayla, Charlie, me, and Ruthie it is!" Uncle Bobby confirmed.

Lucas went to call her, and Uncle Bobby sat down to watch TV with Charlie. Ruthie quickly agreed, and Lucas filled her in on all the details he knew thus far, except that he still didn't know the wedding location.

"Where is the wedding going to be?" Lucas asked once he got off the phone.

"It's a little white church about ten minutes from the hospital. I already have people over there setting everything up. All you need to worry about is taking care of Kayla and looking handsome," Uncle Bobby smiled.

"Thank you," Lucas told him sincerely.

"Anything for my beautiful niece, my favorite nephew, and the best nephew-in-law I've ever had," Uncle Bobby replied, clasping him on the shoulder.

"Is there going to be cake?" Charlie exclaimed.

"Yes! A big cake!" Uncle Bobby cheered, lifting Charlie into the air and swinging him around carefully.

"Hooray! This will be the best wedding ever!" Charlie exclaimed.

Lucas and Uncle Bobby paused for a minute.

"That's right, Charlie." Lucas agreed quietly.

He could feel the horrible realization of the likelihood of her death setting in like a knife through his heart.

"Why don't we make cupcakes for Kayla and the hospital staff for when she goes in the hospital tomorrow?" Uncle Bobby suggested, as Lucas grew silent.

"Come on, Lucas, help me make cupcakes!" Charlie encouraged as Uncle Bobby lifted him into his arms.

"Sure," Lucas agreed, trying to force enthusiasm into his voice.

Lucas made the batter while Uncle Bobby and Charlie mixed ingredients for frosting.

"We should do different colors," Charlie suggested while Uncle Bobby measured the milk.

"Mine can be pink!"

"Pink! You're a boy!" Uncle Bobby reminded.

"Oh, Kayla will love that!" Lucas sarcastically chimed in.

"Can I have purple?" Charlie tried.

"Why don't you pick a boy color?" Lucas sighed.

"Because I like purple," Charlie smiled. Lucas shook his head.

"Hey! I'm the best man, and the one to walk her down the aisle. I wanna pick my own color cupcake!," Charlie demanded. Lucas laughed, "Okay, if you want purple, then you'll have to be the flower girl too... but you have to make a yellow one for Kayla."

"Okay," Charlie agreed.

"Hey! You forgot me! What color do I get?" Uncle Bobby pretended to act offended.

"You can have an indigo one," Charlie told him.

Uncle Bobby laughed, "How do you know what indigo is?"

"I am smart," Charlie retorted indignantly.

Uncle Bobby ruffled his hair. "I know, I'm just teasing. I'll take an indigo cupcake from you any day."

Lucas smiled as Uncle Bobby and Charlie teased back and forth. He was exceptionally grateful to have Uncle Bobby around to lift the mood and help with the wedding.

"Okay, Charlie, I'm going to put these in the oven and check on Kayla," Lucas told him as he placed the cupcake pans side by side on the rack.

"Tell her I said to hurry up and get better so she can eat my cupcake I made for her," Charlie piped.

"Sure! Uncle Bobby, will you keep an eye on him? I just want to check on Kayla," Lucas requested, nervously wiping his hands.

He felt anxious and he wasn't sure why. As he hurried closer to her room, he knew something was wrong.

"Kayla?" he called anxiously as he pushed the door open.

Kayla was curled up in the middle of her bed clutching her stomach.

"Lucas…" she whimpered.

"It's okay. I'm here. What's wrong?" Lucas soothed, sitting on the edge of the bed next to her.

She shivered, and he felt her forehead, "Babe, you're burning up."

"I don't feel good," she responded, hugging her knees closer to her chest.

"You feel like you're going to throw up?" Lucas asked gently as he caressed her shoulder.

She nodded and he moved to get a bucket for her.

She was already shaking her head. "I can do it," she insisted.

"Its fine," Lucas assured.

"I don't want you to see me like this again!" she cried, trying feebly to push him away.

"Babe, I'm not leaving. Come on," he coaxed, helping her into a sitting position.

She was burning with fever, and she was too weak to move. He leaned her against his shoulder for support and held her upright as she began to throw up. Horrified, he watched her suffer through the pain as blood spewed out her quivering lips.

"Uncle Bobby!" Lucas screamed.

The house echoed with the sound of heavy footsteps, and Uncle Bobby burst into the room.

"What's wrong?" he asked, his heart racing. His eyes widened as Kayla threw up another round of blood.

"Call 9-1-1," Lucas commanded.

Uncle Bobby felt frozen watching his precious niece in so much distress.

"Uncle Bobby, *now!*" Lucas demanded.

Uncle Bobby shook himself back to reality and ripped his phone from his pocket. He left the room to check on Charlie as he dialed.

Kayla's body trembled, and she slumped against Lucas, barely able to breathe.

"Kayla, you're going to be okay. We'll get you to the hospital, okay?" He held her close to his side as her eyes closed. "Hey! Stay with me!" he begged.

Kayla sensed the taste of vomit in the back of her throat and swallowed uncomfortably. Her mind rushed, thinking about all the things that she had done with Lucas and Charlie and about how happy she had been. She wanted to be strong for them, but the pain and sickness had bit by bit taken over, and she couldn't hide it anymore.

Looking up at Lucas, she saw his beautiful blue eyes anxiously searching hers. She wished she could stare into those eyes forever... Then...everything went dark...

THIRTY-FIVE

A FEW DAYS PASSED WITH Kayla at the hospital.

Lucas was terrified that she wouldn't get to see her wedding day. But he knew also that she wasn't strong enough to do much but sleep. He didn't know that Kayla was awake enough to hear him talking to himself. Then she moaned something.

"What, Baby?" Lucas asked, lying down next to her.

"When can we go home?" Kayla quietly groaned.

"Not until next week at the earliest." Lucas answered as Kayla carefully rolled over to see Lucas' exhausted face.

"Baby, go home. Charlie's exhausted and you are, too," Kayla encouraged him, watching Charlie's heavy eyes blink slowly.

"But you're my fiancée! I can't leave you alone and so sick!"

"I'm fine. I have people here to look after me."

"Are you sure?"

"Yes! Now go home, and get Charlie in bed."

"Fine."

Lucas finally gave in. This was one of the few nights he allowed himself to go home. He spent some nights in the hospital with her while Uncle Bobby was with Charlie. Other nights, he spent trying to comfort Charlie while Uncle Bobby kept close watch on Kayla. Both boys were worn out from lack of sleep and from constant hospital trips.

Halfway through the week, Uncle Bobby remembered Charlie's birthday was a couple of days away. He had to break it to Lucas that he would not be there for it. In order to get time off for the wedding, Uncle Bobby had taken two weeks off from work. He hadn't anticipated Kayla getting sick so soon. He had to go back to work – at least for a couple of days.

Lucas took the news well enough to Uncle Bobby's face, but after he left, Lucas thought he would collapse.

One night, he decided it would be good to take Charlie home to sleep in his real bed. Neither of them had been getting much sleep in the hospital, and it was running them ragged.

"Can we go to my house and not the apartment, even though Kay's not there?" Charlie asked as they were pulling into the driveway.

"Of course, Bud," Lucas assured, unloading Charlie and bringing him into the house.

Once inside, Charlie frowned.

"What's wrong, Bud?" he asked, noticing the frown.

"It's not the same without Kayla here."

"Come sit with me on the couch."

Lucas gave a tired smile and sat down on the couch, pulling Charlie close to him. He stroked Charlie's hair.

"Is something bothering you?"

"I'm fine," Charlie replied quickly, shortening his tone and whipping his head the other way.

"No, you're not," Lucas corrected, forcing Charlie to look at him. "What's wrong, Buddy?"

"It's just that Mommy and Daddy are gone, and now Kayla's leaving!" he cried.

Lucas lifted him onto his lap. "It's hard, I know, but I'll always be here for you."

They were both so exhausted that they fell asleep there on the couch. Even the couch was more comfortable than the hospital chair.

Lucas awoke before Charlie the next morning. Charlie still lay sleeping on his lap. Lucas didn't want to disturb him – the child needed his sleep.

Lucas sighed. He remembered that Charlie's birthday was the next day. He had no idea what to do. He wondered how he could ever make it special for him without Kayla there. She was too sick to know most of what was going on these days.

Charlie stirred a few moments later and Lucas got him ready for the day.

"Are we going to the hospital?" Charlie asked with fear in his eyes. Lucas knew that it was becoming more and more difficult for Charlie to see his sister.

"Yes, we are, Charlie, but it's good for us to be with her as much as we can," Lucas encouraged, cradling Charlie in his arms.

"Fine. But I wanna do one thing. "

"Uh oh, what?"

"Can I go to the hospital with just a diaper on?"

Lucas was speechless, but he had a feeling that Charlie was probably trying to somehow get Kayla and him to smile.

Lucas could only get out one word. "*What?!?*"

Charlie gave a huge grin. "You heard me."

"Ummm...let me think...*NO!*"

They both laughed and headed for the hospital with Charlie fully dressed.

When they arrived back at the hospital, Kayla seemed to be more awake and alert. She looked at Lucas and motioned him to come close.

"It's Charlie's birthday tomorrow," she whispered while one of the nurses played with Charlie.

"I know, Uncle Bobby told me," Lucas whispered back.

"Can I come home for it?" she pleaded.

Lucas hesitated.

"Please," she begged, tears beginning to form in her eyes.

Lucas sighed. She had been so weak in the last couple of days that she had not even requested a drink of water. How could he deny her now when it might be the last birthday they would spend together? Reluctantly, he agreed to bring her home.

The doctor approved it and discharged her for one day. After she heard the news, she held Charlie and told him about all the surprises they had in store for him.

Lucas could see her getting weaker as her enthusiasm took all her strength. He left her to sleep and took Charlie out for a while.

How was he going to get presents, he wondered as he drove. He was weary – the past week had taken a toll on him. He hadn't shaved in forever, and there was no clean laundry left – he had been wearing the same pants for days. Now he had to get presents? Where would he even leave Charlie so the presents could be a surprise?

"Lord, I have no more strength left," Lucas prayed desperately.

"Lucas, can we stop at the diner? I miss Ruthie and Gerry," Charlie suddenly begged.

Lucas smiled as he realized God's plan.

"You know what, Charlie? How would you like to stay with them for a few hours? Maybe Gerry can teach you how to make pancakes," Lucas suggested.

Charlie smiled broadly for the first time that week. Lucas pulled into the driveway and wheeled Charlie in.

Ruthie noticed them first. Her heart broke for Lucas. He looked ragged and exhausted. The blue eyes usually alight with happiness now seemed sad. His shoulders slumped as Gerry came out from the back and took Charlie from him.

"Hi, Hon." Ruthie leaned down and hugged Charlie quickly before Gerry whisked him off to say hello to all the cooks in the back.

"How are you?" Ruthie placed a loving hand on Lucas' shoulder.

"I'm okay..." Lucas tried to force a smile and enthusiasm into his voice.

"You don't have to pretend with us, Honey. How are things really?" Ruthie asked tenderly.

Lucas hung his head, letting her see his defeat.

"Things are bad, Ruthie...really bad. I just...I don't know what to do," he sighed, rubbing his neck.

She hugged him tightly, praying for him silently as they stood there for a minute.

"I have a big favor to ask," Lucas said as he pulled away.

"Anything, Dear," Ruthie replied, smiling.

"Charlie's birthday is tomorrow, and I don't have any presents for him. I want to surprise him, but..."

"Say no more, Hon. Charlie can stay here with us as long as you need. You go get him some presents and take some time for yourself. You could use it. You can't always take care of everyone else – you have to take care of yourself, too," Ruthie chided gently.

"I know," Lucas nodded, making a hasty escape before Charlie noticed. He wasn't sure the boy would let him leave.

"You enjoy yourself; we will take care of everything. And if Charlie needs a diaper change, I'll make Gerry do it," she winked.

Lucas was too tired to laugh, but he forced a smile.

For the first time in months, Lucas was finally alone. He drove to the beach and parked in an empty space far from the other cars. Lucas turned on worship music and broke down. He sobbed for Kayla never being able to enjoy life, for Charlie losing the last of his real family, and for himself. It was heart wrenching to see her so deathly sick, for Charlie to be so depressed. Lucas felt as if his world was ending. He cried out to God. He shouted in anger, and begged in tears, and finally was still.

In the stillness, he finally heard God speak.

"I know the plans I have for you, and they are good. I will walk you through the valley of the shadow of death, and you will overcome. I will take care of you. I love you," the deep voice whispered.

Peace filled Lucas – a peace he knew wasn't his own. He couldn't yet see the end of the story, but God knew. God had gotten him through enough that Lucas trusted that He would get him through this, too.

Lucas took the promises God gave him to heart and strength filled him. With a renewed hope, Lucas drove to the toy store down the road. He picked up a hammer peg board, a couple of plastic swords, a fake gun, an Indiana Jones whip with real cracking noises, and a new blanket Kayla had asked him to pick up.

On his way back, he stopped at the dollar store and bought wrapping paper, tape, and a card. With one last stop at the candy shop for Kayla, he had everything he needed. Lucas couldn't believe it was already late in the evening. He hoped Charlie had behaved himself for the diner crew.

Hiding all the presents in the back of the car, Lucas drove back to the diner.

"Lucas!" Charlie cheered as Lucas walked in the door.

"Come here, Little Buddy!" Lucas held out his arms for Charlie and Gerry handed him over.

Ruthie brought out the wheelchair from the back.

"Gerry changed me," Charlie beamed as Gerry made a face.

Lucas laughed.

"I hope he had as much fun as I do every time." Lucas winked at Gerry who shook his head.

"He did fine for his first time. Don't worry, Charlie, in a couple of years someone will be changing *his* diapers." Ruthie winked at Charlie and everyone laughed.

"I'll do it!" Charlie volunteered as Lucas placed him in his chair.

"Very funny," Gerry rolled his eyes while Ruthie patted his shoulder.

"You kids have a good night, now. Anything you need let us know!" Ruthie waved as the crew headed back to the kitchen.

Lucas was grateful to have them there. Charlie seemed to be happier than he had been in weeks and Lucas was very glad for that.

Lucas' alarm went off at exactly at seven in the morning. He rolled over to Charlie to see if he was awake.

"Charlie, are you awake?" Lucas nudged Charlie.

"Yeah, what's wrong?" Charlie moaned, rolling over.

"Happy birthday!" Lucas cheered, holding Charlie over him.

"I'm six!"

"I know! I have a surprise for you!" Lucas said getting out of bed and putting his clothes on.

"What?" Charlie asked as Lucas got his chair.

"Kayla gets to come home for a day just for your birthday!"

Charlie's eyes grew dark with worry. "Will that hurt her?" he asked nervously.

"No, she begged to come home for it. If anything, it would hurt her to stay," Lucas reassured him.

"Okay then! Yay!" Charlie cheered.

Lucas drove them quickly to the hospital where the nurses had already gotten Kayla ready. She looked happy and bright in a yellow shirt and new sweats.

Lucas smiled as she grinned. Today was about Charlie, not about sickness. Lucas knew he had to be careful with her, because she would never tell him how sick she really was.

The nurses helped them out to the van and Lucas drove them home. Kayla rested on the couch.

"Happy birthday, Charlie! You're six!" Kayla hugged Charlie tightly.

"What are we doing today?" Charlie asked as Kayla handed him to Lucas.

"Totally up to you, Bud," Lucas placed him over his shoulders.

"Can we bake a cake?" Charlie asked both of them.

"Of course," Kayla answered.

"You mean from scratch?" Lucas panicked.

"Yup," Kayla grinned.

"How?"

"You've never baked a cake before?" Kayla asked Lucas in shock.

"Um, no, should I have?" Lucas answered, embarrassed.

"Even *I* know how to bake a cake, Lucas." Charlie rolled his eyes and punched Lucas' side.

"How do you know, Mr. Know-it-all?"

"Kayla taught me," Charlie answered in pride.

"It's true." Kayla interjected.

Exasperated, Lucas threw his hands up into the air.

"Alright, fine. A six-year-old is smarter than me! Leave me alone!"

Kayla laughed. "Lucas, preheat the oven to 350."

"Yes, Princess."

"Don't burn yourself again," Charlie warned.

"I won't, Bud," Lucas sighed rolling his eyes. With Kayla's help, he gathered all the ingredients and threw them into a mixing bowl.

"Can I crack the eggs!?" Charlie requested from the kitchen table where he was playing on Lucas' phone with his nose.

"You're the birthday boy! You can't do anything except eat cake and open presents," Lucas reminded.

Lucas pretended to wipe sweat off his forehead as Kayla weakly joined them from the couch.

"You could have let him crack *one* egg with me," she teased quietly.

"And ruin the beautiful new shirt I bought you?" Lucas' mouth gaped open in pretend horror.

"You were supposed to buy Charlie presents, not me, and I don't need candy. I saw that huge bag you left," she accused as he placed his hands on her shoulders.

"I didn't leave that, Santa did."

"It's a little late for Christmas." Kayla rolled her eyes.

"I'm your fiancée," Lucas said with a fake French accent. "I can buy you whatever I want."

"Oh yeah?"

"Yes," Lucas answered, reaching around her waist to hold her tightly.

"Well, tell Santa thank you," she teased, running her finger around the edge of the batter bowl.

Lucas smiled. "You should tell Charlie to tell him. He's on the best terms with him."

"Oh, is *that* why he gets everything he wants? I was under the impression that it was *your* fault?" Kayla retorted.

"Who, me?" Lucas asked innocently, spinning her around to face him.

"Yes, you," she accused playfully as he held her close.

She gazed into his eyes for a moment as he looked down at her. She loved those eyes. The same eyes that watched over her so carefully, held so much worry and pain, now burned into hers with a love she felt.

He leaned down and kissed her.

"Not on my birthday!" Charlie protested after a few minutes.

Lucas laughed and drew her close. For one day, everything was supremely enjoyable. Just for that day, Lucas could believe things would one day be all right.

THIRTY-SIX

"WHERE ARE WE?" CHARLIE ASKED bleary-eyed, looking around to figure out where he was.

"We're heading home." Lucas gave an encouraging grin as he turned onto the highway, flipping on his windshield wipers.

Finally, the tires crunched over their wet rocky driveway. Lucas unzipped his coat and covered Charlie with it to keep him from getting drenched.

"You're getting heavy," Lucas grunted, wiping his forehead dramatically.

"I'm not, you're getting weaker."

"You're getting too good at comebacks."

"Is that good?" Charlie raised an eyebrow.

"No, because that means you're growing up."

"Yeah!"

"You're supposed to stay cute and little."

"Whatever! I'm *STARVING!*"

"And tired." Lucas added for him.

Lucas made cookies and milk for Charlie. Charlie practically swallowed the cookies whole he ate them so fast.

"Ready for bed, Bud?"

"Yeah."

Charlie yawned, rubbing his eyes. "I'm worried about Kayla."

"I know, Bud. We'll get through this."

"Maybe when I wake up, she'll be better," Charlie suggested hopefully.

"Maybe," Lucas said quietly as Charlie fell fast asleep.

Hours later, Lucas finally drifted off, trying to force himself to think of something other than the fact that Kayla was getting much worse.

The next day, they went to the hospital early. Lucas knew Dr. Beeoko was supposed to stop by and give them a new update. He wanted to make sure he was there for it.

Kayla was still asleep when they arrived.

"It's time to talk to the doctor, Baby," Lucas whispered as he knelt on the bed.

Kayla dug her head into the pillow.

"I don't want to, though," she murmured into the pillow. "They'll just put me on more medicine."

Lucas laid his head on the pillow next to her, wrapping an arm around her waist and pulling her closer.

Kayla accepted the comfort, rolling over to get as close to him as possible.

"Lady and gentlemen, I have an announcement." Dr. Beeoko briskly entered the room, a look of incredulity on his face.

Lucas only hugged Kayla tighter, waiting for the prognosis.

"I can't believe it….I just can't believe it…" Dr. Beeoko murmured to himself. "Right along, the brain tumor has shown no sign of responding to the chemo…things looked terrible on the scans! But unbelievably, the scan we did yesterday shows that your tumor has finally started to respond to the aggressive treatment. Kayla, I think you have turned the corner. You have a super chance of beating this cancer."

Dr. Beeoko smiled and hugged her.

Lucas wasn't sure he heard right.

"Did you say the tumor is responding to the chemo?" Lucas asked incredulously.

"Yes, Lucas, that is correct. It is because of your love and care that she has made it this far. You three are an amazing bunch, and I'm happy to know you. Now, there still could be complications if the tumor doesn't fully resolve, but right now I do think the chances of survival are excellent. So celebrate!"

Dr. Beeoko stepped back and let in a stream of nurses who applauded.

"Look, Lucas! They're late, but maybe they have presents for my birthday!" Charlie shouted excitedly.

Joy erupted in Lucas' heart as he and Kayla sobbed. He would marry her as soon as possible, he decided. There was no time to waste. She would live!

THIRTY-SEVEN

THEIR WEDDING DAY WAS QUICKLY upon them.

Kayla finished the last few days of chemo and gradually began to improve. Her joyful spirit returned like the beautiful feel of spring after a long harsh winter. Though she was not strong enough yet to do everything she used to, she could walk around for a short while without getting tired, and she could bake without dropping everything.

It was hard to believe she was marrying the man of her dreams tomorrow. She didn't like having so much attention placed on her, or so lavishly. She knew Lucas and Uncle Bobby would spare no expense to spoil her, and though it exasperated her, she also found it endearing.

Since her close call with death, Kayla let Lucas do as he pleased for her, although she didn't have much of a choice! She knew it was his way of trying to make sure nothing would ever hurt her again.

The tumor had scared them all. She realized that nothing in life mattered more than her faith and her family. There wasn't time in life to worry about unimportant things. Real love outlasted smudged make-up, sweatpants, cancer, and all. She was going to marry that real love tomorrow, and she couldn't be happier.

Lucas made everyone go to bed early in preparation for the day. They would need to be up at dawn for showers and breakfast.

Uncle Bobby slept on the couch in the living room, and Lucas and Charlie went back to the apartment for the last time. They had packed everything up to move into Kayla's house right after the wedding. The only things still unpacked were the bed sheets, toothbrushes, and the tuxes.

Lucas stepped around all the boxes to put Charlie into bed, and then he climbed in next to him.

"Lucas," Charlie began as he settled down under the covers. "Do you think Mom and Dad will be watching from heaven tomorrow?"

Lucas paused a long moment before answering.

"I think everyone will be watching – Jesus, your mom and dad, and all the angels." Lucas' voice took on a tone of awe as he thought of it.

Charlie thought about it for a few minutes. Lucas' eyes began to close, but not before he heard Charlie's last question.

"Will you still take care of me like you do every day?" Charlie asked seriously.

Lucas chuckled. "You think I'm not going to change your diaper after tomorrow? Is that what you're worried about?"

"No, I mean…you will still be my daddy, right?" Charlie's soft voice echoed in the darkness.

Lucas rolled over and hugged the little boy tightly.

"No one can replace your daddy, Charlie. But I promise to take care of you, just like I always have. I love you," Lucas reassured him.

For some reason, he felt uneasy. The feeling had haunted him all day, but as he reassured Charlie, it came back stronger than before. He shook it off as pre-wedding jitters.

"More than you love Kayla?" he asked hopefully.

Lucas laughed again and rolled over to go to sleep.

"Maybe…but it has to be our secret. Promise?"

Charlie grinned widely, and threw a fist in the air.

"Yes! I win!" he cheered.

"Go to sleep, Champ! We have a long day tomorrow," Lucas reminded, shutting his eyes.

"Wake up! It's wedding day!" Charlie tackled him like every other morning of Lucas' life for the past year.

They got ready and crossed the yard to eat breakfast with Kayla, just like every morning.

This morning, however, was different. Today, he would marry the girl of his dreams and permanently enter a real family who loved him. It had been a long year, but through all the sadness, there had been good times, too. He had fought to find joy in every bad situation.

Lucas couldn't wait to get the day started. He loaded the car and then checked twice to make sure they had everything.

Uncle Bobby sat in the back with Charlie, and Kayla sat up front while Lucas drove. They were headed to Ruthie's house so she could help Kayla get ready.

"Ready? Here we go!" Lucas announced as he pulled out of the driveway.

"Today is your last day as a single man. How do you feel about that?" Uncle Bobby teased.

"I was never single, I was just waiting for the right one." Lucas smiled at Kayla who blushed.

"Oh, please! Do you have to put up with this all the time, Charlie?" Uncle Bobby playfully rolled his eyes.

"Yup! Tell me about it," Charlie sighed.

Suddenly, a loud pop sounded from the back of the vehicle and the car jerked right. Lucas steered it to the shoulder, managing to avoid the oncoming traffic.

"What was that?" Kayla shouted, freaking out.

"I'm sure it was nothing. Maybe just a tire," Lucas tried to assure her, though he had a sinking feeling in his stomach.

Carefully, he opened the car door after all the traffic had passed. There wasn't much of a shoulder where they were parked, and in order to look at the popped wheel, Lucas had to stand in the right lane of the highway. Most people seemed very careful of him as they passed quickly by.

"Do you need any help out there?" Kayla called as Lucas fished in the back for the tire jack.

"No, but you guys are going to have to get out of the van. Uncle Bobby, will you take Charlie out? Kayla, stay over there with them," Lucas instructed.

Dutifully, everyone obeyed.

Kayla was more worried about Lucas getting hurt than about making it to the wedding on time. She came around the front of the van to tell him to wait for help. At the same time, Lucas stepped back to tell her to go stand with Uncle Bobby.

Kayla had no time to scream. An oncoming car hit Lucas sidelong, sending him flying forward onto the pavement. The back wheels crushed his body. Kayla jumped back as the vehicle aimed for her. It just missed and didn't stop again but drove off.

"Lucas!" Uncle Bobby screamed as Kayla dropped to her knees.

Uncle Bobby carefully put Charlie down by a tree and dashed to the scene.

Blood covered Lucas and soaked Kayla's pants as she knelt in the rapidly growing pool of red.

"Stay with me, Lucas," she pleaded with him as his eyes opened and shut slowly.

"I love you, Lucas…"

The beautiful words of his fiancée were the last thing he heard before the darkness closed in.

The heart monitors beeped rhythmically like a haunting lullaby.

Lucas appeared to be asleep, and for a moment, Kayla could almost believe that he was. She wanted to. She wanted to pretend it was all a dream, but she knew she couldn't. Lucas was dying, and she had to sit and watch.

Uncle Bobby crept into the room carrying a sleeping Charlie.

"Any change?" Uncle Bobby whispered as he transferred Charlie from his arms to hers.

Kayla reached up and gently cradled Charlie to her chest.

"No, he hasn't woken yet today," Kayla whispered, choking up on the words.

They were awful words and she couldn't believe she had to say them.

Uncle Bobby turned a chair backwards and sat down, his chin resting on the top of the chair back. He gazed at his young niece whose shoulders slumped forward, her body exhausted.

"Kayla, go upstairs to the family ICU sleeping area…get some rest." Uncle Bobby placed his hand on her shoulder.

"I'm not leaving Lucas' bedside," Kayla retorted.

"Honey, Charlie's exhausted. Take him upstairs so he can at least sleep in a bed."

"I can't! He to needs be able to see Lucas if he wakes up!" Kayla snapped.

"Kayla, what would Lucas do?" Uncle Bobby asked firmly.

"He'd make sure Charlie got some sleep and was comfortable," Kayla sighed.

"I'll keep an eye on Lucas. You get some rest," Uncle Bobby instructed.

"No! I have to be right here when he wakes up!" Kayla insisted stubbornly.

"You will be," Uncle Bobby reassured. "But you need your rest. You just got out of the hospital a couple of weeks ago yourself."

Kayla knew she was exhausted. She could feel the deep ache in her body telling her so.

"Okay," she agreed. "But please come and get me if anything changes," she begged.

"I will. I promise." Uncle Bobby soothed. "Now get some sleep."

Kayla stood carefully and carried Charlie with her to the family sleeping area the hospital had provided. She lay down to sleep and pulled the bars up on the sides of the bed so Charlie wouldn't fall out.

She had to be strong. The boy who had always taken care of her – the love of her life – needed her, and she couldn't let him down.

She tucked Charlie underneath her arm and tried to sleep.

"Wake up, Kayla."

Uncle Bobby gently shook her awake just as dawn was breaking.

Kayla woke with a start, instantly concerned.

"Come with me," Uncle Bobby whispered.

The three made their way quickly to Lucas' room. Uncle Bobby held Charlie as Kayla ran to Lucas' bedside.

"Lucas?" she spoke softly.

Her heart leaped as he stirred. For the first time in three days, she saw his beautiful blue eyes open.

"Oh, Babe, you're awake!" she exclaimed taking his cold hands in hers.

Carefully avoiding the IV's, she tenderly rubbed warmth back into his hands. His eyes met hers, and her eyes filled with tears.

For a moment, he seemed confused, but as she moved to hug him he recognized the beautiful girl at his bedside.

"Kayla," he whispered, relief coloring his hoarse voice.

"It's so good to hear your voice!" she cried.

"Where am I?" Lucas croaked.

"At the hospital," Kayla replied, stroking his cheek.

"I want to go home," he whispered, fear filling his eyes as he looked around.

Kayla leaned in and kissed him with trembling lips.

"I'm right here. I want you to go home, too, but we can't," she said quietly, smoothing his hair back from his forehead.

"Where's Charlie?" Lucas wondered, looking around.

"Right here," Uncle Bobby replied, coming to stand where Lucas could see him.

Charlie was still rubbing sleep from his eyes.

Kayla dabbed Lucas' forehead with a warm cloth as he coughed up blood into a basin. Tears flooded her cheeks.

Lucas moaned in pain as he rolled over.

The nurse strode in quickly with a syringe.

"I know you want to talk to him, but he needs rest right now," she explained.

Kayla winced as the nurse jabbed the needle into Lucas' arm. His moaning slowly quieted, and Kayla fell apart in Uncle Bobby's arms.

By evening, after Uncle Bobby had gone home for the night, Lucas' weakened body lay motionless in the cold white bed. His pale skin matched the color of the sterile sheets. Even his dazzling blue eyes were sapped from the trauma to his body.

Kayla lay curled against him, listening to his ragged shallow breathing. She reached up and dabbed a small wet sponge on his dry lips.

His eyelids fluttered.

"Hey," she greeted his half-open eyes with a smile.

"Hi," he whispered, cracking a smile and feebly reaching his hand out for hers.

Tears sprang to her eyes as he brought her hand slowly to his lips. He was her light in a dark sky. If anything happened to him, her candle would blow out.

As if he could read her thoughts, Lucas spoke.

"You will be okay, Kayla Rose," he encouraged.

His ragged voice was barely audible over the hum of the machines keeping him alive.

"No, I won't!" she cried. Kayla began to sob. "I can't do this without you. You are everything to me!"

She clutched his hospital gown in her fists and desperately wished it all wasn't real. Her heart felt drowned with sadness.

Lucas' chest felt like it was going to explode, but he had to speak.

"You will be okay. God is your everything. He is the one who brought us together and kept us going. He was the only one who kept me going for you. He will do the same for you and for Charlie. Hang on, Kay. You got your whole life ahead of you..." Lucas' voice trailed off as he quickly lost strength.

The words drained all that remained of his life energy. The heart monitor slowed dangerously.

Kayla drew close and held his face between her hands.

"I love you, Lucas. I will always love you –" she whispered, choking on the last of the words as Lucas' eyes closed.

A hospital volunteer wheeled Charlie in from the TV room where he had been hanging out with some of the staff. Kayla pulled him close.

A nurse came to administer a dose of medicine in his IV.

"He's nearly gone, Kayla. This will help him," the nurse reassured.

Kayla nodded as her tears flowed unchecked. It was all she could do to keep from screaming.

"Why did she give him a shot? I don't want them to hurt him!" Charlie bawled.

Kayla placed her hand over his head and pressed him to her chest.

"He won't feel anything in a few minutes, Charlie, he'll be with Jesus," she soothed.

Charlie whimpered as the heart monitor slowed to next to nothing.

"It's time to say goodbye to Lucas."

Kayla wiped her tears and cleared her throat. She had to be strong for Charlie.

"I don't want to say goodbye," Charlie protested, tears streaking down his cheeks.

"We have to, Baby." Kayla's voice broke.

Tissues were in short supply as the nurses stopped in to check on Lucas. They had watched him tirelessly care for Kayla and Charlie. The nurses had been there in the middle of the night as he sang to her, held her, and took care of her. He had inspired them.

There wasn't a dry eye in the room as Charlie leaned down toward Lucas' still body.

"Goodbye, Daddy," Charlie gulped, not knowing what else to say.

He rested his cheek on Lucas' hand, just as the heart monitor finally went silent.

Lucas was gone.

THIRTY-EIGHT

KAYLA SAT UP IN BED, sweating.

She reached over for Charlie to comfort herself and found...Lucas? In bed next to her??

The realization startled her.

"Wasn't he dead? Didn't I just see him get hit by a car? Didn't I miss my wedding???" Her thoughts ran together in a stream of semi-consciousness as she shook herself fully awake.

"Lucas?" she whispered cautiously.

As he snored loudly in response, her thoughts began to come back into synch with reality. She watched him breathe for a moment, the rise and fall of his chest bringing relief to her previously tortured mind.

The world around her began to stabilize as she sifted fact from the dream reality she had just experienced.

"I have to stop watching the Discovery Channel so late at night!" she told herself. "But I wish I could have seen Charlie walk though...he had CP even in my dream..."

She yawned and curled up next to Lucas.

All of a sudden, the memories came back in a rush. Horror set in as she remembered what had really happened just a few days prior. Her body shook, the awful memories flooding her with the deepest pain she could imagine.

Lucas stirred as grief overtook her.

"What's wrong?" he mumbled, rubbing his eyes with his palms.

"I had a dream about Charlie...that Charlie was alive!...and that he was my brother..." she went on as she burst into tears.

Lucas reached for her, struggling to keep his own tears in check.

"The shooting wasn't your fault, Kay, it was mine. I should have never been involved in that gang when I was younger! I never thought they would find me…" Lucas shook his head regretfully.

"It's not your fault, either, Lucas. God saved you from that gang! I don't know how they found you after all these years…"

Kayla held Lucas close as his body was racked with sobs of fresh grief and guilt.

"We should have never read that article yesterday morning. I just couldn't sleep for the longest time," Kayla sniffed, still teary-eyed.

She had read the story over and over until she had memorized it line for line.

"Handicapped Child Shot by Gang Members!"

"On April 23rd at around 6 P.M., a tragedy occurred. A mom, Kayla McMullen, and her wheelchair-bound son Charlie were outside their Florida home. The husband – former gang member Lucas McMullen - was apparently out at the grocery store. A black Cadillac pulled into their driveway. The people in the Cadillac opened fire. Mom Kayla threw herself in front of the disabled boy a second too late. A neighbor had alerted police to the sound of gunshots. The mom was miraculously unharmed, but Charlie was shot multiple times and died at the scene. Funeral services for Charlie McMullen will be held at Grace Community Church. The community has been deeply affected by the loss of this little light. He was a shining example of love. He will be terribly missed."

The words of the article echoed in Kayla's mind as she lay holding Lucas. One second! – That was the difference between the life and death of her son. She hated herself for not having been faster.

"It's *NOT* your fault, Kay," Lucas whispered, pulling Kayla closer. He knew she blamed herself. But he knew it was his fault. It was his troubled past that was always coming back to haunt him – to haunt them.

After being raised in an abusive family, he had turned to the only people who had offered him protection – the neighborhood gang. He wished he had known then that that bad decision would follow him all his life and ultimately take the life of his son.

They lay in silence for a few moments before Kayla rolled over to look at the clock.

"The funeral is in a couple of hours. We should get ready," she said wearily.

Pulling off the quilts, her feet hit the cold wooden floor. She walked over to the window and shifted the curtains to one side. The day was gloomy – as gloomy as she felt...

Glancing over at the nightstand; she glimpsed her favorite picture of the three of them at the beach.

Lucas followed her gaze and rose immediately from the bed to hold her tightly.

"He's in a place with no suffering. He's healed and doesn't have to use that power chair he hated so much. He's probably up there running around, driving Jesus crazy, and eating chocolate covered strawberries with Moses. He's also probably climbing the ladder up to the tree house, just like he always wanted to do. No more ramp!"

Kayla laughed a short harsh laugh.

"True," she agreed. "He doesn't have to suffer watching us kiss, either!"

Lucas smiled.

"And there are no nightmares or seizures in Heaven," he whispered, wiping the tears which had begun yet again.

"Do you think he'll miss us?" Kayla asked, clutching Lucas' arm. Lucas gently lifted her face to his and cupped her cheeks.

"Kayla, Charlie's the happiest kid ever right now! He knows we'll join him there one day. It's not he who's hurting, it's us."

Kayla lifted a soft, slender hand up to rest on Lucas' cheek. He needed a shave – he hadn't shaved since Charlie's death. Grief had made even the everyday activities difficult.

"Remember how he used to jump on me to wake me up every morning?" Lucas reminisced as Kayla rested her head on his chest.

Kayla smiled. "Yeah – he did that even in my dream last night."

Lucas chuckled. "Really? What else was in your dream?"

"Well, you were from an abused home and your mom was a drunk."

Lucas laughed again. "That's pretty accurate, actually." He kissed the top of her head as she continued.

"The tree house was in my dream. You and Charlie were building it for our policeman dad who was killed on the job. You weren't much better with a hammer in the dream..."

Lucas frowned. "Great! I'm not even handy in dream life!"

"Being handy isn't everything – you have plenty of other good qualities," she assured, winking at him.

Then she continued.

"Then there was my sister who bullied me into dropping out of school."

"Alexis, Nicole, or Autumn?"

"Alexis. She attacked me."

"She's out there for sure, Lucas said. One time she told Charlie that when he was old enough for prom, she was going with him naked."

"Really? How did I not hear about that?"

"It was a joke for a long time. I'm glad it didn't find its way into your dream."

"Me too!" Kayla chuckled.

"What else was in your dream? Or who else I guess I should say..."

"Well...Gerry from church was a cook at the local diner and Ruthie, the church receptionist, was the four hundred pound waitress!"

"WHAT?? What did you eat last night?" Lucas laughed.

"Nothing! I was too upset about Charlie and the newspaper article," Kayla closed her eyes and Lucas kissed her again.

"Now, don't go back down that road. Tell me more about your dream? Maybe it was meant for us to know Charlie is okay."

"He was happy. You spoiled him rotten, like normal. Of course you were his PA in the dream. You know how he always wanted one who would give him everything he wanted."

"That must be God's way of saying he's being spoiled in heaven. Just in case I didn't do a good enough job here." Lucas smiled.

"You most definitely did! But as much as I wish we could just stay here in this room talking about him, we really do have to get ready for the funeral."

Kayla pulled away from Lucas. He let his arms drop to his side. He knew it was time.

"He's in God's hands now, Kayla. We just have to try to get through this. Come on, I'll help you put on that necklace he gave you."

As she prepared for the funeral, Kayla was drowning in memories... Charlie's birthdays! For one of Charlie's birthdays, Lucas had built him a rocking horse with lots of safety buckles so Charlie could ride it by himself.

Most boys play baseball with their dads. Since Charlie couldn't hold a ball or a bat, Lucas thought of things Charlie could do. He'd wrestle with him, bake with him, and even color with him. Whenever he had seizures, restless nights, or when he tipped over on the floor, he would cuddle with him until the last tear was shed. He loved that little boy more than he ever imagined that he could love someone.

Buttoning his dress shirt, Lucas looked around at all the pictures of their once happy little family. He vowed he wouldn't let Charlie's death be in vain. He would do what he knew God was calling him to do his whole life.

Having been in a gang, he knew how gangs pulled in young teens with the promise of protection and provision. Lucas had an idea of starting a center where he could rescue young teens by trying to get them the help they needed there rather than on the streets. Several people had already called him to speak out against gang violence.

Thinking of Charlie's beautiful smiling face, Lucas bowed his head. He would teach these kids about a God who could save them – the same God that now held his little boy in His arms.

"How does it look, Honey?" Kayla turned around for Lucas to see. The little beads he had helped his son string together for Kayla glittered in the sunlight.

"Beautiful," Lucas responded.

Her sad eyes reminded him that though he would dedicate himself to making sure Charlie's death was not in vain, they still had to get through the pain of facing each day without him.

THIRTY-NINE

"I CAN'T DO THIS!" KAYLA cried curling up in the back seat of the car.

"I can't go in there and talk to all those people about my son. I just can't!" She burst into soundless sobs that shook her frame.

Lucas was relieved that they had come early enough for Kayla to process the shock of seeing their beautiful little treasure in a wooden box. He buried his own despair and slid into the back next to her.

"We have to do this. Charlie would have wanted you to say good-bye," Lucas whispered rocking her in his arms.

She tucked her head under his chin and clutched his shirt as waves of sorrow washed over her.

Lucas couldn't find the strength to pray, but his heart cried out to God, knowing He could hold him in that moment.

Kayla's cries slowed and Lucas rubbed her back.

"Come on. We have to go inside now," he encouraged.

Together, they slid out of the car. Lucas took Kayla's hand, and she leaned into him as they walked.

Approaching the door to the private room that had been provided for them, Kayla paused and took a deep breath. Slowly, she entered, and her eyes fell immediately on the little boy who was the son she had treasured and loved.

She made her way to the small coffin where Charlie lay still and un-moving. It seemed so unbelievable to her that he could actually be laying there so still! His CP had always caused him to be in constant motion.

Overwhelmed, her body could no longer contain her anguish. She cried out, leaning her head on the cool wood. She draped her arms over her little boy and stood there sobbing.

Lucas covered his face with his hands, the torment threatening to overtake him. Struggling for air, he walked to the other side of the coffin and gazed at his little boy. He reached in and touched Charlie's cheek, his fingers resting on cold skin. Lucas wished he could pick him up, wrap him in a blanket, and hear him speak.

He leaned down and kissed Charlie's forehead, and a million memories flooded his mind. For a moment, he was transported to a week ago – their very last conversation.

"Daddy, where do you go when you die?" Charlie had asked over their favorite cup of hot cocoa.

Lucas had taken a long sip as he thought carefully.

"You go to heaven," Lucas responded. "Why do you ask, Little Man?"

Charlie didn't seem to hear his question. "Do you think there are puppies in heaven?"

Lucas chuckled, "You can have as many puppies as you want, Son."

"Will I get to meet Grandma and Grandpa?"

Lucas smiled and ruffled his hair, "Yup! Jesus is probably hanging with them right now."

"Do you think they're waiting for us?" Charlie questioned.

"I think you think too much," Lucas responded, laughing.

"Come on, let's go outside and play."

"Okay!" Charlie agreed.

Lucas could still see his broad grin, hear his squeaky laugh, and feel his warm skin as he slept. He stroked Charlie's cheek again and squeezed his pale, smooth hand.

The one hour they were given for private grief seemed like one minute, but all too soon it was time for the funeral services to begin. Lucas stood and helped Kayla to her feet.

"I love you," she whispered to Charlie.

Lucas couldn't find words to speak. All of a sudden, his heart felt crushed with pain.

When Lucas opened the old, creaky church doors, he couldn't believe so many people had come to support them and to say goodbye to his beloved son. From therapists to church friends to family and community members – all were there.

Lucas stumbled up the stairs onto the platform, trying to pull himself together as the tears threatened to overflow. Sadness soaked into his soul.

Lucas approached the microphone.

"Thank you all for coming. Charlie, as you all know, had cerebral palsy, but that never stopped him from impacting all of our lives," Lucas tried to chuckle but failed.

"When he was born, I promised him and myself that I wouldn't let anything bad happen to him. Then without warning, Charlie was gone, and it felt like somebody was stabbing me with a jagged-edged knife. I felt like the worst father ever! But God is our heavenly Father and He alone is perfect. Finally, Charlie is able to take his first steps by himself."

Lucas' words caught in his throat. Tears flooded his eyes.

Kayla stood and took over the microphone with shaking hands.

"It is by God's grace that we will make it through today, and every day we will have to live without Charlie. Charlie made our lives sweeter and brighter. But his death has shown us how precious and short life is. We want to dedicate our lives to protecting other kids from being hurt like this."

Kayla took a deep breath. She could feel herself beginning to lose control of the careful calm she had practiced for this speech. Silence hung in the air as she bowed her head and prayed a desperate prayer for strength. A strange sense of peace washed over her, as if she were being lifted off her feet. She felt Jesus had wrapped her in His arms, and by His overwhelming love and presence, was empowering her to finish.

"God knew this was going to happen. This was part of the enemy's plan to destroy our family. But in Jesus' name, we will not be destroyed! Charlie's physical body is gone, but his mission in life lives on in us. He wanted everyone around him to be happy and full of laughter, no matter what our circumstances.

This tragedy struck us with a sadness I could never describe, but our hope and trust is in Jesus. It will not be long before we see our precious little boy again. When we meet him up there, I want him to see all the people we brought to Jesus through this.

I picture meeting him at the gates of heaven. I will lean down, pick him up, hold him close, and say, 'Look Charlie, see what Jesus did through you?' And I can imagine those little brown eyes shining with love as he looks on each and every soul that heard his story and saw Jesus in it."

Tears fell freely from her eyes and soaked the notes she held in her hands. There was not a dry eye in the place as she finished. Lucas embraced her.

The preacher solemnly stepped up to the microphone as Lucas and Kayla sat down.

"My name is Erik and I am the pastor of Grace Community Church. I was there for Charlie's birth. I knew Charlie for his whole life, and not for a moment did I ever doubt that one day he would go to seminary.

When he had something to say, everyone listened. When he sang, everyone sang along. But he didn't have to go to seminary to be a preacher. He preached to us with his life. Every challenge, he overcame with joy.

I don't know if many of us could wake up every day and allow other people to do everything for us. He loved his life the way it was. He loved Jesus, and that love shined through him. You couldn't meet Charlie and forget him. He was a memorable kid who was loved by everyone, even with his crazy stories and constant questions.

One Sunday, he said to me, 'Why do we have to listen to you preach? Can't we just all talk about the Bible?'"

Erik paused as smiles began to break out across the congregation.

"And I said to him, 'Charlie, you are the most honest person I have ever met.' He looked up at me with those brown sparkling eyes of his and said, 'Does that mean I can tell you your purple Easter Sunday suit makes you looks like an oompa loompa?'"

Small bursts of laughter echoed through the dismal funeral atmosphere like a candle in a dark room.

"Let's not be hindered by darkness today. It is okay to be sad for what happened, but let's not forget that Charlie is not sad right now. Charlie is chasing Noah around begging for a ride on the ark, and he is trying to get Cain and Able to be disciples like Peter and John. Let's celebrate the life Charlie lived and remember how he touched our lives. The funeral procession to the graveside will now begin. Pall bearers please come forward."

Autumn, Nicole, and Alexis came forward, lifted the small, lightweight casket and proceeded outside to the waiting hearse. The crowd slowly followed them out to the parking lot where the sun was shining brightly. Everyone climbed into their cars and followed behind the hearse with purple flags flying in the wind.

A few miles away from the church, a small cemetery sat a little way off the main road. Toward the back of it, a hill sloped gradually upward to meet the surrounding woods. There, beneath a young sapling, stood a small headstone inscribed with the words "Charles McMullen August 28th 2003 – April 23rd 2011."

The cars parked along the road, and everyone filed into the cemetery.

Lucas wrapped an arm around Kayla's shoulder and held her close as they led the slow procession up the hill to the graveside.

The tiny casket was placed carefully next to the grave. People took turns sharing about how Charlie had touched their lives. After they were finished sharing, each threw in a tulip. They were Charlie's favorite flower.

One by one, each person said their goodbye to Charlie, attempted to comfort Kayla and Lucas, and left.

Kayla gave hugs or said a few words to the parting mourners, but was too numb to really know what she was saying or doing. Lucas was quiet, absorbed in his own thoughts.

Erik was the last to leave. He hugged Kayla and clasped Lucas on the shoulder.

For a long time, Kayla and Lucas stood motionless in a gentle embrace, staring down at the headstone and the grave that held what was once their son.

At sunset, Lucas and Kayla finally left the burial site.

With one last glance at the stone with Charlie's name carved on it, they slowly walked toward the car.

Trudging together in silence, Lucas slipped an arm around Kayla as the sun began its final brilliant descent behind the trees.

The beautiful sunset felt to Lucas as if Charlie himself had helped God paint it. Lucas could almost read the scribbled letters in the clouds… "You'll be okay, Dad, you'll be okay…"

And his son's beautiful smile remained in his mind, even as the sunlight vanished.